Romantic Suspense

Danger. Passion. Drama.

Christmas K-9 Guardians
Lenora Worth
Katy Lee

Deadly Christmas Inheritance
Jessica R. Patch

MILLS & BOON

First Published 2024
First Australian Paperback Edition 2024
ISBN 978 1 038 93555 7

Leonora Worth is acknowledged as the author of this work
PERILOUS CHRISTMAS PURSUIT N© 2024 by Harlequin Enterprises ULC
Katy Lee is acknowledged as the author of this work
LEATHAL HOLIDAY HIDEOUT © 2024 by Harlequin Enterprises ULC
DEADLY CHRISTMAS INHERITANCE © 2024 by Jessica R. Patch
Philippine Copyright 2024
Australian Copyright 2024
New Zealand Copyright 2024

MIX
Paper | Supporting
responsible forestry
FSC® C001695
www.fsc.org

Published by
Harlequin Mills & Boon
An imprint of Harlequin Enterprises (Australia) Pty Limited
(ABN 47 001 180 918), a subsidiary of HarperCollins
Publishers Australia Pty Limited
(ABN 36 009 913 517)
Level 19, 201 Elizabeth Street
SYDNEY NSW 2000 AUSTRALIA
Cover art used by arrangement with Harlequin Books S.A.. All rights reserved.
Printed and bound in Australia by McPherson's Printing Group

Christmas K-9 Guardians

Lenora Worth
Katy Lee

MILLS & BOON

With over seventy books published and millions in print, **Lenora Worth** writes award-winning romance and romantic suspense. Three of her books finaled in the ACFW Carol Awards, and her Love Inspired Suspense novel *Body of Evidence* became a *New York Times* bestseller. Her novella in *Mistletoe Kisses* made her a *USA TODAY* bestselling author. Lenora goes on adventures with her retired husband, Don, and enjoys reading, baking and shopping...especially shoe shopping.

Katy Lee writes suspenseful romances that thrill and inspire. She believes every story should stir and satisfy the reader—from the edge of their seat. A native New Englander, Katy loves to knit warm woolly things. She enjoys traveling the side roads and exploring the locals' hideaways. A homeschooling mom of three competitive swimmers, Katy often writes from the stands while cheering them on. Visit Katy at katyleebooks.com.

Perilous Christmas Pursuit

Lenora Worth

MILLS & BOON

Keep thy heart with all diligence;
for out of it are the issues of life.
—*Proverbs* 4:23

To my puppy Bogi. Thank you for the doggy kisses
and the unconditional love.

Chapter One

"Hi, Granny, I'm almost done. How's it going?"

Isla Jimenez held the phone to her ear and glanced at the white-and-black clock on the wall of her downstairs tech fortress at the Elk Valley, Wyoming, Police Department. Almost eight o'clock. She always liked the near silence at the end of the day after most people had gone home. Her brain worked better when she could be alone and hear nothing but the thoughts in her head, the kind of silence she'd craved as a child. No one shouting, no one fighting, no one crying in a corner. Group homes were not for the squeamish.

She'd promised her grandmother she'd be home by now. The last home visit from the adoption agency would take place tomorrow and she wanted to finish setting up Enzo's bedroom. He already lived with her as a foster child, but he'd officially become her child if all went well.

She could finally adopt Enzo and make him her own. She already loved the toddler but a few setbacks had kept the red tape of the adoption tied up. She'd had a busy year. As a technical analyst for the police department and the Mountain Country K-9 Unit, she'd helped solve a serial killer cold case. The investigation spanned eight months. During that time, she'd also been targeted by a stalker—a woman from her past who'd tried to defame her to the adoption agency—who'd finally been arrested. With Christmas fast approaching, Isla was ready to put those difficult events behind her.

"Things are good here, honey," her grandmother, Annette, said. "I can't wait for you to get home so we can finally celebrate. I'm going to be the best *abuela* in the world."

"You are already that, Granny Annie," Isla replied, glad she lived across the street from the station. She'd been a foster child all of her life and when she'd aged out, by the grace of God, Annette, the maternal grandmother she'd never known, had been waiting for her with an offer she couldn't refuse. A home and funding for college.

"I am, aren't I?" her ever-feisty grandmother replied, her bubbly laugh sending sweet chimes out over the airwaves. "Hurry home. I made flan for dessert."

Isla's favorite. Having her grandmother move in with her to help with Enzo did have its perks. Isla had a lot to celebrate this Christmas. The excitement of finally being Enzo's mother kept her going even when she was exhausted. Thankful that her dream had come true, she didn't need anything else for Christmas. Having Granny and Enzo with her, after the year she'd been through, gave her the peace she'd prayed for so long. Now she could truly relax and enjoy this final step.

She closed her files, saving them in an encrypted cloud. Before she shut everything down, she did one last check—she liked things neat—then grabbed a small laptop and some flash drives so she could finish up a few files before taking a week off. Always on call, she planned to enjoy some time with Granny Annie and Enzo over the next few days. Quiet time, so precious, to cuddle and dream of gifts and goodies.

Heading toward the elevator, she stopped and went still when she heard footsteps echoing from the stairs. Who could be coming down to her lab without warning so late at night?

"Isla, you're still here."

"Michael?" The local vet took care of the department's K-9 officer dogs and did a great job at it. Handsome and quiet, his hazel eyes always alert, his hair always needing a comb, he never had much to say, and he had no reason to come looking for her. And yet that shiver of awareness made her glad to see him. "What are you doing here?"

Then she saw the massive dog standing like a stone lion with him. "Hey there, fellow. Don't tell me you want to work in the lab?"

Neither the dog nor the man responded to her humor.

Silence. They both stood with guarded gazes, the tension around them palpable. What was going on?

Michael Tanner filled her electronic space like an oak tree spreading over a rose garden. Granny would call him *fine*. Nice-looking and muscular, with a stoic expression that showed he meant business. And so did the beautiful black-and-tan dog with him. A Malinois.

"I need your help," he said. "In a technical way."

Trying to make things light because she really wanted to get home, she said, "As pickup lines go, that one is unique."

"I'm serious." His gaze flickered from her to the stairs behind him. "Can I come inside?"

Why had she even said that about pickup lines? Lifting her shoulders and chin, she said, "I was about to go home."

Michael ran a hand over his thick gold-brown hair, which matched the dog's fur almost perfectly. "Bogi is in danger. He has a target on his back."

He nodded toward the dog and said nothing else.

"Is this Bogi?"

"Yes, aka Bogi the Narc Shark. Highly trained in drug detection, but he's an all-purpose K-9. He recently sniffed out a shipment of fentanyl and other drugs worth over ten million dollars. A raid down in Texas."

"Wow, impressive," she said, offering her knuckles toward the dog. Bogi gave her a brown-eyed stare down but didn't sniff her hand. More than highly trained. Like lightning on a leash. The big dog shifted his head, the leather collar around his neck jiggling.

She glanced back at Michael. "So how did he wind up in Wyoming?"

"Because his work is so impressive, someone wants him dead," Michael replied, his words low and whispery. "I'm supposed to be hiding him, but these people always find what they want."

"These people?" Isla's heart rate pulsed some heavy beats. How many times had she helped find and put away *these people*? "Define that, please?"

"Cartel people," Michael explained. "It's a long story and I don't have much time. It's top secret—me having him in the first place. But I think they've found out and I can't reach my contact in Texas."

"As in, the cartel people are looking for you two?" she asked, her brain moving into gear even though her imagination created creepy scenarios. "Were you followed here?"

"I don't think so," Michael replied in a voice that made him sound like an undercover spy. "I can't be sure, but the place is like a ghost town tonight what with the holidays coming up. You were my last resort."

"And yet, another great line to win a woman's heart," she said, because she always used sarcasm to hide her fear. And she sometimes blurted out whatever popped into her head. "Get in here, Doc, and let's see what we can find out."

She studied Bogi. "And don't worry, handsome. Sounds like you're a major hero. We'll see what we can find and who we can find to protect you." Glancing at Michael, she said, "I'll need to report this to Chase, of course." When he didn't respond, she went on, "Nora is out of town right now."

The police chief, Nora Quan, had taken a few days off for the holidays.

"They'll both want an explanation."

Chase Rawlston, FBI Special Agent in Charge, and the head of the Mountain Country K-9 Unit, had saved her life when he'd caught Lisa King, a woman who'd been a preteen in the group home where Isla had spent most of her life. Lisa had been her stalker, seeking revenge because she'd blamed Isla for her little brother's disappearance years ago. She'd tried to ruin Isla's credentials and terrorize her into thinking she'd never be able to adopt. It had almost worked, but Chase and the team had watched out for Isla. She trusted him. He'd know what to do for Michael, and she'd help in any way she could. Probably a veterinarian overreacting.

Only, Michael Tanner never overreacted. Some of the team members called him Mr. Cool. Always calm and focused on the animals that came to his clinic, just as he now focused on the trained dog beside him. Isla could feel the tension pinging off him like shell casings pounding the ground. She had to help him. And not because she might have a tiny crush on him. Just part of her job. Or so she told herself.

She'd hurry and call Chase for advice. She couldn't risk getting involved in anything that might mess up what could be her last opportunity to finally adopt Enzo.

Before she could find her phone, however, Michael held up a hand. "Don't make that call yet."

After she gave him a dagger-filled stare, Michael Tanner followed Isla over to the massive desk where she restarted her equipment. He watched as several different screens blinked and churned and sputtered, the bells and whistles of technology humming along at warp speed while his life had come to a complete halt. He considered her the best at tracking down information that could slay dangerous criminals. After all, she'd been put on a task force to hunt a serial killer. She sure didn't need any more danger coming from him.

They barely knew each other, but his gut told him he could trust her. He'd seen the petite, brown-eyed woman in action and he'd always been impressed with her professionalism and her need for justice. She worked fast, too. He could almost see the information he'd given her percolating in her brain. Tonight, he had that same need for justice in mind, and the one person he wanted to talk to couldn't be found. Isla could help. She could locate just about anyone using her tech talents.

But right now she shook her head and glared at him. "What are you saying? I have to alert someone and Chase is the SAC. I report to him when Nora's not around."

"I'm sorry, Isla. I'm trying to keep a low profile, so let's keep this between us for now. All I need is intel on one person—the friend who asked me to do this."

"You're right about this place being deserted," she said, her gaze questioning his every move. "The task force is taking a break, spread out through the whole month, but I still need to report this. I'm taking some time off next week. Monday, I'm signing the official papers to adopt Enzo, and I'm going to enjoy the holidays with him. So let me get you some help before I leave."

He heard the determined inflection in her words. She really wanted to get away from him. Could she sense the danger that surrounded him, the kind of danger that could ruin innocent people's lives? This was why he held friends at bay. He couldn't—shouldn't—have come here.

"I'd heard about that," he said, unable to tell her that someone had tried to break into his clinic. He could handle a fight, no problem. But when it came to animals, he'd go beyond a fight. And he refused to think of those dark days of anger when he looked for the fight and welcomed it. Not now, when Bogi's life depended on Michael keeping his cool.

She pivoted back toward him and Bogi, bristling in an urgent-business mode. "So what happened and what do you need?"

He was about to explain when they heard an echoing crash

overhead. Gunshots on the floor above, followed by a thud. Did an officer on duty get hit? He gave Bogi the silent signal.

"They followed me," he whispered as he glanced over his shoulder. He shouldn't have come here. Now they'd target Isla, too. Grabbing her by the arm, he pushed her toward the stairs. "We have to go. Now."

Isla's eyes widened with a glow of surprise. "Go where? If we're not safe in police headquarters."

He tried to tug her behind a big cabinet.

Isla pulled away, disbelief mixed with traces of fear in her eyes, a gasp escaping her parted lips.

More shots, footsteps hurrying. Then the elevator dinged, and the door slid open to reveal a big man in black with a gun nestled in his hand.

Isla and the man stood face-to-face for a split second while Michael blocked Bogi behind the cabinet. Before the man could do anything, Michael swung around and fired one shot, hitting the intruder in his left shoulder. He fell to the floor.

Isla screamed as Michael dragged her away, Bogi getting between the unconscious man and them, a low growl his only sign of aggression.

"Guard," Michael commanded Bogi. "Isla, don't move."

She gave him a look that shouted at him, then she whirled toward the man bleeding on the floor, but the K-9 stood guard. Michael couldn't explain things right now, but she'd want answers and she deserved to know what was really going on. He'd flipped a switch and she'd witnessed it. No turning back now.

Michael checked the man's pulse. "He'll live, but we have to go."

She shifted back. "Shouldn't we wait until the police come?"

Michael shook his head. "No, we can't. You're not safe. They want Bogi, dead or alive. But mostly dead. And I'm pretty sure they want me, too. Really dead."

"You failed to mention that part," she said, suddenly diving into gathering more equipment. She grabbed electronics she'd need. They both knew to be prepared for anything. But right now, she needed to get out of here.

"Leave it," he said. "We need to go now."

He shoved her toward the outer door while she grabbed her backpack. "I'm taking this," she said in a breathless rush that dared him to argue. "I have one of my secure laptops in here."

"We're gonna need more than electronics," he replied. "My past has finally caught up with me, Isla."

Chapter Two

A thousand thoughts moved through Isla's mind like a gurgling river. Anger and frustration, empathy and understanding, and finally, acceptance and resolve. Michael guided her out of the compound in a way that told her he'd done this before, his body tense, his gaze scanning like a radar zooming in on a target. He told her to put a hand on his shoulder and keep it there. Michael had a gun and a new attitude, now in full commando mode. Something she couldn't grasp right now. Something that made her see why Michael Tanner had intrigued her and made her aware of him each time she'd been around him. Something dangerous, and dark, and disturbing. He was a warrior. He moved with precision, his footsteps light, his grip on her heavy and heated, while they skirted the extreme perimeters of the buildings and parking lots. Bogi followed his every command, sniffing, guarding, watching.

Isla shifted her backpack and wondered since when did an animal doctor know K-9 signals at every turn? Yes, he moved like a trained K-9 handler, like a trained soldier. Maybe he'd worked in that position before becoming a vet? A military position? A lot of veterans came home and found work that involved the police. Or maybe he'd trained so he could be more capable around the dogs?

No. This man—this side of Michael Tanner—showed more than a love of animals. His actions were calculated and deliberate, cautious and determined.

She'd have questions later. But right now, she had to alert someone. "I need to call my grandmother," she said when they were beyond the complex and moving from tree to tree. "She's with Enzo. Really, my house is right there on the corner. We could run over there."

"No," he said, that one word sharper than a knife blade.

Isla stopped in her high-topped turquoise tennis shoes. "What do you mean, no? I have to, Michael. I'm about to sign the adoption papers. In the morning I have one more person coming from the agency to see how things are going. I want to go home."

"They know you're with me," he said, giving her a firm solid-as-a-wall glance. "They'll do whatever it takes to get to Bogi."

Isla's heart raced ahead while she tried to comprehend things. Darkness permeated her with the kind of fear she'd fought against most of her life. The kind that had made her hide in corners and cower in her bed late at night. She didn't cower these days. All in for justice, she'd learned to push fear to the far corners of her mind.

But now she had someone else to protect. Enzo. "They'll try to harm me or my family?"

"Yes," he said, glancing around. "We need transportation."

Isla's heart pierced against her ribs, her throat went dry. "My car's at my house, where I am going right now."

Michael held her arm, his fingers like steel against her skin. "No. We need to keep moving."

"I'm not going anywhere until you explain about your past. Are you kidnapping me?"

"No," he said, his own frustration showing in the dull glow

of a winter moon. "No," he said in a softer voice. "I'm trying to protect you. Turn your phone off. Now."

Isla shook her head, disbelief tearing through her soul. "I have to warn my grandmother. She moved in after we renovated my place because of the fire. She and Enzo are at my house, waiting for me."

She glanced down the street to where Christmas lights sparkled on her front porch, her mind searching like a laptop engine for a way out of this. She wanted to be in that little cottage, where a fresh-smelling tree stood decorated with colorful bulbs and trinkets, and gifts were wrapped and waiting, where the smell of cinnamon and roasted pecans would fill the air. Enzo's first Christmas with her. She couldn't miss that.

But Michael held her, his whisper low and raspy like steel grating against concrete. "If you go home, they'll both be in the line of fire, Isla. It's safer if we get you away from here as quickly as possible."

Isla dug in her boot heels. "I can't leave them."

"We'll get some protection on your home, once we're out of here. This is no joke. I got clearance from high up to protect Bogi. He's got a bounty on his head. I'm supposed to be hiding him and now we've been compromised." He gave her a dangerously determined stare. "And because I came to you for help, that means you've been compromised, too."

"Then *let* me help," she said, thinking he spoke like a commander. "Shots were fired at the police department, so right about now they'll find that wounded man in my lab. They'll want explanations. The cameras will show you and I leaving together. I need to get an encrypted message to Chase. He'll go after whoever is trying to get to Bogi, but first he'll want answers. I want answers, too." She watched his reaction— nothing. Just a stone wall hiding a fortress. "Like right now."

A lift of his chin gave her a hint that he'd heard her. Sirens whined through the night. "It's out on the radio now. That should scare them off for a while. I'll give you answers when I know you're safe."

"Meantime, I'm calling Chase."

He held her arm. "It's still too risky to make your call. Chase knows me, Isla. He'll understand I had to get you out of there."

Isla shivered, the adrenaline wearing off to leave her shaking in her wool peacoat and flower-embossed jeans. She'd worked on hundreds of criminal cases, but she'd never been thrown into the middle of one. But that man could have killed Michael and taken Bogi. She'd been a distraction, at least.

Watching her, he finally said, "Let me get you somewhere safe and I'll explain. Then you can send your encrypted message. Meantime, that wounded man can answer to whoever finds him first. If he's still alive."

She didn't argue but as soon as she could, she would get away from him and his need to protect her. She couldn't go through this kind of thing again, this being afraid, running from the shadows, always trying to find her way to peace. She had to stay out of trouble for Enzo's sake.

They'd made it three blocks south of the police department when a dark SUV came barreling toward them, its big wheels bouncing and growling like an angry tiger as the driver accelerated and headed straight for them.

Michael pushed her down into the leftover early snow and held his body over hers. Bogi dropped in front of them, his head up, his ears out. For a brief moment, Isla felt a shield of protection, something she'd never felt before, something comforting and dangerous all at the same time.

The truck sped by, then did a swift turn, swerving around toward where they were hiding behind a huge mass of evergreen shrubbery. That ended the brief whiff of protection she'd felt.

Isla held close to Michael, bracing herself. The truck would hit them and probably kill both of them. And what would happen to Bogi? What would happen to Granny and Enzo?

She had to stop this. But before she even moved an inch, Michael rolled over and pulled out what looked like a slender grenade from his jacket pocket, his finger tugging at the clip.

Then he threw it toward the roaring truck.

Isla waited for the explosion, bracing herself. But no explosion came. A bright flash of blinding light followed by a huge puff of gray smoke that filled the truck and cut off the driver's ability to see. A flash-bang. Military grade.

She lay frozen until Michael lifted her into the air and said, "Run."

She ran, glancing back as the truck hit the tree and knocked out a light post. When they were about a half mile away he finally stopped to drag her into an alley, Bogi never leaving his side.

After Michael scanned the street, he spotted a hole-in-the wall bar and grill. "Let's go inside there and sit in the back."

"What if they find us?"

"We run out the back into the alley across from this one."

She took a breath and turned to the man who'd ruined her night. Shivers slipped along her spine like fingers trying to grab at her. "Who are you really, Michael Tanner? And don't even try to lie to me. I have enough equipment in my bag to dig deep into that past you mentioned, and I'm pretty sure it's either military or you're a trained assassin." Grabbing him by the collar, she added, "But I'd rather hear the truth from you, here and now. Or I'm walking."

Michael gave her a fierce stare, the shadows around them making him look like a prowling lion. "That would be a big mistake."

Michael didn't know where to begin. He could have hidden out somewhere until the heat was off. Instead, he'd rushed out without a plan, his one goal to get to these people before they got to him. Someone had used Bogi as a lure to reveal Michael's whereabouts, to flush him out. Not that he'd been deliberately hiding. But he had kept a low profile and tried to stay out of trouble.

Now trouble had found him.

As they sat in a grimy booth by the back door of the dank-smelling, crowded bar, he said, "We need transportation."

People gave them surprised looks but Bogi wasn't kicked out. The staff didn't seem to care one way or the other and the few scrappy patrons didn't even take a second glance.

Isla did a scan of the few working red lights on the twisted strings of Christmas ornaments and the sad little fake tree that hovered dangerously close to falling off the corner of the battered bar top. Not exactly romantic, not that he had any romantic thoughts at the moment. He'd always liked Isla and now he admired her, too. She didn't back down and she would get away from him if she found an opportunity.

"Don't worry about a getaway car yet," she replied, her pretty eyes fired up and angry. "You need to tell me the truth. I can't run off with you and leave everything behind."

"I'll make sure things are okay with Enzo," he said. "You'll get to adopt him."

"Wow, you have that much power? What kind of animal doctor are you?"

"The kind that goes all out to protect an innocent K-9 officer dog, a war dog," he said after he'd given Bogi some water from a paper cup he gotten from a waitress. Then he scratched the dog's neck just over his thick collar. "It's a long story."

Isla gave him a sarcastic stare. "I've got nothing but time, thanks to you."

A spitfire, but petite and nice-looking, her eyes dark and open like an unexplored cavern. Only he didn't have time to explore caverns or figure out women. And she was right. He'd pretty much ruined her time off. Depending on how this played out, he might ruin her life.

So he decided to talk. She could guide him through the truth of this maze by following the online footprints. He had his suspicions, but he wouldn't divulge them yet. He needed the kind of proof that couldn't be disputed.

They ordered sodas. "Are you hungry?" he asked her, thinking she had to be.

"No. I can't eat. Too wound up. Start talking, Doc."

He sent the waitress away with their drink orders. Time to level with Isla. He owed her the truth.

"I started out at Lackland Air Force Base in Texas. As you probably know, it's a joint base with Fort Sam Houston Army Base. I've always had a love for animals, so I immediately applied for the Military Working Dogs program at JBSA."

"Wow," she said, filling in the blanks. "Joint Base San Antonio. So you trained with the Army? That's an impressive program. Most of our dogs come from there." Glaring at him, she asked, "Why haven't I heard this before? Maybe because your background is on a need-to-know basis?"

"That's right," he said, watching the door for any suspicious customers. Although most everyone in this dive looked suspicious. "Bogi and I trained together then went into security forces, part of the military special ops program. We worked for the Department of Defense, doing two tours in the Middle East, searching for explosives and narcotics. Bogi is an all-purpose K-9, trained to track anything or anybody. He's good with finding bombs and drugs."

The dog lifted his head but remained settled near Michael's feet, his nose constantly lifting in the air.

"And you?" she asked. "You're obviously trained for something dangerous, and you have a past that doesn't include being a veterinarian."

Michael lowered his head. "You're right. I have a...past that I've tried to forget. My last few months on tour, we were sent on a dangerous mission that went bad. People died on both sides. I got injured, so I decided to leave the military. Which is why I went to Plan B—becoming a veterinarian." He shrugged. "It keeps me close to the K-9s and because of what I went through as a military handler, I can help them both physically and mentally."

He couldn't give her details of his past assignments. That would involve confidential information and put her in more danger. If she knew the truth—all of the truth—she would walk right out of here as she'd threatened.

Isla sat silent for a moment, then said, "I know there's more to that story. I have enough compassion to know most military people don't like to open their wounds to anyone, especially the emotional wounds." She took a deep breath. "And I'm sensing both you and Bogi have an emotional bond."

He tried not to flinch. "You might say that, yeah."

"So how did you wind up here?"

"I saw an ad on a job site. The part about working with K-9s got my attention," he replied. "I needed to start fresh, away from Texas and the memories, and because I had enough experience on both ends of the spectrum, both in handling and providing medical attention to the dogs, I felt like God had given me a nudge. Bogi had moved on with another handler, but his partner got killed only a few months after they were together. I kept in touch through a friend stationed back at JBSA. Bogi suffered even more trauma after his partner's death, and the base brass wanted to put him down."

"No." Isla glanced at the dog sitting there so noble and calm, so alert and sure. "He's a hero." He saw resolve dawning in her light brown eyes. "You said he got hired out for one last mission—to bring down a drug cartel. So, when he found that supply and cut off a big chunk of their income, the cartel put out a hit on him. They won't forget that. They'll kill him to make a point. We can't let that happen."

"Yes, they'll make him an example to scare others," Michael said. "Human or animal, they'll make sure someone pays."

He didn't tell her the rest of his suspicions. Bogi had been handpicked for that last mission because he'd been trained to be aggressive at sniffing out drugs. One last chance to prove himself or end it all in a noble way if he got injured or killed?

Michael couldn't be sure, but stranger plans had gone down. And something about this whole thing—him being singled out to protect Bogi—smelled rotten. But how could he say no? He still did contract work here and there as needed, and this was one of those times. He'd do anything to protect Bogi.

"Because you came to me for deep dives into the dark web—these people will want me dead now, too. I'm beginning to see the picture."

Michael opened his mouth to speak, then quickly hushed when the creaking double doors swung open and two men in black leather jackets walked in and scanned the room. He gave Bogi the silent command, then put a finger to his lips and dropped a ten-dollar bill on the table. Motioning Isla toward the door closest to them, he tugged her up and into his arms while he tried to shield both her and Bogi.

"Lean on me as if we're leaving together. Like a couple."

Shock covered Isla's face as he held her tight, their backs turned away from the men. Michael watched out of the corner of his eyes as he hurried her and the dog out.

The men searched back and forth. Michael glanced back and locked eyes with one of them. "They've spotted us. Run, Isla."

Chapter Three

Isla ran for her life. Not only did she run from those massive men who'd come into the bar, but she needed to get away from the way she'd felt when Michael had swept her into his arms and held her close. Could she ever breathe properly again?

A big truck turned down the alleyway as they slipped off to the right and sprinted as fast as they could to the next street. Isla's heart raced and her backpack felt like a load of heavy stones hitting against her backbone, but she couldn't leave it here on the streets. It was her connection—their connection—to find someone out there to help them.

"They must have trackers on one of us," Michael whispered, his breath huffing as he searched his clothes. "It might be difficult for them to do, but they'll keep coming even if we find any bugs."

Isla's mind went spinning ahead on all cylinders, her thoughts sputtering like a print-out spitting out of a machine while she checked herself and her backpack.

"Nothing," she said. "I can't believe this."

Michael tugged her close. "I'll get you home soon, Isla. I promise."

"I don't know if you can promise me anything at this point."

He put his hands on her elbows, his expression deeply etched with a dangerous determination. "I got you into this and now it will be up to me to get you out. Bogi and I can do that together. I promise. And I always keep my promises."

Still stunned by the way Michael was holding her, Isla tried to stay calm. She had handled delicate, intricate evidence for years, but this was different. This *evidence* chased a man and dog, trying to kill them, and her, too, for that matter. How could she find a way to finish what Bogi had started and end this evil cartel? Not just for her sake or Michael's and Bogi's sake. But for all the people out there addicted to drugs. Hadn't she seen enough of that living in a group home?

How can I make a difference? How can I go up against a cartel?

And still keep the life she'd always dreamed of.

She said a prayer, asking for intervention. *I can't lose Enzo. I can give him the love he needs, a good home, a safe place to grow up. I'm so close. But I can't get myself out of this. I need help, Lord. Michael and Bogi need Your help.*

Could she really help Michael? Doubts started tugging her down as they weaved from street to street, hiding behind buildings, trees and bushes. When would this end? When could she sit down and catch her breath and let Chase know their situation? He'd have a team together in no time and get them out of this mess.

Michael tugged her toward a busy area shrouded in mushrooming oak trees. "I'm going to rent a car."

She saw a shabby car rental building on the corner and nodded. Then her mind went to work. "In your name?"

"I have other names," he admitted. "I'm still backstopped for various reasons."

Backstopped—meaning he had a whole fake background set up in case anyone vetted him. Which meant he probably still did some freelance work for the DOD or the CIA. Contract work. He considered this contract work. Was he a spy?

Or an agent on call? All this time, she'd seen him come and go at headquarters and never once did she imagine this quiet, intense man had a hidden past. And was a hero, too. He couldn't accept that right now. Or maybe, he needed one more fight to become a hero again, to right those wrongs from the mission that had gone bad?

She wouldn't press him any more for now. He'd carried his secrets so well, he had everyone fooled. Or did he?

"Does Chase know everything about you, Michael?" she asked as they hurried toward the blinking lights of the auto rental place.

He didn't respond at first. He was on high alert and she should be, too. Bogi mastered the art, doing his thing, looking aware and intense. Trained. Dangerous. They were both trained and dangerous, and they moved together like one, their shadows merging in the dark night like a giant superpower.

"Michael?"

He finally turned before they went inside the building. "As you said, he is the SAC and the team he put together will continue to work closely with the locals. He knows what he knows, and that's all I can say."

"You don't have to say anything else. Chase won't reveal anything. He's solid."

"I know," Michael said. "He's the only one I can trust right now, besides you."

"You trust me?"

"Only if you'll trust me," he shot back. "Let's get this done so we can be on our way."

She followed him into the dingy fluorescent-lit office, but she wanted badly to ask him where exactly they would be going.

He didn't know where to take her. Finally, he decided he'd rely on one of the safe houses he'd used before when things got dicey. He thought he'd left the worst behind but being a contracted undercover operative for years had left a lot of enemies along the path. Could one of them be tied in with the cartel?

But why? Which one? Revenge? Boredom? Playing games to mess with his head? Or someone going all vigilante on him?

Midnight, and the rental car wasn't the best. A small economy model which used less gas, but a tight squeeze for Bogi in the back. The big dog kept scratching at his collar. For now, Isla and Bogi were safe.

"What's your plan?" she asked, sounding defeated as she accepted what had happened. Her tone went low and raw, the rage she had to be feeling hissing like a live wire with each word.

She'd never forgive him for this.

"Right now, to get you and Bogi off the streets and then you can let Chase know you're with me and safe." He checked the mirrors and did a zigzag across the town center and then out onto a less traveled road with foothills and deep ravines on each side.

Isla kept glancing around. "Think he'll buy that? He's probably reviewed the station's video. He'll see you coming down to my lab, and then shooting that man and forcing me out the door."

"He has to know I got you out of there for a reason. He knows me. Knows how I operate."

"Too bad I didn't know that before now, too."

Michael wanted to explain more, but he had to focus. "Look, I do what I have to do when things need to get done. And right now, this is my mission. To protect this K-9. And you."

She stared at him as if he'd turned to stone. "I think you and I should sit down and come up with a plan *together*. I turned my phone off. I'm sure Chase will have figured out why I disappeared with you by now. He'll likely have put a patrol on my house. But I have my own obligations and I can't risk getting caught up with a cartel. I need to find a way to get that cartel off our backs." She let out a sigh. "I can't even believe I said that."

"I'm sorry," he replied. "I thought if I could do some digging—the kind that needs to stay off the record—I could quickly access the situation and make a solid decision. I must be getting rusty."

"I'm sorry, too. You're obviously trained to avoid such things. Whatever happened to you before, you've let your guard down now. You're doing work you love. I can't fault you on that, but what stirred this up?"

She had him there. "I trusted the wrong people," he said. "I won't make that mistake again."

"Do you bring people here often?" Isla asked Michael when they entered the little cabin nestled at the bottom of a stone-faced ridge near the Laramie Mountain foothills.

"Only when necessary," he said. "It's off the beaten path but it has great internet and cell reception."

"I'm guessing the best, right?"

He gave Bogi the sit command. The dog made himself at home but kept his ears up. "It has to be for obvious reasons."

"So you have this side hustle? I mean, contract work, because of your experience in the military?"

"Yeah, on an as-needed basis."

Isla studied the sparely decorated cabin. A nice fireplace, a galley kitchen with a two-burner stove and small refrigerator, and a lot of windows with the curtains drawn. A front door with heavy bolts, and a back door with a fancy security box attached to it. A safe house masquerading as a quaint cabin.

What had he gotten her into?

She sank down onto the worn plaid couch and tugged out her laptop and phone while he fed Bogi some food he'd dragged out of a closet and poured him some water. The dog lapped it up, then shook his head, the rivets on his collar shining.

"Okay Bogi, you deserve some playtime." Pulling a roped ball out of the same closet, he threw it toward the big dog.

Bogi leaped into the air to catch the toy, then retreated to a corner to enjoy gnawing on his treat.

Those two had a bond that she'd seen working for the K-9 team. Bogi and Michael would protect her, but mostly, they'd take care of each other, too. That brought her a small measure of comfort.

After Michael did another search for listening devices, and checked both their rucksacks for bugs, only to find nothing, she turned to him. "I need to let Chase know I'm okay. I only hope these people didn't go to my house." She pushed at her hair and tried not to panic. "What if they did?"

Glancing at the door, Isla wanted with all her being to run.

Michael stood in her way. "Isla, don't do anything to endanger them or yourself."

"I haven't. You have."

"I know and I'm going to fix it." He guided her back to the sofa, while she wished she hadn't been so sharp with him. But hey—stress.

"They don't know where you live. Yet." He helped her sit down and then checked the curtains and blinds before pulling kindling from a woven basket to start a fire. "Send Chase a message but not on your phone. Send it on your fancy laptop."

"I can do that," she replied. Then she got to work, ignoring the cup of hot tea Michael brought to her.

I might be out of town for a while. Can you water the plants? Use the gold key. And make sure the house is secure since no one should be there now. Sorry—got tied up at the lab but I'm out now and with a friend.

Michael brought over a cup of instant coffee for himself and sat down beside her. "Mind if I read it before you send it?"

She pushed the laptop around and took a sip of the strong

but slightly stale tea, shivers moving down her spine despite the fire burning away. Nervous and worried, she kept talking despite her brain telling her to shut down. "The gold key is code for I'm in trouble. My granny always had a safe word for us to use if something happened. If…my biological dad ever tried to find me."

Michael's eyes darkened, making her wish she'd stayed as mysterious as he seemed. This man would easily commit murder to save Bogi and her. "Did he harm you?"

She did a quick head shake, but the floodgate had been opened. "No. He died in prison when I was twelve. He'd been put there for domestic abuse, but he got out after a few years. Then he was sent back the second time—for murder. I didn't know he'd died so Granny and I were always careful. Even though we finally found out he couldn't hurt me, we still used the code." She inhaled a breath and let it out.

She took a breath then let it out, and the pressure of her situation hit her full force. "He went back after he killed my mother when I was too young to understand. I didn't know what had really happened until I was older. Now, I like having information firsthand." Frantic, she tried to gather her thoughts. "I need to see the whole picture, Michael. I'm not good at trusting people."

Michael shook his head, his eyes full of sympathy and anger, a jagged pain etched in his rugged features. "I'm sorry, and I mean that. I had no idea."

"I've never told anyone and I really don't know why I told you. I don't talk about it, you know."

"I understand, and I won't repeat what you've told me."

She believed him, but now he knew; now he'd seen her vulnerable side. "I imagine you have a thousand secrets inside that head of yours," she replied. "So I'll keep your secrets if you trust me with them, same as you keeping mine."

"That works," Michael finally said. "You've established

you're safe and with a friend, but still in trouble. We'll wait to hear from Chase."

He went back over to the kitchen and pulled cans out of the top cabinet. "I have soup and soup."

"I guess I'll have soup," she replied, suddenly hungry. Nerves. She'd always been that way, eating when anxious, or not eating because she was worried. But she also loved exercising out in the open air and eating healthy food when she could, a delicate balance. Tonight, her world had tilted and gone off balance. So soup.

He heated the soup in a big mug and brought it over with a sleeve of crackers. "Vegetable beef and not-so-fresh crackers."

"I'll take it." She nibbled a cracker and took in a spoonful of the salty mush. "Thank you."

He ate his and then placed his bowl on the battered coffee table. "I'm sorry, Isla."

She studied him, wishing they could have gotten to know each other under normal circumstances. He was a good man, a handsome man, but one she'd kept on the back burner as a coworker and acquaintance, no matter that she got a bit flustered when being around him. But those times had been brief and all business, or at functions with their coworkers. Not like this, alone with him in a cabin that seemed to shrink each time he prowled around the room.

Finally, she spoke. "Yeah, me too, for so many things."

Then she sat up straight. "Tell me who reached out to you to protect Bogi. We start there."

Michael ran a hand down his five-o'clock shadow. "My friend Dillon Sellers. He's moved up the ranks and is now a chief master sergeant at Lackland. He knows how I feel about Bogi. I had mentioned to him that I'd like to petition to take Bogi—adopt him—and retrain him, get rid of his trauma, give both of us time to heal." Michael looked away and then back to her. "I kept getting turned down, but now..."

"He got in touch with you after he realized Bogi had a target on his back?"

"Yes. After a big write-up in a local paper, the cartel got wind of it. The story made the national news, so word got out. And the bounty grew to a million dollars. I agreed on the condition that I'd be allowed to take Bogi. We got clearance to bring Bogi here. I've had him in an enclosed room at the clinic. I cleared my schedule and stopped kenneling any other animals over the holidays. I live right next to the clinic, and I have cameras on at all times."

"How long have you been hiding him?"

"About three weeks now." He shrugged. "I thought we were safe."

"Someone must have been aware, even before you picked up Bogi. The cartel must have hacked into your security system."

"Yes, and that's why I came to you. I think they definitely tapped into my security system and cameras. They could have been watching Bogi and me the whole time with eyes on the street and with monitoring the clinic and my home. Which is why I can't go back there either."

"What tipped you off?" she asked, her head in the game now. But her heart burned with worry for Granny and Enzo, which urged her forward.

"I heard a noise outside." He took the last sip of his coffee and shoved the mug away. "I went out the front door and saw a man running away. A man I thought I recognized."

"You think someone you know could be in on this?"

"Maybe. He's a local—Ralph Filmore—a retired veteran who hires out doing odd jobs. Someone could have hired him and sent him as a distraction so they could get to Bogi, but I scared him away before anything happened. Ralph is a good man, but his issues make him gullible. I've tried to help him, but he doesn't socialize well."

"They took advantage of that."

Michael let out a deep breath. "Yep. Which means they'd

been watching for a while and had seen him coming and going. I knew we'd been compromised so I grabbed some things and got Bogi into my truck as fast as I could. And I came to you because I wanted to see if I could track down the whereabouts of my friend Dillon, and also find the cartel members who've scattered since that big raid. And possibly track some people from my past." He let out a grunt. "Like I said, I think my past has caught up with me. Someone wants Bogi badly, but someone also wants me."

"For reasons other than you having Bogi?"

"Yes, and I think the answers are hidden somewhere deep in the system."

Isla stood and whirled to stare down at him. "The military system?"

"Exactly. I think someone back in Texas is setting me up."

Chapter Four

Isla kept pacing until she had her heart rate under control. "We start with everyone you knew from this raid that went bad. If you and Bogi were involved and someone from your team is after you, what's in it for them? Revenge, the reward, anger, justice or a psychopath getting thrills?"

Michael stared up at her with a mixture of apprehension and pride. "I think you've covered every angle, and frankly, it could be any or all of the reasons you've mentioned. Or it could be the enemy seeking retribution. You seem to understand that kind of thing."

She placed her hands on the back of the couch and faced him. "I have to cover all the bases. It's what I do. Who in your past would have a grudge against you? And could they be working with this cartel that's after Bogi?"

"Well, there could be a long line," Michael said, his eyes distant. "It's war, you know. Things happen and people have to blame someone. But I hadn't connected the two, no."

"And?"

Michael's expression held tight to his secrets, a window closing with a hard click, silence shouting at her. He deflected. "You're good at this, aren't you? Not only the technical stuff, but at asking all the right questions, too."

"I've had a lot of hands-on training and I've been around police officers—on both sides of the law—most of my life."

He smiled, which made him even more intriguing. "On both sides? You mean you've been in trouble with the law at times?"

"When I was in the system, yes," she admitted, her own dark moments bubbling up while she fretted about Enzo. What would happen if she never made it home to him? Michael needed to understand her urgent need to be with the little boy.

"My mother was a police officer. After my biological father killed her, the whole department watched out for me so I always turned to the police when I was afraid or concerned. That's why I studied criminal justice and became a tech analyst. He was an abuser, and he did what they all do. If he couldn't have her, then no one would."

Michael stood and came around the couch and tugged her against his chest. "Again, I'm so sorry and as you said about me, I wished I'd known this before."

"I'm only telling you now because I want to go home to Enzo and my grandmother," she admitted, the panic she'd held at bay breaking through to wash over her. "It's hard to explain. My granny and my mother were estranged because of my father. My parents were never married, but they lived together. Granny only learned about me after years of trying to piece together what happened. She spent a lot of time and money on tracking me down. I'd aged out and had no idea where to go or what to do. She showed up one day and told me she loved me and offered me a home and a college education."

Pulling away, she wiped her eyes then focused on Michael. "Which is why I want to get back to her and Enzo and celebrate this special Christmas with the people I love. I have to get to Enzo."

Michael stood across from her, his gaze dark with understanding and regret, misty with memories and misery. He looked away and then back to her. "I will make that happen."

She took two steps back before she caved and tugged him close again, anger warring with hope. "I'm going to hold you to that. First, let's check your security system for bugs. Then let's figure things out from the beginning. Make me a list of names and I'll research those first. It could be that someone from your past got caught up in this cartel and now has to make amends."

"Isla?"

She ignored the way he'd said her name with a hint of a plea, but she'd told him too much already. She didn't want to bend or break, not now. "I'm okay, Michael. I want to get this over with, please."

Michael went to a drawer and found a pen and paper. "Then let's get started."

Michael watched as she did her thing, going through back doors on the dark web to check his system, her head down, her lips tight, the tail of her ponytail like a soft golden-brown wrap against her neck. Three in the morning, but she kept on going even after she'd revealed her darkest secrets to him. Her mother—a police officer—hadn't been able to save herself. Isla tried to save everyone to make up for that.

And now, she was reliving the nightmare of what could go wrong. They had to hurry.

"See anything?"

Isla's gaze glowed with determination as her fingers moved with ballerina grace across the keyboard. "Oh, yes. Someone definitely hacked into your system." She hit a few buttons. "We could scan your videos, but that might alert them. We know they hired a local to mess with you—a distraction— while they planned to get inside."

Tension filled Michael's body, a burn flaring inside his stomach. "I let my guard down."

"No, they went around the guard walls. It happens."

"Not to me," he said, knowing he'd become complacent. "Well, we can't go back and change that."

"No, but I can alert a colleague to get that bug out of your system."

"Okay."

"I've also sent out feelers on some of the names you submitted. We should hear back on those soon."

"Thank you." He wondered if some of his old team members still blamed him for the loss of life they'd caused that day. Most of them had stood by him, but he had made the call to go forward with the operation based on the intel they'd received. Dillon had stood by him, never once accusing or pointing the finger at Michael. So why did Michael still feel so guilty?

And why couldn't he get in touch with Dillon? Had someone already got to his friend? Twisting his head left and right to ease the tension, Michael knew he couldn't keep Isla on the run. He'd have to think of something, and quick.

She tapped a few keys and sent another encrypted message. "This goes to a private message board, and it has thick, strongly protected walls. If this doesn't work, I have an AA back in the city."

He nodded, even more impressed with her. "Thank you." An AA was an accommodation address—an old-school way of getting messages out to agents and assets, like a private mailbox, a cutout hidden from the world. It could be a facility or a go-between person. It made sense in her line of work. He'd keep that information close.

Isla watched the pings and dings on her laptop screen. "Hey, wait. I think Chase is reaching out."

That got his attention. Chase wouldn't be happy about this, but Michael could handle Chase's anger. "What does he say?"

She read the message:

Plants watered. House secure. No one is there now. Used the gold key. Checked for you in the lab. Saw you'd left with

a friend. Busy at work now. Hope you have a safe trip. Keep
me posted and say hello to your friend. I can't wait to hear
the details.

"That sounds tight," Michael said. "He's moved your grandmother and Enzo. He's good, he's busy."

"He's investigating this," she added. "And us—why we're
involved in that shooting. He might find the truth before we
do."

"He doesn't know about the details behind me doing this
job, so he won't know exactly where to look. We'll stick with
you sending updates. I try to keep things vague."

"You don't have the luxury of being vague, Michael. I might
not be there to tell him the caliber of the bullet that took down
that man, but Chase already knows you fired the shot. He'll
be all over trying to figure out why."

"You're right," Michael said. "I met Chase when I first arrived. Because he's FBI, I had to read him in on my cover.
He's a shrewd man and devoted to serving justice."

"Wait. You came here to work as a veterinarian, using that
as a cover for your other work?"

"I did," he admitted. "But my other work is supposed to be
few and far between. I might not be in special ops anymore,
but I still have credentials and clearance in certain areas."

She glanced up, her chin down, and gave him a direct stare.
"Like a ghost?"

"Something like that."

"But you were wounded. Does that bother you now?"

She was fishing for details so she could vet him even more
than he'd already been checked. "A head injury and a lot of
scans, X-rays and therapy. I'm okay now, but I couldn't go back
out there and risk messing up another mission."

"Did your trauma mess up the last one?"

"No. I was okay when we raided that village. I took a bullet
and hit my head going down. Hard. On cement."

"Ouch. I can see why that would stall things. TBI?"

"A bad case of traumatic brain injury, yes. I still get head-aches when I'm tired, but I've been coping, leading the simple life, taking my meds."

"And now? How do you feel right now?" Her voice held concern coupled with anxiety. She still didn't trust him.

"I'm fine. Tired. Tense. But okay. You have to believe that, Isla."

Glancing at her watch, she said, "You should sleep."

"So should you. I can't sleep but I can stand watch."

Her laptop pinged. "Hold on." She studied the screen and then said, "So far we've found that one of your team members died of cancer last year. George Parton?"

"Yeah, a good man. We called him Dolly. Drove him nuts. We lost touch. He wouldn't have it in for me anyway."

"How about Tennessee Sanders? He's back in Tennessee and working as a security agent."

"Tenn Man? He's clean. I visit him now and then. I could reach out to see if he's heard or seen anything."

"I'll keep him on the list." She moved over all the names associated with his team. "Dillon is here, of course. But then, you'd have no reason to suspect the man who asked you to protect Bogi, right?"

"Right." A tickle went down Michael's backbone.

"Michael?"

"We've had our moments, but Dillon is solid."

"Does he have a nickname?"

"Yes." Michael smiled. "Dill Pickle."

"That alone could make him want to get revenge."

Michael got serious again. "It's not him." He couldn't see Dillon holding a grudge. "We were given the wrong intel, but the responsibility fell on my shoulders. Dillon vouched for me through the whole investigation."

"Okay, then."

"You don't believe me?"

She stood and stretched like a sleek cat. "I want to believe you, on finding your enemies and everything else. I've told you that. But you have to admit yanking me out of my comfort zone when I'd planned to go on vacation doesn't exactly make you one of my favorite people." She smiled.

"Was I ever one of your favorite people?" he asked, mainly to stall her and throw her off.

Surprise shifted to sarcasm in her eyes. "I liked you, but I didn't know you that well. Obviously. I still don't know you, but now I sure know *about* you. You're leading two lives and that is not an easy feat. I can barely deal with one life, so I don't think I'm quite ready to cope with your double identities."

He leaned against a chair and crossed his arms over his chest. Why was his pulse increasing with each second she stared back at him, her defiance moving from her eyes to her lifted chin?

He sent her a straightforward stare. "Would you like to get to know me?"

She let out a laugh and he grinned, glad he could ease her worries for a moment. Then she pushed at her ponytail and let out a sigh. "I would like to get to know you because I'm the curious type and because I find it hard to trust people who aren't honest with me."

He sighed. "I guess I've blown the first-impression thing, haven't I?"

"Pretty much."

They both went silent. He, leaning on the chair—her, standing by the old leather desk chair. Bogi's gaze ping-ponged from one to the other, while they kept eyes on each other. The silence lapsed into something else. A pause that became palpable.

Michael moved toward her, only wanting to reassure her, make her feel safe. She stood, her dark eyes flaring.

Then they heard a crash outside and the moment was gone in a flash of movement. Bogi leaped into the air and snarled, clearly having his own moment, ready to fight.

Isla shut everything down and dropped her small laptop into the dark recesses of her big backpack. "On the run again."

Michael grabbed his weapons and tugged her around the old leather sofa. "You might have to leave that behind."

"I will not," she exclaimed. "I'll use it for a weapon before I let go of it. This is the only thing I salvaged tonight."

She held her pack tight, causing him to realize she must have had one like this, living in the system, and she'd moved it with her from each and every home she'd had to live in, even the bad ones. A group home, before she aged out. How she must have protected that pack that held most of her belongings. Her treasures. He'd had a pack like that when he was on tour. Treasures he could send back home, or someone could send back home, if something happened to him.

"You can hold on to it, Isla, unless things get too hot. I have to save you, not that backpack."

"I can save myself," she whispered as they heard a ruckus outside. "I know how to hide."

"Not from the people after us," he warned, his heart leaping like Bogi's body, a need to protect her overtaking him. "Not from them." He went into action, setting up ways to trip and trick their intruders and buy them some time. By the time he'd finished with wires and moving heavy furniture, she wondered how anyone could get into this place.

A ping hit the window and Michael shoved her down.

"Bullet," he said. "The windows are bulletproof, but they'll have us surrounded if we don't hurry. They could start a fire to draw us out or set off a bomb to blow this place apart."

Those scenarios weren't helping her anxiety at all.

"How will we escape?" she asked, her gaze scanning every window in the same way she scanned the codes moving across her computer screen.

"I have a plan."

"That makes me feel better," she said on a droll note. "Want to share?"

He pushed at the sofa and then pulled up the rug that had been underneath the sofa. "Yeah. A tunnel through a cave that leads to a road where there's a shed with my old Jeep inside it."

Something hit at the door. More bullets or a human?

"It's time to move," he said, grabbing his own gear.

He pushed the sofa toward the front door to stall them, then tugged at the heavy rug again, just enough to open the portal. "Ladies first."

Isla looked at him, then looked down into the dark tunnel.

"Here," he said, nudging her.

A flashlight. "Thank you. I don't like the dark."

"Neither do I." He pushed her down and then sent Bogi in with her and ordered him to guard. "I'm right behind you."

After securing the door, which pulled the rug with it when it shut, Michael reached where she stood hunched over and waiting. He slipped past her, the scent of her floral shampoo wafting after him, a garden he didn't have time to explore.

"Follow me," he said, a sadness covering him in the darkness. She'd never follow him again after this, and they both knew that.

But this long night had to end one way or another.

Because dawn was coming.

Chapter Five

The tunnel held smoky lanterns lined up like mason jars full of fireflies, the silky shadows of spiderwebs and dust merging to give the walls a creepy, moldy glow. That didn't help Isla's anxieties or settle her nerves. She'd never liked dark, dank, closed-in places. Maybe because one of her foster moms had hidden her in closets when she'd acted out? Or had the same thing happened when her mother had hidden Isla from her father? Did babies remember such things?

"Hey, you okay back there?"

She blinked as Michael and Bogi rounded a curve that gradually began to elevate them. "I'm fine. Having a lovely Friday night—I mean Saturday morning—full of revelations and secrets. What's not to like?"

"So you're not fine?"

"I don't like any of this, but I especially don't like this tunnel and any minute now I'm going to have a panic attack if you don't get me out of here."

"We're there," he said, hitting on a button that opened what looked like a hatch out of some kind of dystopian movie. "Feel the cold air?"

She did, she felt the breath of fresh air hitting them. Bogi jumped out as if they were playing in the park, but he did a scent scan that showed this wasn't a park and he wasn't playing.

Michael helped her up the ladder and then tugged her to the left. "The Jeep's about a klick to the west."

A half mile or more, she figured while she studied the brutal terrain. "I can make that because I'm breathing again," she said, taking in a deep breath of the cold dawn air. "First that tiny cabin and then the tunnel. Our time together is nothing short of strange, Michael."

"Okay, got it. You're not happy, but we need to stay in the shadows and we have about ten minutes before the sun crests over that ridge to the east."

"Should we run?"

"No, but we can walk fast and stay crouched near the thickets and rocks, just in case."

"Got it." The man had gone from spy to soldier in a click of his own. How could she ever look at him in the same way after this? If they even got out of this.

They crouched and walked in a hurry until they reached an old shed, their breaths causing steam to lift out over the still, muted air. Michael opened the rickety locked door with a key from a big key chain inside his jacket, where she assumed he also had a change of clothes and some MREs—Meals Ready to Eat. James Bond or Jason Bourne? Or a desperate man trying to save a dog?

Bogi glanced at her as if he'd read her mind. Isla gave the dog her strongest frown but he didn't even flinch. Tough, that one. Exhausted and full of angst, she'd become giddy and a bit bold.

"Where to next—the Riviera?"

"I wish."

She had an image of him swimming in the sea, swimming toward where she sat on a lounge chair in the sun.

"Hey, stay with me."

She blinked again and got her thoughts back on track, back to the worry hole she'd carved in her brain and heart. She wouldn't cry, but bursting into tears would help her feelings. Only not so much her predicament. She couldn't run away now. She needed his protection. And...he needed her.

Another revelation that floored her. Michael needed her. And not just her expertise. He needed someone he could trust to get through this with him. Could she?

As he got them into the Jeep—*old* didn't begin to describe it—she thought of Enzo's dark eyes, so bright with hope, and Granny Annie, her one champion. Did they know how much she loved them?

"Are you going to make it?" Michael asked as he cranked the choking, coughing vehicle and geared it into a fast run along the bumpy mountain lane that would take them away from danger.

"I'm trying," she said, tears burning hot in her weary eyes. She should be home right now, waking up to her new world with Granny and Enzo.

"We've lost them for now, but we don't have much time." He glanced at her, and he must have caught the look on her face because he said, "I can't do this to you anymore, Isla. I'm going to find a place where you can be safe with your family."

Isla burst into tears then. She couldn't speak so she didn't reply.

Bogi glanced at her again and this time he whimpered under his breath, his big, dark eyes full of understanding.

The same as Michael's gaze landing on her for a brief second before he turned to face the road ahead of them.

Once they were safely miles away and headed in a zigzag of back roads, the long way back to Elk Valley. Michael glanced over at her. "I've made up my mind. I'm going to find a place to stop and I'm going to give you a message to send to Chase. I don't want to use my cell phone. I'll need him to set up you and your family in another place, not exactly an official safe house. The people after us might know all of my hidey-holes, so this will be different but somewhere with protection and still nearby, so we can possibly work with Chase on this."

"What have you got in mind?" she asked, swiping her eyes, hopeful for the first time since he'd walked into her lab.

He pulled the old Jeep over onto a lookout surrounded by rocks and trees then backed it off the road to hide it a bit and have it ready to take off if needed, something she'd do in this situation, too.

"A ranch," he said. "A big one with a lot of people around to keep watch and a lot of gun power to back that up."

Isla listened, her laptop ready, while they checked the road several times. Wondering what Michael wanted to convey, she waited to type his message, exhaustion finishing off what little adrenaline she had left. Her eyelids felt like heavy spools of weight and her hands shook a little bit. She missed her home and the life waiting for her.

Michael did one more scan and then started:

Need to find a quiet place for my friend to be alone. MN-Four should do the trick. It's secluded and has great views from every room. Can't wait to see the relatives there? I'll take care of the rest. Thx—Doc.

She looked up at him after she'd typed the words. "MN-Four? As in the McNeal Four Ranch near Laramie Mountain?"

"The very one," he replied, his tone heavy with hope and regret. "It's secluded and Cade McNeal knows his way around guns and horses, which could both come in handy. Plus, he owes me a favor for saving one of his mares and her colt during a rough birth. And another plus—his wife, Ashley, is a K-9 officer."

"I know her," Isla said. "Obviously."

He lifted his chin, his dark gaze on Isla. "Obviously, which means you'll feel comfortable around her. She'll help protect you and your family."

"Is the ranch one of your safe houses?"

"Nope."

She wouldn't get anything more out of him on that point. So she tried again. "That's not a big ranch house."

"No. And they might not agree. But for now, I think it can work. You'll be safe and we can keep trying to protect Bogi from the people after him, whoever that might be."

She would love to stay with Ashley and Cade. Ashley had been a rookie cop with the Elk Valley PD when Isla had been recruited as a member of the team they'd put together to catch a serial killer. The MCK-9 Unit had become a family and had been commissioned to work together on other cases. But Isla didn't want to put anyone else in danger.

"Are you good with this?"

"Yes, as long as we can keep everyone safe," she replied. "Now while we wait, let's consider what we know so far."

"Not much," he said, "but I appreciate your hard work. We've ruled out several people from my past."

"The cartel sends out red flags," she replied, her mind spinning again. "But maybe that's too obvious. We know they have a bounty on Bogi, but we also know they have ways of getting to people that no one ever sees. Why send a lonely retired veteran, and one with issues at that, to distract you? They would have gone in with guns blazing and taken out both of you."

"You make a valid point," he said, his gaze taut and all-seeing because of the image she'd presented. "We still need to consider the cartel members because they do want Bogi gone, and we can keep working on the remaining list of people from my past to jar any memories."

"Or we can consider combining the two," she reminded him. "They could be working together to off both Bogi and you."

"Yes." He went silent on that one, which made her think

he wasn't telling her everything about his past. "Maybe your hacker friends will come through."

"I didn't say I have hacker friends."

"You don't need to. We all know they offer their services in exchange for not going to jail. Assets, of course."

"Of course. We'll leave it at that."

He smiled. The man sure had a nice smile but he didn't quite know how to use it.

"I hope I'll hear more on that," she told him, getting back on point. "Once I'm settled in one spot and have time, I can dig a little deeper in figuring this out."

"I hope the McNeals will take us in," he replied as they got closer to town. "I'm letting Chase do the asking because I'm sure he'll take over once we get there."

"Us, we?" She pivoted on the seat, her heart bumping along with the ruts on the old road. "You're not planning on staying at the ranch, too, are you?"

He gave her a glance that told her this was nonnegotiable. "I plan to, yes."

"Why?"

"To watch over you and your family, and to be close so I can help you research this."

"I'll have Ashley to watch over me."

"I understand and I can come and go. I have to get back to my clinic and tidy things up but I'll be alert and careful. My receptionist has to be wondering where I am, though she's used to me having to leave town now and then without notice. I have a friend who fills in for me at times like this. I need to let her know, too."

Her.

His friend—a her. Well, none of Isla's concern, so why did hearing that rub against her skin like grit. A man like him would draw women like flies sticking to sugar. Quiet, a bit intimidating, mysterious and good-looking. The hard-to-read kind of man that made a woman want to get inside his head and figure him out, change him in places and keep him the same in other places. The wrong kind of man for Isla.

Or so she kept telling herself.

Her laptop dinged, causing her to break free of daydreaming. "Chase," she said.

Michael straightened in his seat. "Read it to me."

Your vacation is all set. Will pick up supplies tonight—and two suitcases. MNFour is booked. Should have some peace and quiet. Can check in ASAP. Will discuss future plans when I see you.

"We're in," Michael said, a long sigh of relief washing over him. "I feel better knowing you'll be with your family and safe again. I shouldn't have done this to you."

"It's okay." Her eyes burned a glistening bronze as the rising sun shimmered over the mountains off in the distance.

"No, it's not okay," he said. "I don't usually panic, but I had to think fast and get Bogi away from there. My mind went to logistics and analysis. I thought I could do this job alone and get intel then be on my way."

Isla watched the sunrise, her voice husky as she turned to glance at him. "I want to help you. I'm trying to do that. What's done is done, Michael. We'll get through this. I'm used to getting through things."

That comment hit Michael in the gut. He had a new perspective on the tech analyst, a new admiration for Isla. She worked hard and did so with purpose. She wanted justice in much the same way he did. She'd been through so much and yet, she rolled with the punches and recovered with a coolness that impressed him. But she shouldn't have to get through things.

"I'll make this right," he said.

Her laptop pinged again.

"Chase?"

She shook her head. "One of my contacts." Her gaze danced

over the screen and then back to Michael. "Michael, the man you saw running away from your clinic last night…"

Michael's pulse quickened. "Ralph?"

"Yes." Isla swallowed and looked back at the screen. "Found dead in a ravine about a mile from your clinic."

Michael hit the dash, causing Bogi to jump to attention behind them. "They killed him. He's no longer useful so they killed him. This is what they do, Isla."

He cranked the Jeep and spun out.

Isla held on and gave him a quick glance. "Michael, be careful. I'm sorry about your friend but you need to stay on the alert. They want you to give them Bogi."

"I'm not going to cave. I'm going to find the people doing this and I'm going to make them pay."

Isla shut down the laptop and held it against her stomach.

"I didn't mean to upset you," he finally told her. "I'm so angry and you're right. I need to control my temper. Anger got me into trouble the first time I made a mess on that mission. I won't let it ruin me again, and I especially won't let it ruin you and your life. That I can promise you."

Isla's eyes had deepened to a burnished brown in the morning sun. The touch of her hand on his sent a warmth throughout his system, giving him strength.

"I won't let that happen either," she said. "Not to you or to me. We'll figure this out together, Michael, because that's what we do, right?"

"Yes," he said. "It's our job, but now it's even more. It's personal. And it ends with me."

Chapter Six

"So here's the plan," Michael told Isla after he'd calmed down. "We need to find a hotel room and stay there all day until dark."

Isla didn't like hearing that, but he made good sense and she wouldn't complain. It wouldn't matter if she did. "Yes, because we can't arrive at the ranch in broad daylight. So where will we find a safe place?"

He watched the road behind them. "I know of a small, out-of-the-way motel near Long Lake. We can hang out there until tonight. We need to let Chase know."

She nodded, so fatigued she couldn't even argue with him. She typed a quick message:

Will arrive around dinnertime. Going to hang out and rest for a bit and enjoy the views.

Michael gave her a nod after she read it to him. "Okay, you do need to rest."

"I have to admit, sleep sounds good right now."

He zoomed to the north and Long Lake. "You can sleep and I'll do some digging of my own."

"How?" she asked. "You said you can't risk using your phone."

"I'll grab a burner," he explained. "I know a place."

"Of course, you do. Why didn't you mention that last night?"

"Last night and up until now, in survival mode, I tried to keep you and Bogi alive. We should be safe using your fancy laptop, but I need to make these calls myself. None of the people I'm calling would talk to you and they'd track your phone right away and probably expose our whereabouts."

"Burner phone it is, then."

She closed the laptop and then closed her eyes, the bump-bump of the Jeep luring her to sleep. But her dreams were dark and full of dangerous people, black closets and screams. She could hear Enzo crying and Granny calling out to her. She couldn't breathe.

She woke with a scream and felt the Jeep accelerating.

"Hold on, Isla," Michael said. "Someone is following us."

This was her nightmare.

Being chased on a winding mountain road, fearing for her life, worrying for her family. What could she do?

She'd pray. Prayer had always gotten her through the worst, and Granny had taught her to pray deep and with meaning after so many years of short chaotic and choppy prayers.

She closed her eyes as the Jeep hugged a curve with rocks on one side and a deep ravine on the other.

Dear Lord, help us now in our time of need. Protect Michael and Bogi and me. Keep my family and my friends safe. Help us to escape these evil people. Give us strength and hope, Lord.

Michael touched her arm. "Hey, you okay?"

"I'm praying," she said as they whirled and bumped, the ravine so close she could see dust and rocks spewing out around the vehicle and falling into nothing but air.

"Good idea."

He gunned the Jeep as they approached a downhill curve, a black truck grinding its gears behind them. "These back roads are a mess and treacherous."

"Really? I hadn't noticed." Her head hurt, and the lack of food and sleep had caught up with her. She'd pulled all-nighters before, but not while she was running for her life with a man who both thrilled her and confused her.

What has happened to my safe, quiet Christmas holidays?

"Yes," Michael shouted. He hit his palm against the shredded leather of the steering wheel. "I had hoped that would happen."

"What? They disappeared?" She twisted to see the truck behind them slowing down.

"Nope. The brakes are running hot on the truck."

"Oh, well." Her heart slowed down at about the same time he slowed the Jeep. "So they can't come after us anymore. For now?"

"Not with hot brakes." He glanced behind them. "Won't do any good to call this in. By the time the authorities find the truck, which is no doubt stolen or unregistered, the people in it will be long gone."

She nodded and inhaled a deep breath, then let it out. "I don't understand how they keep finding us. My equipment is encrypted to the max and you haven't used your phone. We both checked for trackers."

He nodded. "I can't imagine they would have planted anything on you before this started in the possibility that I'd go to you for help, and I've checked my clothes. But either they did plant a tracker we can't find or they've got eyes everywhere and they're toying with us. We'll have to hurry and hide the Jeep somewhere, then walk to the motel."

She went through her backpack again, checking every pocket and every corner. "I have the same things in here I carry home with me every night. My phone and the one laptop that I can use until I get back to the lab, and a few personal items." She stopped, looked over at him, then shook her head.

"What?" he asked, his dark eyes burning.

"What if someone got into the lab while I wasn't there. A cleaning person or someone dressed like an officer?"

"That's possible," he said. "They tapped into my clinic's security system somehow. But why would they bug your lab?"

"Maybe the man who showed up came there to do that but he stumbled on both of us instead?"

"But they'd have no prior reason to bug the lab," he reminded her. "Unless they were trying to bug the entire police station because they know I come and go there a lot."

"All possibilities," she said.

"All possibilities," he repeated. "We need a safe place to get it all together."

"The ranch," she said. "They'll have internet, at least, and I can take it from there. But we have to be careful. We don't want anyone attacking the ranch because we're there."

"No, but right now it's close and it's the safest place I can think of."

"Then let's get to that motel," she replied, ready to fall across a bed.

Then her laptop pinged an alert, causing both of them to jump.

"It's from Chase," she said. Then she read it to Michael. "Meet me at the Chateau. Now."

The Elk Valley Chateau was where most of the task force members who'd come from various states had stayed while trying to find the Rocky Mountain Killer. Now a hotel, it had once been a Victorian home. After being renovated, the huge structure with wraparound porches still held a bit of old-fashioned charm.

Unless your boss had summoned you there knowing you were in danger from bad people. Then it became a concerning place.

"He's mad," Isla said, her tone flat and firm, her exhaustion just messy enough to make her want to scream if anyone approached her.

"He's trying to protect us," Michael shot back on a low growl. "Doing his job."

But in his heart, he knew Chase had to be aggravated with him for going against any type of protocol and taking the department's best tech analyst on the run. Chase might be FBI, but he'd do anything to protect the team members who'd worked so hard all year to crack a big case and solve several murders. Chase and Isla had grown close during that time. Chase fit the big-brother type perfectly. He'd vouched for her so she could adopt Enzo and he'd blame Michael if she lost that little boy.

"But why call us in? I thought we were going to the ranch."

"We'll find out when we get there," Michael replied, trying not to think ahead. "I'll get you to the ranch and I don't care if Chase disapproves."

"Is that it, then? You believe he's not on board with this idea?"

"I told you I don't know. You read his statement. Nothing there to tell."

Isla stared over at him. "Someone else needs sleep, too."

"I'm sorry," he said, agreeing. "I'm to blame for you being here, for Chase having to get involved, for your whole world crashing around you."

"Yes, that's true," she said, without skipping a beat. "But I could have tried harder to sneak away. I believe you, Michael. I want to help you, but I need to know Enzo and Granny are safe."

She wanted to help him.

That told Michael a lot about Isla. Generous and loyal, she'd do anything for a friend. Even a friend she didn't know that well, more of an acquaintance, really. Well, until yesterday, and now they were getting to know each other pretty quickly— both good and bad.

"Let's talk to Chase," he finally said. "I should have gone to him first, but the FBI never likes to get involved with CIA or Homeland Security. We all think we know best."

"But you work for the Department of Defense, right?" She stopped, took a breath. "Wait? So you work for whoever needs you?"

"Yes."

"Are you an assassin?"

"No."

"You told me you do contract work. Is that even true?"

"That is true."

"But?"

"But I can't tell you anything else."

"No wonder several people are after you," she said, the ebb and flow of his ever-changing nocturnal life bringing out the frustration he heard in her words. "You've obviously made a lot of people mad."

"I'm beginning to wonder if they came after Bogi as a cover, but they really wanted me all the time." He didn't say it out loud, but why would his friend send the K-9 here when the base could have protected Bogi? He'd believed Dillon needed his help.

She didn't ask what that might be. They were too close to the chateau now. He pulled around back and parked the Jeep under the mushrooming cover of a giant oak tree, hoping that could hide them for the rest of the day.

"Are you ready?" he asked her. A dumb question.

"I'm not sure what to say," she replied.

When they got inside and headed toward the big conference room, which resembled a large dining room, Michael opened the door and let her go ahead of him. He gave Bogi a command to stay. The dog sat by the door, but his eyes were on the people across the room. The dog had bonded with Isla, same as Michael.

"Enzo," she screamed as she ran toward the toddler and

her grandmother, who were sitting on a small sofa. "And Granny Annie."

Bogi's ears lifted, but he remained in position.

"You're here," her grandmother said as she pushed at her dark curls. "Are you all right?"

Enzo giggled and squirmed to get down from Annette's lap. The toddler's dark hair and big eyes matched Granny's, even though they weren't related. Her grandmother's gaze gleamed with tears of relief. "Isla, I've been so worried."

"I'm okay," Isla replied. Then she reached out her arms.

Michael watched as Isla hugged her grandmother and her son close, his fatigue and the sight of all of them together again making him as mushy as a teddy bear. He didn't do mushy, but he felt the same relief, and something in his tired, burned heart shifted and softened. Isla shot him a thankful glance, then closed her eyes for a brief moment.

Michael looked over to where Chase sat in a chair, watching the scene. Then Chase turned, his smile freezing into a hard gaze as it landed on Michael.

Before Michael could say anything, his friend got up and grabbed him by the collar, anger smoldering like coals in his eyes. "What were you thinking, going to Isla with this mess?"

Michael let out a grunt but didn't flinch. He had to stay cool for Isla's sake. "I had my reasons."

Chase lowered his voice, but his words drilled like a screw being twisted into wood. "Well, you'd better explain those reasons. The police chief who is on vacation in California is not happy with you right now. Nora is upset that one of the few officers working the late shift got shot trying to keep that man out of the lab. He'll survive, but he's on leave until he fully recovers."

"What about the culprit?" Michael asked. "Did you interrogate him."

"He's not going to talk," Chase replied. "He forced an orderly to unlock his handcuffs then knocked the orderly out. He escaped and we haven't located him yet."

"Probably dead for failing on the job," Michael said. Just like Ralph Filmore.

"Yes, probably." Chase stood back and gave Michael a thorough once-over. "Were you or Isla harmed?"

"No, but I had to get her out of there. I wasn't sure how many were coming for me."

"So you decided to take matters into your own hands."

Chase didn't need to remind him that he'd done that very thing in the past and messed up miserably.

"I'm sorry about that," Michael said, his eyes on Isla and her family. "I needed some concrete information. I thought I'd covered my tracks, but someone followed me there. Or, as Isla and I think, someone had already planned to be there. We think someone has been watching my place and the station." He glanced around, not ready to trust anyone right now. "They know I come and go, which made it easy for them to follow me."

"You think?" Chase shook his head. "Michael, you know the protocol."

"Yeah, but they got to me, Chase. I think they set this whole thing up—me watching out for Bogi."

That comment caused Chase to do a pivot and drag Michael away from Isla's celebration. "And why do you think that?"

"Because I believe they're after me, too," Michael said. "They must have been watching me for weeks, even months. They knew my routine, hacked into my security system, sent a homeless veteran as a decoy and killed him when he failed. And somehow, they've managed to track us, even though we've pretty much gone to ground."

"They won't find you now," Chase said. "I've set things up at the ranch but only for a few days. You'll need to keep moving, and Isla needs to be off this case."

"But she's helping me to build this case," Michael argued. "We need a couple of days to dig back into my past."

"Your past? Isn't the cartel behind this?"

"I thought so," Michael said, aware that Isla kept glancing toward them. But she couldn't leave her son. She wouldn't leave her son again. "Now, after we eliminated several people from my past, we think maybe the cartel is working with someone. Rico Saconni could be offering a bribe, a payoff, or they're threatening my former team members. I don't know. I can't abandon Bogi to go hunt them down. I needed intel and fast."

"So you got Isla involved, and at the worst time possible."

"Yes, and I regret that."

"You and me both," Chase said. "I'll give you three days at the ranch and then I'll personally take over protecting Isla, got it? She's in the middle of adopting that little boy."

They both looked over at Isla. She lifted Enzo up and walked toward them. "First, Chase, I'm fine. Second, I'm not happy about this but Michael needs our help—my help. I have to let my caseworker know what's going on or I could lose Enzo."

"You don't have to do this," Chase said. "We could get you back to the lab and put guards on you."

"And put the whole skeleton crew in danger," she replied. "Nope."

"So you'd rather go on the run again."

"I'm not going on the run. We'll be at the ranch with Ashley and her K-9 partner. I do need your protection because Michael can't stay there with us 24/7."

"Well, we can all agree on that," Chase replied.

While he stared at both of them as if he knew something besides danger had been brewing between them.

Chapter Seven

Isla could see Chase wasn't happy with them. She wasn't thrilled about what had happened either, but Michael did at least get her back here as he'd promised. Thanks to Chase summoning them, Michael had suggested the ranch and Chase had concurred. Hopefully they'd get past being mad at each other and get this situation under control.

They both wanted the best-case scenario, but she wanted to get on with this and end it.

"Are we going to stand here all day while you two try to outdo each other like gunfighters about to draw their weapons?" she asked. "Bogi and Michael are in danger."

"And so are you," Chase reminded her, his tone all business.

"Yes, and we can't change that now," she replied as she rocked back and forth and kept smelling Enzo's baby shampoo. He snuggled against her chest, his dark hair curling over her collarbone. Oh, how she loved him already. Always. And she'd do what needed to be done to keep him safe. "We know how this goes. We work the case, same as any other case."

Michael gave her an appreciative nod while Chase stared at the floor.

"We do need to come up with a solid plan," Chase finally said.

Granny rushed over. "Let me take him while you three work this out."

Isla hesitated. "I don't want him out of my sight."

"They have a room upstairs," Chase explained. "I've had them here since last night with a female officer blocking the door, the drapes closed and tight security around this whole place. And just so you know, no one has been near your house. Too close to headquarters, I believe."

"Thank you," Isla said, relieved. Kissing Enzo's forehead, she handed him over to her grandmother. "I'll be up soon, Granny. I need a shower and a long nap."

"I have clothes for all of us," Annette said. "I wasn't sure how long we'd be in hiding. And I'll order some food to be brought up."

"We move you to the ranch tonight," Chase explained. "But I called you back here so you could see your family. We can hide them somewhere else, if you'd rather, Isla."

"I want them with me," she said too quickly. "If that sounds selfish, I'm sorry. But I'm so afraid these people will come after them to get to us, so I'd feel better knowing they're close. That way we can get them to safety."

"Maybe," Michael said, a plea in his gaze.

"Are you thinking differently now?" she asked.

"I'm trying to think of the best way to protect you and them. That might mean splitting you up."

"I don't want to be split apart again."

"He's right," Chase added. "They've harassed you all night long, after all of your attempts to lose them."

Isla took Enzo back. "What should I tell the adoption agency? Have you talked to them?"

"They know you had an emergency and had to leave in a hurry. They know Enzo is safe with your grandmother."

"So we have some time." Her heart rending, she glanced from Chase to Granny. "Would you feel better with me, or somewhere safe with guards?"

Annette touched Isla's hoodie sleeve. "I want to be where you are, *dulce Niña*." She glanced at Enzo. "But we must think of the little one."

Isla blinked back tears. "I don't know what to do. I want to keep you both safe."

Michael ran a hand down his five-o'clock shadow. "I can't promise I'll be able to protect all of you, but Isla, if you want them with you at the ranch, I will do my best to watch out for you and your family."

Chase nodded to that. "You'll have us checking in, and Ashley and her K-9 partner know what they're doing. Cade can handle intruders, too. We'll set it up like a fortress."

Isla stopped and closed her eyes, asking God to show her the way. Could she keep them close and safe?

"How about this?" Michael said, glancing from her to Chase. "We get you all to the ranch and you can rest and recharge. Meantime, Chase and I can do our own recon and research. When you're rested, you can get back to digging into who might be after Bogi and me. If things seems okay in a few days, we can decide then whether to move you or not. All of you."

"We don't want to burden Ashley and Cade," Granny said. "But from what Chase has told us, they're willing to house us for a while."

Fatigue fell over Isla like a smothering hot blanket. She couldn't be any use to anyone until she'd had some food and sleep. With her son close by.

Michael steadied her while Annette lifted Enzo out of her arms again. The toddler started crying, but Granny distracted him with the promise of a book and a good nap.

"I'm okay," she said. "I'm used to pulling all-nighters."

"You're not okay," he replied. "I'm taking you upstairs. Chase and I have some things to discuss."

"Don't fight," she said, a weariness dragging her down.

She'd never felt this tired before, but the stress of the last few months, and now this, almost brought her to her knees.

"We aren't going to fight," Chase replied. "But we do need to talk about strategy and I'll want an official report. Washington isn't too keen on this type of thing."

"Washington isn't too keen on me right now anyway," Michael said over his shoulder to Chase.

"What else is new?" came a quick reply from his friend.

"What's he talking about?" she asked Michael after they'd reached the second-floor suite where Granny had taken Enzo.

Michael turned her toward him, the door behind them. "I haven't always played by the rules, Isla."

"Really?" She giggled and shook her head, punch-drunk with sleep deprivation. "I would have never guessed that."

She made the mistake of looking into his eyes and felt as if she'd plunged off a mountain, about to fall into a deep, dark lake. No one had ever made her feel that way. She'd only been with Michael a full day and she'd come close to dying several times now, but the bond they'd formed seemed like a brand that marked them and sealed them together.

He stared back at her, a trace of his secrets moving with a flicker through those mysterious eyes. "I'm not who you think I am," he said. "I made a big mistake on that mission and we lost a couple of the team members. It's hard to get over something like that. I don't like playing by the rules anymore. But I can now see I'm vulnerable because I've become content, complacent and almost happy here as a veterinarian and helping with the K-9 officer dogs."

"And now?"

"Now, I've put you in danger. You're a good person, Isla. Remember that."

"And you're not?" she asked, seeing through the barriers he'd tried so hard to put up. "Do you want me to remember that, too?"

He drew back. "Remember that, first and foremost," he

whispered. Then he opened the door and checked the room before he tugged her inside and shut the door on his way out.

Isla stood there, thankful for her son and her grandmother. She had been almost happy, too, until last night.

No matter how this ended, she and Michael would have this bond, this tug, this need to know each other. All of each other. Could that possibly make both of them both completely happy?

Isla woke with a start, her dreams dark and full of gunshots and screams, and her on the run calling out for Enzo.

"You're safe. It's okay. You're safe."

In her dream, Michael kept telling her she'd be safe. In reality, Granny stood near the bed, her hand holding Isla's with a grandmother-strong grip, the kind that sent warmth and unconditional love straight to Isla's heart.

She sat up, searching for the clock, grogginess and confusion burning like a fire inside her mind, a sheen of sweat popping out along her backbone. Nine in the morning. "Enzo?"

Granny pointed to the couch across from the bed where her son lay with pillows around him. "He's still asleep."

"Granny," Isla said, all of her emotions bubbling to the surface like a lab beaker full of chemicals running over. "I've messed up again."

"No, you have not," Granny said, sinking down beside her to take Isla in her arms. "You didn't do anything wrong, but your need for justice is still strong."

Isla held tight to the one person who'd fought for her, even when she hadn't known about her grandmother. Granny Annie, as Isla called her, was her anchor in the storm. She clung to that anchor now, thanking God for this spunky, courageous woman.

"Michael is a friend," she replied as she finally left go and looked over at Granny, then wiped at tears. "I couldn't abandon him, but I didn't know all of this would happen."

Granny pushed at her curly salt-and-pepper bob and shook her head, her dark eyes full of concern. "He is also a grown man who has seen and done things you weren't aware of. But then, that's the nature of this kind of work, *sí?*"

"*Sí,*" Isla replied, wondering if she could find something less dangerous to do with her life. "I love my work and Michael needs me. It's natural for me to dive right in. And I need to get back to work."

"Not yet," Granny said, a hint of frustration flaring in her no-nonsense stare. "Chase and Michael left together to see what they can find out about the man who got shot in your lab. I understand he is now presumed dead."

"I would think so."

Her *abuela* gave her a stare that stretched wide and deep, with eyes that could read Isla's very soul. "How close are you and Michael?"

Isla couldn't say much right now, maybe not ever, because she couldn't explain these feelings she'd developed for Michael since last night. Did spending hours with someone really bring out the best in them, or the worst? Used to finding the worst in people sooner or later, she had to tread lightly on this one.

Isla lowered her chin. "We're friends."

Her grandmother grunted, lifted her hands, then dropped them back onto her lap with a shrug. "I see more when I watch him glancing at you, and when I see you trying not to glance at him. So tell me the truth and let's discuss this."

"I've known him for a while since he comes and goes at the department as the K-9 veterinarian and we've all socialized together at times," Isla replied, trying to deflect because her feelings were so twisted right now. "So yes, we care about each other. He's good at his job and he has a love for the working dogs—our K-9s. I've talked to him at work in passing, but I didn't know much about him, really. He came to me for intel that only I could provide."

"I have prayed for you all night and day," Granny said. "I think the adrenaline of this situation has brought you and Michael close. But that might not last once this is over."

When Isla didn't speak, her grandmother lifted her chin, forcing Isla to look her in the eye. "Or can it?"

Isla couldn't hide anything from Granny Annie. "I don't know," she replied. "I will tell you this. Michael needs me, and yes, we've become close. When this is over, he might move on. Or I may decide to change careers. Who can predict that?"

"And if you both stay right here?"

"Then we'll still be friends and we'll see where that takes us. Enzo is my first priority right now."

Granny nodded, satisfied for a while at least. "You'll eat," she said. Then she stood and pulled over a cart full of sandwiches and fruit, a water carafe and a thermal coffeepot, with oatmeal cookies on the side. "Where do you want to start?"

"I'll have a huge cup of coffee and a cookie," Isla said, her love for sweets nagging at her empty stomach. "Then I might eat a sandwich half."

"Okay," Granny replied. "But drink some water, too. You need to stay hydrated."

"Yes, *Abuela*." Hydration was the least of her worries right now, but a grandmother was a grandmother, no matter the situation. Somehow, that brought Isla a huge amount of comfort.

They both smiled at that. Then Isla heard a giggle and saw her son's sweet little head peeking out from behind a fluffy pillow. "I think someone else might be hungry, too."

Enzo grinned and pointed his finger at her. "Mama."

For a brief moment, the world around Isla melted away and her life seemed almost normal again.

But she knew as soon as the sun went down, she'd have to make another move. And this time, she'd have her family with her. Would she save them from harm, or put them in danger?

Chapter Eight

Tension danced throughout Michael's body with a fast-paced beat that ticked right along with his universal military watch. The sun disappeared and several undercover vehicles lined the street, discreetly yards apart, but ready for business.

They'd take Isla and her family out the back way and get them into a dark van. Then their detail SUVs would lead and follow behind as they circled town and took a zigzagged path to the McNeal Ranch, where Ashley and Cade, along with Ashley's black lab K-9, Ozzy, would be waiting to take over.

Snow covered the night, but the roads were clear for now. According to the latest reports, the weather would soon change due to heavy snow predicted for the next few days, which could be good or bad. They could be snowed in, thus keeping any intruders unable to get to them, or they could become trapped by intruders who'd do anything to get to them.

Not a great scenario either but at least Isla, Enzo and Annette would be surrounded by people who were used to doing their jobs in any kind of weather. Protectors.

He used to be a protector, then he'd turned rogue and become something he didn't even want to think about. A machine that moved only to take down the enemy. That had worked until he'd hurt and killed innocent people based on the wrong intel. But he couldn't prove who had given him the wrong information, so he'd taken the fall for the team. Would it be the same situation now, all these years later? He'd vowed after that mistake to always have the best information before he made a move, to trust the people he needed to trust or else. But once again, he knew in his gut someone had fed him incorrect details to throw him off. He'd gone slack, enjoying his work at the clinic, being normal.

Nothing about this situation was normal.

And now, he'd messed up by getting innocent people involved again. This time, he wouldn't take the fall and he wouldn't do the dirty work. This time he'd be the one to track *them* down and do what needed to be done.

The right way.

"All set," Chase said over the radio when Michael's watch hit exactly 18:00. "Roads are clear and we've made sure we're not bugged or being watched. You ready?"

"Ready," he replied. "I'll go collect the cargo."

"Roger. Help will be waiting."

Michael knocked on the door to the suite where Isla and her family had been all day. He hadn't spoken to her in a few hours, when he'd stood at this door with her. A moment that he'd never forget for so many reasons. One being his attraction to Isla. He couldn't be attracted to her. Not now, maybe not ever. He put people in danger even when he tried so hard to keep a low profile and keep his nose to the ground.

Chase had interrogated him about what had happened, pulling out details regarding the last few hours, but when it came to the personal stuff, Michael had shut that down.

"What's the deal with you and Isla?"

"What do you mean?"

"I know those kind of looks between a man and a woman."

"You're in love now, so you're imagining things."

"Don't insult me, Michael. Isla is in a delicate place right now and you getting her caught in this mess isn't helping. Don't do anything you'll regret."

"Maybe you mean don't do anything *you'd* regret, Chase. I thought you trusted me."

"I do, but Isla is special. She had a tough life until her maternal grandmother came along. Now she's about to finally have the life she's dreamed of, adopting a kid and loving him so he won't have to go through what she went through."

"I know that. I understand that. I know what I need to do."

"That's what I'm concerned about," Chase had replied. "Now is not the time to go rogue, Michael."

"A little late for that," he'd responded.

He'd already done some of the recon work while he was out today. After going over every inch of the clinic with a keen eye, he'd found nothing to clue him in, so he'd shut it down, glad he didn't have any patients kenneled there right now. Then he'd called his assistant from a secure phone Chase had cleared for him and told her to take the week off with pay. Later, he'd circled around town and gone to the motel where he'd planned to hide Isla and left a few traces in a room he'd rented for the night.

He'd explained to Chase, "We can put surveillance on the Lookout Motel and see if they show up there. Then I'll have certain proof they've got me bugged somehow, or they have someone who's good at the job of tailing me."

"I'll send an undercover to watch," Chase said, after a couple of grunts. "You shouldn't be taking risks like that right now."

"I have to take risks to get this done, Chase." Then he'd looked his friend in the eye. "But I can promise you this. I'll go by the book this time. I won't get impulsive. I'll have solid proof when I bring these people down."

"And you'll abide by the law?"

"Yes. I will. I have to for Isla's sake."

Chase's grunts turned into a sigh of acceptance. "I'm counting on that, Michael."

Now it was showtime.

Chase came on the radio again. "Your instincts were spot-on. The Lookout Motel had a break-in in room 202."

Michael's heart dropped. "The room I booked this morning."

"Yep." Chase inhaled a breath. "We captured the intruder and he's in custody now."

"Just one?"

"Yep. On foot. Found an abandoned vehicle two blocks over with a stolen tag. The techs are dusting it for prints and anything else they can find."

"Is he talking?"

"No. Not yet. He's fidgety and says we'll regret messing with him. Let's get this deed done and we'll see if we can shake something out of him later."

"We can't have them following us or attacking us tonight. I have to get Isla's family to safety."

"I'm bringing out the cavalry," Chase replied. "I've talked on the phone with Isla, so she knows security will be tight. I've got patrols everywhere. We need to get started."

Michael wished he could have talked to Isla, but he'd decided to give her some space. He needed that, too.

"I'm on it."

After ending the call, Michael nodded to the patrolman on guard near the door. The officer let him in.

"We're ready," he said when he saw Isla turning to face him.

He inhaled a breath of air. She'd changed into dark leggings and a long beige sweater with a big turtleneck collar. She wore sturdy brown lace-up boots. Her bronze-colored hair hung in loose coils around her shoulders. She should be in a fashion catalog instead of sneaking around in the night with him.

"For the weather," she explained because he couldn't stop

staring at her, and because she kept staring back at him, her dark eyes wide with questions. And something he couldn't read right now.

He cleared his throat and glanced away. "Good. I mean— that's a good idea."

Annette gave him a look that said *Back off*, and she did it with a smile that didn't quite reach her stern eyes.

Michael peeled his gaze away from the women. "Okay, let's get you two and Enzo out of here."

He grabbed their duffel bags and the diaper bag, noticing Isla had her beat-up leather backpack tossed over her quilted black coat. After he'd put their things in the SUV, he turned to see Enzo reaching out to him.

Michael glanced from the boy to Isla. "May I?"

She nodded as she handed her son over to him. For a moment, Enzo was caught between them. The little boy grinned up at Michael, then touched a chubby finger to Michael's face.

Isla gazed at Michael, something sweet and intense moving between them. He'd die for them if he had to.

The moment ended, but he sure hoped whatever she had in that bag of tricks would help them get out of this situation. They couldn't keep moving from pillar to post forever.

Or at least, she couldn't. He, on the other hand, could draw these people out and bring them to justice. That thought uppermost in his head, he hustled them to the waiting vehicle, marked as a cleaning van. Getting them quickly inside and settled, he hopped in the front passenger seat and did a scan of the area. Nothing. Nobody. Very few cars nearby and they'd all been checked and cleared.

"We're good to go," he said, earbuds transmitting the message on a secure line.

Nodding to the driver, he turned to check on the passengers. Granny sat in the far back with a female officer, while Isla and Enzo were in the captain seats, Enzo in a sturdy car seat and Isla buckled in.

"Everyone okay?" he asked, glancing at Isla.

"We're fine," she replied, her tone low and quiet.

He gave her a quick okay, then said, "We have a lead vehicle up front, and another one following. We've cleared everything—watching for any activities or anyone who might try following us. So far, we're clear."

Isla gave him a smile he could only see as the streetlight glided by. Her tense smile that told him she didn't really feel all that safe with him. He hated that. He wanted to protect her and the child and her grandmother. He wanted them safe.

They were a tight-knit little family.

His heart pierced with a deep longing, but he'd given up on a family a long time ago. Pushing that and the way she'd looked him in the eye earlier to the back of his brain, he focused on the mission.

Because he couldn't guarantee anyone's safety, really.

Even when he'd promised Isla that with every breath.

Isla kept glancing around, checking on Granny and Enzo. Relieved to have them with her, she prayed they'd all made the right decision by sticking together. She couldn't imagine them off somewhere with strangers, scared and worried.

But she didn't want to think about any harm coming to them if they were with her either. She'd be diligent in protecting them, and her instincts told her Michael would do the same.

The ranch sat several miles from Elk Valley, and about fifteen minutes from Elk Valley Park, located on the foothills of the Laramie Mountains. She'd never been to the ranch, but she'd heard Ashley talking about it several times.

She reached across and took Enzo's little hand in hers. The toddler giggled and kicked his legs, the tiny leather booties he wore knocking against the seat.

We'll be safe, she told herself. *We have to be okay.*

Ashley was a good officer, and Ozzy was a well-trained

K-9. She didn't know Cade that well, but Ashley loved him so that counted in Isla's book.

Now she waffled between praying and hoping everything would work out. Chase had informed her earlier that he'd started his own investigation with the absent police chief's go-ahead, and Isla could add to the equation by pulling up phone records, bank account transfers and travel details on several people who might be involved in this. Michael wanted to dig deep into the whereabouts of the cartel boss, Rico Saconni—who had originally put out a hit on Bogi. He was still a suspect. Isla had suggested early on that Saconni and the cartel could be working with someone from his past. Now that seemed to be the case.

Possible cartel connections inside the government or the military.

That would make her work even harder, but she could focus on finding the truth so her family and Michael and Bogi would be safe.

She glanced out the window, the streetlights fading away as they drove through roads carved into the mountain toward another valley. Ranch land miles outside town. Isla rarely ventured this far out since she worked so much, but she had hiked in Elk Valley Park a few times with friends. She knew those trails, at least. Doubting she'd be able to leave the ranch house, let alone hike, Isla took in a breath.

Michael glanced back at her, his expression as stony and stoic as the mountains around them. She usually could read people, but not this one. Not this man who'd disrupted her life and dragged her out on the run with him. And yet, she knew he had a good heart underneath that rock-solid exterior. He was a believer, maybe one who'd lost his way. She could see that at least in the way he protected people and spoke of God. She'd caught him with his head down and his eyes closed a couple of times.

Had he been praying? She sure hoped so.

"How you doing?" he asked, looking back at her again.

"Nervous, worried, but safe for now," she admitted. "And so glad I have my family with me."

"We'll be there soon and you'll feel even better. Ashley is cooking chili and has hot dogs for Enzo."

"That's good. His favorite." Isla wasn't sure she could eat anything. "I'm thankful for Ashley and Cade."

"Yeah, me too."

He turned back to the front, his head moving back and forth while he checked the road and scanned the few vehicles driving it. From what she could tell by turning to face her grandmother now and then, no one tailed them.

Michael saw her glancing back and nodded.

Isla suddenly wanted to know more about Michael. She had the resources to find what she needed to know about him and she'd use those resources to help him and also get the truth about what had happened on the last mission that had sent him into hiding. He'd kept fighting the good fight as some sort of spy and as he'd said—a machine. Punishment? Or redemption?

He was a confused human being who needed people in life, people he could trust and…and love. Whatever she found out, she had to trust Michael right now. What else could she do?

Chapter Nine

Michael went back over the protocol.

"Guards 24/7 around the perimeters of the ranch. I'll stay here tonight and check back in during the next few days. But no one else other than people who've been cleared can enter the house or the grounds. Understood?"

Cade and Ashley both nodded. "Understood," Ashley said, Ozzy by her side. The black Lab looked like a lovable lump of fur, but he would go to work in a New York minute.

"I've got a couple of hands watching out for things, too," Cade added, nodding at Michael. Then he glanced at Isla and Enzo. "You'll be as safe here as you would in some isolated safe house. My wife is a pro."

Ashley laughed at that. "Why, thank you, handsome."

Michael could see the love between the two of them. He looked at Isla and her eyes met his briefly before she lowered her head to kiss her son. The sight of them together tore through his gut like a fish-knife, jagged and painful.

He'd never thought of family before, but now this family stood front and center in his mind.

Getting back on task, he went on, "Okay, so now that we're all here and settled in, we can wait to hear from Chase on what he's found out. He's got feelers out on this situation. Meantime, Isla and I will do some online sleuthing and hope we hit pay dirt."

"How about supper first?" Ashley asked, getting up to move to the stove where a huge pot bubbled, the spicy smell of homemade chili wafting through the air. "You both need nourishment."

"I could eat," Michael said. "How about you?"

Isla's smile showed the strain of the situation. "I do like a good bowl of chili."

"And we have the hot dogs ready to cut up for Enzo," Ashley said, her grin making Enzo laugh. "I also have peas and carrots that I chopped up and cooked for him. Cade gets credit for the chili."

"Thank you," Isla said, giving them a smile. "I appreciate you doing this for us."

"We owe both of you," Cade said. "Michael is the best veterinarian in Wyoming. And, Isla, you helped me find my sister."

"I was doing my job," Isla said, clearly not wanting to take the compliment. "But I'm glad I could help."

"And we're glad we can do the same," Ashley said. "It's my job, but you're also my friend. So let's try to enjoy this meal and then you and Annette and Enzo can settle into the big bedroom we showed you down the hall. It's perfect since it's the main guest room." Glancing at Michael, she added, "We have a small office I carved out of the corner of the living room. You can have privacy there. Ozzy and I will keep watch across the room on the old couch, until Cade takes over around daylight."

"She's rearranging a few things and making the place a bit spiffier," Cade explained as he got them all to the table and passed the bowls full of chili. "I'm not that good with decorating a house."

"It's our *home* now," Ashley replied, smiling at him.

"It is that—now." He smiled back.

Michael felt the discomfort of watching two people in love while his own heart beat a strange flutter each time he looked at Isla. Crazy since they'd only been around each other for over a day or so. But maybe he'd known the good in her all along. Maybe he'd gone to her because he knew without speaking it that she'd be the one he could trust.

Chase has asked him why he didn't let him know this. "I could have taken you in and helped you. Isla didn't have to be involved. And don't give me that lame excuse about needing technical intel that only she could give you. You have contacts all over the planet."

Michael didn't have a good answer to that statement. He couldn't tell Chase he thought this might be an inside job. He'd speculated that, yes, but to put Chase off the trail, he hadn't confided in him all the way. Chase had agreed that Isla was the best at getting onto the dark web and getting into websites through back doors.

For now, his cover and Isla were safe. Thankful that Chase had put himself in the middle of this, Michael accepted that he couldn't do it alone. He needed to remember God was the one in control here, not him.

He'd prayed last night. Real prayers. Not just the brief choppy requests he'd carried around in his head. His faith had become stronger since he'd moved here because Chief Nora Quan and FBI SAC Chase Rawlston considered their strong faith as part of their shields. It protected them through good or bad.

He'd begun to lean on that again, even if he didn't think he deserved God's grace.

"How's the food?" Cade asked, studying him with an intense expression. "Giving you heartburn already?"

"No, it's good," Michael said, shoving more of the steaming, spicy taco soup into his mouth. "The corn bread is amazing."

Isla grinned and bobbed her head. "I guess I was hungry

after all. Or maybe it's knowing that I don't have to go on any more wild rides in Michael's Jeep."

"You don't like old Bessy?" he asked with a mock frown.

"*Old* is a good word for Bessy," she retorted. "I'm sore all over from the bumps and whiplash."

"She got us this far," he replied, his tone fun while the look he gave her had to be shouting his feelings.

"That's true," Isla said, growing somber. "You kept me alive and I appreciate that."

Michael wished they weren't sitting here in hiding. He shot a glance at her again and something flared like a firecracker between them. He saw so much there in her pretty eyes.

Cade cleared his throat. "More corn bread, anyone?"

Michael glanced around and then back to Isla, mortified.

From the interested expressions on their faces, everyone else sitting at this table had also seen that flare of awareness sizzling between Isla and him.

Two hours later, Isla and Michael were cloistered over her laptop in the far corner where a small desk and chair had been set up behind a partial folding screen. *Cozy*, she thought while her finger typed away. *Too cozy.*

Michael leaned over her, watching the screen. The fresh outdoors scent surrounding him made her very aware of him and caused her to miss keys and hit the wrong buttons. He'd taken a shower earlier and smelled like fresh snow on cedar.

And they were alone in this tiny corner of the now-quiet house.

True to her word, Ashley sat on the couch on the other side of the room, pretending to read a book. But Isla had peeked around the screen a couple of times and had seen her friend near the windows or checking the doors, Ozzy by her side. Ashley had discreetly left them alone so they could get on with their quest. And this had become a quest. Like going through a round of a fantasy game maze on a lonely Saturday night.

Isla sighed and kept working, trying to find out more on Rico Saconni. What else could she do? Enzo and Granny were asleep in the big bedroom, him in a crib borrowed from Cade's sister and Granny in the queen bed she'd share with Isla. A female patrol officer sat guarding their door.

"So other than pictures of him with beautiful women hanging off his arms, Rico Saconni is hard to track down. But after breaking through some back doors and calling in some favors from some of my hacker assets, I finally found this." She stopped and downloaded a file, then pulled it up so he could see it. "RSC Trust."

"And what's that?" Michael asked, his gaze scanning the spreadsheet. "I'm afraid I already know."

"Well, after pushing through layers of companies, I found the owner of all of these *wrapped* companies."

"A company behind a company behind a company." Michael let out a sigh. "Saconni?"

"The Saconni family, yes." She pointed to some figures on the sheet. "Rico is the son of Ricardo, who is deceased. But Junior likes the good life and he owes a lot of money to a lot of people."

Michael glanced over at her. "Yes, a source told me after the big bust, Rico has let the family firm turn into a mess, even more trafficking of drugs, guns and humans, but not in the controlled and protected way his father did. Yet nobody can capture him or pin anything on him, and somehow the money keeps rolling in."

"And he keeps rolling it right back out. A gambling problem, too many cars and homes across the continents, and probably payoffs to a lot of women he's loved and left."

Michael nodded at that. "So what else do we have?"

"He's got all these shell companies lined up right here in Wyoming," she explained. "He's taking advantage of tax breaks and a lack of oversight that would control secret finances. And I'm guessing the drugs Bogi found would have been funneled through our great state because of all the LLCs his lawyers here have set up to hide and launder dirty money."

"A *Cowboy Cocktail*," Michael said. "Secret arrangements too good to resist."

"Yes," she replied. "Exactly."

"So a connection here means it would be easy for them to know about me, but how and who would have given them information?"

"They set these things up with independent managers and financial advisors," she said. "Do you know anyone who works as such?"

"No," he said, "I can't think of anyone but I'll see what I can add to this. Let's keep looking at the list I gave you—see where these people are now and what they're doing."

Isla planned to track both Michael and Bogi, too, from the time they'd been partners until now. She might notice something he'd skim right over.

When he went quiet she noticed his expression changing, going blank, a frown forming. "Do you remember something?"

"No, just a tickle. Kind of like I used to get when we were about to complete a mission. Like the missing piece of a puzzle that snaps into place at the last minute."

"We need that piece right now," she said, hoping he'd remember. "Let me know if you get it figured out."

He shrugged and rubbed a hand through his hair. "I still get memory lapses from my injury years ago. So this could mean nothing. Or it could mean that someone on the outside is working with the Saconni family, and if I can find the missing piece, I can find out who that is."

"This does prove that whoever is behind this has ties right here in Wyoming."

"And probably homes and legitimate businesses covering their crimes," he replied. Then he rubbed his forehead. "Now this will nag me until I figure it out. It's a start, so let's keep at it."

Isla didn't push him to remember. Fatigue etched his face and gave him a craggy, stone silhouette. He would work through this, she hoped.

"If we connect the two, we might find out who's after Bogi and you, and more important, the motive behind it—something that can stand up in a courtroom. They want Bogi gone so he can't track illegal drugs anymore. But why do they want you dead, Michael?"

"That is the million-dollar question, isn't it?" he replied, his tone low and grim. "And that is the missing piece of the puzzle in all of this."

"Yes." Isla yawned, then put her hand over her mouth. "I'm sorry."

He pulled her out of the chair. "Don't apologize. It's past midnight. Let me escort you to your room."

Her heart did a fast pump as his strong hands held her arms. To counter that, she swallowed and said, "It's like…right there down the hallway, Michael."

"I'm walking with you." He turned to where Ashley sat. "Why don't you go to bed and Bogi and I will take the couch."

Ashley nodded and gave them a sleepy grin. "Ozzy can help Officer Mira guard the back of the house."

Michael waited until Ashley got to her room. "Get some sleep. You've uncovered a lot of good information. I was thinking of Saconni from a distance, but if he has ties right here in the state we have an even bigger problem."

"Yes, because this explains how they keep finding us. Someone local—someone we trust—could be leading them to us."

"Exactly." He still had one hand on her arm when they reached the door. Mira, an officer guarding the house, greeted them. "All's quiet in there and nothing much happening on this side of the house."

Michael motioned to the comfortable chair Mira sat in. "Take a break, Mira. I'll roam the hallway for few minutes."

Mira took off to the front of the house. "I'll be right back."

Isla almost giggled. "You are one smooth operator."

"Comes with the territory."

She poked a finger against his solid chest. "One day, I'm going to dig deep into who you are, behind all that intriguing spy-shield stuff."

He grabbed her hand and held it tight, his eyes flaring with a heat that seemed to spark right down her backbone. "Careful. You might not like what you find."

Then he stepped back and gave her a soft smile. "Sleep."

Unlikely, she thought as she watched him stalk back up the hallway, her heart racing after him.

Chapter Ten

Ashley was in the kitchen the next morning when Isla got up, the smell of coffee and bacon enticing and wonderful. She'd slept all night, but her dreams were full of distorted faces and dark alleyways, a sense of being chased hanging over her sleep.

"Hi," she said, pushing at her hair. "Where's everyone?"

Ashley handed her a cup of coffee and motioned to the table where bacon, eggs and biscuits were ready. "Cade is taking care of the animals and checking in with the guards. Mira went home, but I'll be here with you and we have patrols all around. They're searching the grounds and will be back in soon."

Isla sipped the strong coffee for fortitude, and trying to be casual, asked, "And Michael?"

"I wondered when you'd get to him," Ashley said, her eyes as bright as spotlights that shouted, *Tell me everything*. "He said he had some business to attend to—following up on some of the intel you discovered last night."

Isla worried about Michael out there alone, but she had to remind herself this man knew how to take care of things. Or at least he'd done so up until now.

"Well, he's not safe out there." She nibbled on some bacon

and glanced over to where Bogi lay with Ozzy. The big dog lifted his snout but didn't move. "And he left his K-9 here."

"For you," Ashley replied as she leaned against the counter and sipped a cup of tea. "Eat up before it gets cold. How are Annette and Enzo?"

"Still sleeping," Isla replied, noticing Ashley wasn't eating with her. "They're both worn-out."

Ashley looked at the food, set her cup down and then bolted. "I'll be right back."

Surprised, Isla watched as her friend headed into the bathroom. Ozzy stood, a worried expression on his dog face.

Isla tried to eat, but between worrying about Michael and wondering if he'd ever come back, and trying to figure out what was wrong with her friend, she could only take a few bites.

Granny came walking up the hallway. "I need a biscuit."

When she saw Isla stand, she waved her hand. "He's still asleep so enjoy this quiet time."

"I want time with him," Isla replied, about to head to the bedroom to watch Enzo sleep.

But Ashley rushed out of the bathroom, her face pale. "I'm sorry," she said as she hurried back into the kitchen.

Isla turned around. "Are you all right?"

"I'm fine," Ashley said, blushing.

Annette's gaze settled over Ashley and she let out a gasp. *"Ella esta embarazada?"*

Isla gave her friend a second glance after hearing that declaration. "Are you expecting?"

Shocked, Ashley held a hand to her stomach, then with tears in her eyes, started bobbing her head. "We found out last week. I wasn't going to say anything."

"You glow," Granny said, a soft smile on her face. *"Bonita."*

"She's right," Isla said. "You look beautiful. I'm so happy for you." She hugged Ashley. "But this means we need to leave and soon."

"Why would you want to do that?" Ashley asked, sinking onto a chair. "I'm capable of taking care of things. My sister-in-law and nephew, Melissa and Danny, are visiting friends, so I need some company."

"I know you're capable," Isla replied, remembering Cade's sister and her young son. "But Cade would never forgive us if something happened to you or the baby."

Ashley laughed and waved away Isla's worries. "I'm having morning sickness but I can still do my job."

Ashley stood, but Granny ordered her back down. "I'll make you some tea and you can nibble on some soda crackers."

Ashley nodded. "I hope this won't last too long." She put a hand to her mouth. "I'm sorry, Isla. You're adopting and here I sit talking about morning sickness."

"It's okay," Isla replied. "I might not have a husband but Enzo will be my son—if I can get through this."

"Michael might have other ideas after you get through this," Ashley teased. "The man is smitten."

"Sí," her grandmother said from the stove. "I'm not sure how I feel about that."

Embarrassment did a heated path over Isla's face. "Michael is a mysterious man who has a target on his back and he's trying to save a K-9 because he has a strong sense of duty. He is not interested in me right now, nor will he be later."

"Are you interested in him?" Ashley asked. "Please spill. This is keeping my mind off of being sick again."

"There is nothing to spill," Isla said, shaking her head. She didn't like the scrutiny or the questions. "We barely know each other."

"We think there is lots to tell." Granny handed Ashley tea and crackers. "You don't need to have feelings for a *desperado, chica.*"

Cade and Michael came into the room and glanced at the surprised women. Cade laughed. "When you walk into a kitchen full of women staring at you with too much interest, you'd best walk away, buddy."

Michael grunted. "Oh, no. I want to know what they've been discussing here."

His gaze washed over Isla but before she could absorb it, one of Cade's hired hands came in. "Breach in the west pasture, Mr. McNeal. Two motorcycle riders, wearing all black."

Everyone went into action. Ashley forgot her tea and crackers and called out to Ozzy, "Guard."

The big Lab rushed to her side.

Michael alerted Bogi. "Stay. Guard."

"Take them to the back of the house," he told Ashley. "This could be another distraction, but we need to check it out." Then he turned to Isla. "Bogi will guard the front door. Stay here inside until we get back, understand?"

"I'm not leaving," she replied. "We'll be in our room."

Ashley quickly retrieved her gun from the hidden cabinet inside the kitchen hutch, then glanced at Cade. "I'll stay with them and Ozzy can stand guard with the officer watching their room."

Cade kissed her on the cheek. "We'll see about this. Could be tourists out on a ride. If not, we'll try to hold them off."

"Be careful," she replied, hugging him close.

Cade held her tight, then pulled away and glanced down at her stomach before he looked back at her. "You, too."

Isla's heart beat a swift warning. She could feel her pulse pushing through every vein in her body. She held Enzo as he cooed at a stuffed teddy bear, her prayers caught in a web of fear.

Ashley and the officer by their door kept checking on Bogi for signals of stress or to alert them. Isla hoped he wouldn't let anyone come through this house.

Granny sat still, her eyes closed as her lips moved in an

ongoing prayer. Ashley came into the bedroom and sat by the window, her phone on the table, her gun in her hand.

"Bear," Enzo said, giggling as he held the little blue animal up to Isla. "Mama, bear."

"That is a bear," she said, kissing his dark curls. His big brown eyes held such trust she almost lost her breath. "Enzo's bear."

"Mine," Enzo said, snuggling close to her with a breakfast cracker in one hand. Thankful she had some snacks for him in a bag on the dresser, she'd feed him a real meal later. She couldn't think beyond that one thought—they'd have a later.

"Mine," she replied, hoping Enzo would truly be hers soon.

"No movement so far," Ashley said after lifting back a curtain to check the area around the barn. "But we have people stationed in the trees, watching."

They sat quietly, waiting for what seemed like hours, but really had only been a few minutes. When Isla thought she'd scream from the pressure, they heard gunfire echoing over the hills and woods. Several shots in rapid succession.

Then a crash sounded outside the house. Ozzy started barking and Bogi's hard growl echoed across to the hallway.

"Stay down." Ashley crouched by one of the windows facing north from where the shots had come. The officer in the hallway opened the bedroom door. "I'll lock this door and check the perimeters."

Ashley nodded and silenced Ozzy. Isla heard noises, footsteps and what sounded like a scuffle near one of the bedroom windows. Then there was another crash as a gunshot pinged and glass from the shattered window went all over the room.

Granny kept praying and slid into the corner. Isla dropped behind a chair and held so tight to Enzo, he pushed away and squirmed out of her arms and wobbled toward the glass-covered floor.

"Enzo," she whispered, trying to grab him as cold air filled the room. She stayed down and belly crawled on the floor and rolled a ball toward him. "Bring it to Mommy," she said in a wobbly plea. "Pretty please."

He picked up the ball and threw it. The shattered window jiggled. Isla glanced at Ashley. Her friend put a finger to her lips and moved toward the window. Ozzy was ready to attack on her order. Bogi barked loudly now and snarled.

Isla managed to grab Enzo, her heartbeat sounding through her ears, while the intruder kept pushing at what was left of the window. Then they heard a distinctive sound. The sound of another round being put into the gun's chamber.

Ashley braced herself, her gun aimed at the broken window. Ozzy stood still, his focus on the intruder.

The tension in the room stretched like a cable wire about to pop. Enzo gazed at Isla. Then he burst into loud sobs.

Isla gritted her teeth and hugged him tight, knowing they could all be shot. Then came a shout from outside. "Riders on horseback. Let's get out of here."

The footsteps departed toward the back of the house, followed by more shots ringing across the countryside like fireworks.

Ashley crawled to the window and peeked out a sliver in the curtains. "I see our men. We're safe."

"For now," Isla said in a whisper, her arms wrapped around her son. But not for long, she knew.

Michael rushed inside the house and gave Bogi the clear sign, then rushed down the hallway, the intense dog behind him. "Isla?"

"We're here," she called as he whirled by the officer who'd returned inside. "We're all here."

He rushed to her and pulled Enzo into his arms. "Are you all right?"

"We're okay," she said, nodding, her dark eyes filled with relief. "You?"

He held the child close, relief washing over him. "We're

good. We chased two off before they made it to the house. Checked the woods and put out alerts, then shot at the two trying to get into the house. Last we saw, an official SUV was chasing them up the highway."

"But they got away?" Ashley asked as Cade held her tight.

"For now," Michael replied. "They now know the ranch is being heavily guarded."

"Did they see you?" Isla asked.

"No. We were hidden behind some trees, waiting for them to approach, an Elk Valley Police SUV blocking their way."

"That and a few rifle shots did the trick," Cade said. "We held them off, but we can't be sure they'll stay away. They were trespassing but that won't matter much with this kind."

"Nothing matters to these kind," Granny said from her corner. "Evil to go after someone who is innocent."

She glanced from Isla to Michael, the meaning behind her statement clear to all of them.

Michael lifted his chin and returned her glance. "You're right. This has to end. And I'm the only one who can make it stop."

Chapter Eleven

"What does that mean?" Isla asked a few minutes later after they'd been cleared to come back to the den. "Don't do anything to put yourself in danger."

"I'm putting you and all these people in danger," he said, already pulling away. "I thought I could get you away safely. But now, this thing keeps escalating. They will be relentless because they've failed. It's a matter of power and pride now."

And he still hadn't heard a word from Dillon Sellers. "I'm afraid they've already taken out Dillon. If they have, then they probably have all the information they need on me, too."

"Call someone else," she said. "You can't go all noble on me now, Michael."

"I'm not the noble kind," he replied. "I can't call anyone else. Top secret and too risky. I think Dillon sent Bogi to me because someone on that base is connected to Saconni. Like I said before, we need that one more piece of the puzzle to figure this out."

"Then you stay put until I can dig some more," she said, the look in her eyes daring him to make a move. "You walk now and you risk the lives of everyone here protecting us. Neither of us could live with that." Glancing around to where Granny stood helping Ashley make sandwiches, she said, "But this has gone from protecting a K-9 to finding out what these people really want. And I can help with that. It's my job."

Michael paced, his head down, his mind whirling. "Do one more search to see if any of your connections can come up with something. If we don't get anything by tomorrow night, I'm moving you and your family again."

Isla nodded and headed straight to the corner desk. "I'll be over here until Enzo wakes up from his afternoon nap."

He nodded, then pulled out one of the three burner phones he had. Ashley had called in a report to Chase and he would update the police chief. Michael tried one more time to reach Dillon, using an old number he'd memorized years ago. Still no answer, but at least the number seemed to work. It wasn't like Dillon to ghost him, but then again they hadn't had an opportunity to talk much when Michael had gone to a deserted airstrip to pick up Bogi. Dillon and the pilot he'd hired had been waiting and they'd gotten Bogi on the plane pretty quickly with nothing more than a "thanks and I owe you one" from Dillon.

He went over to Isla. "Anything?"

She turned to him and nodded, then looked over at the others. "We need to talk."

He sat down beside her. "What?"

"I got a hit from a source in Europe. Another shell company with a branch right here in Wyoming. River Purses. Ever heard of it?"

Michael's mind buzzed like a bumblebee. "Yes, I have heard of it." His stomach roiled as the puzzle seemed ready to fall into place. "I can't remember where."

Isla's eyes lit up but held a track of fear. "The name Saconni is a variation on *saccone*, which mean *maker of purses*. River Purses manufacture Italian leather goods—expensive handbags, like maybe thousands of dollars for each purse."

"Okay, so what's that got to do with us and this case?"

"A lot. The Saconni cartel owns River Purses. It's one of their deeply buried shell companies, but there is a River Purses store in Laramie. I looked it up. They are all over social media, selling all kinds of leather goods, even coats and jackets."

"Okay, tell me more," he said, that sick feeling settling in his gut.

"My source says that's a cover and a way to lure people into selling drugs. He says this cartel has a wide reach from America to Europe and South America, which means the store here must cater to rich clients and vulnerable people who want to be like those rich clients."

He studied her face, thinking she was so beautiful, and so smart. "And that could mean they definitely have a stash house here and plenty of loyal underlings who'd do anything to win favor."

"Yes," she said. "Should we visit that store?"

"No. Too dangerous." He held a hand to his head, memories misting just out of his reach. "I wish I could remember where I heard about these purses. It must have been someone I know because I don't go purse shopping a lot."

Isla touched her hand to his. "Maybe it will come to you. The good news is we can put surveillance on that particular store, see who's coming and going."

"Good idea."

"I've also been searching Bogi's background since you and he left the military," she said. "He wasn't always back at Lackland. For a while after he retired as a war dog, Dillon had him, and interesting thing—according to his vet records, that's when Bogi became even more aggressive." She took a breath and looked down to where Bogi sat, guarding. "This dog hasn't been aggressive, not once since I've been around him. I'd trust him with Enzo. I'd trust him to alert because I believe he knows the truth, too."

Michael's brain dinged and pinged with reality. "You think

Dillon has something to do with all of this, right? You've been leaning toward that angle since I told you about him."

"I'm following the leads and yes, this one stands out to me. He is your only source of information and yet, you can't get in touch with him. Think about that, Michael."

Michael had to agree with her, whether he liked it or not. "If Bogi has heard or seen something that brings out his aggressive nature, he can't really show or tell us that until we have this figured out."

"Yes, because alerting is his only way of telling us the truth," she replied.

Michael stared at the K-9, then looked back at Isla, his mind reeling. "But who? And where and when will he be able to do that?"

"Only Dillon can help us there," she said. "And he's missing in action."

Michael told Chase he wasn't leaving the ranch again. He and Isla pulled the information they'd found and Isla saved it on a tiny flash drive and hid it in the desk drawer, taped inside a box of envelopes. Michael still couldn't remember where he'd heard about River Purses but figured it had to be from someone he knew. But mostly, his mind couldn't accept that his friend and former teammate might have betrayed him. Yet the puzzle pieces were beginning to fit.

"They're tracking us somehow," he reminded Isla at the dinner table that night. Annette and Enzo had gone to bed, while Isla and he sat with Cade and Ashley. He glanced at Bogi. "I wish he could tell us what he knows."

As if on cue, Bogi grunted and scratched at his collar.

Isla looked at the dog and then back to him. Ashley gave Bogi a curious stare. "He scratches at that collar a lot, you know."

Isla let out a gasp. "What if they put a tracker on Bogi?"

Ashley nodded. "I was thinking the same thing."

Michael called the dog to his side. "I haven't given him much attention since this happened, but I have noticed him always pulling and scratching at his collar. That makes perfect sense."

Michael lifted the heavy brown leather collar and undid it, then ran his hand over the worn back side. Silently, he pointed to a small flat button embedded between the leather and the metal label on the front. He didn't put the collar back on. "This is how they've been able to get to us."

Later that night, Cade and Michael slipped out with Bogi wearing the tracker. At a neighbor's remote ranch, and with his permission, they'd taken it off Bogi and placed it on a long bridle around a mean bull's massive neck. Ashley had followed to make it look like everyone in the house would be moving on and they'd left her SUV at the other ranch.

"That will keep them guessing for days," Michael told her after they'd returned. "We got a call from the hired hands guarding the woods. They heard motors cranking and off-road vehicles leaving the premises, so the patrols up on the road will coordinate with Cade's friend and hopefully capture a few of our lurkers."

Now, two nights later, Isla sat with Michael on the sofa, the house quiet and the fire mostly embers, but she couldn't get over the jitters. Or the way Michael made her feel when they were alone like this.

"So nothing's happened since you removed the tracker. Could this finally be over?"

"Not yet. We did capture two of them trying to sneak onto the other property, but we need to locate their headquarters. We've got them busy and confused but the two in jail aren't talking."

While the quiet times had been nice and she'd felt safe again, Isla wanted to go home. "We still need to be careful. That's why we have a guard, right?"

"Yes," Michael said. "I've lost my edge. I didn't consider them putting a bug on Bogi. I don't think I've thanked you at all for figuring that out." He looked over at her, their gazes clashing. "I don't think I've thanked you for any of this. So thank you, Isla."

"It's about time," she replied with a muster of snark, her heart hammering. She liked being close to him but it was also torment. "Maybe now at least we can finish this up."

"We have some other things to finish, too," he said, leaning close. "Like this." He kissed her, his warm lips touching hers with such a gentle sweep, she couldn't help but sigh and kiss him back. They both pulled away, awe crackling between them like kindling starting a fire.

"A nice surprise—that's what you are," he whispered as he reached for her again. "I like sitting by the fire with you."

Bogi suddenly jumped up and stood, his whole body trembling.

"Maybe he's jealous," Michael teased.

The big dog growled and stared down the hallway. They heard a pop and Michael grabbed her. "Silencer," he whispered.

Ozzy started barking.

Isla twisted away, panic in her eyes. "Granny?" She rushed to the bedroom and opened the door, then screamed.

Michael and Bogi ran in, Ashley, Michael and Ozzy right behind them. Isla was kneeling on the floor, sobbing. "They're gone," she shouted, looking up at him. "Gone."

Michael scanned the empty room and saw a blue teddy bear lying by the crib, his heart bursting with a pain like none he'd ever felt before. Enzo loved that teddy bear.

"Isla," he said, bending and reaching out to her. "Isla, I'm so sorry."

"Get away from me," she screamed as the others gathered in the room. "Where is the guard, where is my protection? You promised me, Michael. You promised me."

Still sobbing, she pushed past all of them and ran out into the night. "Enzo, Enzo. Where are you?"

Michael watched, her pain cutting him like a knife. Then he turned and saw a figure lying on the ground by two Adirondack chairs. He hurried and turned over the still body. The patrol officer who'd been guarding the door lay dead, a bullet wound in his temple, his own gun still clutched in his hand.

And suddenly, Michael remembered where he'd seen a River Purse. Dillon Sellers's latest girlfriend had been holding one when he'd last visited Dillon about a year ago, before any of this had happened. The purse had been rich brown leather, but with a bright red emblem that had reminded him of a clear-shot wound. Just like the one on this officer's forehead.

He looked at Isla as Ashley tried to comfort her, then he turned to where Bogi stood growling and shaking with rage. Michael commanded the K-9 to come, then stalked out to his Jeep and left. He planned to find Dillon Sellers and make him pay, and he had no problem dying in order to seek justice. What did he have to live for if Isla had lost her family because of him?

Isla sat on the bed, the blue teddy bear clutched to her chest. She couldn't sleep, couldn't eat, didn't want to talk to anyone at all. Ashley kept checking on her, and finally came in and sat beside her without saying a word. They both started crying.

"I don't think I can live," Isla whispered. "I've survived a lot of things, but I don't think I can survive this."

Ashley only nodded. Then she whispered back, "We have search parties everywhere, looking. The flash drive with the information on Saconni is with Chase now—good thing you told me where you'd hidden it. That information could lead us right to them. We've got people watching their store."

Isla tried to speak, but her sobs increased. "Where is Michael?" Not that she wanted to see him again, but he'd left without a word. Did she want that? To *never* see him again?

She only wanted her Granny Annie and Enzo safe. After that, she didn't care. At all. She'd get out of this bed and find them her way.

Ashley didn't answer her question.

"Where is he?" Isla repeated, her voice rising this time.

Ashley gave her a level stare. "He's doing what he needs to do. He's heard from the cartel, so he's meeting them tonight to hand over Bogi in exchange for your grandmother and Enzo."

"What?" Isla got up and started putting on her clothes. "Take me there now, Ashley. I have to get to them." When Ashley didn't readily agree, she said, "I know who's behind this. It's not the cartel, but Dillon Sellers. He's been running the whole show, but I can't prove that."

Ashley stood, her phone out. "Chase needs to hear this."

"No, Chase needs to take me there. I mean it. If he doesn't, I'll find out where they are and go alone."

Chapter Twelve

Two hours later, Michael sat in his Jeep with Bogi, tapping his fingers on the worn leather steering wheel. He had to do this. Had to give over Bogi to save Annette and Enzo. He hadn't slept since last night after he'd gotten the call he'd been waiting for.

"Mr. Tanner," the smooth accented voice had said. "I see you've wised up now that we have collateral damage to discuss."

"I'm wise to you," Michael told the man. "The dog for the woman and child. See how easy that was."

"Smart decision." The man had named the place and the time.

After that, Michael had geared up back at his place only to find two of Elk Valley's best along with Chase, waiting for him.

"You're not doing this alone," Chase said, shaking his head.

"I have to. They've made that clear without even reminding me. Do you want Annette and that little boy to die?"

"No, what I want is for you to be sensible so nobody will get killed."

They had a SWAT team lined up, and they'd called in

some favors. Several K-9 officers from other units would slip through the woods and be ready to help the SWAT team.

After Chase threatened to lock him up, Michael finally agreed. He couldn't exactly take down more than a half-dozen people and he had no idea how many would be waiting for him.

For once, he wasn't going rogue. He had to do this by the book. He checked his watch and got out of the Jeep, Bogi jumping out behind him. He walked up to a dark building that looked like a giant garage and waited about ten yards from the front door.

When a lone man came out that door, Michael wasn't surprised at all. But he sure wished he'd listened to Isla about this.

Dillon Sellers stood dressed in a black leather jacket and black jeans. "MT, you finally decided to do the right thing."

"Nice jacket," Michael replied, his gut burning with a heated rage, his plan to follow the rules going up in smoke. "I'm guessing that's the kind of jacket I'd find in a River Purse store?"

"They do sell all kinds of goods, yes."

Bogi growled and lifted up with a snarl, but Michael held him by the new protective working collar and vest he'd put on him earlier. "I see Bogi and you aren't on good terms anymore."

"Nope. Bogi knows too much about the cartel and, well, about me."

"Because you're the one, aren't you?" Michael asked. "The one who made sure I'd get the wrong intel on that mission and cause innocents to die. Just like you've done with this whole mess we have now."

"No, I made sure you had the best intel to get that stupid mission over with and done. You always were a softy."

"So if you kill Bogi and me, no one can ever prove you set me up to take the blame for all those deaths."

"You got it, buddy." Dillon glanced back. "That and I get

a sweet deal. Two million in cash—double the original asking price."

"Why not turn him over yourself? You'd still get the reward."

"Because it would be too obvious—he's only aggressive around me. I sent him on that last mission, thinking he'd get shot, but no, he had to become a national hero. I decided to get you two back together, kill two birds with one stone and end this thing that's been hanging over me for years."

"Why not take us both out when we met at the plane?" Michael asked.

"Too many eyes, even if that place did seem deserted," Dillon replied. "It would have been too obvious."

The puzzle pieces had finally fallen into place.

Michael stared at the man who'd once been his best friend. "So after all this time, you decided it was time to end the very things that have also haunted me for years. Let me guess— Bogi was about to give you away because he always alerted around you."

"Sorry, but I can't have you and that dog undermining my position now, can I?"

"No, but positions come and go," Michael said. "Before I hand over Bogi, I need proof of life."

Dillon gave a signal to someone at the open door of the big building. Michael held his breath when he saw Annette coming out with Enzo in her arms, her expression cold and blank.

He lifted his chin to Dillon. "This is it, Bogi. Goodbye, boy." Then he leaned down and let go. "Attack."

Dillon shouted as Bogi lunged toward him. Then the woods went wild with barking dogs and camouflaged officers. Gunfire hissed and sizzled through the cold black night. Michael didn't call Bogi off. The sound of Dillon's screams merged with the team rushing into the building. Michael stood and watched the K-9 he'd trusted with his life finally giving him the answers he'd always needed.

Chase came rushing up. "Michael, call off your dog."

Michael glared at his friend and then shouted, "Let go."

Bogi dropped Dillon like a sack of potatoes and stood still, guarding, while Dillon wailed and tried to get away. Chase handed Michael the cuffs.

"This is for all the people who died," he said on a hiss as he grabbed and handcuffed the man who was once his best friend. "And for Bogi, a better officer than you could ever be."

Back in the SUV where Chase had left her and Ashley, Isla heard all the noise and jumped out of the vehicle. She couldn't stay put, knowing her little boy and the grandmother she loved so much were in danger.

And Michael. She had to see Michael.

Ashley called after her, but she kept running toward the noise of barking K-9s. A sound like music to her ears.

By the time she got there, it was over.

She saw Granny and Enzo standing off to the side with Chase. "Granny! Enzo!"

Chase whirled and glared but didn't say anything. He watched as she hugged her sweet little boy and her amazing grandmother, tears of relief falling down her cheeks. Glancing around, her head held against Enzo's, she spotted Michael.

He nodded then turned and walked away, Bogi by his side.

Two days later, Isla hurried out the door with Enzo and Granny, praying she'd still be able to officially adopt the toddler. They were headed to the courthouse to make her longtime dream come true. If it *would*. Fatigue tugged at her brain. She hadn't slept well, but then she never did. And she hadn't heard a word from Michael Tanner.

Dillon Sellers was in jail, and most of the cartel members had scattered after Rico Saconni had tried to escape the stash house where they'd held her family. He been caught hiding in a shed, K-9s barking all around him. He'd go to prison along with Dillon.

She wanted to talk to Michael.

Not that she expected to see him again. She'd told him to leave her alone and blamed him for her grandmother and son being taken, but now she regretted being so cruel to him. In the end, he hadn't gone rogue. He'd gone against his grain to save her family—and Bogi, too.

Only a good man would do something so heroic and noble. Only a good man would kiss her with such tenderness, he'd melted the walls around her heart.

But only Michael would do that and walk away because he didn't think he was worthy of a family. She'd believed that about herself once, but she knew they were both worthy.

She'd gotten Enzo strapped into his car seat when a blue pickup truck pulled up to the curb.

Michael.

He got out and walked up to her. "Hi."

"Hi," she said, glancing to where Granny sat in the back of her small SUV with Enzo. "What are you doing here?"

"I came to go with you to court. Annette called me."

Isla glanced back at her grandmother. Annette shrugged and nodded. Not sure how to react, Isla studied his face.

"I would have been there anyway," he clarified. "But I want to drive you there. If you'll let me."

She tossed him the keys and went around to the passenger's seat. "Let's go."

When they got to the courthouse, Isla's nerves had reached a high pitch, but with Granny on one side and Michael on the other, she held her child close and held her head high.

Then when they got inside and she saw the whole K-9 team and most of the police force, including Nora Quan, there waiting, tears fell down her cheeks.

The judge took note and listened as Chase, Michael and

Nora all explained what had happened and how Isla had fought so hard for those she loved. The judge had tears in her eyes by the time everyone had given their testimonies, and the adoption went through without a hitch.

She was Enzo's mother now.

After they filed out, sniffing and crying and hugging, Granny invited everyone for an early Christmas dinner. "I've been cooking for days, so you can't say no."

They all showed up at her house at about the same time snow started falling in beautiful big flakes. After putting Enzo down for his nap, Isla stood inside the short hallway and marveled at all the wonderful friends in her life.

Michael had been quiet, but he and his shadow, K-9 Bogi, approached her. "Can we talk?" he asked, motioning toward the backyard.

She put on her coat and followed them out, then turned to face him, her heart so scattered and shattered, she wasn't sure if it could ever have a normal beat again.

"You have your family now," he began, his words jittery and his expression bordering on panic. "But I was wondering. I mean Bogi and I were wondering…"

"Yes?"

"You're not going to make this easy, are you?"

"Easy?" She laughed. "Nothing has been easy with you, Michael." Then she tugged him close. "Except that kiss."

He grinned, relief washing through his eyes. Eyes that held honesty now, and hope. "I wondered if you might find it in your heart to forgive me and let me and Bogi hang around?"

"That depends," she replied. "Will you disappear in the night to do all your spy things? Or can I depend on you to hang around for a long time?"

He smiled and held her there. "I'm a veterinarian full-time now. No more nefarious missions. I'm here to stay."

Bogi barked in agreement and rolled in the snow.

Isla kissed Michael and then touched a hand to the map that was his face. "I'd like that, Michael. I'd like that a lot."

"I'd like that, too," he said, no more secrets shadowing his eyes. "And I think I love you. A lot."

Isla opened her heart. "I think I love you back. A lot."

They kissed, then the back door burst open and the team got involved in a snowball fight, dogs included.

Granny brought Enzo out all bundled up and handed him to Isla, then turned to Michael. "Remember what I told you."

"Always," he replied, saluting Granny.

"What did she say?" Isla asked.

"She said it in Spanish, but I'm pretty sure she explained how she'd hurt me in bad ways if I break your heart."

"You won't do that," Isla told him. "I trust you, Michael."

And she knew it was true. Her spy had come in from the cold and she had a family to love, a family full of faithful guardians. The best Christmas present ever.

* * * * *

Lethal Holiday Hideout

Katy Lee

MILLS & BOON

Commit thy works unto the Lord,
and thy thoughts shall be established.
The Lord hath made all things for himself.
—*Proverbs* 16:3–4

To Isabella, my groupie leader
and motivational mate of all the things.
I'm so thankful God brought you into my life.

Acknowledgments

I want to thank my new editor, Katie Gowrie,
for her enthusiasm about my work. I'm excited to
create more wonderful books with her in the future.
Her dedication and commitment to bring
wonderful stories to our readers only make our
books shine even more.

I also want to thank K-9 trainers for their time and
investment into these powerful and intelligent dogs,
particularly the K-9 unit at Hill Air Force Base
for their willingness to demonstrate and
share their skills with me.

Chapter One

"Mocha, down!" Special Agent Cara Haines, Washington, DC, and K-9 Task Force boss, ordered the unruly chocolate Labrador to quit jumping and barking in her crate. At this rate, the dog would never qualify for the Mountain Country K-9 Unit that Cara oversaw. She righted her glasses that had slipped when wrestling the dog inside the vehicle and prepared to lower the SUV's rear door. She had taken Mocha to the outdoor training facility in Alexandria for some exercise and fresh air, not ready to give up on the recruit. Being December, the K-9s did most of their training on the inside course, but Cara thought a change of scenery would do Mocha good. Cara wasn't sure if the dog was going to pass the assessment to become a full-fledged K-9 officer. The dog's rambunctiousness told Cara she might be sadly right.

However, Mocha wasn't the only one who needed some fresh air that day. Cara needed a little breather from her stuffy city office as well. She spent most of her days on conference calls and doing paperwork up to the top of her six-foot frame, rarely having time with the dogs anymore. Ten years ago, she gave up being a trainer out west and took on the role of the big boss in the FBI DC offices, overseeing task forces around the country instead. Some days, she just wanted to be with the dogs—she *needed* to be with them, even the unruly K-9s. Today was one of those days.

Last week, Cara received a notification that her ex-brother-in-law would be released from prison this week. The state of California reduced his twenty-year sentence to ten. Cara angrily thought of all she had given up because of that man. Moving her home across the country from Wyoming to DC was only one of them.

Mocha continued to whimper but still strained to be released from the confines of the back of the FBI SUV. Her black eyes alerted on something in the vicinity.

Perhaps there was more to Mocha's rambunctiousness than Cara realized.

"What do you see, girl?" Cara's own senses spiked and the hair on the back of her neck stood to attention. She flipped the safety strap on the holster beneath her black suit coat and had her weapon in her palm before she turned and raised it.

Every corner of the outdoor facility remained empty.

Cara's gaze darted to each structure and obstacle of the fenced-in course. Tires, boxes, jump poles became places to hide behind. Cara targeted her focus on the shadows the structures caused. As far as she could tell, there was no sign of anyone else around. The outdoor course wasn't as protected as the official training center, and she thought she might need to change that in the future. Anyone could easily get in here.

But it didn't appear anyone had. As best as she could see, she remained alone.

Cara lowered her gun and reholstered it. She left the flap undone just in case she needed a quick draw again. Turning back to the dog, she reached to close the rear hatch.

"False alerting is not a good sign for you, Mocha." She issued a warning to the dog and pushed the button to close the door. Cara came around to the driver's door, but before she opened it, a firm hand went around her mouth. Her back hit against a hard chest. She went for her gun but found the holster empty. She heard the gun hit the ground, leaving her weaponless.

Mocha jumped around in her crate, barking profusely inside the SUV, now useless to Cara. Whoever this man was, he recognized the need to wait to make his move until she'd secured the dog.

A pocketknife appeared in front of her face in the man's other hand. One flick and the four-inch blade opened inches from her nose.

At fifty-two years of age, thirty of which were in law enforcement, she didn't think she'd ever been in this situation. Decades of technical practice and self-defense classes rushed to the forefront of her mind, but none of them prepared her for the real thing. Cara knew she had seconds to live if she didn't kick her mind into gear.

Kick was the operative word, she thought.

"We're going to do this slow and easy," the man said in a low voice. "One wrong move and I will slit your throat. Simple as that."

Cara tried to breathe deeply through her nose, but his thumb covered one of her nostrils, making it difficult to fill her lungs. Remaining calm was her only choice. She nodded her compliance once.

"Good. You're a smart woman. Smarter than your sister."

So this was about her sister. The sister Cara hadn't seen in ten years. If Cara didn't know better, she'd think this man was her ex-brother-in-law. But he was still behind bars, so how could it be him?

"You're going to take me to her."

Cara shook her head as much as she could. His request was impossible. She tried to speak through his hand pressed against her lips. At the shake of her head, he brought the knife closer.

"You don't get to choose." The knife came away from her face, and the next thing she heard was the clinking sound of her handcuffs removed from her belt. She had no more time to wait to make her move. If this man apprehended her and stuffed her in her car, there was no telling where he would take her next.

Closing her eyes, she pulled on the memories of breaking out of a person's hold. With the knife gone, she used her foot to find his instep. With as much breath as she could take in, Cara grunted and stepped down on his inner ankle, twisting around at the same moment to grab his arm and flip him. In less than five seconds, she threw him to the ground, ripped the handcuffs from his hand and slapped one cuff on his wrist.

The man struggled and squirmed. Suddenly, with his free hand, he reached for her gun on the ground. Cara lunged forward to beat him to it, but just as she grabbed the handle of the gun, he seized the barrel.

She let go of the cuffs to fight him for the gun, spotting another officer entering the facility.

"Stand down!" The young woman rookie officer raced in with her own gun drawn.

The perpetrator let go of Cara's gun for his knife. Before Cara knew what he planned, he threw the blade in her direction just as the rookie's gun discharged.

Cara ducked as fast as she could, but the knife sliced through the shoulder of her suit coat, throwing her body back against the car.

As the echo of the blast died down, and Cara regrouped over what had just happened, the man lay dead in front of her.

"Are you okay? Don't move!" The woman crouched in front of Cara, unsure of what to do with the knife protruding from Cara's shoulder.

"Kick the gun away," Cara instructed her. "Just in case." Although judging by the way his eyes were wide with no life in them, she knew the girl's shot had been accurate.

The rookie called for an ambulance while Cara examined the protruding knife, expecting only minor tissue damage.

Mocha jumped around in her cage. Cara knew she might hurt herself if she wasn't informed that the perpetrator had been silenced.

"Open the back door and try to calm her down," Cara said through clenched teeth. Pain set in with a slow burn. She glanced at the rookie's name on her badge. "And thank you, Officer Vasquez. Good work today. I'd say I probably owe you my life."

"Not necessarily, ma'am. I'm sure you'd have taken him down at any moment." The young woman smiled, allowing Cara to keep her pride intact. "Do you know what he wanted?"

"Yeah. He wanted my sister, and he wanted me to lead her to her."

"Well, I'm glad your sister's still safe. And you too. Wait until you tell her you saved her life today."

Cara frowned, knowing that conversation would never happen. "I saved her life ten years ago by getting her into the witness protection program."

Vasquez gasped at what that statement meant. A sad expression settled on her face. "That must've been a hard decision to make."

"It was the only decision to make. Her husband was Luis Morel."

The woman's eyes widened. "The head of the Mexican mob? How did your sister get mixed up with him? That organization is more dangerous than any cartel. They run every gang in California's prisons."

"And most likely the guards too, if Morel's made parole. My sister met him on vacation down in Mexico. She didn't know who he was until after she was married and living with him in California four weeks later. With over fifty thousand foot soldiers and assassins at his disposal all over the continent, I had no choice but to let her go into Witness Protection. He would have killed her, and not before torturing her."

The woman looked at the dead guy. Her face blanched. "You think Morel sent this man?"

The ambulance's siren rang off in the distance. She'd take the ride to get stitched up, but that would be it. "I don't *think* Morel sent this man. I *know* he did."

"Do you think your sister's still safe?"

Cara reached for her cell phone inside her coat. With her good hand, she thumb-dialed the only person who would know the answer to that question.

The phone rang three times before US Marshal Sullivan Briggs answered the call. "I'm surprised to see your number on my caller ID, Cara." His deep voice rumbled through her speaker. It still had a way of soothing her nerves, but she wouldn't tell him that. "I'm surprised you even remembered my number. How long has it been since you called?"

His cynicism was anything *but* soothing.

Cara ignored his question and cut right to the chase. "I was just attacked by one of Morel's men. Luis will be out of prison this week, and he's already looking for my sister. You need to find out if she's safe right now and make sure she has a detail on her."

"Attacked? Are you okay?" Sully sounded stunned through the line.

She glanced at the knife protruding out of her left shoulder. "I'll need stitches, but that's nothing to what Jeanette will need if Morel gets ahold of her. Call her handler right now."

"I'm making the call as we speak. But are *you* safe? I want the truth, Cara."

"He's dead." She left out the part about nearly being taken out by him. Cara could kick herself. She'd let her guard down when she should have been expecting something from Morel.

"There'll be more coming, Cara. You know it."

"Yeah, but I'll be ready next time. What have you heard? Did you reach her handler?"

"Hold on. I'm trying his other number."

The paramedics pulled in and before Cara knew it, she was being lowered onto the stretcher, carefully on her good side. Her adrenaline still surged as she waited for the answer.

"Answer me, Sully. That's an order!" She bit back the pain radiating through her body. A weakness overcame her, causing dizziness. Shock, maybe, she thought. Minor wound or not, she was losing blood.

"An order?" Sully chuckled, which only grated on her nerves more. "He'll call me back soon, I'm sure. Don't worry. Your sister has been safe for ten years. She's happy doing what she loves most. I made sure I assigned her a good life she could love. You just need to make sure you're safe."

"I'm coming out there." Cara felt her weakening body lifting into the ambulance. She grunted with the landing. "As soon as I get this knife out of me," she mumbled.

The line went quiet. Then Sully said, "Neither of those statements makes me feel good. First, you stay right where you are in DC. You can't know where your sister is, so there is no reason to come out to Wyoming."

The paramedics in front of her blurred and when she spoke, her tongue got in the way. "I have to…" The rest of her sentence made no sense, even to her ears.

"Put the paramedic on the phone, Cara. Now!" Sully demanded.

Cara heard him speaking somewhere in the darkness of unconsciousness, but she couldn't form any more words.

"Cara! Don't leave me!" he shouted.

But somewhere in her mind, she knew those words weren't said by him today.

Those were the words Sully said to her ten years ago when she did just that.

Chapter Two

Sully hung up one phone, only to make another call to Logan Doyle. At this rate, he'd have an entire head of gray hair by tomorrow morning. Jeanette Morel, now known as Jennie Monet, had lived out in Jackson, Wyoming for the last ten years, without a hint of a problem. Sully had put his best man in the role as Jennie's handler, but now Logan had yet to answer any of his calls. Sully reasoned that the handler would have a good explanation for ignoring his calls.

Except Cara had just had surgery after being stabbed by one of Morel's men. Not to mention the fact that if her attacker knew where her sister was living, he wouldn't have needed Cara to begin with. As far as Sully was concerned, Jennie was still in expert hands.

And so was Cara.

The doctor had assured Sully that Cara was stable now. Her surgery had been smooth, and she was resting.

Sully chuckled at the term the doctor used. *Stable* was not a word Sully would link with Cara Haines. The word *stable* reminded him of something uneventful, predictable, maybe even boring.

No, Cara had never been boring and never would be. But

that didn't mean her life had always been secure. Sully knew all the strife that Cara had had to grow up with, forcing her into a role as guardian for her little sister. An absent mother and a drunken father had led Cara through a life of hard knocks and an unhealthy need for control over every aspect of her being. But never one to let her past define her future, Cara became the best cop Sully had ever met. She was by the book, never wavering from doing what was right. Even saying goodbye to her sister forever to keep her safe.

That ultimate act from the big sister put Sully in awe of Cara. He just never thought she would leave him because of it.

Sully thought back to when he had first partnered with Cara, long before she oversaw the Mountain Country K-9 Unit, which he still partnered with. Ten years ago, Cara had been a supervisor with the Wyoming FBI, quickly rising high in the ranks because of her diligence and expertise in the department. When DC offered her the position as the big boss at FBI headquarters, she'd shrugged it off and kissed him, assuring him she wasn't going anywhere. Then Luis Morel entered their lives and destroyed everything.

But then, Morel didn't break them up. Cara did that all on her own.

As a US Marshal supervisor, Sully would always know Jennie's location and identity in witness protection, and he could never tell Cara. Just as Cara was by the book, so was he. She'd said there couldn't be two big bosses in the relationship. So DC became her next rank, and he was relegated to part of her past.

Sully's cell phone rang on his desk. He glanced quickly, but it wasn't Logan. Instead, the number alerted Sully to Chase Rawlston, the MCK9 task force leader. Sully accepted the call.

"I'm assuming you heard about Cara," he said before Chase wasted his breath on relaying the message. The sound of Christmas music wafted through the phone line. "Sounds like the office is getting ready for the holidays." A glance around his own drab office at the Cheyenne US Marshals building made him wonder if he should hang something to recognize the upcoming day next week. After all, it was his Savior's birthday. Maybe a few brightly colored lights around the door would liven the place up.

"How are you holding up?" Chase asked.

"Me?" Surprised, Sully cleared his throat. But what would be the sense of denying the stress he'd experienced that day? How he had stayed on the phone with the paramedics for the longest twenty-five minutes of his life, and how he had barked at the doctor to hurry and get Cara into surgery. "She's going to live. That's all that matters," Sully said.

"I heard. She just called me."

"Did she really?" Despite having no reason for the surprise, Sully huffed in disbelief. "The woman just got out of surgery. What's she thinking?"

"You know Cara, nothing keeps her down. She'll most likely work right through Christmas and New Year's too."

"Don't let her take you away from your new bride-to-be." Chase Rawlston had recently asked Zoe Jenkins to marry him after a harrowing case that brought the two of them and her little baby girl together. This would be their first Christmas as a couple, and that took precedence over work. Considering Chase's tragic loss of his wife and child in DC five years ago, they both deserved this time together. Cara should show more empathy, given what Chase had been through.

Chase laughed. "Well, Cara is my boss, and by the sounds of it, I'll probably be inviting her to dinner."

Sully's stomach bottomed out like a rock. Chase had to be mistaken. "I hope you're not saying that Cara is planning a trip out west, are you?"

Silence ensued. "Um… I assumed she told you."

"She hasn't called me since before she went into surgery." Sully left out the fact that she was unconscious the last time he spoke to her. "I told her there was no point in coming out here. Did she say when?"

"Yes, she called me to tell me she was taking the first plane out in the morning. This visit isn't out of the ordinary. She flies in all the time. She was just here at Thanksgiving after the RMK arrest. You know that. You were there."

Sully remembered being in the same room with her all too well. They barely said two words to each other. "Fine, but she was just stabbed. The anesthesia hasn't even worn off yet. She needs to heal. Did she tell you why she was flying out here?" As if Sully didn't know.

"Does she need a reason? She *is* in charge of MCK9. Why are you so upset about this?"

"Because I know she isn't coming here for an inspection of your work. She's coming here to inspect *mine*."

Cara stepped out of the jetway with Mocha beside her. After the dog's keen detection at the training facility, Cara wanted to give her some extra attention and training. Cara also felt better with having a K-9 by her side in case Morel sent another one of his soldiers after her. To burn her trail, Cara bought two tickets, one to California and one to Wyoming. She sent her assistant to California with the ticket in Cara's name. Tracy bore an uncanny resemblance to her with the same short black hair. Whereas Cara's eyes were green, Tracy's blues needed contacts and a pair of crystal-framed eyeglasses to finish the disguise. Tracy would appear in LA and quickly return to DC. By the time Morel realized Tracy wasn't Cara, Cara hoped to be already on her way to her sister's house, and Tracy's protection detail would make sure she made it back safely as well. Cara exited to the passenger pickup area and spotted the MCK9 SUV waiting for her at the curb. Chase had come through in picking her up.

Gingerly pulling her luggage behind her with one hand and holding Mocha's leash with the other, she approached the black vehicle from behind. As she neared it, the passenger window lowered.

"Thanks for picking me up." She approached the door. Only it wasn't Chase behind the wheel. It was Sully. She stopped short of opening the door. "What are you doing here?"

"I should ask you the same question, and it's nice to see you too. Why aren't you in a hospital?" He didn't wait for an answer, as if she owed him one. He opened his door to step to the back of the vehicle. Pulling the hatch wide, he revealed two dog crates, one occupied.

"Mocha, in," she commanded. As her dog settled inside the crate, Cara said, "I see you still have Deacon. He must be getting on in years." The sleek, black Doberman pinscher raised an eyebrow at her. Cara gave him a brief smile.

"He's a dependable dog. We work well together. He's devoted and in it for the long haul. Ending our relationship for no reason doesn't feel right."

Cara eyed Sully with a sideways glance. She noticed his brown hair graying at the temples, but other than that, Sully, at fifty-three, was still in prime shape. She ignored his dig, obviously meant for her, and said, "Since when do US Marshals drive K-9 unit vehicles? And where is Chase?"

Sully closed the rear doors and headed back to the driver's seat. "Chase had a prior engagement with Zoe's family. I offered to pick you up. I took his vehicle so you could easily find me." He settled in behind the wheel, leaving Cara with no other alternatives. "Are you coming or not?"

Suddenly, a loud noise echoed from behind. The blast sounded like a gunshot, and Cara dropped to her knees. Pain shot from her shoulder wound on the impact and the next thing she knew, Sully was beside her.

"Hey, it was just an old truck backfiring." His face leaned close and his intense, hawklike eyes she remembered well leveled on her. For a moment, she let herself catch her breath. Then she pushed herself up and away from him. "At least let me help you up," he said.

"I got myself down here. I'll get myself up." She gritted

her teeth as she used her good arm for leverage. She was on her feet and inside the car before Sully moved from his spot.

When he stood, he leaned in through the opened window, once again coming close to her. She faced forward but could feel his warm breath on her cheek.

"Why are you here, Cara?" he whispered. "You know there is nothing you can do for Jeanette. Nothing has changed in ten years. Nothing will ever change. What do you hope to accomplish by this impromptu trip?"

She slowly turned his way. She knew he was right but couldn't tell him that. He'd always been right to keep her in the dark. "I have to know that she's safe. That's all. No one has to know that I checked on her. And Jeanette will never see me."

The intensity in his eyes softened. "Aw, Cara. Jeanette is alive and well and loves the life that was created for her. She's happy, believe me. She's safe and spends her days painting, just as you wanted. You know if you see her, you risk her losing all of that."

"I want to speak with her handler. Once I'm satisfied that he's up for the task, I'll go."

Sully's gaze averted from hers. The shift happened so quickly that she knew something was wrong. "It's not possible." He moved away from the window and circled around the front of the truck to the driver's side. Putting the vehicle into gear, Sully drove off from the pickup area in silence.

"You never were a good liar, so you might as well tell the truth. You haven't heard from her handler, have you?"

Sully took the highway entrance to Elk Valley, glancing her way with his mouth open to respond. After a moment, he closed it and shook his head. "Just let me do my job, Cara. This doesn't concern you."

"We'll see about that."

Chapter Three

Ten minutes in Cara's company and Sully remembered why they never would have made it as a couple. Her distrust in him never made sense. He used to take it personally, thought that if he tried a little harder, then maybe next time, he would get it right. But that next time never came. And eventually, she walked out on him without even a backward glance.

"I'll be heading to Jeanette's," he told her. "If there's a problem, you'll be the first to know."

"So does that mean she's nearby?"

Sully held his tongue from saying more, not wanting to give away Jeanette's location.

"I'm going with you."

Sully shook his head and took the turn into the Mountain Country K-9 Unit headquarters. He pulled into Chase's designated spot and cut the engine.

"You know that's not possible. For once, you're going to have to trust me to do my job."

She sent a heated gaze his way. "For once? I trusted you for ten years with Jeanette's life. It's not you I don't trust, it's Morel. He's coming for her."

"He'll never find her. She's in the most remote area, with

nothing around for miles. And by the way, your decision to leave the hospital and come here contradicts your claim of trusting me." Sully observed the building. "I filled everyone in. They're going to keep you safe while I investigate the matter."

"I'm not the one with the target on my back. I can't involve the people at the unit in this. That's letting too many people in on Jeanette's whereabouts. If Morel learned that anyone at the MCK9 knew where my sister was, all their lives would be at risk. I'm not dumb, Sully. I know how to keep people safe."

"Everyone but yourself, you mean." He stepped from the vehicle and retrieved Deacon from his cage. Cara guided Mocha out as well. Sully slammed the doors. "Go inside and have some eggnog. Enjoy the holidays with your team. Celebrate their victory over finding the Rocky Mountain Killer this year. Make yourself comfortable because you're not going anywhere."

Sully made his way to his own vehicle, an unmarked SUV, and loaded up Deacon in his crate. A glance back at Cara showed she'd followed his orders. He saw no sight of her or her dog. Sully figured she must've gone inside, and he climbed behind his wheel. He tried Logan one more time before hitting the road.

"Pick up." Frustration set in. Why would Logan Doyle choose this time to go AWOL? The man would lose his job unless he had a real good reason for stepping off his post.

Sully pulled out onto the road, preparing for his seven-hour drive west. He thought of the quaint ranch he had put Jeanette on, going above his duty to give her a nice new life. He took the ribbing for playing favorites, not caring what his colleagues said. All that mattered was that Cara's sacrifice of giving up the only family she had would have a silver lining.

Snowflakes hit his windshield, light at first but soon requiring the wipers. He turned the radio on and listened to the mindless chatter of the hosts as the snow picked up. Any worse and his trip would double in time. If the weather worsened, the roads might even close completely. He thought about calling Logan again, but he needed to focus on driving.

A few cars pulled off to the side of the road, unable to pass through. He drove by them in his four-wheel-drive vehicle and glanced in his rearview mirror. Another SUV drove behind him a short distance away. He recognized the vehicle instantly. It appeared Cara hadn't gone inside the MCK9 building after all. Rather, she climbed back into Chase's SUV and now tailed him.

Sully chuckled, knowing that if he didn't laugh, he might just shout in anger.

"What do you want from me, Cara?" he spoke aloud into the cabin of his vehicle, having a notion of turning around.

He already knew the answer. She wanted him to lead her to her sister. But at what cost? If he drove on, he could lose his job. If he didn't, he could lose Cara.

I already lost her.

The thought echoed in his mind. He may have lost a future with Cara by his side, but the two of them had found a way to coexist amicably in their lines of work.

Sort of.

He watched the vehicle pull back and chuckled. She knew he was onto her.

He had to give her credit. Cara was fantastic at her job. And she was the most responsible person he'd ever known. Perhaps he could lead her to Jeanette just this once, let her see from afar that her sister was happy and safe. Cara may struggle to trust him, but in this moment, he trusted Cara would do the right thing later.

Sully slowed down a bit to give her time to catch back up again. Soon, the two of them drove on at a comfortable pace. It felt almost companionable, as though they traveled together. This little game they played could be disastrous, but it could also end beautifully.

Sully imagined the look on Cara's face when she saw her

sister again. He grinned ear to ear, his reflection in the mirror as dopey as ever.

Then he caught sight of another vehicle speeding up to pass Cara, and his smile slipped from his face. A black four-door sedan moved dangerously close to Chase's SUV. It stopped at Cara's window and moved in closer.

The driver didn't mean to pass her. He meant to hit her.

Cara's vehicle jolted to the right, the steering wheel slipping in her hands. Through the snow hitting her windshield, she saw Sully bring his SUV to a stop in front of her at the same moment.

It took Cara a moment to realize that someone had hit her. A glance out her driver's window showed a black sedan coming too close. Metal against metal collided again before she could move out of the way. Maintaining control of her car took precedence. One more hit like that and she could end up in the ditch. She didn't dare take her eyes off the road, but she also couldn't remain in this vulnerable spot. With Sully stopped up ahead, Cara sped up and yanked her wheel to the left to take the next turn by surprise.

"Call Chase Rawlston," she stated, directing her phone to make the call through Bluetooth. After two rings, he picked up.

"Is everything all right, boss?" his voice spoke through the vehicle's speakers.

"I'm going to need backup. I followed Sully, heading west. Now I have someone trying to push me off the road." Cara had known Sully was onto her. He wasn't a top US Marshal for no reason. She just didn't expect him to realize she'd tailed him so soon. Now she was glad he had. She glanced in her rearview mirror to see if Sully had followed her.

"Did you get a good look at the driver?"

"It's snowing too hard. I did everything I could just to get out of his path." She gave him the make and model of the car, keeping the man in her rearview mirror.

Sully was nowhere in sight.

"Did you get that?" she asked when Chase hadn't responded. Still no response.

"Chase?" She sighed when she realized the connection was lost. "Great. Now I'm out here in the middle of the prairie with nothing but my sidearm, an unruly K-9 in the back and a beat-up SUV."

SUV. A plan formed.

Cara's vehicle, even damaged, would stand up against the weather better than a sedan. She may need to take this thing off-roading.

Removing her weapon from her side holster, Cara placed it within quick and easy reach. She picked up her speed, hoping to give herself a cushion. A forest of thick trees came into view around a bend. As soon as Cara reached the outskirts, she drove off the road and down into the thick of them. Turning the wheel, she came to a stop, grabbed her gun and flung open the door. She raced to the rear of the SUV and released Mocha from her crate. She grabbed Chase's bag of ammunition and removed enough bullets to make her point with this man.

"Stay." The command had Mocha sitting at the ready while Cara settled in behind her car door with her gun at eye level.

The sedan raced in, following her tracks off the road, bumping along the unpaved portion. The uneven terrain and weather didn't seem to bother her pursuer. She understood he had a job to do and his own boss to answer to. Cara needed to send a clear message back to Morel, one that told him he'd messed with the wrong woman. If he thought she would be as naive and controllable as Jeanette, he would learn today that he was wrong. Cara had devoted her life to being the one in charge. No one could hurt her when she was at the top.

Including this goon.

Morel would learn fast that if he wanted to deal with her, he would have to do it himself. At least make the playing field equal. She may have been caught off guard yesterday, but it wouldn't happen again. That was his one given.

"Stand down!" Cara ordered the man as he jumped from his vehicle with his gun in his hand.

He took three shots as his answer.

That was all Cara needed to unload her own.

The passenger door of the car opened, and a second shooter appeared, firing rapidly. Mocha whined from behind her. Cara wasn't ready to send her out into the spray of bullets. One command to bite should be enough for a K-9 to apprehend the assailant. But relying on Mocha to act without hesitancy wasn't possible. Fear could get her killed.

Cara reloaded her gun, staying low behind her door. Bullets pelted off the side of the SUV as she took aim.

One bullet hit the first shooter's thigh. Her second hit his arm, and he dropped the gun. The other assailant ran closer to her, shooting haphazardly.

She heard the pop of her tires and knew she wouldn't be going anywhere in this car. They could take out her tires, but they wouldn't be taking her out. She reloaded again. But before she could lift her gun, another gun blasted from behind her and the second assailant fell to the ground, dead.

The first shooter raced back to the car and spun his wheels to get out. He made it back up the embankment and slipped and slid all the way down the road in his escape.

Silence fell over the scene as Cara looked around to see who had taken the death shot.

One moment she saw no one around, but in the next, Sully stepped out of the trees, his gun at his side.

With less than twenty feet between them, she locked gazes with him. The anger in his intense eyes spoke volumes. *Go home, Cara.*

She shook her head.

"It's too late. I won't go until I see her with my own eyes."
But with Chase's SUV now undrivable, Sully wouldn't just
lead her to Jeanette. Sully would take her to her sister.

Chapter Four

Sully stepped away from the local law enforcement who were processing the scene. He'd been given the all-clear to continue with his plans and trip to Jackson. Halfway between the scene and where he parked his car, he stopped in indecision. Ahead, he could see Cara standing by his vehicle, talking on her phone. Her strict mannerisms and body language showed her level of power. She most likely was giving the MCK9 unit her orders and laying out her own plans, which conflicted with his own. As he stood on this middle ground, he felt himself wavering in his position. The thought dumbfounded him. He had never been double-minded.

Sully called on his beliefs, digging deep to where he held tightly to the word of God, Scriptures hidden in his heart for moments such as these. He drew on the promise that God had not given him a spirit of apprehension. God gives a sound mind, power and love.

But then, had God known Cara Haines would come into his life and disrupt everything? It was as though the two of them picked up where they'd left off ten years ago. Who would be in charge? It was all-or-nothing for her.

Sully began the trek toward her, mentally preparing reasons for her to return to the MCK9 and let him do his job. But when he stepped up in front of her, she clicked off the phone and began a whole briefing of everything she'd set in motion with her team. All Sully could do was stand and listen with no way to get a word in edge-wise.

"Are you listening to me?" she asked.

"I'm hearing everything you're saying," he said. "And I'm hearing everything you're not saying."

"What's that supposed to mean?"

"The fact that this is not your jurisdiction. I don't work for you. I am a United States Marshal, and the witness protection program falls under my responsibility."

Cara's eyes widened behind her glasses. "Excuse me, but I was attacked...twice. The current threat takes precedence over witness security from ten years ago. These are crimes in progress that must be stopped."

"So does this mean you'll return to the MCK9 and handle these crimes?"

"I have my team working on it. Chase is pulling in as many of the local officers who are available. They can handle things in Elk Valley and the vicinity around."

"I had a feeling you would say that." Why was saying no to her so difficult? *Just say it.*

She turned and opened the passenger door, stepping a foot inside while the word hung on his tongue.

No.

"Are you coming, or should I drive?" She stopped halfway in the car, leveling her stare of authority at him as if he was a low-level rookie.

Frustration set in. *I have a sound mind.* He repeated this promise quietly to himself with a deep breath. "Why are you doing this? Why can't you trust me to handle this and make sure Jennie is safe?"

"Jennie? That's her new name? You couldn't even change her first name to something like Wanda, or something vastly different? Why don't you just drop a pin on a map so Luis can track her right down?"

"I gave her the name she wanted. I did everything you asked me to do. By you going to see her now, it'll all be for nothing. There's no guarantee I can get her this life again. Right now, she's safe. Do you really want to risk everything?"

"I could ask you the same question. Deep down, you know you could be wrong. Do you really want to risk her life? Now get in the car and drive." She climbed the rest of the way in and shut the door. He watched her put her seat belt on. Then she raised her slender wrist and tapped her watch.

A sudden laugh escaped his lips. Did she just tap her watch at him? His first thought was if she was serious. But he didn't have to think too long. Cara was always serious.

He felt his smile slip from his face. He wasn't sure he'd ever heard Cara laugh in all the time they dated. Had her tough exterior been from more than the badge she wore?

But there was one time he caught her smiling.

Sully moved around the front of his SUV and climbed in behind the wheel. Even as he started the engine, he questioned his reasoning. Cara had him second-guessing himself. Was he caving into her demands because of his doubts about Jennie's safety? Or was it because everything he'd ever done for Cara was for the hope of seeing her smile again?

In the back of the SUV, Mocha jumped in the crate while Deacon remained still and poised. Cara sighed as she stared out the window, watching a snowy Wyoming drift by. Five hours in, and she didn't know where Sully was driving to. He remained as still as his dog.

And silent.

Cara needed to break the tension somehow. She knew he had a protocol to follow. She knew all about those rules, every painful one of them. Cara reminded herself daily of those rules, and even as she moved closer to her sister's location, she knew she couldn't breach them.

"I'm not sure Mocha will make it as a K-9," she spoke the first thing that came to mind, but not what was really in her heart.

The dog whined at the sound of her name, proving Cara's statement about her.

Sully glanced in the rearview mirror before shrugging. "Perhaps not, but I'm glad to see you not giving up on her so easily."

He was back to his passive remarks about the dogs that weren't really about the dogs. Cara weighed her words carefully. Regardless of their past and how things had been left between them, she would remain professional throughout this trip. Their relationship had been ten years ago. It was time for him to get over it.

"What you see as giving up, I see as what's best for all parties," she said. "There are good reasons for goodbyes."

He put his turn signal on and took the next exit. She glanced around the wide-open terrain for a sign of their location. Was this the town where Jeanette lived? Before she could ask, he said, "As long as both parties have a say. Otherwise, it's giving up."

Cara faced him directly, ready to deny his accusation. She took a deep breath instead. "And how would you like me to ask Mocha about her wishes? She doesn't have a say because she can't talk."

He shrugged again and pulled into a rest area with fast-food restaurants. He parked in front of a dog area. "Maybe relinquishing some of your control and demands so she can show you she's worth the effort. She's a dog, not a robot. If she truly wants to please you, she'll do it without command. It's part of the trust you build with her, not order from her. You used to be an amazing K-9 trainer. How could you have forgotten this crucial component?"

Cara readied to deny his accusation but held her tongue. She questioned if he was right. Did taking the DC job cause a lapse in her training skills, or had her choice to leave training for a desk job been more about her unwillingness to loosen the leash?

In more ways than one.

She opened the door to retrieve Mocha. At the back with doors opened, Cara clipped the leash onto the K-9's vest collar. Circling the leash around her wrist, Cara guided the dog down and toward the dog area. She stood away from Sully and Deacon as though they didn't know each other. But it wasn't true. Sully knew all about her. In a lapse of judgment during a night while they dated, Cara spilled all about her past to the man. Jeanette had just married Luis and found out about the monster he was. Cara remembered feeling as though she'd lost all control over her life with no way to protect her sister. Cara had broken down and pleaded with Sully to help, and before she knew what she was doing, she'd told him everything. She vowed to never make herself so vulnerable again. It was a moment of weakness that became a wedge between them after that night. The strong and fearless woman she portrayed to the world was proved to be false. And Sully knew it. But then Sully knew everything, even things she wasn't allowed to know.

And that was the heart of the matter.

Cara moved to return Mocha to the vehicle. "Crate."

"Wait," Sully called from behind, halting Cara in mid-step. When she turned his way, he held a red rubber ball in his hand. "When was the last time someone played with her?"

Cara scoffed. "There's no time for that. We need to get back on the road. Who knows who's on our tail as we speak?"

"Then all the more reason to make sure she'll be there when you need her." Before she knew what he was about to do, he threw the ball at her.

It hit her on the cheek and fell to the ground.

Cara pursed her lips. "I don't think you're funny."

"I can't believe you didn't catch that." His eyes danced with suppressed laughter. He walked toward her and picked up the ball. This time, he placed it in her hand. "Play with her. It's the best way to build trust."

"If this will get us back on the road, fine." Cara released the leash from Mocha's vest. She pulled back her arm and let the ball sail through the air. Sully held Deacon in place, commanding him to stay. Mocha glanced at the ball and back at Cara. A look of longing in her black eyes mixed with confusion irked Cara. She hadn't expected for Sully to be proved right over something as silly as a game of fetch. "Go. Fetch."

Mocha took one tentative step, then picked up her pace until she was in a full-blown run. She swooped down and, in her open slack jaws, scooped up the ball and stopped. With the ball in her mouth, she glanced at Cara, but didn't return.

"Get down on your knees," Sully said. "Lower to her level and hold out your hand."

The whole thing seemed ridiculous. This was a working dog. Treating her like this could ruin her completely as a K-9. And yet, Cara bent down on her knees.

Slowly, Mocha approached her, both of them broaching unfamiliar territory. She dropped the ball a foot away from Cara. When Cara moved to reach for it, Sully stopped her.

"Tell her to fetch it," he whispered. "And bring it to you."

Cara understood why Sully wanted her to carry this through. But what if Mocha didn't complete the task? What if it was too late to earn trust because Mocha failed crucial training to be a K-9 officer?

"Fetch the ball and bring it to me," Cara ordered.

Mocha tilted her head, then lowered it to the ground to scoop up the ball again. This time, she took the remaining steps and placed the ball into Cara's waiting hands. The dog stepped back, but Cara reached out and tussled her fur quickly for reinforcement.

Suddenly, Mocha raced up to Cara, huffing in satisfaction. She slobbered a bit on Cara's cheek.

As Cara tried to avoid the dog's tongue, she said, "Now I fear she's really ruined."

When Sully didn't respond, Cara looked up at him. A strange expression filled his eyes as he watched her intently. Just as quickly as the look had come, it disappeared, and he turned toward the SUV.

"Let's get the dogs back inside and we'll grab some food before heading out."

Cara followed him to the vehicle and once the dogs were secure, she and Sully went into the rest area.

Sully held the door for her, and Cara paused before entering. "When I'm wrong, I say I'm wrong. And I might have been wrong with Mocha."

"Might have?" Laughter filled his voice.

"Time will tell," she said, passing through the door.

The interior of the rest area was bright and cheery. Someone had painted a mural on the far wall that depicted beautiful Jackson Hole. Ski slopes overlooked the quaint Western town that Cara remembered fondly from when she lived in the state and frequented the town. Slowly, she approached the wall, taking in the stunning image.

"It's beautiful. Seems wrong to be at a rest stop." Cara walked along the painting, studying every fine detail from the bear on the mountaintop to the child's face on the ski slope. Twinkling lights warmed the downtown. As Cara came to the end of the mural, she found the artist's signature.

Jennie.

She thought back to when Sully had called Jeanette Jennie, but it had to be a coincidence. This couldn't be her sister's work. Her sister was in hiding. She would be foolish to be commissioning her skills.

But when Cara turned and faced Sully, the shocked expression on his face told her he knew who the artist was as well.

"Did you authorize this?"

He shook his head. "She was only supposed to paint for herself. That was the deal. Her handler knows this."

"The handler who is MIA? It seems to me your man isn't doing his job. Which means neither are you."

Chapter Five

"Why am I not surprised your sister would go against the rules?" Sully asked around the last bite of a cheap burrito. It was the fastest food available because they needed to get back on the road. He climbed in behind the wheel and started the engine. He hit the windshield wipers to swipe away the accumulating snow that had built up while they were inside the rest stop. "After everything I did to make sure she was safe. What was she thinking? She might as well have posted a neon sign on the ranch that said, 'Here I am. Come and get me.'"

"I'm glad to see you're finally believing Jeanette's in danger," Cara said smugly from the passenger seat. "Or I guess it's Jennie now." Cara buckled up. "No more denying the facts. Call in backup."

Sully drove out of the parking lot. "For what?" He sped up and reentered the highway. "I never said I believed she was in danger. I still don't think her identity's been breached. The only threats have been on you."

"Then what's the hurry?" Cara leveled her self-assured gaze at him.

Sully let off the gas a bit. He nearly growled at her keen awareness. He'd let her see his worry. For a moment, he drove through the storm in silence, considering his next move. He could call in his team, but under what evidence? At two days before Christmas and a snowstorm, he doubted that would go over well.

"I'm eager to have a few choice words with Logan, that's all," Sully said. "The marshal shouldn't have allowed her to take her painting so public. It was only supposed to be a pastime."

"My sister has always been an artist. It's all she ever wanted to be."

"You coddled her. You still are. If she's in danger, she brought it on herself."

"I protected her. There's a difference. Something Logan is failing to do. But it looks like he's not the only one." An underlying threat laced Cara's insinuating words.

"I have always protected her, just as you asked. You can't keep sacrificing your life for her." Sully huffed and took the next exit.

"Sacrificing my life? I didn't give up my life for her."

"No, you gave up the life *we* had." Sully cringed, wishing he could inhale those words back in.

Cara faced forward in silence. Her eyes drifted closed, and she dropped her head back on the headrest. "I thought we were past this, Sully. It wouldn't have worked anyway. *We* wouldn't have worked."

"Funny, I don't remember weighing in on that discussion."

"There was no point. I made the decision."

"Right. And your opinion is the only one that matters."

"Yes." Her response was blunt and cut deep. But he wasn't surprised.

Sully took another turn, but the snow accumulation made the side roads difficult to navigate. The tires spun a bit and slipped around. The number of trees picked up, and the forest grew denser with each mile toward the secluded ranch tucked in a small mountain town.

The snowfall picked up, making visibility near zero. Sully slowed the SUV, trying to see the road ahead.

Suddenly, a loud crack echoed through the air. He strained to see where it had come from.

"Stop the car!" Cara shouted. She raised her arms over her head.

Sully hit the brakes, skidding, still uncertain what she had seen. Then a louder crack, followed by a large tree crashing down directly in front of them, had him gripping the steering wheel even as he knew they were in a slide. The distance between his SUV and the tree lessened by the second.

"Hold on!" The moment of impact sent his SUV to a jarring stop with a portion of his truck jammed above the trunk of the tree and the rest on a perilous angle. Any amount of gas he applied only spun the wheels, going nowhere. The heavy thud of the tree trunk falling still shook his bones.

And frazzled his nerves.

The dogs barked in unison and jumped in their crates.

"Down," Sully commanded as he sat in shock over the sight before him. If he hadn't listened to Cara, they would be dead. *Dead.*

"This was the third attempt on your life," he said.

"Or the heavy snow brought it down."

"You don't really believe that, do you?" He felt his eyes widen in disbelief at her silly notion. She couldn't be serious.

Cara turned his way, and he expected her to fight him on this too. Instead, she simply said, "No. Someone wants us dead. Someone who knows our location. We're being hunted."

"No, not us. Someone wants *you* dead."

"How much farther to Jeanette's?" Cara asked after observing the fallen tree across the road. Even if they could get the tree off the truck, the undercarriage of the vehicle was clearly damaged. Various fluids leaked out onto the pristine snow. But these were still better than their spilled blood.

"I can't just walk up to the ranch," Sully said while trying to push the vehicle off the tree trunk. He strained with no amount of budging from the car.

"You're wasting your energy. We need to get a lay of the land and find the closest residents. If not Jeanette's ranch, then someone else's."

"There is no one else around here. It's why I chose this place. She would be in complete isolation."

Cara folded her arms, a bit out of annoyance but more out of the cold setting in. "Witness protection wasn't supposed to isolate her. It was supposed to reinsert her back into society with a new life. How is living out here all alone doing that?"

"Morel has people everywhere. And she isn't all alone. It's an artist colony. People come for various lengths of residence to work on their artwork. She was among her own people. She chose this. I made her the owner and permanent resident."

Cara cocked her head, considering his words. "I suppose that sounded like a dream to Jeanette. It would have been what she always wanted." Cara knew she should thank him, but they weren't out of the woods yet. Jeanette's new life would most likely be uprooted after today. "I see how a breach of her new life could ruin this for her."

His eyes widened, and he stepped down off the trunk. "It's a little late for that."

Cara frowned, understanding his reason for wanting her to stay behind. But he was right; there was no going back now. She avoided his stare and approached the base of the tree trunk about ten feet from the side of the road. Cara figured the tree to be at least three feet wide at its base. She inspected the wood and saw no decay inside its bark. The tree had been alive and well.

A scan of the snow around the base displayed evidence of someone cutting the tree down. Sawdust showed through the first layer of snow even as more flakes fell from the sky. And though the newly fallen snow-covered footprints, the evidence of a pair of large men's boots trailed off into the woods.

"Our lumberjack went this way." Cara pointed.

"We're not going that way. First, he most likely wants us to follow him, and it could be an ambush. Second, we don't have much time out here if we want to stay alive. The sun is going down and we have nothing but the coats on our backs to keep us warm."

"But if we go to the ranch, we'll lead him right to Jeanette."

"We have the dogs. They'll alert us to his presence."

"Deacon, maybe. I doubt Mocha is up to that task."

"Alerting is a requirement for a K-9," Sully said as he approached the rear of the vehicle and opened the door.

Cara followed him. "You don't have to tell me twice. Taking her on this trip was my last-ditch effort to train her."

"There's a chance she becomes a liability instead."

"Are you suggesting we leave her here?"

"That would be cruel on our part." He reached into Mocha's crate and rubbed the black fur by her nose, lifting her gaze to his. "Sit."

Mocha sat back on her haunches with a little huff. Her breath puffed to vapor in the cold.

Sully opened a backpack and removed booties for the dogs' paws. "She's following commands. I think she'll be okay." He passed a set to Cara while he fitted Deacon into his boots.

"Down," Sully said, and both dogs jumped out. "Guard," he gave, issuing the next command, and headed in the opposite direction of the footprints.

"Is it far?" Cara asked.

Sully didn't respond right away. She realized he had an ear turned to their surroundings, and she took his unspoken command to walk in silence. Knowing the distance wasn't important. Getting there alive was.

Two hours passed by, and Deacon whined and alerted to his right. Mocha followed Deacon and did the same. Sully put his arm up to stop Cara, jerking his head to the right and nodding to the left. He wanted her to go left behind a wide tree.

Cara frowned and instead removed her gun from inside her coat. As she gripped the pistol, she noticed her fingers struggled to clench it. They were stiff from the cold temperatures.

"Are you all right?" Sully whispered.

"I don't need to be coddled. I'm a trained FBI agent who can handle her own." She tightened her fingers and lifted the weapon. Her wounded shoulder said otherwise, but she kept that to herself.

"Fine. He's cutting us off. We'll need to take the longer route if we're going to avoid him."

"Why don't we just apprehend him?" Cara heard the exasperation in her voice.

"And then what? Take him with us? I'd like to avoid that until we have backup. We need to get to the ranch first."

Cara didn't like leaving this man free to continue to hunt them, but with each moment, the sky darkened, and they needed to find shelter.

"Come," she called to Mocha.

But instead of responding to the command, Mocha only had eyes for Deacon.

Cara glanced at Sully to see if he noticed and, at his nod, he directed Deacon in the opposite direction. Mocha immediately followed.

Interesting. Perhaps there was hope for the dog yet.

With the K-9s at the lead, Cara and Sully fell in behind them, each with their weapon in their hand. The terrain rose in elevation on this alternative route. An icy wind picked up at the higher elevation. Cara's work boots didn't hold up to the deep snow. At some point, she realized she couldn't feel her feet any longer. Her hand also stuck to her gun.

"Frostbite is setting in," she whispered. She heard a strange sound coming from her voice. "Am I slurring my words?" She hoped it was her imagination, but then, if she hallucinated, that wouldn't be good either.

"It's not much farther. I think," Sully replied. "I've never walked these woods, but I'm pretty sure we're coming in from the rear of the property. I hope anyway."

Cara realized he put an arm around her shoulders and pulled her close to him, but she couldn't feel him. She leaned in, knowing something was wrong, but she struggled to form the words to say it.

No, she didn't want to say it. The idea of admitting to a weakness made her want to scream in frustration. She should be able to hold her own. Even more, she should be able to be in charge. She was the big boss. She'd earned that title for a reason. Admitting defeat now would make everything a lie.

It would make her a liar and a fraud.

Heat scorched her cheeks and neck. She pulled at her collar and stumbled.

"Cara?" Sully's voice seemed so far away, not mere inches. "I got you. Stay awake."

Cara jolted and thought she had fallen asleep on her feet. Except she wasn't walking anymore. For a moment, she realized she was being carried. How long had she fallen asleep for? Before she could ask, darkness overtook her completely.

Chapter Six

Finally, the outline of the barn came into view beneath the moonlit sky. They'd made it to the ranch. But were they too late?

Sully glanced down into Cara's unconscious face as the dogs walked on either side of him, keeping guard. This was his own fault. He should have locked her up to keep her safe. But he couldn't deal with the what-ifs right now. He needed to get her someplace warm and revive her.

He passed by the barn and neared the single-story ranch house. All lights were off, and no one looked home. The sight boiled his blood. If they came all this way for nothing, risking their lives, Logan would pay for it. Moving the witness without permission was against protocol. Logan knew he needed to inform Sully if Jennie needed to be moved to a safe house. "I'll have his badge," Sully said desperately as he trudged through the knee-deep snow toward the house.

A sound came from behind just as Deacon alerted to it. How had the dog not heard sooner?

Sully had no time to figure it out. He picked up his steps and trudged through the snow at a fast clip, spraying the loose powder all around. The back door loomed ahead, feeling forever out of reach.

A gunshot blasted through the night, its bullet banging off the roofline. Sully turned to the left and then the right. Back and forth, he evaded the gun's scope. Bullets sprayed the surrounding snow, and then one took him down. Hot, searing pain emanated from his back, but he pushed up onto his knees and targeted the last five feet to the door.

A moan escaped Cara's lips as he placed her on the threshold, her back against the wooden door. He tried the doorknob, and it turned. He caught Cara before she fell into the house.

"Inside," he commanded the dogs, and they ran in behind him. He pulled Cara the rest of the way through and slammed the door, locking it. "Hang in there, Cara." He tapped her frozen cheek to wake her up. Taking her hands, he tried to warm them by rubbing them with his own. He was also too cold to make a difference.

"Please, God, don't let me be too late."

Staying low, Sully carried her closer to a heating vent. Thankfully, hot air poured forth. Placing her by it, he scanned the room for a blanket. A sofa about ten feet away had one folded neatly on the top.

"Guard her," he ordered Deacon, and crawled over to the sofa. He had to stand to get it, and as soon as he did, a bullet blasted through the window and landed in the wall above the sofa.

Sully dropped to the floor with the blanket and crawled back to Cara. He wrapped her tightly with the wool, realizing she was already coming to. Her eyes fluttered before closing again.

"We're at the ranch, but no one's here," he whispered. He looked around the wide-open space. "At least I don't think so. I need to search the place to find out if we're alone inside. We have company outside."

Cara trembled fiercely, and he tucked the blanket up to her chin, staying close to her and rubbing her frozen hands. He was glad to see her trembling again. When she had stopped, he knew hypothermia was setting in. Living his whole life in

Wyoming, he'd seen enough people succumb to the cold to know the signs. He also knew the slow and steady warmth would revive her. Sully would just rather not have a predator outside waiting to take them out. He needed to eradicate that threat as well.

He also needed to tend to his own wound.

Feeling around his back, he felt the place his skin burned. From what he could tell, the bullet only grazed his side and the pain he experienced was probably more of a bruised or broken rib than anything else.

As Cara awakened further, he leaned close to study her eyes. He looked for coherency. But what he found was disappointment.

"I did my best," he said as she turned her face away from his.

"But I didn't," she replied. "I was nothing but an anchor for you. If we die here tonight, it'll be my fault. Not yours."

"That's not going to happen. Guard," he ordered Deacon. Pushing back, he took his gun into his hand and said, "Mocha, come."

Cara tried to sit up. "No. Don't take her. Leave her with me and take Deacon."

"You're not in charge of this one." He held the gun up. "Stay here and warm up. And stay low."

"Sully, you can't let the shooter leave here. He'll go right to Morel and tell him of this location."

"You got it, boss." And with that, he slipped out into the dark night, now the hunter himself.

I can't stay here like a useless lump. Cara forced herself to sit up, still clutching the blanket to her trembling body. Her skin burned and ached as feeling seeped back in. Knowing Sully needed backup and his dog pushed her to her knees. If she thought she could stand without falling on her face, she would go out there to help him.

But I've done enough damage already.

As Cara moved away from her spot, her hand encountered a sticky substance. In the darkness, she couldn't see what she touched, but she recognized the feel.

Blood.

She knew she wasn't cut, which meant the blood belonged to Mocha or Sully. Judging by the way Mocha left with no symptoms of being hurt, it could only have been Sully.

More guilt flooded through Cara. *He's hurt because of me. But then I always caused his hurt.* Nothing had changed as far as she could tell. She was still a hazard to him. The best thing she could do was to organize her team here as fast as possible.

Figuring Sully would not have put Jeanette in a place with no way to contact her, there had to be a satellite phone somewhere. From her coat pocket, she withdrew her own useless cell phone to use as a flashlight. Making her way toward the kitchen, she crawled along smooth wood floors. Shadows of Jeanette's artwork lined the walls above her. From what Cara could see, the home was pristine with her sister's artistic touches everywhere. She'd filled even the kitchen with everything a gourmet chef could ask for. Stainless steel appliances and stone counters made for a wonderful artistic retreat. Cara envisioned her sister hosting many artists over the last ten years. She must have been in her glory.

All because of Sully.

He really outdid himself, providing more than what Cara had asked of him. *Take care of her, give her a good life, one she can love forever.* He had done just that.

All the while saying goodbye to her.

Don't leave me, Cara! His words still haunted her. She may have left him ten years ago, but she would not leave him now.

Slowly, she made it to her knees. Just as she had thought, a satellite phone sat at a desk against the far wall of the kitchen. She shut her flashlight off and crept slowly through the dark.

But before she made it to the desk, she slipped and fell to her face. Her hands landed in more blood.

Too much blood.

How was Sully still standing? He had to be bleeding out with this much blood loss. And now he was out in the freezing cold. Even if Morel's man didn't get Sully, a wound like this would kill him.

Cara crawled through the huge puddle of blood and made it to the desk. She reached up for the phone and made the call to Chase.

"Where are you?" he asked.

Cara gave him the directions Sully had taken to get here. "But the road is closed. A tree fell on us. You're going to have to helicopter in. It's the only house in the area. You shouldn't have any trouble getting to us. Fast, Chase. Sully is badly hurt."

"I'll get our team out there as soon as possible. I'll also have Ian chopper in from Montana. He's a lot closer to you than I am."

One of the K-9 officers, Ian Carpenter, lived in Cattle Bend, Montana, staying there after he became engaged to Meadow. He now covered that territory for the MCK9 Unit.

"Do you have this number in case you need to reach me?" Cara asked.

"Yes. I have it on my caller ID. Stay safe. We're on our way." Chase ended the call and Cara sat back against the wall with the phone in her lap. She turned on her cell phone's flashlight again. Lifting it, she took in the room's image.

On a sharp inhale, she knew she couldn't wait for backup to arrive. She needed to get outside and help Sully immediately.

"Deacon, come." Cara skirted around the puddles and met the dog on the other side. Wiping her hands on her pants, she reached inside her coat and found her gun, thankful Sully had returned it to its place. She took hold of Deacon's collar and found his leash, and standing, she walked to the front door.

Frigid cold whipped at her face, and she wondered if she

was ready for this. Her body still hadn't thawed completely, but she refused to stay inside and do nothing while Sully bled out trying to apprehend this man alone.

I owe him everything.

With that thought in mind, she stepped out into the dark night. The snow had stopped falling at some point, but it left a good foot on the ground.

"Seek Sully," she commanded the dog in a low whisper, putting her hand beneath the dog's nose.

Deacon whined in response, but began tracking.

Quietly, Cara followed the dog until they reached the tree line. Then, the dog turned left while Cara saw two men fighting near the barn on her right. She wondered why Deacon would go in the opposite direction, but that answer would have to wait. Cara pulled on the leash and picked up her pace through the snow.

Beneath her coat, at her back, she removed her handcuffs and had them at the ready to apprehend the man. Mocha had her teeth locked tight around the man's leg, but her grasp wasn't strong enough to deter him. When Cara came within a few feet, she ordered Deacon to hold the man down. The dog launched into the air, sunk his teeth into the man's arm, pulling him down to the ground.

Cara moved in, reaching for his free hand to pull behind his back. She slapped the first cuff on.

"Release," she commanded. Deacon immediately let go and sat down on his haunches as she took the man's wrist and put the other cuff on it.

Standing, she pulled the man up with her and Sully stood quickly in front of him, reading him his rights.

Cara strained to see through the dark. "Where are you hurt?" she asked Sully.

"It's just a scratch. I'm okay. Let's get him inside and call in the authorities to pick him up."

"I already did. MCK9 is already on the way."

"That could be a while."

"Chase is taking a helicopter. He has Ian also flying in from Montana. But I don't understand how you're standing. You've lost too much blood."

Sully grabbed one arm of the perpetrator while she grabbed the other. They walked toward the house with the dogs beside them. "It's just a scratch. I barely bled."

Cara stepped first into the house and turned the lights on. She looked down at where Sully had placed her and could see a few bloody spots, now smeared. She led the man toward the kitchen and turned that light on.

"You bled more than you think you did. Look."

Sully inhaled sharply, shaking his head. "Cara, I never came into this room. This is not my blood."

Stunned, Cara looked from Sully to the floor and back. "Well, if it's not yours, then whose is it?"

A strange look came over his face. He tilted his head to the right.

Cara heard the air expelled from her lungs as the realization of what he wasn't saying settled around her. "Jeanette's."

She stepped back until her legs hit a chair. Slowly, she dropped into it. Glancing up at the man in Sully's grasp, she leveled what had to be her most lethal stare she'd ever given anyone. "Where is my sister?"

Chapter Seven

Sully stood back with Deacon by his side and watched Cara with her team. Chase had arrived with Meadow, Ian, Rocco and Ashley. Being Christmas Eve, they impressed Sully with their dedication to the MCK9 Unit. He didn't know Rocco well, but he knew Ashley, or more like he knew her father. Agent Hanson was a bigwig out at the FBI DC offices. Many believed Ashley was hired on because of her father's influence. Sully would wait on Ashley to prove otherwise before making an assumption of nepotism. So far, she showed seriousness about her job and proved to be dependable. For Cara's sake, he hoped so.

Even though Cara's emotions ran high, and this case was personal, she handled herself with poise and authority. The team had traveled in two helicopters and the choppers had landed in the rear yard. The apprehended perpetrator sat in one, and the pilot prepared to lift off the ground to take him to the closest jail in Jackson. If the man knew where Jennie was, he wasn't saying. Sully didn't believe the man knew anything. Morel sent him to kidnap Cara to use as bait. It's all he would say. He was supposed to bring her in, dead or alive. But he wouldn't say where he was to bring her and to whom.

Sully approached Cara and Chase and told Deacon to sit. Sully then overheard Cara explaining her plan to stay on the ranch. But that was something he couldn't allow.

"That's not possible," he interjected. This was her team, but this was his case. "I need you to return to Elk Valley. I'll take it from here."

Sully expected Cara to fight him, as usual. She didn't like being told what to do, even if it kept her safe. He braced himself for her retort.

"My being here put you in danger. For that, I am sorry," Cara said, stunning him into silence. She glanced at Chase. "Would you give us a moment, please?"

Chase nodded and stepped away, rejoining a few of his team members with their K-9s.

Once again, Sully braced for what Cara planned to say. He held up his hand to warn her. "Don't fight me on this."

"I won't." She reached for the hand he held up, shaking it. "Thank you."

He stared at where she so formally shook his hand, waiting for her to release him, but she squeezed harder. "For what?" he asked with uncertainty in his voice.

"For coming to my rescue. And for giving Jeanette this life. You did more than I could have ever asked for."

"I'm going to find her, and I'll give her another wonderful life. I promise."

Cara frowned, glancing back at the house. "There's too much blood. I have to face the fact that my sister..." Her throat sounded clogged, and she let go of him to brush at her eyes to wipe away tears.

Sully didn't think he'd ever seen her cry. Not even the day she said goodbye to her sister forever. And definitely not the day she said goodbye to him. Cara was always stoic, with a tough exterior. But in this moment, the shell of her outward appearance just cracked, and she let him see inside. The rarity of such an occasion touched his heart.

At one time, he would've leaned in and kissed her gently. But those days were long gone. That wouldn't be a line he would ever cross with her again. He knew if he did, then he crossed it alone and with a risk of her putting him back in his place once again.

He kept both his hands at his side but didn't step back. At her height, they matched eye levels, but they were not equals here.

"I'll inform you of every step of the search," Sully said. "I expect to have a team here within the hour." The team wouldn't just be searching for Jennie but a missing marshal as well. One of their own could be in danger, if not already dead, taken out by the cartel to get to Jennie. It wasn't like Logan to fail in his duties.

Cara nodded, already straightening her shoulders and lifting her chin. The tears were gone. "I would appreciate a brief every two hours." She frowned. "I mean, if that's possible. Sully, I know you don't owe me anything. And you don't work for me."

No, but I care about you.

The words stayed locked inside as he reached for Deacon's collar. "I'll be in touch as often as I can."

Deacon leaned his nose into Sully's hand and immediately alerted. He turned his body toward the front of the ranch, ready to run off, just waiting for the command to seek.

"He's onto something." Sully grabbed the leash and tightened his hold.

Cara followed the dog's attention. "That's the direction we had been going in when we were looking for you." She looked down at her hands, still red with dried blood. "I thought this was your blood, and I had told him to seek you. But..."

"But that's not my blood. That's someone else's. He was tracking whoever's that is, leading you to them."

Cara scanned the terrain behind her, the direction the K-9 had been taking her in. "Possibly my sister's."

Or my marshal's. "Or one of the gang members themselves."

Sully couldn't let her jump to conclusions with speculation. She was too close to this case, but still driven by her profession to catch the bad guys. Could he really send her away now?

The rising sun speckled the new snow like a billion diamonds around them, but the look of determination in Cara's eyes shone brighter than any gem. To deny her this search felt wrong.

"Get Mocha," he said. "We'll check it out. Then you can go."

The look of gratitude filled Cara's face. "Thank you. I know you don't have to let me do this."

In the next second, Cara reached her good arm around his neck and hugged him. The embrace was short and awkward, but it was something she had never done in all the years he had known her. Not even the year they dated. Any act of affection had always been on his part. Cara would never have let herself be so vulnerable.

As she walked to her team to retrieve Mocha, Sully felt sad for her, more than he ever had. That a simple hug was hard for her to offer made him realize the lack of affection she received growing up. Hugging him wasn't easy for her, but she did it. Letting her take the reins in this search wouldn't be easy for him, but he would do it.

Cara returned with Mocha by her side. "I'm ready to check this out. Lead the way."

Sully stepped back and waved her forward. "No. You have the lead."

Cara tilted her head, confusion on her face. "But this is your case. You should call the shots."

"And I say you're in charge now, boss."

Cara frowned. She reached for his chest and tapped him twice. "You were always too good for me, Sully." She turned to her team and began giving orders like the most efficient drill sergeant he had ever heard. Soon they all lined up with their dogs and Cara gave the K-9s the scent they were to track.

As he watched her excel in her FBI duties, Sully feared how

finding Jennie's body might change Cara, close her up more. He silently prayed to God to be there for her. Her nightmare, the one thing she tried to stop by putting Jennie into the program in the first place, may be about to come true.

If it was only Deacon tracking, Cara might have thought the dog was bringing them to a dead end. But with her whole MCK9 team's K-9s heading in the same direction, Cara felt confident the trail was hot. Even with a new-fallen snow, the dogs could sniff out her sister's blood and lead the way.

The unit spread out behind in a line about ten feet apart and trudged through the smooth snow that to the human eye appeared tranquil and untouched. But beneath its surface, a trail of blood had been left to follow. Yesterday, before the snow fell, there were footprints that would have shown if her sister walked alone or if someone carried her.

Or dragged her, dead or alive.

Cara refused to let her mind go to that dark place of the torture Jeanette must have experienced to lose that much blood. It surprised Cara that the interior of the house showed no evidence of foul play. Things appeared to be in their place. Although Cara wouldn't have any idea if that was the case. The life her sister now led was foreign to her, including her home life.

That Sully gave her an artist colony to run stunned Cara with more evidence of his caring heart. She always knew he was a good man, but never to this extent.

That's a lie, and you know it.

Cara's conscience got the better of her. Sully Briggs was the most genuinely caring man she had ever met. And it scared her.

Cara didn't know what to do with such kindness and tenderness. It was foreign to her and made her uncomfortable. She'd much rather go toe to toe with him than hand in hand.

"Mocha is holding her own," Sully said from behind Cara. He had taken her dog and given her Deacon for the lead.

Cara surmised, "She may just be following Deacon's direction. I'm not sure she could handle this on her own. It's still too soon to tell with her."

"You could direct her now to take the lead and find out."

"No. This is too important to risk any misdirection."

"I don't want to sound rude, but every case is important. You'll never know what she's capable of if you don't put her to the test."

Cara looked at the sky and took a deep breath. She knew he was right, but she couldn't let Mocha take the lead. "I just can't, Sully. Right now, I need one hundred percent from everyone. And I need assurance that I'll get it."

"I understand." He walked in silence for a few moments, but she could sense he had more to say, and she probably wouldn't like it.

"Don't hold back on me now," she said. "Say what you need to say."

He chuckled, a deep, rolling, smooth sound that calmed her frayed edges. Still, she braced herself for his painful truth. He always saw too deeply into her. Thankfully, all he saw right now was her back.

"All right, have you ever asked yourself why you must be in control of everyone around you? You know it's impossible, right?"

Daily, she thought. But he didn't have to know that. "Which question do you want me to answer first?"

"Your call."

Cara contemplated her words. She pressed her lips tight and lifted her face to the sun. Its warmth gave her the courage to speak freely. Sully walking behind her helped as well. She wasn't sure if she could be honest to his face.

"Yes, I know it's impossible, but impossible never stopped me. I faced impossible things my whole life and have overcome nearly every single one."

"You've defied the odds—I grant you that. Now for question number one."

Cara smirked and rolled her eyes. "Fine, but let me ask you something first."

"Shoot. My life is an open book."

She nearly stopped and turned around. "Nothing about you is open. That was our problem. You knew things I could never know."

"I said *my* life was an open book. The lives of the people I protect are not." The seriousness in his voice kept her walking forward, his point made.

Cara questioned how much she wanted to share with him. He knew the crux of her past situation. In a moment of weakness, she had told him her deepest secret fear.

"You know things about me, so I don't think I need to go into them again. But to answer your question about why I need to control my environment, it's because I know what it feels like to have no control. I refuse to be that little girl again. I learned the hard way that no one was coming to help, and I vowed that I would be that help for someone else. *I* would be the cavalry. I don't trust anyone else but myself to fill that role."

"Because no one came for you," he said in a low voice, but it sounded as though he walked closer to her now.

She didn't need to respond. He understood what she was saying.

After another minute of the quiet shushing in the snow, he asked, "What if I told you someone came for you?"

Her foot tripped, and she turned her head slightly. "What are you talking about? No one came for me."

"Jesus did."

Cara chuckled. "I appreciate the thought, but a man from two thousand years ago didn't come to my rescue. I rescued myself."

"Yes, you are a brave, selfless woman. But just consider this for a second. What if God made you this way because

He knew you would have to endure a harsh childhood? What if He gave you everything you'd need to rise above your circumstances? What if He's been cheering for you to overcome the things that were meant to destroy you? Would your ideas of Him change, knowing He's been with you the whole time?"

"No. Because I don't need Him to be. In fact, I don't need anyone." Cara could practically hear the frown she knew he was wearing. "Look, if you don't mind, can we change the subject? Because if I let myself believe God has been with me the whole time, then I'd have a hard time trusting anything He says and does."

"Because you'd think He let it happen and didn't care enough," Sully said, speaking her thoughts aloud.

"Seems like a logical conclusion to me."

"God's plans don't always look logical to us. But He promises He will work them out to their proper and perfect end. If we are willing to let go and let Him take over."

Deacon picked up his pace, surprising Cara with a quick pull. Speaking of taking over.

Sully continued, "I think you've dealt with enough bad guys to know they acted of their own free will. Should we punish God for their actions?"

Cara understood what Sully was getting at, but it felt as though he was trying to chip away at her resolve.

A resolve that had taken her years to build up on purpose.

She scanned the area of rolling hills and rugged snowcapped mountains in the distance. The Tetons were a formidable range with a strength she envied. Their gray peaks dominated the horizon, and nothing would ever topple them.

"I'm not punishing God," Cara said. "I just don't want to need Him. I don't want to need anyone."

Deacon stopped abruptly. He pushed through the snow to sniff, turning in a circle until he faced left and started in that direction.

Cara let the dog lead, and Sully stepped beside her. Deacon led them into a thick growth of trees.

"There," Sully said and picked up his steps to pass his dog. Cara struggled to see anything but a forest.

"What do you see?"

Sully knelt and moved the snow-covered brush aside. He revealed a hole in the ground. Cara held her breath as she prepared to find her sister's body. But was that kind of preparation even possible?

She closed in and peered over the opening of the hole but saw no body. Blood was evident but no remains.

"Did an animal take her?"

Sully jumped down, landing with a hard thwack that didn't sound like earth. It sounded like wood.

"A coffin?" Cara asked.

"No. A door." Sully bent and reached for the handle. Before he could lift the cover, a bullet blasted through the wood, sending them both falling backward.

Chapter Eight

"This is the US Marshals! Stand down!" Sully ordered, with his gun drawn. He kicked open the trapdoor and stood back in case they took another shot at him. "Drop your weapons and put your hands up!"

"Don't shoot! It's me. Jennie!"

He heard the gun fall to the ground and, as he peered inside, he saw Cara's sister with her hands up. "Are you alone?" he asked.

"No. Logan's with me. But he's hurt. Real bad. He's lost a lot of blood. I don't know what to do."

"What is this place?" Sully asked.

"It's a bunker. Logan built it for me in case the ranch was breached. Please help him, Sully!"

Sully had to give a hand to the handler for his ingenious plan. But first he had to save his life. "We're coming down."

Sully reached a hand up for Cara. His hand hung in the air as he realized she no longer stood above the hole. Moving to the other side, he looked over the edge to see her standing back with the dogs and her team. He locked his gaze on hers and waved her forward.

A small shake of her head told him she would not breach

his protocol. She would not alert her sister to her presence. It would be as if she had never been there. True to her word, she only needed to know that her sister was alive and well.

"She'll need a new life anyway," he said. "You were right the whole time. You saved her life."

Cara frowned, not basking in her keen awareness skills, but conflicted. "I don't know if I can say goodbye again. I'm not strong enough."

Sully lifted his hand and chuckled. "You will because you are. Come and meet Jennie. She needs you right now."

Sully wasn't sure if his words broke through Cara's tough exterior. She gave no expression if they did. Even as she took a step forward and closed the gap between them, he still wasn't sure if she would see Jennie.

At the top of the hole, she said, "Ask Jennie if she wants to see me. I will honor her wishes either way."

Sully didn't like it, but nodded and climbed down into the bunker. It took a moment to adjust his eyes to the small room. Logan had carved a ten-by-ten cavern into the ground, supported with beams and stocked with supplies and a couple of cots. One of which he used on the far side of the bunker. Jennie knelt beside him, speaking softly and encouraging him to wake up.

"Help is on the way. Stay with me, Logan," Jennie pleaded.

The sound of Logan shifting on the cot told Sully that the handler was still alive. "We'll get you out of here, Logan. We have a chopper ready to go."

"I won't leave her," Logan replied in a pained voice. "Morel's men know where she is."

Sully stepped up beside Jennie. "We won't let anything happen to her. We'll take her right to the safe house. You just worry about staying with us." Logan Doyle's blood drenched his clothes. Sully wasn't sure where the injury occurred. "Where were you hit?"

"Near my stomach." A moan escaped his lips. "I don't think it punctured it, though."

"Has the bleeding stopped?"

Jennie looked up at Sully. "I think so. I did the best I could."

He smiled down at her and rubbed her shoulder. He immediately felt the tension coursing through her. "You did good. And well done to you too, Logan, for building this place."

Jennie took Logan's hand, rubbing it with her other hand. "He's so good to me. My only complaint is the peppermint air freshener he hung in here. He didn't know I can't stand the scent. Luis had an addiction to peppermint gum. But other than that, Logan thought of everything."

"You sure gave Morel's men a run for their money. When they couldn't find you, they got creative."

Jennie asked, "How? What'd they do?"

Sully considered his words. "They went after your sister."

Jennie stood with widened eyes. "Please tell me Cara's okay."

Sully brushed her forearm. "Alive and well. In fact, I'd like to know if you want to see her before you're taken to the safe house."

Jennie quickly looked up at the ceiling. In a breathy whisper, she asked, "Is she here now?"

"Only if you want to see her. If you don't think that'd be a good idea, she will make herself scarce."

Jennie swallowed a few times before tears filled her eyes and she nodded multiple times. "I need to see her. Yes, I want to see my sister."

Sully turned to return to the opening but stopped short.

Cara already stood there, waiting in the shadows. At Jennie's words, Cara stepped forward. In the next second, the sisters ran into each other's arms. He could hear crying from Jennie, but Cara embraced her sister stoically and without emotion.

"Did he hurt you?" Jennie asked through her tears.

"Nothing that won't heal. Don't you worry about me," Cara replied, locking her gaze on Sully. The message was obvious. He could say nothing about her attack. "We don't have much time. We need to get Logan to the hospital and you to the safe house."

Jennie lifted her head and stepped back from her sister. "I have to go to the hospital with him."

Sully said, "Jennie, we can take it from here. Cara will go with you."

Suddenly, Jennie stood just as tall and strong as her sister. She shook her head once. "Where Logan goes, I go."

Sully glanced at Cara. She wore an expression of confusion on her face that must have matched his own.

Cara said to Jennie, "You have an army looking for you. We don't have much time to get you someplace safe. Logan's job as your handler is done. You'll be assigned a new one."

Jennie returned to the edge of the cot, kneeling beside it. She took Logan's hand again and brought it to her lips. "I don't want another handler. I just want Logan."

Sully looked at his agent, realizing what Jennie wasn't saying. Had Logan crossed the line? Relationships were forbidden between the handler and their charge.

"What are you saying?" he asked. "Doyle, explain yourself."

"Sir, nothing has happened. Please, take Jennie and keep her safe."

Jennie reached for Logan's cheek. "I'm not going anywhere without you." She turned back and looked at Sully, a defiant lift to her chin. "I love him. And he loves me. I would rather die than be apart from him."

Sully glanced at Cara, and he thought he saw flames in her eyes. He lifted his hand to hold her back, but he wasn't fast enough.

Cara's drill sergeant's voice was back. "After everything I have given up for you, after everything I have done to keep you safe, you would choose to throw it all away? You *will* go to that safe house, even if I have to drag you there myself. And that's an order, Jeanette."

Sully knew he should jump in and take over, but Cara's statement about all she gave up startled him. What did she mean?

He told himself that it was about giving up her only family. But what if that included him? Had Cara cared more about him than he had thought?

"The road is open, and the truck is running," Chase informed Cara back at the ranch. "We'll still fly Logan to the hospital, but the rest of the team will need to drive back. Sully's SUV is drivable. I just need to know what to do with Jennie. She's adamant about going with Logan, but Sully says she must go with him."

"Sully's right. She'll be going back into witness protection and will go to the safe house right away. Every moment that she's out, her life is at risk."

Chase nodded but didn't move to follow the orders. He hesitated a little too long for Cara's comfort.

"Is there a problem, Rawlston?" she asked with a tilt of her head. Ordinarily, she wouldn't invite an opinion, but she had known Chase long before their time together in DC. Their careers intersected many times when she lived and worked in Wyoming. She might have even considered him a friend if she wasn't his boss.

"That depends on who you ask. I completely understand the necessity of getting Jennie to the safe house. But, ma'am, there are enough of us to keep watch. It seems almost cruel to separate her from Logan when she…"

"She what? Loves him? All the more reason to make a clean break quickly. She'll love again. Don't worry, Chase. This is how my sister is. When she's in her next life, she'll fall for the next handsome man that smiles at her. This is why she's in this mess with Luis to begin with. The team has put their lives at risk for her. The least she can do is follow orders, so no one gets hurt."

Chase frowned. "All I know is that giving up someone you love can fill a person's life with no hope."

Cara sighed and walked to the table, taking the chair at the head of the long oak. "But you found someone. You're about to be remarried. Zoe is a wonderful mother. You're going to be a father again. There *is* hope in loving again. You've just proved it."

Chase nodded and stepped up to the adjacent chair, placing his hands on the top rung. "But it took years. And there's no guarantee that Jennie will. Look, all I'm asking for is if she can go with him to the hospital to make sure that he makes it? At least give her that peace."

Cara looked up at her team leader and remembered the pain he felt for years after losing his wife and daughter in that bomb.

"Peace," she said. "Peace comes from order."

"I used to believe that too. But now, I know that true peace is not something we can create ourselves. It comes by letting go and letting God bless us. It's committing our work to Him and letting Him establish our plans. He's in control."

Cara did her best not to roll her eyes as she mumbled, "You sound like Sully."

Chase smirked. "So you've heard this before."

"It's not that I have anything against God—it's that I've learned I need to make my peace. My sister will do the same. It will just take time. She'll find a new life and make her own peace."

"Tell that to Ian," Chase said, referencing their team member Ian Carpenter, who had spent time in WITSEC, the witness protection program, with a new identity. "It's not always about making a new life. It's about getting your old life back. Jennie's done well in her new life. She knows more than any of us what it's like to start over and knows what it'll take to do it again."

Cara folded her arms on the table and eyed her team leader suspiciously. "Are you suggesting that she not return to the program?"

Chase put his hands in the air and shook his head. "Not at all. If that's what keeps her alive, then that's her only option. I'm just saying ten years have gone by for her. She's not in the same place she was when she went in. The clock didn't stop for her, even though your image of her may have stopped for you. She's a different person now, and I'm not talking about her new identity. A lot has happened in this time frame. I believe she's fallen in love and now has more to lose. Let her go to the hospital. I'll put both Ashley and Ian on as her detail. Along with their K-9s, no one will get through. She'll be safe. If she has to say goodbye to Logan, give her some time to do it."

Cara dropped her forehead in her hand as she contemplated all that could go wrong. Morel had his soldiers all over the world, most of them well trained in prisons. They held no code of honor and wouldn't think twice of taking out the team to get to Jennie.

"You're asking a lot of me. I'm responsible if someone gets hurt, or worse."

"I understand, boss. But it's Christmas Eve."

Cara took a moment and realized he was right. After such a harrowing few, she'd lost track of days—not that she had any big plans for the holiday. She frowned at the thought.

"I suppose it'd be nice to spend Christmas Eve with my sister one last time."

He smiled. "There's that too. I'll make sure you're not disturbed, and you have this time together."

Standing, she reached for Chase's hand to shake. But just before she made contact, the kitchen door opened, and Sully stood in the doorway. His face was pale, and his chest heaved as though he'd run the whole way. Something was wrong.

Cara dropped her hand and walked his way. "Logan? I thought they stabilized him."

Sully shook his head and reached a hand to her. Cara closed the gap and took it, never losing eye contact. "Your sister…" He shook his head and closed his eyes.

"What about her? Morel?"

"Not yet. But I'd say anytime now. She stole my car."

"What?" Cara dropped his hand and tried to move past him to the door.

"They're gone. I thought they were in the helicopter. When I went to check on them, it was empty, and the SUV was missing."

"She took the SUV? What is she thinking?"

"There's more," Sully said. "I was just radioed in the chopper that Luis Morel was released early because of the holiday."

Cara took a few seconds to process this information. Slowly, she turned and locked gazes with Chase. "Now, I'm *really* not feeling too peaceful about this situation. Get the helicopter ready. We fly in ten minutes."

Chapter Nine

As the pilot flew them over the towering treetops, Sully scanned the roads below, looking for his vehicle. Cara sat beside him, looking out the other side, and they each wore a set of headphones. Although, she had yet to say a word since the helicopter lifted off from the ranch. Up front, Chase sat beside the pilot. He had left his K-9 with the team, but Deacon and Mocha were secure in their crates in the chopper's rear. Sully thought it best to bring their dogs, just in case they ran into trouble.

"Even if Morel was released this morning, it would take him a few hours to get here from California," Sully spoke his thoughts aloud.

Cara stayed facing toward the window. "If that's supposed to comfort me, it's not." She leaned closer to the window but shook her head. "The tops of these cars all look the same. If only we knew a direction that she went in. She knows this area better than either of us. She could be anywhere from here to Yellowstone. Or maybe she went south into Colorado."

Sully replied, "Logan needs medical attention. If she loves him as she says she does, that would be her only concern."

"Chase," Cara said through the microphone. "Find the nearest hospitals. Have the team call to see if Jennie brought Logan into any of them. Tell them to be on the lookout for her and to notify us the moment she walks in."

"You got it," Chase said, picking up his phone.

Cara rubbed her forehead, removing her glasses to touch her eyes. A quiet sniff captured Sully's attention.

Cara was crying?

"We're going to find her and get her to safety," he assured her.

She put her glasses back on and looked out the window. Shaking her head, she said, "Was it all for nothing?"

"Was what for nothing?"

"Everything." Cara faced him. "All you did for her. Aren't you the least bit angry about her throwing it all away?"

Sully thought about the question, but not for long. The answer was simple. "Not at all. I did the best job I could. Whatever happens after is out of my control. I'm not responsible for the outcome. That will now be between Jennie and God. But, Cara, you should know, everything I did for Jennie wasn't for her. It was for you."

"Me?"

"You asked me to give her a good life, one she could love. It was all for you."

Cara bent her head and broke eye contact with him. "You were always so good to me. I don't—"

"Don't say it," he said, covering her hand on her lap. "Just say thank you. I mean, if you want to."

"Thank you, Sully. But it should be Jennie telling you that. And she should be right here to do it." Cara turned her palm up and grasped his fingers. "I don't owe you a thank-you. I owe you an apology."

"For what?"

She sent him a sideways glance. "Uh…for walking out on you, of course."

Sully chuckled uncomfortably. He caught Chase removing his headset and knew the man was giving them privacy.

Sully let go of Cara's hand, feeling unsure about hearing what she was about to say. "Leave it be. There's no reason to rehash those days. You were right—we never would have made it anyway. Don't let today's events cloud the truth."

Cara nodded and faced the window again. "I suppose you're right." She glanced back at him with the slightest frown. "But I guess we'll never know, will we?"

Twice in one day, Sully questioned Cara's words. First back in the bunker when she mentioned how much she had given up, and now this reference to never finding out if they could have survived as a couple.

Sully faced forward, not letting himself dig into her words. He caught Chase putting the headphones back on.

"Boss?" Chase said. "No hospital has seen Jennie or Logan come in. Any ideas?"

Cara glanced Sully's way with a question in her eyes. "You know this area. Would there be any other places she might bring him?"

Sully shrugged. "Hospitals, or maybe a nearby clinic, would have been my guess."

"Did you try the clinics, Chase?" Cara asked quickly.

"Not yet. I'm on it." Chase removed his headset again and typed on his phone.

Cara fisted her hands in her lap and closed her eyes. She looked like she was at her wit's end. She looked like she was losing control.

But control was a facade, and it always had been. How to get her to understand this was beyond him.

Sully closed his eyes and prayed for God's guidance and words that would break through the tough exterior of Cara's beliefs. He knew those beliefs were planted in the pain of her childhood, and it would take the power of God to pull those roots up. Sully hadn't been enough to help her ten years ago, and he wouldn't be now.

"I'm sure this isn't how you planned to spend Christmas Eve," Sully said.

Cara shook her head. "No, but it's part of the job. I'm sure the entire team would much rather be hanging boughs of holly than tracking down my foolish sister. But they won't complain, and neither will I."

"What had you planned to do?"

Cara stared out the window. "I was invited to a friend's house for dinner. Now that I think of it, I don't think I told them I wasn't coming." She reached into her coat pocket and removed her phone to type out a text. "There," she said and hit Send. "I hope they aren't too mad."

"Mad about what? You just said this is part of the job. They must know that things come up for you. Bad guys don't follow a calendar."

"No, but I made a commitment. I said I would be there."

"This is out of your control."

Cara smirked his way and narrowed her gaze. "Don't remind me."

"It's really hard for you to let things go, isn't it?"

She shrugged. "It's dangerous to let things go. People get hurt when I do."

"You let *me* go." Sully said the words before he thought them through. He was about to apologize, but she spoke first.

"Yeah, and it hurt."

Sully paused. Once again, Cara struck him speechless with her words. But even though her words led him to believe Cara had suffered from their breakup, her aloof composure said otherwise. She acted as though it wasn't a big deal.

He looked down at his hands and said what was on his mind. "But not enough to come back."

He knew he sounded flippant and maybe a little whiny, but it felt good to talk freely with the big boss of the MCK9 and FBI Special Agent in Charge. He always knew she would eventually outrank him in their pursuits, but it never bothered him until she turned her back on him and all they had. Then he felt inconsequential.

He felt forgotten.

He felt small.

"You should be happy I didn't," she said. "You would hate me by now."

Hate you? I loved you.

"Why do you say that?" Sully asked instead.

"Sully, I'm not partner material. The truth is, I would never have been able to rely on you. I don't trust anyone but myself. It's why I left a hospital bed and hopped a plane to fly out to Wyoming."

"The whole 'it's not you, it's me' excuse? You can't be serious," Sully said pointedly. "You never let me prove to you that you could rely on me."

"Exactly. That would mean..."

"Letting go," he finished for her. "It would mean choosing to believe in us. Tell me, did I let you down when you asked me to find a wonderful home for your sister?"

Cara frowned and looked out the window. Eventually, she shook her head. Without turning back to him, she whispered, "When I saw what you did for her, I knew you went above and beyond what I asked for. You didn't just give her a home. You granted her dreams."

"I wanted to give you yours as well. What's your dream, Cara? What do you wish for more than anything else?"

"You're being frivolous and ridiculous," she said, but didn't turn his way. "I don't need anything. I'm perfectly content where I am."

"I don't believe you. Deep down inside you, there's a little girl who once had a dream that was squashed. You say that you can only rely on yourself, but you've let that little girl down. What did she dream of? What was that little girl's dream? Be honest."

Slowly, Cara turned his way. Sully saw Chase fit his headphones back on. He wanted to tell the man to hold off sharing his update. He may never get Cara to be so open with him again.

"The team found her," Chase said, turning his head to look at Sully. "Or at least they found your car. And you were right. She took Logan to a clinic. Beacon Falls Medical Clinic outside Jackson. We haven't gone in yet. What do you want them to do?"

Sully caught Cara watching him intently. Whose call would it be? She said she couldn't rely on him, and he knew his next move would prove if she was right about him or not. He also knew he had to make this call, not her. Legally, Jennie was his responsibility.

"How far are we from the clinic?" he asked.

Chase looked at the pilot to ask.

The pilot held his hand up with all five fingers. "Five minutes," he shouted.

Cara tilted her head. "A lot can happen in five minutes."

She was right. If they scared Jennie, she could run again. If Luis's men were already on her, she could be dead by then.

Sully took a deep breath and decided. Looking directly at Cara, he said, "Send them in."

Cara's eyes widened as she pursed her lips. Apparently, he had chosen wrong.

"You would rather the team wait?" he asked. "Or did you want to be the one to go in? They're your team, Cara. How much do you trust them?"

Chase looked behind the front seat at Cara. "They're the best, boss. I have complete faith in them to handle this correctly. I know this is your sister and personal to you, but you can count on them."

Cara closed her eyes for a moment before nodding. "They're

a good team and have proved themselves this year with the Rocky Mountain Killer. Still, please tell them to be careful. Luis Morel is a career criminal the likes they have never seen."

Chase turned back with a nod and set out to warn the MCK9 team. When Sully looked at Cara, he found her slightly smiling at him. If all went down poorly, he would still be to blame.

"You trusted me with your sister before," he said. "You can trust me again. You can trust me always."

Cara faced forward without responding. The next five minutes ticked on in excruciating slowness. When the clinic roof came into view, he spotted his SUV as well as a few others from the team. There were a few cars he didn't recognize, most likely the employees of the clinic. Off in the distance, he could also see the red-and-blue flashing lights of the local police racing toward the clinic. Then he saw an ambulance speeding behind the police cars.

"What's going on, Chase?" Sully asked.

Chase held up his finger for a moment as he read his texts. "She's not there. But Logan is. He's unconscious. There's also a doctor and nurse who are dead."

Cara dropped her head and clasped her hands in her lap. "We're too late. Morel has her."

Sully had to agree but kept his comments to himself. After a moment, he thought he saw Cara's shoulders trembling. In the next second, clear liquid fell on her hands, and he realized she was crying.

Sully reached a hand to her, but Cara quickly pushed him away and turned to face the window.

"Whether you want to believe it, I'm on your side. I always have been. You may think you survived on your own, but the truth is you survived because there are people rooting for you and praying for you, and I am one of them. I'm not your enemy."

"No."

Sully frowned, frustrated in her ability to believe him. Then she turned his way and let him see the tears streaming down her face.

"You're not my enemy. You're my dream. But, Sully, dreams are for free spirits like my sister. Dreams are for people who chase sunsets. I chase bad guys before they can hurt anyone else. I don't dare dream. Dreaming is a waste of time for me. So don't bother praying for me anymore. Just be real with me. That's all I want."

Chapter Ten

As soon as the helicopter landed in the rear yard of the medical clinic, Cara opened her door and jumped down to the ground. Before she made it to the back entrance, Sully ran beside her with Mocha and Deacon. Thankfully, the man let her confession go…for now. She knew him well enough to know he wouldn't let it go forever. It had been foolish and risky of her to admit such things. It had been…well…it had been a loss of control.

Never again.

Cara held her arm up to stop Sully from entering the building. "Wait until I hear if the scene is under control. Chase, what's the situation with the team?"

Chase headed up to her side. "We're clear to enter. Logan just came to, and the paramedics are prepping him for transport. The scene is secure, and they already know we're here."

Cara nodded but still shouted, "FBI!" to announce herself as she stepped inside.

The MCK9 team was already processing the scene and covered the two bodies. Bullet holes riddled the walls and Cara figured Morel's man must have come in with guns blazing. At least two people were killed, but what about Jennie?

Cara stepped up to the stretcher with Logan on it. His eyes were closed. "Is he coherent?" she asked the paramedic.

Logan turned his head slightly her way. His voice was weak. "Find her. Please."

"Was she shot?"

He shook his head back and forth. "I failed her." His voice caught and sounded gargled with tears that dripped down the sides of his head.

"I need you to stay with me. Did you see who took her? Were they in a car?"

He shook his head again. "I didn't hear a vehicle. I couldn't do anything to stop him. I didn't get a good look. One moment, the doctor stood beside me, and the next...he fell onto me, pulling me down with him. I could hear Jennie screaming, but I lost consciousness once I hit the floor."

Cara sought Chase. He stood by the exit with Sully and the dogs. "Start a search through the woods out back."

Deacon sat in perfect compliance, but Mocha had her nose to the floor, sniffing. Cara frowned, about to give up on the dog. Mocha just couldn't follow commands.

"Leave Mocha behind. She'll hold you up," Cara said, moving to take the dog's leash from Sully.

"Wait," Sully said, kneeling. "She found something."

Cara narrowed her gaze on a tiny piece of paper. She reached for a pair of latex gloves on the table and picked up the tiny square. On the other side of the paper was the label for a stick of peppermint gum.

"Peppermint gum," Cara said, wondering if it was important at all, or if it had been here before Morel's man arrived. There was no way to tell.

"Did you say peppermint?" Logan asked from the stretcher.

Cara stepped up beside him again. "Yeah, why? Does it have any importance?"

"Luis used to chew peppermint gum all the time. Jennie can't stand the smell."

Sully said, "Right, she said that at the bunker about you putting a peppermint air freshener in there. It was her only complaint."

Cara looked down at the piece of paper and considered what this evidence meant. "But if the shooter left this here, then it wasn't one of Morel's men at all."

Sully shook his head. "It was Luis Morel himself."

Even though Cara had figured this was the case, hearing Sully say the words felt like a punch to her gut.

"Luis took her? She'll be dead within the hour." Logan tried to sit up.

Cara put her arm on his chest to push him back down. "You're not going anywhere."

"I have to. She was my charge. I have to find her."

"You're going to the hospital. *We're* going to find her." Cara nodded to the paramedics to take him. She held the wrapper beneath Mocha's nose. "Seek."

Immediately, the K-9 put her nose to the floor and turned for the rear entrance. The hunt was on.

Cara passed the wrapper to each member of the team for their dogs, and soon the MCK9 group was heading into the woods, following Luis's favorite scent.

Sully stepped up beside her. "Mocha came through."

Cara had to agree, though she still wasn't sure about the dog's future. "It's promising, but I'm not ready to rely on her completely. She could have just been curious."

"Or she wants to earn your trust."

Before Cara could respond, she heard a helicopter firing up. It had to be Morel's getaway. Cara picked up her pace to an all-out run. "Up ahead! Quick, before they fly out!"

Sully ran up beside her, keeping her pace. She pushed herself harder, and when she broke through the trees, the helicopter tilted as it lifted off the ground.

"Stop!" she shouted at the top of her lungs, pulling her gun.

But before she could hold it out, bullets sprayed in her direction from the helicopter.

"Get down!" Sully shouted beside her, pulling her back behind a rock. They riddled the place she had been standing with bullets. "He'll kill you first. You're her only family. Let us handle this."

"He's getting away!" Cara never felt so useless. She knew Sully was right, but how could she just stand down? How could she let Luis get away? How could she let go and let everyone else handle this? What if they failed?

She would fail. After everything she did to protect her sister, it all would be for nothing. All her plans and sacrifices were for nothing.

Her plans, not God's.

Cara sought the words Sully had told her about how the Lord would establish her plans. And how He would work it all out to its proper end.

But that meant letting go and no longer being in control of the situation. *Was I ever really in control to begin with?*

Cara knew the answer, but it didn't make stepping back any easier. Taking a deep breath, she watched the helicopter rise to about ten feet in the air, then looked at Sully and nodded for him to take over.

In the next second, Sully turned back to the team, shouting orders to each of them. He sent Chase and Ashley to his far right. Meadow and Ian went to the left. Rocco was told to handle the opposite side. Suddenly, Cara's team had surrounded the helicopter and opened fire. From her vantage point, she could see Ashley stand behind a tree. She held her gun close to her chest and stepped out. But Cara noticed the officer didn't unload her weapon, but narrowed her focus on something in particular. Suddenly, she took five shots, and in the next second, the helicopter spun around in circles.

Cara realized Ashley had targeted the helicopter's tail, rendering it useless. The helicopter spun itself right into the ground, its blades still swirling until one hit a rock, coming to a grinding stop. If there was still any doubt in Ashley's abilities as an agent, she'd just put them to rest. So what if her father was an FBI head honcho? Ashley continued to earn her place on the team all on her own.

Sully jumped to his feet and waved everyone in from all sides. "Go, go, go, go!" he shouted, and the MCK9 team jumped into action in perfect unison.

Cara crouched low and watched the handlers with their K-9s take down Luis Morel and two of his men on the helicopter. She had never been so proud of this team as she was in this moment. Seeing the threat vanquished, she sought her sister.

Jeanette appeared to be slouched in a rear chair. Suddenly, Cara realized her sister may already be dead. She nearly jumped to her feet and ran into the fray. This morning, she probably would have. Instead, she looked at Sully and waited for his orders.

As if reading her mind, he turned to her and gave her the nod to go.

Cara raced from behind the rock and across the clearing. The helicopter had landed on a tilt, and she had to pull herself up inside. She immediately saw her sister had a gash on the side of her head and she was unconscious. Cara felt her neck for a pulse and thanked God when she felt the beats of life still in her sister.

"Jeanette, it's me, Cara. You're safe now. Wake up." Cara tapped her sister's cheek a few times, but Jeanette only moaned.

The helicopter tilted as Sully climbed up. "Here, let me try this." He cracked open a tiny vial and put it under Jeanette's nose.

"Where'd you get that?" Cara asked.

"Smelling salts. I grabbed them off the wall in the clinic before we headed out."

"Brilliant," Cara said. "Why didn't I think of that?"

Sully chuckled as he waved the vial closer to Jeanette's nose. "That's why we make a good team, boss."

Before Cara could process his words, Jeanette jolted awake and immediately screamed in fright. Cara could only focus on calming her sister down and holding her tight.

"We've apprehended Luis. He's going back to jail for a very long time. I'll make sure of it."

Jeanette continued to fight and flail against Cara. She burst out in tears.

Sully put his hand on Jeanette's head, pulling her attention up to him. "You're safe again, Jennie. And so is Logan. He's at the hospital now. He's going to be okay. You're safe. Do you understand what I'm saying?"

Jeanette let out a deep sigh and focused on Sully. Slowly, she nodded and looked down at Cara. A smile flickered on her parched lips. She touched her hand to Cara's cheek. "My sister."

Cara stood and brought Jeanette to her shaky feet. Wrapping an arm around her, Cara led her out of the helicopter and steered her away from where Luis was in handcuffs and being taken to a police car.

Jeanette leaned on Cara's shoulder, reminding her of the years she protected her little sister from their father.

But she wasn't a little girl anymore. And it was time to grow up.

"You put many people in danger today," Cara said. "Why would you leave like that?"

"I know. I'm sorry. I just wasn't ready to say goodbye yet. I just wanted a little more time with him."

Cara pursed her lips, stopping herself from saying her sister's answer was frivolous and irresponsible. Her decision to walk away from Sully ten years ago had been quick, like tearing off a Band-Aid, but how many times had she wished for one more hour together?

"You really love him?" Cara asked.

Jeanette nodded her head to let out a little cry. "It's going to be so hard not to have him in my life anymore." She turned to look Cara in the eye. "How did you do it? When I heard you left Sully, I didn't believe it. I felt so guilty. I knew you did it because of me."

"I did what had to be done. And so will you."

They walked the rest of the way to the helicopter and boarded in the back. Sully returned the dogs to their crates and sat up front. The pilot climbed into the cockpit and looked back at them.

"Where to?"

Both Jeanette and Sully looked at Cara, waiting for her to decide. Would it be the safe house, or would it be a hospital to say goodbye to Logan?

Cara sought Sully's expectant face. She knew he would go along with whatever she decided, but maybe her plans weren't the right ones right now.

"I suppose a stop at the hospital would be okay. Morel's in custody." She looked at Jeanette. "We'll give you fifteen minutes to say goodbye."

Jeanette inhaled a shaky breath but nodded. "Thank you. I know I don't deserve that."

Cara faced forward and caught Sully smiling at her. He gave her a quick wink and turned back around to face forward in the front. She bit back a smile and pressed her lips tight, finding a tree outside to focus on. Slowly, a thought came to her. She would also need to say goodbye to him. Somehow, the idea of walking away again seemed impossible. It made no sense, as the two of them had parted ways so long ago, disconnecting their lives from each other, other than the occasional forced work proximity.

But she would do it because it was the right thing to do. Her sister would be back under his charge and put into witness protection once again. He would give her another good life, and Cara fully believed he would. The way he came through with the MCK9 team back at the clearing, she knew he would come through with her sister as well.

The flight to the hospital was quick and quiet, with no one speaking. It was as though they all could feel the rising tension of what these last fifteen minutes would be for each of them. The helicopter landed on top of the building, and even their walk through the hospital to Logan's room mounted with more dread.

They entered the room to find him sitting up in the bed with his eyes closed. Jeanette approached his side slowly.

"Logan? Are you awake?"

Immediately, his eyelids flew open, and he reached for her. "I've been sitting here praying for you. Oh, thank God you're okay." He brought her hands to his lips and kissed them repeatedly.

"And you're okay too?" Jeanette asked.

He nodded. "I just came out of surgery. I'm all stitched up. I'm going to be fine."

Tears streamed down Jeanette's cheeks. "Logan, I can't stay. I have to go back into the program."

Logan smiled big. "I know. You're going to have a good life. Sully will make sure, right, Sully? Please give her a good life."

Sully said, "The best." He looked at Cara. "Shall we give them a few minutes alone?"

Cara couldn't see why not. "We'll be right outside. Fifteen minutes."

Cara and Sully turned to the door, but when they reached it, Logan called out to Sully.

"I quit," he said, halting their steps. Turning back, Logan held Jeanette's hands in his. He looked at her. "I love you. I have always loved you. Wherever you go, I want to be with you. Whatever identity and home you're given will be mine as well. I mean, if you'll have me."

Jeanette brushed his hair from his eyes. "Have you? But that would mean you give up your whole life and your family."

"You'll be my family." He looked at Sully. "Do you accept my resignation?"

"Have you thought this through?" Sully asked. "This is not something to enter lightly. You'll be sacrificing a lot."

"I'm a handler in WITSEC. I know what it means. And yes, I have thought it through, and I've prayed about it. I know this is where God is leading me. I know Jennie is my future."

Sully nodded and glanced Cara's way. As she watched her sister lean in to kiss Logan, Cara tried to be happy for her. And she was, but there was still a part of her that wondered if her sister realized how many people gave up so much for her happiness.

"I'll wait in the hall," Cara said and turned away from the joyful couple. She could hear Sully explaining to the two of them what would happen next for them. They would be given new names as a married couple. Cara continued to walk down the hall until their voices became muffled. She didn't want to know the details, nor could she. As she reached the elevator, her phone rang.

She retrieved the phone from her pocket, needing to jump back into her work. As long as she was busy chasing bad guys, she didn't feel any pain. It was how she got through the last ten years, and it would be how she got through the rest of life.

Chase's number showed on the screen. "What's up?" Cara asked.

"Morel made a break for it when he reached the police department. There appears to be some sort of breach in the force. One of his soldiers must've infiltrated. Where are you?"

Cara swung back around to look at Logan's door at the end of the hall. She was the only person in the wing. She took a few steps, slowly at first, then speeding up.

"We're at the hospital. We'll fly out to the safe house right away." She hung up the phone and raced into the room. "No time to pack. We need to get to the roof. Now."

"But he can't walk," Jeanette whined. "He just had surgery."

Cara pulled up a wheelchair from against the wall. "Sully. Help him into it."

"What's happened?" Sully asked as he followed her orders.

"Morel's on the loose. Made a break for it at the police station. We need to get to the roof and fly to the safe house."

Sully growled under his breath as he wheeled Logan to the door. "I should have planned for something like this."

"No one could have planned for something like this," Cara said. "Not even me. The man was in custody. We had him."

"Then the police took him into custody. You said yourself he has soldiers all over this world. Sadly, some of those soldiers wear police uniforms."

They took the elevator to the roof and rushed out the metal door to the helicopter. Cara ran ahead of them to open the helicopter door, hearing the dogs barking profusely in their crates. Then she saw the pilot slumped dead over the controls, a bullet hole in his forehead.

Cara circled, eyeing every hidden location on the rooftop. She drew her gun. "Get back!" she shouted to everyone. "Get back inside!"

"Not without you," Sully said, drawing his own weapon.

"Get my sister to safety!"

Sully ran back to the metal roof door just as a bullet pinged off it. Jeanette pushed Logan through the door, but Sully continued to hold the door open.

"Hurry!" he shouted. "Cara!"

In the same moment, Cara spotted the shooter from behind a mechanical box. The man, dressed in all black, pointed his weapon at Sully.

"No!" Cara struggled to give her orders, feeling her throat close. She ran toward the man. "Drop your weapon!"

But the man took his shot, then turned the gun on her.

Cara glanced at Sully to see he'd dodged the bullet. He held his own gun, pointed in her direction.

No, not at her. He pointed his weapon at the man behind her.

Sully shot off multiple bullets as pain ripped through her back, sending her flying and landing facedown on the concrete.

A bullet struck her, and the world around her fell silent.

Chapter Eleven

Sully dropped to his knees, scrambling to Cara while still shooting at one of Morel's men. Three more shots landed in the shooter's chest, taking him out completely. Scanning the rooftop for any other shooters, Sully reached Cara and scooped an arm under her to pull her toward the door.

She groaned but opened her eyes to look at him. She reached her hand to his cheek. "We should have gone to the safe house. This is my fault."

Sully shook his head. "No. I would've made the same call. Hang in there. I'm going to get you downstairs. The doctors will fix you right up good as new."

Her eyes closed, but she opened them wide. "Sully, I'm so sorry. I wish… I know I hurt you. I wish I was stronger than I am."

He cradled her close and lifted her. "What are you talking about? You're the strongest woman I know. In fact, I'm pretty sure you'd top a few men I know too."

At the door, she said, "Listen to me. There may not be time."

Sully's ears blared in defiance at her words. He refused to listen to them. Opening the door, he saw Jennie and Logan were gone. He could only hope Logan was smart enough to hide Jennie someplace safe. Sully couldn't protect Jennie while getting Cara into the ER.

"Listen to me. That's an order, Sully." Her threat sounded strained and fell short of her typical position.

"No, you listen to me. You're going to be fine." He raced down the stairs three floors, doing his best not to jostle her.

"I never wanted to leave you," she said. Her eyes drifted closed and flew open again. "I did what had to be done, but I didn't want to. I wanted a life with you. You made me..." She swallowed hard. "You made me feel safe."

Her statement proved to be a lie. As he held her, feeling her blood seep out on his hands, he hadn't been able to keep her safe at all.

"You made the right choice, love. Don't think twice about it. I would have held you back. You were meant for so much more. I'm so proud of you. I don't think I ever told you that." He leaned down and kissed her forehead in sheer desperateness. "So proud of you."

Cara's face paled quickly before him, and her eyelids continued to flicker. At the ground floor, Sully burst through the door to the ER.

"I need a doctor!" he shouted as he reached the desk.

A nurse stood and came around the front. "What happened?" she asked as she pulled up a gurney.

"Gunshot in the back. Shooter on the roof."

"What?"

"I'll tell you after. Just get her into surgery. Go!"

The nurse pushed the bed down the hall, but Sully saw Cara's hand reach out to him.

"Sully!" she cried out.

He moved to keep up with her. "I forgive you. Don't worry. Just fight, Cara. Please, fight!"

"Don't leave me, Sully!"

His shoes squeaked on the sterile white floor as he came to an abrupt halt.

Cara reached the doors that he couldn't bypass, but it was her words that stopped him cold.

In a whisper, he said, "Oh, Cara, I never have."

Watching her go, he felt as useless as before, standing alone as the doors swung shut.

But he didn't have to be useless.

He would find Jennie and get her to the safe house. He could do that for Cara while she fought for her life. *God, help her fight. Please, give her Your strength so she can live. She still has so much to do. This world needs her. Mocha needs her.*

Jennie needs her.

Sully stopped short of admitting that he needed her and jumped into action. Raising his voice as he turned and ran for the security booth at the front of the emergency room, he shouted, "Lock this place down! No one in and no one out. We have one active shooter extinguished on the roof, but there could be more."

The security guard tried to ask a question, but Sully showed his badge and kept giving orders to secure the building and call the police. The guard picked up the phone and made the calls throughout the hospital. Doors closed automatically while sirens rang off, with red flashing lights down the halls.

Sully ran for the stairwell again, making it to the roof in record time. It wasn't until he ran out into the sunlight that he realized his hands and clothes were covered in Cara's blood.

Too much blood.

He pushed the thought aside, believing she would make it. She had to. And he had to find Jennie and Logan.

Running for the helicopter, Sully kept his gun in front of him. He opened the rear door and freed Deacon from his crate.

"Guard," Sully ordered while he unlatched Mocha's crate. The dog whined and shied away. Maybe Cara was right about the dog. It might be best to leave her behind. "Cara needs you, Mocha. Now's the time to show you're up for the task. Come."

Sully stepped back and took up Deacon's leash. He gave

Mocha a few seconds to decide. If she refused, he would have his answer about her ability to be a K-9 officer.

She didn't move.

Sully reached to close the door, but Mocha let out a loud bark and bolted from her crate and out of the helicopter door. She ran past Sully and leaped into the air. Sully turned just in time to see Mocha take down another gunman.

The man cried out in pain from Mocha's teeth, holding him in a tight grip. Sully ran to the man and handcuffed him.

"Release," Sully ordered, commanding Mocha to stand down. To the man, he demanded, "Where's Morel?" Sully pulled the man to his feet.

The man turned his head and spit at him, but Sully pushed the man forward to walk. "That's how you want to play it? Just remember, you mean nothing to Luis Morel. This is your last offer to play nice. Tell me where he is."

"You'll never find him. He'll find you, and by then you're a dead man." The man laughed. "Just like your FBI girlfriend."

Sully felt his lip curl at the back of the man's head. He bit his tongue from saying what was really on his mind. "I will find him. You can count on it."

Sully brought Morel's soldier down the stairs of the hospital. On the ground floor, police swarmed about. He approached two in uniform. "Can you hold on to this one?" He knew his comment came across a bit too snidely, but so be it.

The two officers nodded. "I guess we have that coming," one of them said. "Rest assured, we have dealt swiftly with our weakest link. It won't happen again."

"Great to hear. I'm going to need a few vests. I need to get two people out of this hospital safely. I'll also need a car by the entrance."

The two men found the items Sully needed and then led the man out the doors into the back of the cruiser. Satisfied, Sully returned to his task of finding Jennie. This time, he didn't have anything of hers to give to the dogs.

But he had something of Logan's.

With his free hand, Sully reached into his pants pocket and removed the badge Logan had given him after the US Marshal had given him his notice. He stared at the badge and thought of Logan's choice to give up his life for the woman he loved. Sully thought back ten years to the time Cara walked out of his life because of the conflict of interest between them. He never once thought about quitting his job and wondered if that's what she had wanted of him. But if he had done that, he would have had no say in where her sister lived, and he would have never found her this week when her life was being threatened. As much as it hurt to watch Cara leave him, he knew it was for the best for Jennie's sake. He fully believed Cara would say the same thing. Her sister's safety always came first.

Sully returned to where he last saw Jennie and Logan and was glad to see Mocha take the lead in the search.

"You'll make a great K-9," he said. Sully could only hope that Cara would make it through to see the dog earn her badge. He prayed this would be the case as the dogs tracked Logan's scent. Within fifteen minutes, the path ended at a door.

"Logan? It's Sully. It's safe to come out."

No response followed.

Just because the path ended at this door didn't mean the two of them entered this room alive. They could have very well been killed and dropped behind this door.

Sully gave the command to the dogs to be on full alert. He readied his gun and turned the knob. With a quick turn, he pulled the door wide and maneuvered his body out of view.

A quick gasp came from inside, telling him at least one person was alive.

"Jennie, it's me. Sully. It's safe to come out. I need to get you to the safe house immediately."

"And Logan?"

"Yes. And Logan. We need to move fast."

In the next second, Jennie stepped into the hallway's streaming light. She pulled Logan out of the shadows. He still sat in the wheelchair.

Sully passed him a bulletproof vest. "Put it on." He then helped Jennie with hers, securing it around her frame.

"Where's Cara?" she asked.

As much as Sully wanted to tell her, words didn't come. All he could do was shake his head. "Just pray. And worry about you. That's what she would want."

A small wail escaped Jennie's lips and Logan reached for her hand.

"The dogs will guard you both. There's a car waiting at the ER entrance. Follow my lead and move quickly."

No one spoke a word throughout the hospital or on the ride to the closest safe house. Sully drove the borrowed police cruiser, keeping an eye out for anyone following. As far as he could tell, they weren't being tailed.

He pulled into a rear garage of a small medical building that acted as a front. Once inside, he took his first deep breath and let it go. *She's going to be all right, Cara.*

"Your new life begins now," he spoke to the two of them through the rearview mirror. "You both know the drill. You will receive new lives. Jennie and Logan are no more. Forget everything."

Sully opened his door and stepped out. He pulled the rear door open for Jennie to exit. But all she did was look up at him.

"Is there a problem?" he asked.

"I can't let you do it again," she said. "My sister has sacrificed her whole life for me. My new life may begin today, but you will know nothing about it."

The US Marshal stationed at this post stepped from a door and approached the car. "Is everything all right?"

"Yes, we had a breach, so I'll be starting over."

Jennie exited the car. "What he means to say is I'll need a new handler."

Sully touched her arm. "You don't know what you're say-ing. I need to be sure you get the life that Cara wants for you."

"I'll get the life that I make of it. The life that Logan and I will make together. I release you of any obligation that you think you have. Tell my sister that I love her, and I will never forget the sacrifices she made for me, including giving up the love of her life. But that ends today. Now go and be with her. She would never admit it, but she needs you."

Jennie helped Logan from the car, as Sully could only stand dumbfounded at her words.

"Sir?" Logan spoke, leaning on Jennie. He offered his hand. "Thank you for everything. I can take it from here. Cara will never have to worry. I promise. Tell her wherever we land, Jennie will be safe and happy."

Sully dragged his hand down his face, half stunned and half afraid of what Cara would say. "She may never talk to me again."

Jennie giggled. "Give her time. Once she realizes what I've done for her, she'll come around. Now get back to the hospital and be there when she wakes up."

When?

Sully tried to have the same hope as Jennie. He opened the driver's door and climbed in. He looked up at the couple in obvious love. "Goodbye."

Jennie smiled and dropped her head on Logan's shoulder. "Merry Christmas, Sully. May all your Christmases be filled with love from now on."

Sully drove out of the garage, feeling unsure of what had just happened. He radioed for an update on the hunt for Luis Morel, hearing that the man was still at large. By the time he returned to the hospital, Cara was out of surgery, alive but unconscious.

Sully entered her post-op room and stood at the end of her bed. She was still in critical condition and the doctors wouldn't know if she would make it until she woke up. He moved around to the side of her bed and took her hand. He stared at it as he ran his thumb around her palm.

"You have to come back to me," he whispered. "Wake up, Cara. I need you to tell me what to do. I find myself at a loss. After ten years of knowing that the best way to make you happy was to protect your sister, she's made that impossible now."

Sully studied Cara's sleeping face. Right now, she looked at peace. But that would all change when she learned her sister had released him from his duties. Jennie may think Cara would be grateful, but Sully knew otherwise.

He put her hand down and turned for the door. As he opened it, she spoke to him.

"She has a way of controlling a situation, with no one realizing she's calling the shots."

Sully turned quickly and approached the bedside. "You're awake."

Cara squirmed and winced.

"Don't move. You had surgery for a gunshot."

"Yeah, I figured. Now, tell me, how has Jeanette made it impossible for you to protect her?"

Sully hesitated to explain. But Cara's raised eyebrows showed impatience. "She fired me. At the safe house, she asked for a new handler and caseworker."

Cara huffed. "How ungrateful. After everything—"

"She did it for you. For us," Sully said quickly, pausing for Cara's reaction.

"What? How would her putting her life in jeopardy be for us?"

"She thinks we aren't together because of her. She thinks if I'm not her caseworker, then I won't know where she is and then we can be together."

Cara shook her head. "That's not true. You can always find out where she is."

"We know that, but she doesn't. She thinks she's sacrificing for you."

"And you let her believe that?"

He shrugged and smirked. "It's Christmas."

Cara laughed, but quickly closed her eyes in a wince. After a second of recovery, she said, "Tomorrow, you will explain to her you will still oversee her case. Understand?"

Sully nearly responded with a yes, but something stopped him. For ten years, he took Cara's orders out of his love for her, but what if compliance wasn't what she needed?

"I said, do you understand?"

"Did you ever love me, Cara?"

She winced again, but seemingly not from the pain. "What kind of question is that?"

"It's an honest question that deserves an honest answer. I have a right to know. Did I imagine our love? Was it all a lie?"

Cara dropped her gaze to the blanket covering her. "It…it wasn't a lie. It just wasn't…sustainable."

"This isn't some sort of brief on a case. There was love or there wasn't. It's as easy as that."

She lifted her chin and captured his gaze. "Love is never that easy." The pain staring at him through her eyes weakened his knees. He stepped back toward the door. "Love comes with responsibility. That's the only love that I know how to give. It's the only love that I know how to receive. I don't trust any other kind. So tomorrow, you will take Jeanette's case again. If you love me as you say you do, it's the only way to show me."

"I disagree. I love you, Cara, and it's because I do that I won't be taking Jennie's case back. You'll have no reason to deny your love for me any longer. And if you try to order me, I will quit." He turned and opened the door. "Merry Christmas, Cara."

"Sully! I'll have your badge for this!"

A glance back showed her angered and shocked expression. "You could have so much more," he said just before the door closed.

Chapter Twelve

Cara felt useless lying in this hospital bed. Twice in a week she'd been nearly taken out. The first time, she called on Sully and he answered the call. But then, hadn't he always answered her calls?

Until today.

A tap on her door alerted her to someone about to enter. Her heart skipped a beat as she prepared for Sully to return. She wasn't sure what she would say. She needed his help. But had she pushed him too far?

"Come in," she said.

"Boss?" Chase peeked his head in. "You up for an update?"

Cara released a breath, letting her disappointment go. "Yes, have you found Morel yet?"

Chase moved to the end of her bed and crossed his arms. "Not yet. There's a possibility he's out of the state already. We have an APB at the Canadian border and the surrounding states and airports."

Cara shook her head. "He hasn't left. He had Jeanette in his clutches. He's too arrogant to retreat now. He'll do whatever he must to get her back. If he wanted to just kill her, he would've done that at the clinic. In his weird, sick sense, he loves her. Keep the team local. I'm sorry they have to work on Christmas. I'll make it up to them."

Chase lifted his hand. "No one's grumbling. Crime doesn't stop on the holidays, and they knew that signing up." He turned to leave, but stopped. "I have Mocha. Do you want her in here with you? I would feel better knowing she's guarding you."

"Me? Morel wouldn't waste his time coming after me." She winced as she shifted on the bed. "This one's going to take some time to recuperate from."

"I'm thankful that you're okay."

She expected him to leave, but at his hesitation, she knew there was more he wanted to say. "Is there something else I should know?"

Chase frowned. "This is probably none of my business, and I'm probably the last person to offer advice, but all I know is I could have missed out on a second chance at love. Sometimes we believe we're better off alone, that we'll only get hurt if we take the risk. And maybe we will. But what if we let ourselves be loved, and it's more than we could ever imagine? What if we let ourselves love someone else, and we're better people for it?"

Cara listened intently, swallowing hard before she told her team leader that he was right, and it *was* none of his business. But she knew his confession didn't come easy. He took a risk, and it turned out well for him.

"You think I should give Sully another chance?" she asked.

Chase shook his head. "No. I think you should give yourself another chance. I don't know too much about your past, but I know you tried to love. You don't make half attempts at anything you do, and I know that included loving your father. Perhaps he didn't know how to love back, but I tell you he's the one that missed out. There's no reason for you to continue missing out as well. I know you won't regret it." Chase nodded and backed up toward the door. "I'll bring Mocha in."

Cara closed her eyes and rested her head on the pillow. She

heard the door click closed and felt the tears streaming out from the corners of her eyes into her hair. Her lips trembled as her heart yearned to be loved.

But what if I get hurt? What if I can't love back? I don't want to hurt Sully.

You already are.

The realization that she had withheld her love from him for so long had already caused him so much pain. And yet, he loved her from afar.

"Oh, Sully. I'm so sorry."

The door clicked open again and Cara opened her eyes, expecting to see Chase with Mocha.

Except it was Luis Morel running to her bedside. His hand covered her mouth before she could say a word. A knife appeared in his other hand.

Cara muffled a scream beneath his grip. She tried to move her arms, even knowing she was tearing stitches from both her wounds, wounds from the hands of this man's men. He may want her sister alive, but Cara was another story. Cara's adrenaline surged as she reached for his wrist with the knife. She had mere seconds to live. With all her strength, she pulled his hand away a few inches, but nothing more. She tried to force her mouth open beneath his grip. She managed just enough to bite down on his little finger.

Morel let out a scream just as the door swung wide. The sound of Mocha's barking filled the room just before she leaped into the air and sunk her teeth into Morel's back. He swung around with the knife still in his hand and lifted his arm to bring the weapon down on the dog.

"Drop the knife!" Sully stood in the doorway with his gun drawn. If Morel heard, he ignored the command and brought the knife down on Mocha. The dog let out a piercing yelp.

Sully shot his weapon three times, and Luis Morel fell back into the chair beside Cara. His head turned her way, and she watched the life go out of him.

"Is she okay?" Cara asked, catching her breath, only concerned about the dog. From her prostrate position, all she could see was Sully kneeling over the K-9 on the floor. "Sully, tell me. Is Mocha hurt?"

Sully lifted his gaze at her. He wore a soft, encouraging expression. "She'll need some stitches, but she'll live to be a great K-9 officer."

Cara closed her eyes in relief. "Yes, I'd say she's passed the test." Cara's voice shook, and she felt her body trembling as the adrenaline escaped her and the realization that her wounds were open sunk in. "I'm going to need more stitches too."

Sully's smile evaporated, and he stood to his feet in a rush. He ran to the door and shouted, "We need a doctor in here!"

"Sully, come here," Cara said.

"Doctor!" Sully remained at the door, looking down the hall.

"Sully, come here right now, and that's an order."

He turned to her. "An order?"

Cara smiled at him. "Fine, a request. Come here and kiss me."

"What?" His mouth gaped.

She lifted a hand to him. "Please." She sounded like she was begging, and maybe she was. "Kiss me, Sully, and show me what I've been missing all these years."

His steps toward her were slow, but when his gaze fell on her lips, her eyes drifted closed, and she lifted a silent prayer of thanks to God for the second chance to love and be loved by this amazing man.

At first, Sully's touch was nothing more than a warm breath. He lifted his head just enough to capture her eyes. "Are you sure? Because, Cara, I don't know how many more goodbyes I can take."

"Me neither. But I do know I need to love you. I need to let myself give you everything I have to give. Even if it means that love isn't returned. I have to do this for myself."

"Not returned?" He took her hand and put it on his chest.

She felt his fast heart rate beating against his chest. "My heart belongs to you, and it always has."

Cara closed her eyes and Sully's next kiss took her breath away. Even while nurses moved her bed back toward the operating room, Sully walked beside her with his hand holding hers until they were forced to let go of each other.

"Wait for me," Cara said.

He chuckled as his intense eyes locked on hers. "Always. You'll never be able to get rid of me again."

Cara laughed, even though it hurt so much.

"I love your laugh," he called to her as she went through the doors. "It's as beautiful as you are. You're going to marry me. Do you hear me, Cara? You're going to marry me."

Cara felt her smile grow even wider. "Is that an order, Briggs?"

He shook his head. And just before the doors closed on him, he said, "It's a promise. Because God's plans always work out to their proper end, and we were always meant to be together."

Epilogue

New Year's Eve promised to be the most exciting day in Cara's life. She was getting married to a man who loved her completely and whom she loved more than life itself. Sully had already put in for a transfer to DC, even though she had been willing to leave her position for him. He was having none of it, adamant that he would not stand in the way of her calling.

Now, Cara was being released from the hospital with Mocha by her side. The nurse wheeled her down to the exit to where Sully waited for her in a striking black tuxedo. Cara glanced down at her typical teal blouse and black pants and wished she had a pretty gown to wear for the ceremony.

"I thought you said this would be simple," she said. "I want to be dressed up for you too."

Sully leaned down and kissed her, lingering against her lips. All week, he had been making up for lost time, not that she was complaining. "You will be. I have a car waiting out front to take you shopping. We'll meet back up again at the church in a few hours."

Disappointment filled Cara. "I had hoped to be with you for the whole day. Are you sure you can't bring me?" They had already been apart for too long. They had so much time to make up for.

Sully lifted away from her and moved to the back of the wheelchair. He pushed her toward a black limousine in the parking lot. "I meant what I said. I'm never leaving you again. You can believe me, Cara."

"I do." She angled her head to catch his gaze, wanting him to know she meant it. "If this is what you want, I'll go buy a dress alone and meet you at the church."

"Good. But you won't be alone. Now go enjoy yourself." At the car, he opened the rear door and suddenly, her sister peeked her head out with a big smile on her face.

"Jennie!" Cara pushed forward on the chair, stunned at seeing her sister out in the open. "How? I thought you left for your new life."

"First, it's Jeanette. Jeanette Doyle." Her sister stepped from the car and flashed a diamond ring and a wedding band on her left hand. "Second, I'm free. Because of you, my beloved sister, I am free to be me for the rest of my life. I will never forget the sacrifices you made for me, and I look forward to making up for them long into our future together."

Cara pushed up to stand and wrapped her arms around her sister. Over Jeanette's shoulder, she caught Sully beaming at her with more love in his eyes than she had ever seen.

He did this.

Thank you, she mouthed to him. Tears filled her eyes.

"It's only the beginning, my love." He took her hand and led her to the car door, helping her inside. "I'll see you at the church."

Cara smiled at him. "I'll be the one running to the altar."

He leaned in and kissed her. "And I'll be the one ready to catch you. Now go buy your dress and hurry. I don't think I can wait much longer."

Cara giggled, feeling twenty years younger. Sully really had given her a second chance to love again, and she planned to love him with her whole heart for the rest of her life and never look back.

* * * * *

Deadly Christmas Inheritance
Jessica R. Patch

MILLS & BOON

Jessica R. Patch lives in the Mid-South, where she pens inspirational contemporary romance and romantic suspense novels. When she's not hunched over her laptop or going on adventurous trips with willing friends in the name of research, you can find her watching way too much Netflix with her family and collecting recipes for amazing dishes she'll probably never cook. To learn more about Jessica, please visit her at jessicarpatch.com.

Books by Jessica R. Patch

Love Inspired Suspense

Texas Crime Scene Cleaners

Crime Scene Conspiracy
Cold Case Target
Deadly Christmas Inheritance

Quantico Profilers

Texas Cold Case Threat
Cold Case Killer Profile
Texas Smoke Screen

Cold Case Investigators

Cold Case Takedown
Cold Case Double Cross
Yuletide Cold Case Cover-Up

Love Inspired Trade

Her Darkest Secret
A Cry in the Dark
The Garden Girls

Visit the Author Profile page at millsandboon.com.au for more titles.

The Lord is merciful and gracious, slow to anger,
and plenteous in mercy. He will not always chide:
neither will he keep his anger for ever.
He hath not dealt with us after our sins;
nor rewarded us according to our iniquities.
—*Psalm* 103:8–10

To my nephew, Taylor. You probably think I've
run through the whole family and you're the only
one left for a dedication. I mean, you're not wrong.
But maybe I'm just saving the best for last. *Wink. Wink.*

To the host of people who make these books work!
Susan L. Tuttle, Jodie Bailey, Shana Asaro, the team
at Harlequin, Rachel Kent and my husband, Tim.
I couldn't do this without any of you!

Chapter One

The Landoon mansion loomed over the grassy knoll, boasting its grandeur and alluding to hidden secrets.

Teegan Albright, Lorna Landoon's next-to-newest employee and her full-time caregiver for the past six months, approached her fairly new home. As she rounded the curving drive, she bypassed the side road that branched toward the stables. A sleek black SUV whizzed by, the driver glaring in her direction.

Charlie Landoon.

Lorna's spoiled-rotten great-grandson. Privileged, wealthy and attractive. He exuded total letchy vibes. Teegan wasn't sorry she'd missed him. Though he rarely visited the main house. That might mean speaking with his great-grandmother, and all Charlie cared about was the winning racehorses he bred on her estate.

After leaving Hollywood in the late '70s, Lorna had returned to her home state of Texas, where she'd established a well-known stable that bred thoroughbreds. Over the years, fifteen of her champion lines had won the Kentucky Derby, earning her a second fortune that could rival Katharine Hepburn's acting career. They had been good friends. And Teegan would know. Her love for the classics filled her with all sorts of trivia about the golden age of Hollywood and it's why she enjoyed and appreciated all of Lorna's stories about film, filmmaking and acting. Teegan had even done some theater—her passion. She adored local theaters, but these past two years she hadn't had much spare time.

Now, Teegan parked behind a beat-up red Jeep. Who did that belong to? No one in Lorna's family.

She glanced at the grand double doors decorated with large holly wreaths and classy red bows. Bloated clouds signaled storms rolling into the Texas Hill Country. Christmas was only one week away, and it might take her that long to wrap all the presents. She jumped out of the car and headed for the trunk. The eight-tiered fountain with a lion head bubbled, and silk poinsettia blooms floated along the largest pool on the bottom.

They decked the house out—even the white horse fencing had wreaths with red bows, and that was a lot of horse fencing. Teegan was thankful she wasn't in charge of the holiday decor. Lorna's newish estate manager, Olivia Wheaton, had made that happen. Teegan had helped Olivia get the job since they'd been close friends in high school.

The only thing Lorna wanted to be kept for family was trimming the tree—a tradition done on Christmas Eve after a festive dinner, though often they bailed, according to Lorna, but she kept it going regardless. Teegan had put her private tree up the day after Thanksgiving. That was her new tradition— one she'd established after her fraternal twins had been born.

She popped the car's trunk and winced. She might have gone overboard on gifts. River and Brook would turn two in January. Probably wouldn't even remember the holiday this far back, but...

Growing up, she and her identical twin, Misty, had had little. When Dad couldn't handle Mom's drinking anymore, he'd left them. They'd been seven. Their mother had surprised them that year by simply remembering it was Christmas. Most years, Teegan and Misty had been on their own for the holidays. Once they'd turned fourteen, they'd walked to the Goodwill and purchased a banged-up tree, missing several lights, and brought it home to decorate using popcorn and coloring pages. On Christmas Day, they'd given each other gifts they could afford from babysitting.

Misty had given Teegan a megaphone for when she directed local plays someday—which she'd done a few times. *Little Women. Our Town. A Christmas Carol.* She'd loved every single second of it, especially helping teenagers who needed a place to belong. Theater provided community for children who had no one—like herself when she'd been that age. She'd thrust herself into movies, Lorna's movies at the top, and joined a local theater where she'd been loved and valued. The costume director, Mrs. Salvatore, had taken her to church on Sundays, and she'd found a place to belong there, too, in God's family.

But at home...it wasn't warm and welcoming. Some Christmases, Mom had never even left the bedroom unless it was to find another bottle of wine. Teegan's children would never know that kind of life. They would know stability, consistency and, while she may not ever make it rich, they'd know unconditional love and that their mom was sober.

God had truly blessed Teegan—which never went without feelings of awe and reverence. She didn't deserve the kind of love God had lavished upon her. Lorna had not only given her a good-paying job, but had offered her the entire east wing of the main house as her and the twins' living quarters, without docking her check for rent. God's grace was often unexpected—though maybe it shouldn't be. Maybe she *should* expect it since it's who He was—gracious.

But her past wasn't clean.

She didn't deserve such grace and mercy. Yet it had absolutely been God's mercy carrying her through the hardest and darkest of times. Looking back, Teegan had almost bypassed filling out the application to be Lorna's caregiver. Nursing school hadn't been required, and it was one of her favorite actresses. She hadn't expected to be hired, especially having two rowdy twin babies. What ninety-two-year old woman wanted to be saddled with that every day? Granted, Lorna was spry for her age and her mind was sharp.

As it happened, Lorna was the mom, grandmother and friend Teegan had desperately needed. A true godsend.

Taking her bags out of the trunk, she looped the handles on her arm until she had no room left. Her phone dinged with a text from Yolanda and she asked Siri to read it.

"'Take your time and pick them up later. They're sleeping like the sweet babies they are. No trouble at all. I love having them.'"

Lies. They were curious little tornadoes that left a disaster in their wake wherever they went, and now that they were walking, that was everywhere. River had figured out how to scale baby gates and Brook liked anything sparkly, which meant pretty much everything in Lorna's mansion.

"Siri, text Yolanda."

"What do you want to say?"

"'Thank you, you big liar. I'll bring you a cookie and a hug.' Send."

Yolanda, a friend from church, had also been a godsend. She had offered to watch the babies so Teegan could shop a few hours and enjoy a peppermint latte without it growing cold. Now she had time to bake a few holiday treats and maybe even enjoy an hour of a good mystery novel or just stare at a wall in silence. She loved her children but she was flat-out exhausted and forgot what a free minute was.

She opened the right front door, bags teetering and clanking on her arms. Lorna really did need to keep her home locked up, but she'd never been one for safety precautions. No guards and no security. Lorna was well aware people had sneaked onto the property hunting for the decades-old rumor of a hidden treasure buried by Lorna herself. What on earth would she have buried and why?

Teegan wasn't buying it. Nothing was hidden on Lorna's property, but that hadn't stopped scads of teenagers—and some adults—from searching; a few times those teenagers had gotten lost in the labyrinth. With shoddy cell service out there, they'd relied on screaming and crying, which had reached Teegan's ears and she'd had to fetch them.

Lorna never prosecuted a single one. It was some kind of fun game. Leave it to the old sadistic lady she loved so much. For all Teegan knew, it was likely Lorna who had begun the rumors simply to be mischievous.

Using her leg, Teegan kicked the door closed behind her, juggling the toys and rolls of gift wrap piled so high she couldn't even see the floor in front of her.

"Lorna, I'm back. You hungry? I'm going to make oatmeal cookies and gingersnaps. You want a cup of tea?" She'd adopted the proper English teatime, and Teegan loved joining Lorna for tea and biscuits—which were really shortbread cookies, but if one had tea with Lorna, they must be called biscuits. They sipped tea, nibbled biscuits, and Teegan hung on all Lorna's stories. Maybe she'd have a few more today. "Lorna?"

She might not have her hearing aids in and, even with them, Lorna's hearing wasn't that great. Teegan was often hoarse from all the hollering, but Lorna didn't go far these days. Kept to the sitting room and her bedroom on the main floor.

Stairs were difficult now and she refused a walker or cane. That kind of pride was going to result in a broken hip, but Lorna never listened. Probably why caregivers cycled through employment like a revolving door.

Dropping the bags on the massive dining room table, an antique piece that sat twenty people, she headed for the sitting room where Lorna often spent her days reading with her huge magnifier or working her arthritic fingers crocheting, though she never finished a project and admitted she was right terrible at it. Still, she said old ladies were supposed to crochet, knit and quilt, and she was going to finish something some-day even it was a potholder.

Teegan knew what to expect for Christmas—a half-done potholder.

"Lorna, I'm back and the kids have more toys than any child should. I might have gone into debt." She was kidding, but she also liked to rile Lorna just to hear her mid-Atlantic accent go into a spiel about being a good steward of what God supplied. The accent of course was a fake one—an upper crust dialect old actors and actresses had made up. She sounded like Hepburn, and Teegan liked to mimic it because it was rather beautiful and refined-sounding. Teegan's dialect was what she'd call Texan bumpkin. Nothing cultured about her or her life.

"You hear me, Lorna? Debt. I'm going into debt." She waited for something. Anything.

That's when she noticed the house was quiet.

Too quiet.

Only the pops and creaks in the old settling wood and the crackle of the real fireplace could be heard. Icy fingers walked up her spine, prickling her scalp.

"Lorna," she called weakly, swallowing hard as she inched toward the sitting room, the chill growing colder with each shaky step.

The Jeep. The red one outside. Someone was here at the main house.

A separate drive led to the stables, bypassing the main house. If the driver of that vehicle had business with Harry Doyle, the manager, they'd park out there. Like Charlie. There was even a sign to let drivers know to go around.

As she approached the winding staircase, she halted. Her feet froze to the marble flooring as her heart thudded in her chest.

Blood oozed along the white-and-black-checkered squares like thick cherry juice. Her mouth flew open at the sight of Lorna lying broken at the bottom of the stairs. Her stomach roiled and she pressed a hand to it, as if pressure might keep her from vomiting.

But Lorna wasn't the one producing so much blood.

Lying near her, slashed multiple times, was Misty.

Her twin.

The red Jeep.

A sob erupted from her throat and she knelt, feeling her sister's pulse, but it was clear she was dead. If the multiple slashes through her skin hadn't revealed that, her vacant eyes staring up at her did. Teegan scrambled to Lorna's side, slipping in the blood and shrieking. She felt for a pulse, praying she would find one.

Nothing.

Lorna had gone to be with Jesus.

Teegan stared in a stupor, gazing on her own bloody hands and back at two people she dearly loved. Finally, her senses kicked in and she scrambled to the dining room table where she'd left her cell phone. The bloody soles of her Converse left a trail of prints. As she grabbed her phone, a sudden awareness struck her and she froze again, hand trembling on the phone.

She was not alone.

She forced herself to turn.

A looming figure dressed in jeans, a black hoodie, and wearing some kind of mask—a jester's mask?—stalked toward her, predatory-like, a very large, very bloody butcher knife gripped in his black-gloved hand.

Teegan darted around the dining room table and her shoes slipped against the marble from the red, wet soles. She crashed to the floor, pulling a dining room chair down with her. Unable to regain her footing, she began crawling toward the kitchen.

To the back door.

To freedom.

The jester continued to come for her. Not rushing or running. But slow and methodical, as if he knew he had plenty of time and no one would hear her cries or screams.

TV background noise reached her ears; the newscaster calling for a vicious storm that would bring lashing winds.

Using the kitchen island as an anchor, she pulled herself up to her feet and darted for the door, but the jester gripped her head, ripping hair from her scalp as he yanked her to him.

The sharp tip of the blade cut into her side with a searing burn and she cried out. A copper pot caught her eye and she snatched it from the counter then slung it toward the jester. The pot caught the side of his shoulder and he released his grip, giving her the chance to dart for the door again. She swung it open.

Freedom!

Just as she crossed the threshold, he wrenched her inside the kitchen.

River and Brook's little faces entered her mind.

She had to fight. For them.

Teegan spotted a rolling pin on the bottom of the open stainless-steel island and dropped to her knees. She grabbed it and sprang up. As he brought the knife down, she counterattacked, whacking him upside the head and shifting his mask, which revealed a white male with a dark stubbly chin.

He stumbled and she swung again, and the jester crashed to the floor. Teegan bolted outside as thunder cracked and lightning split the sky, the wind blowing the trees low to the ground in forceful submission.

Harry. She had to get to him. Harry always carried a gun and kept more than one shotgun in his office. The wind fought against her but, hunching forward, she kept running, her legs threatening to buckle underneath her.

Chest heaving and lungs begging for oxygen, she made it to the stable and hollered for Harry.

He was nowhere to be found. He was always out here!

"Somebody help me!" She closed the stable doors, her side burning like wildfire and blood coloring her sweater with a dark stain. She locked the doors from the inside and ran for

Harry's office and to the phone. Horses protested her shrieks with neighs, pawing at their stall doors. Blood whooshed in her ears like cotton rubbing against skin.

She grabbed the receiver and dialed 9-1-1. "Help me! Someone is trying to kill me. He's killed Lorna and Misty. Help me!"

"Ma'am, I need you to calm down and tell me—"

"Calm down? I'm about to be butchered!" Tears streamed down her face. "I have babies!"

"Are your babies in the house?" she asked.

Teegan wiped her running nose. "No." She forced herself to settle enough to give the dispatcher information to send the police and an ambulance.

"Stay on the line with me. Cedar Springs PD is on the way."

"Thank you. Thank you." She remained on the line, shaking uncontrollably and wondering who would have wanted to kill Lorna Landoon. And why had Misty been at the house? She hadn't planned a visit. But Misty was known to find trouble. Had trouble followed her here, leaving Lorna a casualty and Teegan an almost-casualty?

Sirens pealed.

Crouching in the office, she continued to listen to the dispatcher and answer her questions, but her mind reeled and she missed what the dispatcher said.

"I hear them," Teegan said. "They're here."

"Stay where you are. They know which stable you're in. You're going to be okay."

That's when she heard the gunshot.

Rhode Spencer pulled up behind his older brothers, Stone and Bridge, at the Landoon mansion. Rain battered his vehicle as thunder rumbled. Rhode wasn't exactly excited to step out into the downpour; instead he gazed up at the old mansion with its Gothic turrets and towers. He and his brothers and friends had sneaked onto the property dozens of times as teenagers hunting for the rumored fortune buried on the estate.

Rhode had always envied the grand home and property with its many amenities such as the Olympic-size swimming pool, hot tub, tennis courts and the labyrinth and English garden. He'd been raised on a modest ranch twenty-five minutes away, and now, in hindsight, he'd have had it no other way. But back then, he'd wanted to live the luxurious life and keep up with his friends like Beau Brighton—Texas royalty. He'd attempted to compete and it had struck him like a venomous snake, saddling him with the poison of debt up to his eyeballs.

So. Much. Debt.

So much stress.

That's when the real drinkin' had begun, holding him hostage. His career as a Cedar Springs' homicide detective had disintegrated, after which he'd spiraled hard. Went on a weekender with tequila and been hauled from the hotel room in Dallas the next day by his brothers. That's the only reason he even remembered that weekend. They'd hauled his sorry sack to a Christian rehab center where he'd sobered up and returned to his faith. Now, his life was much different and he'd been on the straight and narrow almost three years.

Some days went smoothly. Others, his throat ached for the sauce, especially after his twin sister, Sissy, had almost died at the hands of a vicious serial killer eight months ago. But she'd survived and received her happy ending. Now his best friend and business partner, Beau Brighton, was also his brother-in-law.

Two out of four of his siblings were hitched, which left him and his middle brother, Bridge, riding the bachelor train. Tossing the hood of his poncho over his head, he grabbed his gear and jumped out into the downpour. The crime scene had been cleared an hour ago and their card had been given to Miss Landoon's caregiver, who had called Stone at the advice of their cousin, Detective Dom DeMarco, who was working the case.

Rhode raced to the stoop next to his brothers. Bridge removed his hood and raked a hand through his light brown hair. "You think there's treasure here? Because I haven't found it."

"Well, if *you,* a former FBI agent, didn't find it," Rhode quipped with brotherly sarcasm, "I reckon no one can." He slipped into his white hazmat gear, hating the cold rain.

"Shut up," Bridge muttered. "I'm just saying, I've even scuba-dived in that lake. Nothing. I think it's a farce."

Rhode wasn't thinking about the treasure anymore. Not now that he wore the gear necessary to clean up a crime scene. A young woman had been stabbed over seventeen times, and Lorna Landoon had fallen down the stairs to her death.

The caregiver had narrowly escaped and the stable manager had spied the killer, given a warning shot and chased him, but lost him in the woods behind the house. Said he'd worn a creepy white mask. If it hadn't been for Doyle's showing up at the stables, they'd have more than one location to clean.

"What do you think of this crime? Don't you find it odd that the very day the caregiver's identical twin shows up, she dies?" Rhode asked.

His eldest brother, Stone, set the biohazard containers—their red boxes as glaring as the bloodstains inside would be—beside him. "She here?" Stone asked, ignoring Rhode's question.

"I don't know. Depends on if she parks in the garage or out front. Dom thinks that someone followed the sister from California and killed her, but that doesn't explain the Texas bluebonnets left beside her in a pool of blood."

"I don't know," Stone said. "That's not our job anymore. Our job is to deal with the aftermath."

"I know." But that hadn't stopped Stone from inquiring about the murder that had led them to discover their other sister, Paisley, had been murdered, not died by suicide. He didn't bring that up.

"What's the caregiver's name again? In case she is here."

Rhode scratched his stubbly chin. Needed a good shave. "Teegan Albright."

Bridge raked a hand through his damp hair again, and Stone nodded as he zipped up his hazmat suit. Crime scene cleaning was never easy and often tragic and depressing. That was why Stone had started Spencer Aftermath Recovery and Grief Counseling Services after their eldest sister had died. They'd had no idea who was going to clean up the mess. Stone, seeing a need, had left the Texas Rangers, which was about the time Bridge had resigned from the FBI and Rhode had been deep in his drink.

Rhode had left rehab and begun working for the business, but a few months later had also opened up his own business— Second Chances Investigations. The need to solve mysteries and help people find justice wouldn't leave him. Being a private investigator fulfilled that need. He and Beau had been working hard to build a reputable business, though Rhode couldn't afford to leave the aftermath recovery biz. He owed too much money and needed both sources of income to skate by.

Rhode lived in the apartment above his family's garage for free and was as broke as a beggar in downtown Austin. Not exactly the life he envisioned at thirty-five. No wife. No kids. No American dream for him. No one to blame but himself, even though for a time he'd tried blaming anyone and everyone else, including God. But at the end of the day, he'd had to come to terms with the fact that the mess he was in was due to his own sinful choices.

Sissy's blue SUV whipped into the drive. Beau had bought her a new vehicle with hopes of children coming into the picture. Her two Cavalier King Charles spaniels, Lady and Louie, bounded out and raced like greyhounds to the stoop, jumping on his pant legs for ear scratching. Sissy shrieked at the torrential rain and hurried onto the stoop with them.

"I hate the rain!" she said.

"Why are you even here? There's blood inside," Rhode said.
Sissy didn't work assignments with blood. She was squeamish.
His twin was a licensed counselor and often helped families
with grief counseling, her little Cavs being emotional therapy dogs.

"I'm not here for the blood. I'm here to offer grief counseling services to Teegan and any other employees, as well as
family members that might want it. Free of charge to Teegan.
She's my friend."

"Who knew near fatalities would bring together besties,"
Rhode teased. Sissy had almost died on this very property a
few months ago when a killer had chased her down inside the
labyrinth. Beau had rescued her.

"Oh hush. Teegan is great. She's smart and snarky and... I
can't imagine losing my twin." Her voice cracked as she held
his gaze.

Rhode couldn't imagine life without her either. It had been
hard enough losing Pai all those years ago and then their dad.
But he and Sissy shared a special twin bond that was hard to
explain to others. Sissy was literally half of him.

He rustled her hair. "Me neither."

The front double doors opened and Teegan Albright
emerged. Rhode remembered seeing her when he'd arrived
after Sissy had been attacked on the property. Calling Teegan
hot would be disrespectful and not even accurate. She was...
like sunshine bursting through the clouds. Not so bright you
couldn't look on her, but so beautiful you couldn't look away.

Her shiny blond hair was piled on her head and a few strands
fell around her heart-shaped face. She smelled like she'd recently showered—probably washing away the blood. He in-
ternally winced.

Her blue eyes were watery and rimmed in red, which
matched her pert nose. When she looked at him, his insides
shifted and that fuzzy feeling returned.

Did he know her other than seeing her at the estate before?

She hadn't grown up in Cedar Springs or gone to school with him. He wouldn't have forgotten her.

"Teegan!" Sissy said and embraced her, the dogs jumping on Teegan's jeans. Teegan cried on Sissy's shoulder.

It shifted Rhode's heart and sent an ache through him as he remembered the agonizing grief when they'd lost Paisley and their father.

Stone stepped up and broke the embrace. He shook Teegan's hand. "I'm sorry for your loss, Miss Albright."

Rhode hung back, unsure why he didn't want to face her, because she definitely drew him. But he wasn't there for anything other than making it look as if a violent death hadn't occurred. And besides, he had nothing to offer a woman presently. He was the poster boy for Loser. Still, something odd niggled at him. Something like...shame.

"Thank you for coming. It's... I can't..." Teegan sniffed again and shook Bridge's hand. Bridge looked back, his amber eyes boring into Rhode's. Yes, he was being rude, but he couldn't make himself approach. Finally, Bridge said, "This is our other brother, Rhode." He shot Rhode a scowl and Rhode stepped up and shook her hand.

"I am very sorry for your loss, ma'am," he said through cotton.

She studied him and, for a moment, he saw a spark flash in her eyes before they narrowed as if she were trying to place him too. "Thank you. I know I should have left. My friend Yolanda said I could stay with her, but the family will be here any time, I suspect, and I want to be here."

"Understood," Stone said and followed her inside, then Bridge, Sissy and, finally, Rhode entered.

They made their way to the grand staircase. "So, it happened here," Teegan said without looking at the smeared blood. "I was attacked at the dining room table and from there ran to the kitchen where he stabbed me." She pressed her hand to her side. "From there I ran to the stables."

The place was a frenzy of bloody foot-and handprints. Rhode's insides pulsed with fury from his bones to his brain as he envisioned what had transpired. The feelings were intense and fierce...and weird.

"Are you okay?" he blurted. Teegan Albright was absolutely courageous and a fighter. Good for her.

She touched her side again. "I am. The cut was shallow. I've been treated and given antibiotics for possible infection."

"You get a look at him?" he asked.

Stone shot him a glare.

Rhode wasn't a homicide detective anymore and questioning a victim was no longer his job. Unless, of course, she'd hired him as a private detective—which she hadn't. No, his job was to clean up the aftermath. But he couldn't help himself. A protective instinct had kicked in hard and he couldn't fight it. Nor did he want to.

Teegan shuddered. "He wore a jester's mask. Plastic. The kind that has a string around it. It shifted when I hit him with the rolling pin." Her eyes shifted toward the window, but Rhode was sure she wasn't seeing anything other than the frightening moments she'd endured. "He was a white male with a dark, scruffy chin. I saw that. I think his eyes were dark but I'm not sure if it was dark blue or light brown."

"You were so brave," Sissy said as she squeezed her hand.

Rhode agreed. "He say anything?"

This time Bridge passed him a warning eye.

"No."

If Rhode were the detective on the case, he'd call the PD where Misty Albright had lived in California and inquire about other possible attacks by a man in a cheap jester mask. Then he'd run the MO through the Violent Crime Apprehension Program, or VICAP. See if any matches popped.

A jester's mask was particular.

What did it mean? Why that mask?

Why not an easy-to-find, hard-to-trace black ski mask? The

disguise clearly held significance. His investigative instincts kicked into high gear, but this wasn't his job or his case. He stepped out the kitchen door Teegan had used to flee the attacker. Blood crusted the doorknob. Outside, on the patio, the rain beat down and Rhode scanned the area. The water had washed away trace evidence. No blood. No footprints.

Back inside, he reentered the foyer area where his brothers conversed in hushed whispers. Teegan and Sissy had disappeared. "What's going on?"

Stone pointed to the gruesome aftermath. "Stabbing is often personal and the number of stabs reveal Misty Albright was murdered in a rage. But Miss Landoon fell down the stairs. Before or after Misty was stabbed to death? And what was she doing upstairs?"

"Thought that wasn't our job?" Rhode asked. "I saw both y'all's glares."

"In front of the victim's family and close friend? No. Between us, speculation is fair game," Stone said.

He was right. Rhode had no business interviewing a survivor.

Stone continued. "Sissy said Lorna lives on the main floor. How did she get up all those stairs?"

"Elevator?" Bridge asked. "I saw it near the kitchen."

Rhode shook his head. "Dom told me the elevator has been broken for a couple of months. He also mentioned that Miss Albright saw Lorna's great-grandson, Charlie Landoon, on her way up the street. He'd passed her, leaving the estate. She assumed he'd been at the stables. Said he rarely visited Lorna, and used the road running alongside the estate, bypassing the home. Dom's going to question him. Might be right now."

Stone grunted. "Well, we'll leave it to Dom."

Nodding, Rhode said, "I just want to get this done and go." His chest continued to squeeze and it felt like the house was closing in on him. Not so much the house...but Teegan's presence.

"What's up with you?" Bridge asked.

"I don't know." He sighed and combed his hair with his fingers, unsure if he would continue to grow it out or chop it. Currently, his bangs hung to his cheekbones and drove him a little batty. "I…think I know the caregiver."

"Know her how?" Stone asked warily.

Heat flamed in Rhode's cheeks. "Like…in the biblical sense."

Bridge huffed and rolled his eyes. "Really? Is there anyone in fifty miles of Cedar Springs you haven't *known*?"

"That's a low blow," Rhode muttered.

"Fitting, don'tcha think?" Bridge asked, sarcasm dripping like acid.

Bridge might be exaggerating, some, but in Rhode's drunken days, he'd done a lot of shameful things he'd have never considered if not under the influence. He'd made things right with God but the burning shame and guilt continued to dog his heels on the daily.

"I'll take the kitchen and work my way into the dining area." Work would help keep his mind from fixating on what might have happened with Teegan and his past. Collecting his supplies, he marched to the kitchen and began the aftermath recovery. The irony smell of blood wafted on the air, but Rhode ignored it and worked, ensuring that traces of blood didn't contaminate the other areas of the kitchen. Once he'd disinfected and deodorized the large room, he tested the area to confirm it'd been freed from pathogens.

The process wasn't difficult, but it was time-consuming and meticulous. An art he and his brothers had perfected. No one would ever know that a violent crime had been committed in the kitchen. "Clear," he called to inform his brothers that he'd finished the kitchen. As he collected his gear bag and material to work on the dining room, Teegan Albright stepped inside. Her eyes weren't as red as earlier.

She startled. "Oh!" Bringing her hand to her chest, she said, "I didn't realize anyone was in here."

"Sorry," he said, feeling a digging in his chest again. "I, uh, just finished. It's all clear for you."

She stared at him and he shifted uncomfortably.

"Do we…do we know each other?" he asked.

Teegan shook her head. Too fast. Too hard. "I don't think so."

Lie.

Rhode had been trained to detect those as well. His suspicions had now been confirmed. He had a past with her. But from when? How long ago? Maybe she was also feeling the shame. Or she might be unsure and afraid to admit it for fear of facing embarrassment too. He'd let it pass. "If you're sure." He hung on to the last word, allowing her the chance to backtrack.

"I am. I'm sure."

"Okay," he said. What else was he supposed to do? Push and say, *Are you sure we didn't sleep together at some point in time?* Who said that other than some arrogant tool? "Again, I'm sorry about what happened to you."

"Thank you."

He pivoted to leave as the door from outside opened into the kitchen, the covered porch keeping him from getting wet. A man stalked inside, his murderous eyes focused on Teegan.

"I'll kill you!"

Chapter Two

Teegan's heart lurched into her throat at the venomous words Glen Landoon hurled at her. Rhode Spencer jumped in front of her, his arm out like a barricade to block Teegan from harm. This was the first time since she'd returned from shopping that she actually felt safe.

"You murdered my grandmother and your own sister. It's the money, isn't it?" Glen, Lorna's grandson, said, accusation in his dark eyes. "I have news for you. You aren't getting a dime!"

"That's enough," Rhode said with a deep, menacing tone. Glen paused and sized up Rhode. Several inches taller than Glen and made like the Man of Steel. "You just threatened her, and I heard it. If you're willing to threaten homicide, then how do we know *you* didn't kill them? You clearly have murderous intent. Back. Up. Now."

Neither Glen nor his mother, Evangeline, had been fond of Teegan. Anyone new to the estate was a fortune-poacher in their eyes and they'd never shied away from being vocal about it in her presence. Truth was, it was Lorna's own family who were money-grubbers.

Teegan peered over Rhode's shoulder. "I did not kill my sister or your grandmother, Glen."

Glen glared, but didn't make another move toward her. He must have calculated that Rhode Spencer was formidable, not an opponent he would want to go up against.

"You might as well pack it up," he said. "My mother is arriving and you will not be allowed to remain in our house. I don't have to go anywhere."

Rhode's nostrils flared. "Maybe not, but it will be in your best interest to leave the kitchen immediately and to stay away from Miss Albright while she's here."

Glen eyed Rhode. If looks could kill, Rhode would be dead on the floor and Teegan next to him. Without a word, he blew past them into the dining and foyer area.

Teegan clung to the kitchen island to keep upright. She hadn't thought about her living arrangements or the fact she was now out of a job. She was still reeling from shock. Her twin sister had been butchered and Lorna had taken a terrible fall. She'd been attacked and almost killed herself. Jobs and homes hadn't registered.

Teegan's lungs tightened and the room spun. She couldn't breathe and gasped for air.

"Teegan," Rhode murmured. "Hey." He laid a strong hand on her shoulder. "I think you may be having a panic attack. I have them sometimes. Just breathe slow. Easy."

She did as he suggested, but the thought of being homeless with two babies and no job returned and a cold sweat broke out over her body.

"Easy. Breathe."

She'd spent way too much money on gifts, overcompensating because of her meager holidays. She'd have to return most of the presents now.

Rhode's voice was deep, smooth like velvet, and had a steadying effect on her and she did as he instructed until the episode passed and she could breathe easy again.

"Better?" he asked.

She nodded. "Thank you."

"You've had an intense and traumatizing day. It's no surprise you had a panic attack. You going to be okay now?"

She nodded again. Something about him… She'd seen him a few months ago after Sissy had been attacked, and she'd had an odd sensation then. Like she should know him, but her memories were disjointed and fuzzy.

"I'll get out of your hair now. I don't want to stay if you don't want me to."

I don't want to stay if you don't want me to.

Those words felt oddly familiar. As if he'd said them verbatim before. He turned to leave and she caught sight of the back of his head. His hair.

That head of hair. She recognized it.

Over two years ago, she'd woken to the back of that gorgeous head of hair. Everything else had been a haze as she'd slipped from the hotel room in the walk of shame, keeping quiet so as not to wake the stranger in the bed.

But she remembered the hair. Pathetic.

She also remembered one other thing.

A brass bullet that had been engraved with *Congrats. Love, Dad.*

In a scramble to leave, she'd hastily scooped up the contents from her purse, which had fallen off the dresser. Once she'd returned home, she'd found it. Teegan had accidentally swept it into her purse that morning. With no way to return it—because she hadn't even remembered his name—she'd kept it as a reminder never to touch an ounce of alcohol again. A promise she'd broken that night. That one time. After Darryl had broken their engagement three days before their courthouse marriage. She'd already been grieving her mom's death of cirrhosis and Misty had been out of control from pill popping and cycling in and out of rehab. The crushing weight and pain had tempted Teegan to break the vow with herself to never drink.

That weekend, she'd driven to Dallas to simply get away. She'd gone down to the bar to listen to live music and she'd ordered a drink. And then another, until she couldn't remember anything but fuzzy moments.

Meeting a gorgeous man.

Having a conversation with laughter, though they were only slivers of recollection. Something about twins. Names. Sadness. Flirtation. Sloppy slow dancing. Stumbling to her room. The invitation for him to come inside.

I don't want to stay, if you don't want me to.

I do. I want you to stay.

Teegan pinched the bridge of her nose as the past reared its head. A head of gorgeous hair and a face that rivaled Johnny Depp. What on earth would she tell her children when they grew up and asked how they'd come to be? That she'd conceived them with Captain Jack Sparrow?

Rhode Spencer was her children's father, and she had no clue how to broach the subject. But she might not have to. He'd asked if they knew each other, but it was obvious he was as fuzzy as she was, or he'd been pretending to be unclear and had been feeling her out to see if she'd cop to knowing him. When she hadn't, he might have thought they were free and clear of the embarrassment. Could they play it off this way?

No.

Because she was now positive and he deserved to know he had children. If he didn't want them, fine. She would continue to raise them alone, and if he did, then they'd have a different conversation and figure out the future—but she would get to know him first. She might have made a mistake concerning herself, but now she had the children. And she wasn't going to let some guy she'd slept with once jump into their lives. What if this was a habit of his? What if he had a string of children all through Texas? She doubted it, but she wasn't taking chances with her children.

"Is there anything we can do to help you?" he asked, turning back just before the dining room.

"I don't think so." If anything, he was going to make life

more complicated. She was in this alone, starting with figuring out how to handle Misty's arrangements. Her sister was dead. Gone. Not a stitch of blood kin left. She pressed the heels of her hands to her eyes. "I have a church family that can help me." Yolanda. She needed to ask if the babies could stay with her a little longer. She had a lot to figure out and unless Yolanda had turned on the news, she didn't know what had transpired today. Things had been a blur and Teegan hadn't even called.

The national news was running headlines about Lorna Landoon and social media was rampant with RIPs and how much they'd loved her movies, talking as if they'd personally known her.

Teegan had. And she'd loved her dearly. Misty hadn't made national news, other than a snippet, or been raved about online, but she was as loved by Teegan as Lorna.

"That's good that you have a church family." He scratched his head and she noticed the tattoo snaking up his forearm—a scorpion with a Scripture written along the stinger.

Another blurry memory flashed.

O death, where is thy sting.

Then she remembered a fuzzy conversation. He had said, "Scorpions are like death but I'm not afraid of dying..." Something about mistakes made...something about his faith.

She remembered that now, too, reconfirming Rhode Spencer was her baby daddy.

"Yeah." Awkward tension built between them. He shifted as if as antsy as she was to flee the kitchen and the past. He might want to escape a shameful night, but she hadn't been able to and never would.

"Teegan! Oh, Teeg!" Yolanda's alto voice echoed through the house and then she rushed into the kitchen, the beads in her long braids clicking against one another. She all but slung herself on Teegan, squeezing her like a boa constrictor. "Oh, girl. My mama called. She saw the news. I couldn't get your cell phone, so I called Harry at the stables. He told me you were here and I could come and bring the babies too. I'm so sorry."

Babies.

Yolanda had brought the babies with her.

"Where are the babies?" Teegan asked.

"Oh. Right there." She pointed to the entrance to the kitchen. Brook and River were sitting in their double stroller, their sippy cups in the cup holders and butter cookies in each hand.

But it wasn't her children that captured her attention.

It was Rhode Spencer.

He'd gone deathly quiet and was now standing within inches of the children, his mouth agape and confusion forming a divot along his bronzed brow.

Staring at his son, he clearly saw his own reflection. Both children had his Mexican heritage in skin coloring, eyes and hair. River especially looked like Rhode from the cupid's-bow lip to the dimples.

Rhode blinked a few times then slowly met Teegan's eyes. "How...how old are they?"

She swallowed hard, her stomach churning and head buzzing. "They'll be two in January."

"Fraternal twins."

"Yes," she squeaked.

His hand trembled and he balled it into a fist. "Well, I see you have someone here to help you. I need to finish up." He walked through the kitchen, giving the children one final glance.

Passing them off.

Pretending he didn't remember or now know. But his face had revealed the hard truth. He knew he'd fathered twins. If he wanted to pass the buck and keep pretending, Teegan would let him. If he didn't want to be a dad, she wouldn't force him, but the rejection of his children throbbed deep into her bones.

"Who was that?" Yolanda's amber eyes narrowed, hands on her hips.

"No one."

He was no one. Wanted to be no one. Fine.

Her children deserved better anyway.

Twenty minutes ago, the sun had set and Rhode crumpled on the couch in the living room of his family ranch in Cedar Springs. Stone's wife, Emily, had taken Mama to her chemo treatment earlier today, and now Mama was sleeping. Emily had gone out to do some Christmas shopping. Their mother had been diagnosed with cancer last Christmas and had been battling it ever since. She was on a new round of chemo and the tumors were shrinking, which was great, but the chemo was doing her in. The oncologist said things were positive and he was confident this treatment would work, and Rhode clung to that.

He'd endured so much loss. So much pain.

His throat ached for a drink. Since he'd laid eyes on Teegan, a pool of dread had formed in his gut, the ache dogging him to dull it with a shot of bourbon. The smooth burn would numb the pain and calm his nerves. Loosen his tight muscles. He'd fought it every single minute and was fighting through it even now. Praying and repeating Scriptures that reminded him he could overcome because God was greater than the enemy of old and the bite of the bottle.

When he'd spotted the two chubby babies, it was like looking at old photographs of him and Sissy. Unmistakable. Undeniable.

And the ache turned into a raging wildfire of need.

Rhode was a father to babies he'd had no clue existed because neither he nor Teegan knew one another. If she'd wanted to inform him, she'd had no way. Shame kicked him while he was already down and a thought entered his mind: *Daddy kept a bottle of Buffalo Trace in his closet in the shoebox.*

Rhode's drinking had begun as a teenager, but after Pai died, then Daddy, it had become a crutch and coping mechanism.

A crutch made of rubber.

Instead of heading to the closet to check to see if the stash remained, he closed his eyes and prayed for strength to fight it, to be delivered from temptation, until slowly, painfully, the ache dissipated and he could open his eyes without making a beeline to the closet.

Bridge leaned on the doorframe, one ankle crossed over the other as he scrutinized him. "You fighting through it?" he asked quietly.

"Yep." Some days he was sick to death of the fight. The fact he had to fight at all.

"You want to talk about the trigger?"

Bridge was no fool. He already knew the trigger. "You saw them," Rhode murmured. "You know."

"We do. When the friend arrived, we helped her inside with the babies due to the rain and…yeah, it was pretty clear, especially after your confession about possibly having been with her."

"She doesn't remember me. I barely remember her. Time-line fits."

"You know their names?" Bridge asked.

"No." He hadn't even asked. He'd panicked, wanted a drink, and had felt absolutely wrecked by his past behavior. He'd bolted like the cowardly lion.

"Brook is the girl and River is the boy. That's kinda interesting, don't you think?"

Yeah. A fuzzy conversation surfaced. Stone. Rhode. Bridge. All places to walk or stand on. Places that get people from one point to another and are solid. Mama had done that on purpose. Appeared the conversation had stuck, if even subconsciously. His children had water names. "I have no idea what to do. I mean do I just say, 'Hey, I noticed you had babies that look like me. I think maybe we had a moment a few years ago. That was you, right?' Real romantic or mature. It's just the stupidest thing on the planet. I am a total idiot."

"I'll never not argue that you're an idiot." He smirked. "But, dude. You're a dad. You have to man up and talk to her. Maybe just say…" He grinned and shrugged at a loss. "I don't know. This is weird, but you need to have a conversation. I mean maybe they're not yours."

"We both know that's not true." He sighed. "How am I going to be a dad? Bridge, I'm broke. I have no home of my own. My private investigation biz is getting off the ground, but it's not making consistent money, and I can't go back…" Not to any police department. Not after accidentally contaminating evidence in a homicide because he'd been under the influence. The perp had walked because of Rhode and, two months later, had bludgeoned another woman. That was blood on Rhode's hands. He'd been canned, and rightly so.

That was the day he'd driven to Dallas and drunk himself stupid.

"I know," Bridge whispered. "But I don't think being a dad is all about having hordes of money. If it was, then our dad was a failure because he never had a lot of dough. But he loved us and was a good father. I never remember what he could or couldn't buy me. I remember fishing with him, horseback riding. He taught me how to change a tire and treat a woman right. He worked hard, loved Jesus, and his family. Remember how he and Mama used to dance in the kitchen after dinner? I always groaned but, really, I loved it. I felt safe knowing they loved one another."

"'Kay, but I barely know their mother. I don't see me dancing in the kitchen with her. Pretty sure we danced at a bar though—that's real classy. This isn't that. It's not two people who fell in love, married and had a family. It's the opposite. It's two people who were too dumb to restrain themselves." He hung his head. "I always wanted a family. I'm not going to run from it—forever."

"Good. Because I think a couple of babies would make

Mama feel better again. And they are pretty stinkin' cute, bro. You did good. Well, you know what I mean."

"Yeah." He laughed, but it wasn't funny. "Can't blame the babies for our mistake or hold it against them. And it's pretty clear I'd produce adorable children."

Bridge snorted at Rhode's teasing. "Helps that their mom is a knockout."

It was an innocent statement but Rhode's blood heated a degree. "Yeah, well don't go making moves. My kids don't need an Uncle Daddy." They needed their father. Rhode. He stood. "You think it's too late to go over there?"

"You know, Rhode, I don't think it's ever too late to make something wrong right." He slapped his thighs. "I'm eating some leftovers for dinner and going to bed." On the way out, he paused. "What are you getting Sissy for Christmas? I feel like we need to outdo Beau, but how do you outdo a man with millions?"

Rhode laughed. "I have no stinking clue."

"Well, I can always count on you for great ideas." Bridge rolled his eyes then sobered. "If you feel like you want to drink, please call me. Praying for you."

Tears burned the backs of Rhode's eyes. "Thanks. I will."

As he geared up to return to the Landoon estate and face the music, his throat started the dry ache again. God would get him through this. God was in this. He had to be, or Rhode was doomed.

Grabbing his keys, he headed to the vehicle and drove to the estate, his stomach in a million little pretzels, all twisted and corkscrewed.

He parked where he had earlier. The rain was now a steady sheet but the thunderstorms had subsided. Teegan's car was in the drive. Guess the Glen guy hadn't forced her out yet. That man grated Rhode's nerves. How dare he threaten Teegan? Or accuse her of murdering for money. Seemed he was the one who wanted his hand in the coffers.

He did not like that guy. At all.

As he approached the front door, he heard a bloodcurdling scream.

Teegan's scream.

Chapter Three

Someone had appeared in the second floor sitting room.

Out of nowhere!

This time he wore a ski mask in place of his plastic jester mask, but the knife in his hand appeared the same. Big and shiny and sharp.

She raced toward the grand staircase, away from the nursery where the babies slept. They were early to rise and early to bed. He chased after her and she was going to lead him outside, away from the children. But she stumbled on the stairs, letting out a shriek. She tumbled down several before she crashed against the wooden rail.

Images of Lorna's fall popped into her mind and she scrambled to her feet, the attacker coming right for her. She dashed through the foyer and was reaching for the doorknob when the door flung open, knocking her off balance.

Rhode Spencer was there.

His sight landed on the stairs where the intruder stood as startled as Teegan had been to see Rhode. Rhode's eyes glazed over in a hot fury that burned through Teegan's bones. He bolted past Teegan, lightly brushing her shoulder in comfort, and rushed toward the man with the knife, who was already sprinting up the stairs.

No way he'd escape now.

Unless he made it to the back staircase and down them before Rhode reached him.

Her babies were upstairs and helpless. Except they weren't. Their father was upstairs.

But she was their mother. And their father didn't want to be one. He all but flew out of here earlier upon seeing them. Without weighing the consequences, nothing but the twins on her mind, she took the stairs two at a time. Halfway up, Rhode appeared.

He held a gun in his right hand. "I think he made it down the back staircase. I followed and went outside. Didn't see him. But I want to clear the place before I call it safe."

"My babies. I need to be with my babies." Her heart raced and no one, including Rhode, was going to keep her from them.

"Okay. Go to them and stay in the room until I let you know it's safe."

Teegan followed him upstairs and he escorted her to the nursery. River and Brook were sound asleep in their crib, and he silently checked the nooks, crannies and closet. Then he nodded and slipped out of the room, leaving her to keep watch over the babies. Had the intruder known children were present? Would a monster with a knife even care?

After what seemed like an eternity, Rhode returned. "All clear," he whispered, glancing at the crib and his sleeping babes. "Doors are locked. I've called Dom and he's on his way with the Cedar Springs forensic team. They'll want to comb for evidence, and Dom will need a statement. It's safe though."

For now. Someone wanted her dead and maybe even her children. The word *safe* did little to comfort her. Not when all she kept seeing was a big sharp knife coming for her.

Teegan motioned to the door and they left the room. Outside the babies' room was a hall that led to an open loft area with a couch, love seat and rocking recliner. The back wall behind the couch was lined with floor-to-ceiling bookshelves. Lorna had been an avid reader—a romantic at heart—and hundreds of Harlequin romances lined the shelves along with Agatha Christie mysteries and some classics.

"What are you doing here?" Teegan asked, covering her heart with her hand, hoping the racing would slow. "I'm glad. Don't get me wrong."

His sad eyes and apologetic smile sent her heart into a tremor.

"I, uh, came by because we need to talk, and I'm fairly sure you know why." He searched her eyes and she reluctantly nodded.

"Hold on." She left the loft and hurried to her bedroom on the opposite side of the nursery. She retrieved the bullet that belonged to Rhode and grabbed the baby monitor as well. When she returned, she held the bullet out to him. "I think this belongs to you," she murmured.

He rolled it between his fingers. "My dad gave me this when I finished the police academy. I thought I'd lost it. But... I couldn't remember where. Now, I know." He closed his fist over it and peered into her eyes. "I don't know what to say."

Teegan was speechless, too, and her nerves worked overtime. Between this awkward conversation and the fact someone had tried to kill her and might still want to, she was overwhelmed and a ball of knots. "I don't remember that night much, to be honest. I'd been dumped three days before my wedding—I probably told you that but—"

"We don't remember," he whispered.

"No. I was stupid. Angry. Hurt. Depressed. And that was the first time I'd ever drank in my life. My mom was a drunk until she died. But in that moment, I didn't care, and I got drunk fast. Everything else is hazy."

"I understand."

What if he thought this was normal behavior for her? Would he want to take the children away? He didn't understand, but needed to. "I broke a promise to myself that night. But since then, I haven't touched a single drop of alcohol."

Rhode nodded. "I believe you, and I'm sorry. For then and for earlier today." He glanced away. "I thought you might be familiar when I saw you a few months ago, but I wasn't sure then or until I saw the babies. That's when I knew and I... I panicked."

She appreciated his honesty and owning up to running away. But he had returned, and it had been perfect timing. She could not let this jester hurt her children—or her. "It's a lot to process, and I've had plenty of time, so I get it."

"I appreciate the grace, Teegan. I don't deserve it."

"I guess that's why it's called grace." She half smiled. "I thought I'd put that night behind me until eight weeks later. With no way of contacting you, I wasn't sure what to do. I couldn't even remember your name." Shame flushed her cheeks.

"I'm not mad you didn't contact me. That you didn't—couldn't—find me."

That was a relief. "I don't want anything from you. So, you don't have to worry about that. I'm not going to force back child support or anything."

"No," he said and shook his head. "I want to make sure you have what you need—what they need. I'm not a heartless man. Just a... I don't what I am. Sorry. That's what I am. I'm so sorry. Two babies. That can't be easy for you."

It wasn't. "We're making do. Lorna was good to us, but, now I'm not sure where we'll go. Glen's mother, Evangeline, did come by and she gave me a whole forty-eight hours to evacuate. Because she knows I have babies. Whatever." Tears filled her eyes and she wanted to kick herself for not being stronger. "Yolanda, my friend who brought the babies back, said I could stay—"

"Stay with me." He reached out from the couch where he perched and grabbed her hand. "Please."

Teegan froze. "I…uh, I don't do things like that. That was a drunken one-time mistake."

Rhode stood. "No. No. I don't mean that. I mean my family ranch. My brother Stone and his wife live there, and my mom. She'd love to meet the babies. My other brother, Bridge, told me they're named Brook and River."

She grinned. "Yeah. I liked the idea of them having meaning together. Both bodies of water. Fresh springs representing new life. Living water. I kinda feel we talked about that?"

"I think so." He kicked at the floor runner. "I'd like to meet them, Teegan. Have a chance to know them. I'm not a bad man. I just made some bad choices."

Teegan never thought she'd find their father. Sharing the kids now seemed odd. And yet a sliver of her found relief in knowing she might not be alone. But she didn't truly know Rhode Spencer. Spending time with him and his family might be what she needed to get to know him. She might have made a one-night mistake, but what about him? Was it a one-time drink that had blurred his moral lines? Was drinking a part of his life? She would not allow the babies to be around someone who couldn't control his drink. Like Mom. How was she supposed to ask about that? She decided to be bold. It was her children involved here.

"The drinking. That night was a one-time thing for me, but what about you?" Rhode appeared to be honorable. He'd already protected her twice and he'd returned to own up to his responsibility.

"I haven't had a drop of alcohol since that night either. Teetotaler," he said and glanced away.

Tightness lightened in her shoulders. Good. That was good to know. "I guess we need to get to know each other better." Her face heated. How much more could they know one another? This was beyond uncomfortable and weird, and it was no one's fault but their own.

Rhode returned to the couch and she sat opposite him on the

love seat, placing the baby monitor on the end table. "So...you work with your brothers in the aftermath recovery business?"

"I do, and I'm a private detective."

"How'd you decide that?" she asked and rubbed her hands on her thighs.

"I used to be a homicide detective with Cedar Springs but—"

"But you went into the family business. That's nice. I always wanted a tight-knit family—a big family—but it was just me and Misty. Man, I miss her so much. I haven't even had time to grieve."

Rhode cleared his throat. "I lost my oldest sister, Paisley, about five years ago now. She was murdered by a serial killer, and it was made to look like a suicide. We thought for four years she'd taken her own life until Stone's now wife, a Texas Ranger in the Public Integrity Unit, worked a case that connected Paisley to a serial killer. They caught him. We also lost our father."

"I'm so sorry." She sat quietly a few moments before speaking again. "I remember reading about that. Does it ever get easier—the loss?"

Rhode shook his head. "No. Just different. You eventually sort of adapt."

The doorbell rang.

Rhode stood. "That'll be Dom and the forensic team." They headed downstairs, Teegan with the monitor in hand. She opened the front door and Dom DeMarco stood with a kind smile on his face.

With all the police and Rhode here, she should feel calmer and safer, but she didn't. Leaving this estate might be the best thing but that didn't mean the jester wouldn't or couldn't find her. Why? Why her? Why Misty?

"We meet again, Miss Albright." Dom took her statement, and she told the CSI team where she'd been and that her babies were asleep in the second room on the right upstairs.

They went to work and Dom left Teegan with Rhode to join the forensic team.

"You want a cup of tea or coffee?" Teegan asked. "I could use a cup of tea." Her nerves buzzed and her heart was stuck in her throat. "I have decaf, since it's evening."

"Sure. Tea sounds fine."

Rhode followed her into the kitchen where she went to work filling a kettle with water. "You ever ride Miss Landoon's horses?"

"No. I'm skittish. I fell off a horse once during a petting zoo at the school and broke my arm. I haven't ridden since but I do like to go out to the stables and see them, watch them graze. What about you?"

"I like horses, and dogs. I ride often. The horses—not the dogs." A sense of humor. She liked that; a few memories surfaced of her laughing at the bar, though his face was still fuzzy.

"This is weird." She might as well be honest.

"It really is." His laugh was nervous. "But I'm glad to know that I have kids, Teegan. I don't shirk responsibility and I appreciate your wariness about me concerning them. That's being a good mom. Protecting the kids."

Teegan almost cried again. Other than from Lorna, she hadn't heard she was doing a good job at being a mom; she didn't have a role model. She only knew she didn't want to be anything like her own parents. Often, she felt inadequate and lost. Alone. "Thank you. I'm trying. I'm a Christ follower, and raising them in church, though you wouldn't have known it from that time in Dallas. I was in a really dark place and sometimes when…"

"You're in a dark place, you do dark things you never thought you would," he finished for her.

"Yes. Exactly that." What a relief to know he didn't count her sin against her like so many others had.

"I'm a Christ follower too. And I get dark places. Dark

things. I thank God for grace and forgiveness or we'd all be in eternal trouble."

She smiled then. Good. He was a man of faith. A fallible man. But one of faith. She could work with that. It would be good for the babies. "Amen to that."

They sat quietly at the table until he finally spoke again, changing the subject.

"Teegan, who is after you?" He leaned forward with his elbows on his knees. "The theory was that your sister borrowed trouble and it found her. But this attack with yet another knife...is it possible—and I even hate to suggest it—is it possible that your sister's killer had a case of mistaken identity? That you were his target, not her? You are identical twins."

She hadn't thought of that, but with the fact she'd been nearly killed again... "I don't know." Fear crept into her veins and turned her blood cold. "I can't think of anyone who might want me dead." Or Lorna. Although her fall appeared to have been an accident. But because Misty was murdered, they hadn't ruled it out yet. Plus, they still had to do an autopsy. She shuddered.

"Tell me about that jester mask. He wasn't wearing it tonight, but he was earlier."

"It was one of those plastic ones, no hat or bells. It was white with black diamonds around the eyes and a ruby-red mouth that stretched into an evil grin. It was horrifying!"

Rhode took one of her hands in his. "I'm sorry you went through that. Does that mean anything to you? A jester mask?"

She shook her head.

"What about the Texas bluebonnets that were in the blood? Did you see them?"

If she did, she didn't remember. She shook her head again. "I know he must have brought them. Lorna said the state flower is overrated and refused to grow them or have them in the house. She was funny that way. A real card, you know?" She already missed her terribly. And Misty. It was almost impossible to imagine life without her other half, even if they had been estranged for years.

"I used to sneak onto the property as a kid—with my brothers—and search for the rumored treasure." His voice was wistful. Seemed like everyone wanted a piece of that pie, believing a pile of money would solve their problems and provide security. Even Teegan had wished for a cash cow, but she'd learned from her scraping by that God alone was her safe place and security. She might not have had much, but she'd never starved or gone naked. She reminded herself of that now. God would take care of her like He always had.

"I sneaked onto the property once too," she confessed. "We grew up in Round Rock, so it was about a forty-minute drive here."

"Never found the treasure then?" Rhode smiled and she realized he was serious.

"No. I wish."

"Same. You come out here with a boy?"

She blushed at his teasing. "Hardly. I wasn't as popular as my sister."

"Never even asked to a dance?"

"Once or twice but I never went."

"Two left feet?" he teased.

Teegan snickered. "No. I just… I didn't like leaving my mom alone. If she spent too much time alone, she'd find a bottle. Go out and buy one. Misty didn't seem to care, but I did. I wanted her to stay sober. I needed her to."

Rhode dropped his head and his eyes filled with sorrow. "I'm sorry. Alcoholism is a wicked monster unleashed, breathing its fire and devouring anyone in its path."

"You've known a drunk then?"

"A drunk," he whispered. "Yeah. Yeah, I have."

"Then you know why I've never touched a drop and would never let our children be in that kind of environment."

Rhode let out a long, heavy breath. "I do." He sat up and

the pain etched over his face turned resolute. "I want to take this case. Pro bono. You're in danger, which means the children are too."

"Really?" Was he serious?

"Yeah. Cedar Springs is down a detective and they could use the help. I can work with Dom off the books."

"You don't want to go back? I mean if they're short." Maybe he made more money going solo.

He looked away and she caught a flicker again in his eyes. She knew the look. One of loss and regret. "It's a complicated story for another time, but our agency is doing well, and it's personal to me."

"Alright then."

"I'm putting that Glen Landoon on the top of the list. Anyone else belong there?"

Teegan wasn't a fan of Lorna's grandson, but she wasn't sure he was the jester. "He's a lot of bark with no bite. His mother, Evangeline, is all bite with no bark. Truth is, the whole family has been estranged from Lorna. They visit because they want her money, and she knew that. She wasn't stupid. In fact, she was quite brilliant. Did you know she was allowed to help direct a movie? Unheard of in that time! She created literacy foundations as well as programs for theater for girls. She was ahead of her time, that's for sure." Teegan admired Lorna and even more so once Lorna became a Christian. "She traveled the world helping children learn to read and use their creative abilities. She even wrote a play they could perform that shared the gospel with other children."

"She really was amazing. And the money trail is always the first one to go down." He looked around again. "This place is massive and you shouldn't be here alone. I can bunk in the sitting room. Keep y'all safe for the night. Then consider staying on the family ranch with us. My mama's heart would be so happy to be around the grandbabies. She's been sick. Cancer. I think it would cheer her up."

How could Teegan say no to that?

She couldn't.

"Okay, then."

She wasn't sure what was scarier. Meeting Rhode's family or facing a killer.

Rhode awoke to baby chatter and Teegan's soft hushes. Last night, he'd slept on the couch downstairs, as promised, and had done perimeter sweeps every thirty minutes. He'd only dozed about an hour ago.

He rubbed his dry, gritty eyes and stretched his stiff neck then rose and combed his fingers through his hair before popping two breath mints.

Barely 6:00 a.m.

The smell of toast rumbled his stomach as he entered the kitchen. The babies sat in identical high chairs, each with a plate of scrambled eggs and triangle slices of toast with butter. Brook gummed her toast, a glob of butter on her chubby pink cheek, and River banged his little plate on the tray, his eggs smooshed everywhere.

"Did we wake you?" Teegan asked. She'd dressed in an oversize sweatshirt of the Grinch decorating a Christmas tree and black leggings. Her hair was in its usual bun on her head, with a few strands hanging.

"No. I wasn't sleeping sound. Just dozing." He glanced at the children. Brook had fisted her toast and was staring at him with big, brown eyes while River continued to beat the eggs into oblivion.

"Yes," he said to Brook softly and inched closer, "I'm someone new."

She raised her toast and said, "Sose."

Rhode's insides became as mushy as River's eggs. This was the most beautiful little girl ever born on the planet. "You got sose. Yu-ummm," he said, dragging out the word. Rhode didn't have a ton of experience with babies, but he'd had baby cousins growing up and he'd always gotten a kick out of them.

"Umm," Brook mimicked, her smile revealing four perfectly adorable teeth.

River joined in. "Ma-ma. Ma-ma."

Teegan turned from the sink where she was washing the pan. "What you want, baby?"

"Ma-ma. Ma-ma."

She grinned. "Yes, Mama's cooking."

He knocked his sippy cup of apple juice from the tray and Rhode returned it. "Here ya go, bud." He rustled his thick cap of dark hair. "You're gonna break every heart in Texas, dude," he muttered.

"I hope not," Teegan said. "I hope to teach him how to be a better man than one who simply breaks hearts."

Rhode agreed and turned. "I just meant he's a good-looking guy and—"

Her smile was soft and full, creating a ripple effect through his system. "I know what you meant. It's okay. You hungry? Want coffee? I have until eight to be out of here. I packed us up last night. Not like I have much."

"I'll grab a cup of coffee, but you don't need to cook for me, Teegan. Thanks though." He headed for the counter and poured a mug of black coffee. "Have you decided on arrangements for your sister?" He hated bringing it up, but she was alone and might need some help. "If you need anything, I can be there for you."

"Thank you. That means a lot." She dropped her head as a choked sob forced its way from her lips. "We have no family. Misty cycled through friends and, once she used them up, they abandoned her. I don't have a lot of money, so I called the funeral home director back last night as well. I'm having her cremated and her ashes will stay with me. No service or anything. There's no one to attend but me." She wiped a few tears. "Lorna put her wishes for rest in a will." Her lips quivered and the dam broke loose.

Rhode gently wrapped his arm around her, unsure if she'd be cool with his comfort. She surprised him by turning into his chest and allowing him to draw her closer.

"Let it out. We ain't goin' nowhere." At least not until eight.

Teegan's world had crumbled in a day. One horrific and painful thing after the next. No Lorna. No Misty. No home. No job.

Rhode tightened his hold on Teegan as the babies banged sippy cups, tossed eggs on the floor and squealed in utter delight at their mess. River rubbed eggs in his hair and Brook threw her wet, soggy crust onto the floor. No wonder his mom had always been exhausted when they were little. This was only breakfast and the sun hadn't risen yet.

Finally, Teegan's sobs quieted and she peered up through blue watery eyes, shifting his heart like it was a fault line. Rhode scraped a strand of hair glued by tears from her cheek then tucked it behind her ear. "You're not alone, Teegan. I'm not going anywhere."

"Thank you," she whispered, breaking from his arms and leaving a chilly empty space that unsettled him. "I have to clean up and bathe the babies."

"I can help. If they'll let me."

"They will. Neither are bashful. Brook is more vocal and picking up words faster than River, but he makes up for it in grunts and throwing things."

Rhode chuckled. He'd been a rowdy boy too. Teegan snagged a clean washcloth and, as she ran it under warm water, Rhode unrolled several paper towels from the holder. They worked in tandem washing up the children and the high chairs. While Teegan picked eggs from River's jet-black hair, Rhode lifted Brook from her highchair, toast crumbs sticking to her pink footie pajamas.

"Hey, darlin', you want to get a bath?"

"Ba-ba-ba."

"You're smart. Like your mama." He grinned when Teegan glanced his way.

"How do you know I'm smart?"

"Because these babies are smart, and they sure didn't get it from me." He ran his finger down his daughter's cheek. How did one man lose his heart to a baby this fast? There was nothing he wouldn't do for these two. He was like a volcano of love and protectiveness waiting to erupt.

"I don't know about that. Detectives and private detectives have to be smart to catch killers." She settled River on her hip and they carried the babies to the stairs.

Teegan sighed. "The elevator is broken, but I don't mind too much. Stairs benefit me healthwise, and now I have no choice. Can't be lazy on purpose."

Rhode smirked and they started up the stairs. Teegan was absolutely perfect to him, but he refrained from scoping her out. Not exactly respectful, and he didn't want to flash on any memories he shouldn't.

Once upstairs in Teegan's east wing, they bathed and dressed the kids then packed up the rest of their things, including the breakdown of the crib. Last night, Stone had swapped out Rhode's SUV for his pickup so they would have more room for Teegan and the babies' belongings.

By eight on the dot, Evangeline Landoon, her son, Glen, and her grandson, Charlie—who looked like a live Ken doll—stood in the foyer. Evangeline was tall, with wide blue eyes and long lashes. Her platinum-blond bob was a little longer in the front and her grubby hand was held out for Teegan to deposit the keys. She raised her sharp chin, peering down at Teegan. "You can pick up your check on Friday."

That was it. No sentiments about caring for Lorna these past six months. Not a single word. But it wasn't Evangeline's arrogance that caught Rhode's eye. It was Charlie's lecherous sneer that raised his hackles.

Teegan carefully handed over her keys and silently walked to her car. They buckled up the babies. And Rhode turned back one last time to see them with their smug smiles evicting them from the property. "Let's get out of here. Just follow me."

Rhode left the estate and, as he neared the family ranch, his stomach twisted and turned. Anticipation. Nerves. Everyone would be at the ranch. Bridge lived in a cabin on the backside of the property, but he always came up to the house in the mornings for coffee and a muffin. Stone and his wife, Emily, lived in the ranch house, with Mama. Sissy lived about a half a mile away. Beau had built them a new home before their wedding.

He pulled into the driveway and Teegan parked behind him, but she remained inside the car. He approached and she rolled down the window. "I'm nervous," she said. "I don't want your family to think I'm some kind of tramp."

He opened her car door and clasped her hands, gently coaxing her out of the driver's seat. "You are no such thing, and no one is going to judge you." Not when they could have judged Rhode so much harder and never had. "We were broken people who did a broken thing. It doesn't define us. And we got something good out of it in the end."

She nodded. "You're a good man, I think."

Oh, for grace… And she wouldn't think that if she knew he, too, battled addiction like her mom. But that was a conversation for another time. Once she'd gotten to know him— the real him. "Let's go see the fam. Also, prepare to eat again. My mom usually feels pretty good the day after chemo. It's about day three or four when the fatigue and nausea hit. She's probably baked something. Or Emily has, in which case, just smile and pretend to like it."

She laughed as they hauled the babies out of the car seats and went inside.

As predicted, the whole family was home and at the large farm table in the kitchen, no doubt awaiting their arrival. "Everyone," Rhode said, "this is Teegan Albright, and these most adorable things you have ever laid eyes on are Brook and River. My kids."

Mama approached first and hugged Teegan. "I'm Marisol, and you must call me that. Welcome to the family, Teegan. We're happy to have you and the babes. I love their names. So perfectly perfect, dear."

Teegan visibly relaxed and thanked her. "Would you like to hold him?"

"I would."

Teegan handed River over to Marisol and he went right to her, grabbing at her bottom lip with a slobbery grin.

The whole family oohed and aahed over the babies, passing them around like hors d'oeuvres and baby-talking them. Even his gruffest brother, Stone, fell into the baby trap. "Are you so cute? Yes, you are so cute."

Rhode would rib him over it later.

Mama had made cinnamon rolls from scratch and the house smelled like yeast and cinnamon…and the holidays.

Sissy and Emily drilled Teegan with baby questions, and Stone gave Emily a look that said he was ready for fatherhood. Beau kissed Sissy's head when she held Brook and they exchanged a glance. Well. Well. Well. Rhode thought he'd noticed a rosy glow in his sister's cheeks these past few weeks. No secrets between them, not with twin radar. But he'd let them announce it on their own.

Were there secrets between Teegan and Misty?

Someone wanted one of them dead. He had to find out if Misty had been the intended target or if it had been a case of mistaken identity. Once he concluded that, he could dig deeper.

Teegan's phone rang. She frowned and answered. "Yes, of course. When? And why me?" She listened and nodded. "So, I have to be?" She tucked the corner of her bottom lip into her mouth. "Okay then," she said weakly and ended the call.

"Is everything alright?" Rhode asked.

"I don't know. That was one of Lorna's attorneys, Scott Carmichael. I have to be at the Landoon estate at ten this morning for a reading of the will." She rubbed her hands on her thighs. "I don't understand."

"She left you something," Bridge said through a mouthful of cinnamon roll.

"But why? What could she possibly want to give me?"

"She loved you," Sissy said. "You know that. She talked about you all the time to me. She considered you a granddaughter. I think it's great."

"Well, the family won't. Evangeline, Glen and Charlie detest me. Dexter—Evangeline's brother—and his grandson, Peter, don't, but I'm not sure how they'll react."

"What about Peter's parents?" Rhode asked.

"No one knew who Peter's father was. Dexter's daughter—Peter's mom—died in a horse accident when he was young. Dexter raised Peter."

"So much tragedy," Marisol said.

Teegan nodded. "Dexter and Evangeline are fraternal twins."

"My, that's a lot of twins," Marisol commented.

Teegan smirked. "It's one of the reasons Lorna offered me the job. The twins reminded her of Evangeline and Dexter."

"Do you know anything about them?" Rhode asked.

"Peter and Charlie are more like brothers than cousins, and he has a hand in the thoroughbred business as well. Peter's actually quite nice. A little quiet. He visits Lorna more than the others. But I don't know how he'll respond if she leaves me something he might want."

"Maybe it's the treasure," Bridge said, his eyes alight with excitement.

"Get over that," Rhode said. "You'd think you were still fourteen."

Bridge shrugged and snagged another cinnamon roll.

Teegan clutched her stomach. "I'm going to be in bloody water with sharks. I dread it."

"I'll go with you." Rhode laid a hand on her shoulder.

"I can keep the babies," Sissy offered, and Emily and Mama nodded enthusiastically.

"Are you sure? I don't want to be a burden," Teegan said.

"Oh, child. This is family, not a burden." Marisol bounced River on her lap and played patty-cake with him. "We'll be right as rain. And the children will be good and spoiled."

Teegan's eyes filled with moisture. "You have no idea how much that means to me." She looked at Rhode. "We better get going then. I'll follow you in case you need to go, but I want to leave the car seats."

Rhode checked his watch. It was after nine. He grabbed his keys, then removed the car seats from Teegan's car and left them for Sissy in case they needed to take the babies somewhere. On their way to the vehicles, a foreboding swept over Rhode.

What if Lorna and Misty had been murdered over Lorna's fortune?

But the jester got the wrong sister.

Chapter Four

Teegan's stomach lurched as she pulled into the circular drive at Lorna's estate. Rhode parked his modest SUV beside luxury sedans and sports cars that cost more than the average American's yearly income. She met him at the front door, and he laid his hands on her shoulders. "These people are nothing but skin and bones like us. But I can tell you, from running in these elite circles, that they love the smell of inferiority. If you don't go in there with your head up, like you belong, they'll attempt to eat you alive. I won't let it come to that."

Teegan peered into his rich dark eyes, the resoluteness infusing her with the strength she desperately needed. "I'll try. I'm so far removed from this kind of wealth and life that it's intimidating."

"I understand. Trust me. Head up." He lightly lifted her chin and searched her eyes, holding her head until he seemed to realize she was ready.

"Head up," she whispered, and he removed his hold on her chin and nodded once.

Rhode didn't bother to knock. He opened the door and swaggered inside as if he belonged there more than anyone else. She admired the boldness, and it helped her straighten her shoulders and walk with more authority than she felt.

An attractive man with broad shoulders and dressed in a fitted and flashy suit met them in the foyer, his chestnut hair cut short but trendy. A few fine lines crinkled around his amber eyes as he grinned.

He waited a moment, but when Teegan didn't speak, he held out his hand. "Teegan, I presume. Scott Carmichael of Lindenstein, Carter and Brumm. I'll be handling the reading of the will today."

"Nice to meet you."

The lawyer eyed Rhode, waiting for an introduction. Teegan wasn't sure how to answer this one. "Um…"

"I'm Rhode Spencer. Teegan's fiancé."

Her what? Teegan opened her mouth but remained silent.

"I see," Scott Carmichael said. He dropped his gaze to Teegan's left hand, but Rhode had already discreetly taken it in his, hiding the fact she wore no engagement ring. "Follow me. Everyone's in Lorna's sitting room awaiting your arrival."

Rhode squeezed her hand and whispered, "Sorry, had to improvise. Mentioning that I'm a PI would be frowned on, and saying I'm your baby daddy didn't really feel right either."

She grinned, unable to help herself. "I don't think I would have put it quite like that." Although it was exactly like that.

His lopsided smirk swirled into her belly. Rhode Spencer. Mercy, he was beautiful. Men didn't care for that description. They preferred rugged or hot. But Rhode was exceptionally beautiful, and she was swiftly learning he was every bit as beautiful on the inside too.

Surely, she wasn't crushing on her children's father. Right now, the last thing she needed was a romantic entanglement. She was homeless and the list went on. Still…she couldn't help the way he made her feel. Not that he felt the same. He'd never once mentioned anything personal. Only interaction due to keeping her and the twins safe.

Inside the sitting room, Glen and Evangeline stood by the piano and paused their conversation when they spotted her. They might as well be wolves licking their chops as the chicken ventured away from the henhouse. Rumor around the stables was Evangeline never married because she didn't want to share her piece of the Landoon pie if a marriage didn't work. Of course, Teegan had no idea about Evangeline's personal life.

Glen's son rolled his eyes at seeing her and sipped his whiskey neat.

Dexter was in Lorna's favorite chair, scrolling on his phone as if bored with the event. Peter gave her a weak wave and smile, but at least ventured over to talk. Poor Peter had lost so much of his family and never known his father. His grandmother—Dexter's wife—passed a year ago to cancer and now Lorna.

"Teegan, how are you?"

"I've been better."

He touched her shoulder. "I was in Dallas when everything happened. I'm so sorry for your loss—of my great-grandmother and your sister." His sharp brown eyes met Rhode's, and he extended his hand. "Peter Landoon. I'm Lorna's great-grandson."

"I gathered that." Rhode accepted the handshake. "I'm Rhode Spencer, Teegan's fiancé."

"Oh." Peter's dark eyebrows raised and his mouth parted. "I didn't realize."

"It's new," Rhode said. "But we've known each other awhile. I'm the twins' daddy."

Peter's mouth hardened. "I see. Well, welcome." He excused himself and returned to his father, who continued scrolling on his phone.

"He have a thing for you?" Rhode asked. "How old is he?"

"Late thirties, like Charlie. Actually, he may be early forties. And no, he doesn't." He'd once invited her to ride horses, but

Lorna had interrupted with the fact she was being paid to work. Peter had politely seen himself out. He'd never asked again.

A throat cleared and Teegan spun around. Harry Doyle stood with his cowboy hat in hand, dirty work jeans, and weathered skin. "I, uh, I was called to be here?" he said, but it felt more like a question. He was as out of place in this hoity-toity environment as Teegan. Standing beside him was her friend and estate manager, Olivia Wheaton. She said nothing, but waved at Teegan.

"Yes, please, everyone come and have a seat."

"Why are they here?" Evangeline asked. "Let them get their treats and go."

The lawyer cleared his throat and caught Teegan's eye, silently apologizing. "Miss Landoon, I'll get to that."

Evangeline huffed and Dexter shot her a warning look, his phone still in hand.

Scott began reading. "'I, Lorna Landoon, a resident of Cedar Springs, Texas, declare this to be my Last Will and Testament, and revoke all previous wills and codicils, made by me, either jointly or severally. I am of sound mind and not under any duress, and this expresses my wishes.'"

"What does that mean? 'Revoke all previous wills'?" Glen asked.

"It means that anything previously written before this is void," Scott said.

Evangeline's face paled and she touched the hollow of her throat. "And when was this new will written?"

"November twenty-ninth of this year, ma'am."

The family exchanged worried glances. Had Lorna amended her will? Sylvia Bondurant, the senior attorney on her team, had visited a few times these past two months, but Teegan hadn't realized it might be to amend or change the will.

Scott read the amounts of money Lorna had willed to charities and organizations. "Before I announce the executor of her estate and the divvying up of money, property and assets, she'd like me to read this letter, which was written on November twenty-ninth of this year."

Scott opened the letter.

"'My dear family,
You undoubtedly thought I'd never kick the bucket but clearly I have.'"

Teegan imagined Lorna's upper-crust mid-Atlantic accent speaking the words.

"'I've made a lot of mistakes in my life," Scott read with perfect enunciation. "One was staying in Hollywood too long. Fulfilling your desires without hesitation. By the time I realized what was truly important in life, you'd already become part of a dark world full of selfish ambition, greed, and, well, quite frankly, bratty behavior. I regret that.

I own it as I own all my sins. I never should have given you each a trust of ten million when you hit twenty-one. You never learned hard work. Not like I did before I hit it big. You don't know what integrity or nobility means. You do not know any life other than one of privilege—which isn't a bad thing, children, if it's balanced. And that is why, through diligent prayer and consideration, I am leaving you one-hundred and fifty thousand dollars. And that is all. Whatever is left of your trust is yours.'"

Gasps echoed and Glen shot to his feet, his cheeks redder than a male cardinal.

Scott continued.

"'I make Teegan Elizabeth Albright the executor, and I leave to her all my property, estate, which includes every asset on the estate, including the thoroughbred business, as well as all my accounts domestic and foreign. Harry Doyle has done well by the horses and me, and he is a good man. Therefore, I request that he stay on as the manager of the stables and I give him forty percent shares in the business. Well done, thy good and faithful servant. To Olivia, I give you the option to remain on as estate manager and two million dollars regardless. You've been a gem to me. Well done, thy good and faithful servant.'"

Scott finished reading, but Teegan's mind buzzed as she tried to process.

Lorna had left everything—every single thing except forty percent of the thoroughbreds—to her. Why? Why would she do this?

"This is an outrage!" Evangeline shrieked. "My mother would never do this to her family."

Glen insulted Teegan with names. "What did you do to my grandmother? How did you swindle what is rightfully ours? I demand to revoke this will. My grandmother was clearly not sound in mind even though she said otherwise."

"I have to agree," Charlie said.

Dexter sighed. "We will contest this, Mr. Carmichael. You'll hear from my lawyer this afternoon. Peter."

Peter stood but said nothing as they left.

"Well, I'm not leaving this house." Evangeline crossed her arms over her chest, her chin raised. Glen and Charlie flanked her in a united front.

"I'm afraid that is up to Miss Albright. She's the owner of the property and the home," Scott said.

"You will pay for this," Charlie Landoon snarled and stalked toward her.

Rhode stood again as her barrier. "Don't you threaten her. Or you'll have me to deal with, and that's not a threat. It's a promise."

Charlie held his gaze, a murderous glint in his eye.

"And you'll need to drop your keys on the table on your way out. All of you. Give back Teegan's keys as well."

Charlie backed down and stormed from the house, his father glaring at Teegan as he followed, the sound of keys crashing to the floor echoed. Only Evangeline, Olivia and Harry Doyle remained.

"You'll regret this, Miss Albright," Evangeline said. "You may have the house for the moment, but when I'm finished, you and those little babies of yours will be on the street, and from there I don't care what happens to you, but you will not win." She cast her gaze on Rhode. "That's not a threat," she stressed. "It's a promise." She threw the keys down at their feet and raged away.

"I don't understand," Teegan said. "Why me?" She slumped in the chair by the window.

"I don't know, Miss Albright. She also left you a private letter." The lawyer handed it to her.

"What are the chances they contest and win?" Rhode asked.

Scott inhaled and tapped the papers. "The lawyer who drew up the documents would have to testify that Lorna was of sound mind. They will interview doctors as they investigate her mental health. If she was as sharp as it appears in her letter, I'd say nil. This is all yours, Miss Albright. I left the papers with the financial numbers on the piano up there. You're a very wealthy woman now." He nodded once and exited the room.

Harry and Olivia approached. Olivia leaned down. "Lorna knew what she was doing. I'm not surprised she didn't give them a dime. I am surprised she left me what she did. I'll stay on if you'd like. I enjoy the job."

Teegan grasped her hand. "I would love that. Thank you. Just keep doing what you've always done. Harry, same for you, I guess."

He stood shaking his head. "I'll be where I always am if you need me."

They both left, leaving Teegan and Rhode alone.

"How wealthy am I?"

Rhode picked up the papers from the piano and flipped through them, then low whistled. "Let's just say the twins can go to an Ivy League school hundreds of times if they want and then some."

Tears filled her eyes. "Lorna was in her right mind. But leaving everything to me makes me want to reconsider."

"Or maybe she knew you possessed all the traits to handle this kind of money. You're a hard worker. You're kind. You're everything her family isn't. Didn't you say she often thought of you as a granddaughter?" Rhode asked.

Teegan nodded. "I need a cup of tea."

"And we need to change all the locks on these doors. I don't trust her family. They weren't making idle threats. And I have to wonder if she was killed because they didn't realize she'd already amended the will and wanted it to stay the same. Misty might have been in the wrong place at the wrong time and had to die differently to throw off law enforcement."

Teegan couldn't imagine that, but money had motivated many murders. "You think one of the Landoons murdered Lorna for the money and my sister was a casualty?"

Rhode handed her the papers. "I think it's possible. And if you're dead, contesting the will becomes a lot easier."

After the reading of the will, the suspect pool had skyrocketed. The amount of money Teegan had inherited was easily enough motivation to kill her. More than Rhode would make in several lifetimes. The kind of dough that would catapult him from debt and pay off all his mom's medical bills. And then some.

But money didn't solve all problems. Sometimes money made things worse.

After everyone had made their dramatic exits earlier today, Rhode had first called Dom to inform him of the situation. Dom was looking into Evangeline, Glen, Charlie, Dexter and

Peter Landoon. Next, he'd had a locksmith come out to change all the locks. Teegan had agreed to install a security system, but they couldn't come out until Monday morning. Rhode only wished he could have been the one to foot the bill for all this, but about all he could afford was a doorbell camera. It had hit him then: what would Teegan need him for now? She had everything—security, stability, and a massive estate for the babies to grow up on. What could he realistically bring to the table? Offering meager child support was now laughable.

And Teegan had the funds that Rhode didn't, which meant if she didn't want Rhode to see the children, she could hire fancy lawyers and take him to court and win. She'd never mentioned he wasn't going to be allowed to see the children, and had welcomed his help. But then, she hadn't known about his alcoholism. That knowledge might change her mind.

A pit formed in his gut as he climbed the stairs to check in on Teegan. She'd skipped lunch in favor of a nap. That was a few hours ago. It was now four o'clock. Maybe she'd have the elevator fixed too; these stairs were steep and many.

Rhode knocked on her bedroom door.

No answer.

He knocked harder and called her name. A shuffling noise met his ears and then the door opened. Teegan's eyes were puffy and her hair in disarray. A jagged line creased her cheek from her pillow.

"Hey, I'm sorry to wake you, but you haven't eaten, and I thought you might want a bite and then head back to the ranch for the twins."

"Right." She rubbed her eyes and yawned. "I guess I've been sleep deprived way too long, and today has been emotionally draining. I didn't realize I'd crashed so hard. I'm sorry. I don't want your family to think I'm taking advantage."

"I've already talked to them and they're fine. You needed the rest."

"I can fix us something."

Teegan always thought of others first. "I didn't wake you up to be my chef, Teegan. I know how to cook...some things."

She raised an eyebrow. "Oh yeah? Like what?"

They descended the stairs. "Well, I can make scrambled eggs or even an egg sandwich. Egg salad. I make a great omelet and—"

"Anything that isn't egg related?" she asked as the staircase rounded.

"I make homemade pizza and tacos. I can grill a mean steak and bake a potato."

She paused near the bottom of the stairs, staring at the place she found her sister and Lorna.

"Hey. Hey," he said again, and she finally looked at him. Her face was pale and her bottom lip quivered. "It's going to be okay." He prayed he wasn't giving her false hope.

With no leads, anyone could be the murderer.

"I don't know that it is. In fact, I fear it could be even worse. I've taken what the Landoon family should have and been threatened. I've been attacked. I don't understand why or by who. My sister and Lorna are dead. And I'm constantly feeling watched. In fact, I woke up once and it was like someone was in my room. But I didn't see anyone."

She undid her ponytail holder and pulled her hair back, twisting it into a messy bun on top of her head as they walked into the massive kitchen.

Now Teegan's kitchen. If she would even want to stay in this place after what she'd endured.

"I'm going to make us some dinner. Pizza, if the ingredients are here, and we'll just take it minute by minute."

Teegan glanced around the kitchen as if checking to make sure they were truly safe and nodded.

"The kids are fine at the ranch."

"Are you sure? I know what little terrors they are." Love filled every syllable.

"Are you kidding me? They're loving it. Sissy used to babysit for free. Stone had to remind her it was a job and she was to ask for money, but she loved babies so much, she didn't feel right about asking or taking payment. Mama told him to leave her alone, but Stone hounded her until she asked Mrs. Freezy for ten dollars, then cried and returned it."

Teegan snorted. "Sissy is sweet."

"Sissy's a sucker." He smirked and opened the fridge. Well stocked, it appeared to have what they'd need for pizza. Rhode washed his hands and went to work making dough and stealing glances at Teegan. She had every reason to feel on edge, but he had hoped his presence might calm her some.

After letting the pizza dough rest, he then went to work on the homemade sauce and browning Italian sausage. The kitchen smelled amazing. Basil, garlic, onions and tomatoes with that delicious yeast dough. But Teegan didn't appear to have an appetite. Her knee bobbed and she continued scraping her hands on her thighs.

Rhode popped the pizza in the oven and walked to her. "Hey, I know you're scared and us making dinner isn't going to change what happened, but I need you to eat when this timer beeps and keep up your strength. I'm going to protect you, Teegan. And our children."

"I'm going to go wash my face and pray. I'll be right back." She left the kitchen and Rhode leaned against the counter, letting his mind work out the puzzle pieces they had at the moment. Barely a few edge pieces. He rubbed his shoulders just as a shriek filled the air.

Teegan.

Rhode raced up the stairs and met a shaking Teegan at the top. "What is it?"

She pointed to her room. "My bed. It's on my bed!"

Rhode didn't waste any time. He bolted past her and into her room. Curled on one of the pillows was a bloody snake. A note had been nailed into the middle of the body.

Grabbing a tissue box from the end table, he poked the

snake to make sure it was dead. It was a rattler and deadly if alive. Once he was sure it was dead, he lifted the note with a tissue and read the bright red letters.

Snakes die!

Teegan stood in the doorway, eyes wide and her arms wrapped around her middle as if trying to shield herself from this nightmare.

"I don't know if it's safe for me and the children to be here." Her voice cracked and popped with each word. "Do you?"

"Honesty?"

"I'm not a fan of lies."

That was why he had to find a way to tell her about himself before she found out on her own. She'd assume he was deceiving her. He wasn't. He was just scared he'd lose his kids before he ever truly had them. "I'm not sure you're safe anywhere. You own millions—"

"I never asked for that. I don't think I want that kind of money. I mean, I'm honored Lorna would think me to be responsible enough for this, but I don't want a family tearing each other apart because of me. I'm not a snake. I didn't try and finagle an inheritance from Lorna. It's obvious one of the family members did this. But how? How did they get inside the house? I wasn't imagining someone in my room watching me. Someone was!"

He planned to investigate that immediately. "Teegan, the Landoon family has been fractured for a long time and they'll find a way to shred each other regardless. Lorna wanted you to have it. Anyone with a brain knows you're not a snake. Did you read the letter she left you?"

Lorna had included a personal letter for Teegan.

She nodded. "Before I fell asleep. I was going to talk to you about it. Rhode, I think there's a legit treasure."

If that was true it explained the lengths this person was going to in order to rid the world of Teegan—and Lorna for that matter.

"Let me read it to you." She opened her nightstand drawer and pulled out a piece of paper.

"Hey, why didn't Lorna fix the elevator?"

"She never went past ground level."

And that was another thing bothering Rhode. If a ninety-two-year-old woman never went upstairs, how had she gotten up there to have fallen?

Dom had said the autopsy report showed she'd died from blunt force trauma and the medical examiner had ruled it an accident. She'd also broken several bones, including both hip bones, but the head wound had immediately killed her. Guess God was merciful in that—she'd never felt her body break.

Her manner of death hadn't explained why she'd been on the second floor, though. Rhode and his brothers had discovered traces of blood on the side of the banister.

What if Lorna's death wasn't an accident, especially if there had been a treasure? He'd told Teegan he would take the case, and he'd meant it. Beau was already looking into the family members. They all had motive, but who had the most motive or the guts to murder two people in cold blood?

Teegan unfolded the letter with shaky fingers and began reading.

"My dearest Teegan,

How you have brought me such joy. You've been a treasure to me—one that is in front of me and yet buried deep within my heart. You, more than anyone, deserve what I've given you. I know you'll steward it well. I hope it will give you the relief you need to go back to local theater and help teach young people how to love the art, but also to recognize it's not fame they should long for but God. Help them use their talent for the Lord and not for themselves.

Speaking of treasure, it's raining outside, but my heart

is warm with sparkling delight. Let's drink to the occasion, love.
Sincerely,
Lorna"

Teegan lowered the letter. "She used the word *treasure* twice. The rest is a little cryptic, but I think there's a clue in it. I also think I was given this privately because it's so cryptic, it sounds like she's out of her gourd. I need to talk to Sylvia—the senior attorney who visited often."

"Maybe she'll tell us who the beneficiaries of the previous will were." That would help them with their suspect list. "Read the letter again."

She did. "I'm not sure what it means, but because it's so weird—and she uses *treasure* twice, as if for emphasis—it makes me think she's talking in code to me. I'll chew on it."

"That reminds me, I need to check the pizza and get rid of this." He dumped the snake in the bathroom trash and carried it downstairs. Rhode threw it out back but kept the note. "You got a plastic bag?"

"Yeah." She retrieved one and handed it to him. He tucked it with the tissue into the bag as evidence to give to Dom.

The oven beeped and he removed the pizza.

"It's nice on the patio. You want to eat outside?" she asked.

"I'll try to eat but I'm not making any promises."

He nodded, and they carried their plates, napkins and drinks to the outdoor table. The pergola over their heads had been woven with multicolored lights, and the air was crisp.

"I love Christmastime," Rhode said, hoping to lighten the moment so she could stomach the food.

"I do too. I bought the kids so much, it's ridiculous. I have to wrap it all, and I kinda dread it." She laughed and nibbled her pizza while Rhode wondered which family member had been in the house and how they got inside her room with that snake.

Not to mention the death threat that came along with the dead creature. *Snakes die.*

The peal of a car alarm snapped his attention to the front of the house and away from his thoughts.

"That's my car," Teegan said, dropping her pizza on the plate.

"Stay here." Rhode jumped up, pulled his gun from his holster and raced through the house and out the front door.

Chapter Five

Teegan braced herself at the kitchen island, her fingers trembling. A bird flying into the windshield could have set off the alarm. But too much had happened in the past twenty-four hours to believe that. What if Rhode had been ambushed?

Teegan crept through the kitchen toward the foyer, the car alarm's shrill growing louder. She peeked out the front door. Rhode stood in front of the vehicle with his gun in hand, darting his sight around the lawn. Snagging her keys off the side table by the front door she stepped onto the porch and hit the button.

Silence permeated the air and Rhode pivoted in her direction.

That's when she saw it.

Her car.

Painted on the side in white: *You're Dead!*

Teegan's heart lurched into her throat, tightening it. This had now gone from a cryptic and terrifying message to making it clear. She was the snake. And she was dead. She licked her bottom lip and worked to breathe. "Did you see who did it?"

Rhode shook his head. "They're gone."

Teegan was certain this claim was a promise, one someone

had already tried to make good on. "What if I gave the money back and the estate? I mean… I don't need it. I'm doing okay on my own and the kids are healthy and happy. If I don't give them what they want, I could end up like Misty. And my kids… what would happen to them? I'm all they have."

Rhode's face crumpled and he ate up the ground between them. He gently gripped her shoulders. "We are not going to let them scare you into doing what they want. And…you're not all they have now. They have me too. I want to be a part of their lives. I won't let anything happen to you, Teegan. You have my word."

Teegan barely knew Rhode. How could she trust his word? Yet, deep in the marrow of her bones, she believed she could. She weakly nodded. "Now what?"

"Now we lock up and go to the ranch."

"Should we come back at all?"

Rhode's lips twisted to the side and his brow furrowed. He was quiet a few moments then nodded. "If they're serious about coming after you, then they're going to do it no matter where you are. I say show them you aren't scared—"

"Except I am. I am scared, Rhode. My sister is dead. Lorna is dead. This is no joke. I can't take chances. I have to do what is safest for my children." Teegan couldn't care less about showing a brave front. All she cared about was staying alive and protecting the twins.

"I know. I'm not saying this to use you as bait or to antagonize them. This is your home. For as long as you want it. I'll stay here with you."

"Okay, I trust you."

Twenty minutes later, they barreled down the dark backroads to his ranch.

"You give any more thought to that letter you think is about hidden treasure?" Rhode asked. "You've been quiet."

She had a lot to think about. "It's teetering on the edge of my memory, but nothing is clear. Not yet. It's the last line that's cryptic and why I think she's telling me something without outright telling me."

It's raining outside, but my heart is warm with sparkling delight. Let's drink to the occasion, love.

Teegan pictured Lorna writing it in her shaky but gorgeous penmanship. "Let's drink to the occasion" made no sense. Lorna knew how Teegan felt about alcohol and Lorna only had red wine once a week for the antioxidants. "Lorna would never suggest a drink with her for any occasion. Lorna knows my whole story and never judged. I really am going to miss her, and my sister. I wish we'd been closer."

Rhode reached over and clasped her hand. "I know."

After pulling into the drive, Rhode grabbed a bag from the back seat. The air was crisp and the moon was full, but it didn't feel romantic. No, it was like an ominous spotlight on her, revealing her position to an unseen enemy.

Christmas might be coming. But so was a killer.

She shuddered and they entered the warm ranch. The scent of cinnamon and vanilla enveloped her senses before being met with the aroma of fresh coffee. She hoped it was decaf.

River was engaged in building a huge tower of blocks in the living room with help from Stone. Bridge was playing peek-a-boo with Brook's big pink brick. Brook's giggles were infectious.

Rhode leaned down to Teegan's ear. "Bridge is mush when it comes to babies and kids. Stone, on the other hand, is more about making sure River—at barely two—understands architecture."

"And where do you land when it comes to kids?" she asked.

He grinned. "I'm Mrs. Doubtfire meets Indiana Jones."

She laughed and it drew the attention of the twins and Rhode's brothers. Brook tottered toward her, River right behind calling, "Ma-ma. Ma-ma."

She scooped up each baby in an arm and kissed them. "Have you been good?"

"They're awesome," Bridge said. "Super smart. So it's obvious that comes from you."

Teegan laughed at his teasing.

"River could be a great architect one day," Stone said.

"Told ya," Rhode said under his breath. "Where's everybody else?" he asked his brothers.

Stone stood and stretched. "Mama went to lie down awhile. She let the babies help make cookies, so that was a disaster, and then she cooked dinner to keep Emily from the kitchen. We wanted to actually enjoy the meal."

"That woman is super, but she is the worst cook on the planet, and that's including me," Bridge said.

"Preach," Stone said through a chuckle. "Anyway, Mama said she'd be recharged in about an hour." His eyes softened. "Rhode, she had the best time with these babies. I haven't seen her that lit up in a long time."

Bridge agreed. "He's right. She was so alive tonight. Thank you for letting the babies stay, Teegan. They're good medicine for us all."

Teegan's heart warmed and she looked around. "Where's Emily now?"

"Had to go into work. Case came up," Stone said.

"She works for the Texas Ranger's Public Integrity Unit, right?" Teegan asked.

Stone nodded. "Beau and Sissy will be here—"

The back door opened and Sissy's two adorable Cavalier King Charles spaniels bounded into the living room. The babies squirmed to get down, so Teegan complied and the dogs licked their cheeks. "Play nice with the puppies." River could grab their hair too tight. They were good sports but children needed to be taught how to respect animals so they didn't hurt them or end up nipped themselves.

"Teegan," Sissy said, "how are you feeling after the big news?" She pointed to her husband and Rhode's business partner. "Beau told me about the case."

Beau's bright blue eyes met Teegan's with compassion. "I'm looking into the bluebonnets left behind at the scene and into Misty's life in California. I am sorry for your loss. Miss Landoon was a wonderful person. I always enjoyed it when I had the chance to see her."

Teegan appreciated his sentiment. "Thank you. Have you found anything?" She glanced at the babies to ensure they were playing nicely with the Cavaliers.

Beau glanced at Rhode and then back to Teegan. "Misty had been working as a receptionist for a dental office. She was let go and charged for stealing pain meds and coming into work intoxicated. A neighbor lady told me that she'd been doing well prior to that incident and had been sober for almost three months. But she had a bad breakup with a man named Kenny Lee—we're tracking him down."

Rhode winced and Teegan's shoulders tightened. She and her sister had gone in two different directions. Teegan refusing to touch anything that might enslave her—sans the one night. Misty had gone down the road their mom had traveled.

"Do you believe this Kenny Lee came from California to Texas, targeting Misty?" Rhode asked.

"I'm not sure, but it's a lead worth tracking." Beau massaged the back of his tanned neck. "According to the neighbor, Kenny Lee was no good. Misty didn't make good choices in men and when it didn't end well, instead of being thankful, she tanked it all."

"What kind of no good?" Teegan asked.

"She'd heard fights and things breaking inside Misty's apartment before. She called the police three different times and noticed bruises on Misty. Misty denied the abuse. Made up lame excuses," Beau said.

"Who broke off the relationship?" Teegan asked.

"Misty. But it was reluctant, and Kenny didn't take it well. That's why I'm trying to track him down. Revenge is a strong motivator."

Beau was right about that. "Why continue coming after me? If he knows he killed Misty then it should be over. Right?"

Beau sighed. "I thought about that."

"And?" Rhode asked.

"She might be a reminder. He could think you're actually Misty pretending to be the sister and so he's bent on taking you both out. Or...or a family member is using her death to orchestrate yours so that we'll think the same person—possibly Kenny—is the cause of Lorna and Misty's deaths as well as yours."

Rhode rubbed his chin. "Did Misty have ties to bluebonnet flowers? And have you heard from Dom?" he asked Beau. "He was running the signature through VICAP."

"Not yet. He said he'd call as soon as he hears something."

River rubbed his eyes and yawned. The family had tuckered him out. Teegan was exhausted too. Rhode squatted and stroked River's chubby cheek. "You tired, bud?" He held out his arms and River reached for him. Rhode scooped him up and laid his nose to River's sweet button nose. "Do you like to rock?"

"He does," Teegan whispered as a lump grew in her throat. Seeing River with his father tugged her in deep places. "It's their bedtime for sure. I wish they could be in their home."

"We can go back, Teegan. I know you packed everything up this morning, but I don't believe geography is the problem."

She nodded. "You're right." She was going to be afraid no matter where she slept. Her kids needed routine and if she were being honest, so did she.

He pointed to the kitchen. "I left our pizza we didn't get to finish on the counter. Dig in."

Teegan wasn't hungry but knew she needed to eat. She and Sissy headed for the kitchen, but River and Brook had crawled into Rhode's lap in the rocking chair. Marisol woke from her evening nap and the house was full of chatter and laughter. For now, it felt like a normal family.

Although she wasn't sure what normal was. Teegan had never been a part of people who razzed each other, laughed together and clearly loved one another. She was happy her children had a large family of people who adored them.

But Teegan was on the outside. She and Rhode weren't together. Weren't married. And, while she was attracted to him and they got along, it didn't mean family.

She was on her own. As she always had been.

Rhode stretched his arms over his head and yawned. "I'm glad you had a portable crib for the babies. The other one is a beast." After leaving his family's ranch, with sleeping babies, they'd carried them upstairs and put them in their portable crib, snoozing soundly. "My family is exhausting. Even for babies," Rhode teased through a whisper.

Teegan smiled and turned on the monitor then clipped the receiver on her waist. Nothing but the sound of static and baby breaths.

"I've been thinking about that letter."

"What did you come up with?"

"Let's go to Lorna's theater room. I have a suspicion." They descended the stairs and marched to the back of the home where Lorna's theater room housed leather recliners with cup holders, red-velvet curtains flanking a massive movie screen, and a projector booth at the back of the room. It even had a popcorn and drink machine at a bar in the right corner. "Lorna loved movies and often had friends come to watch a flick. But she especially loved her own movies and often watched them. I've seen them all, but some more than others. I believe that last sentence in my letter is a line from one of her movies."

Teegan headed for the projector booth.

"She won an Oscar for her role as Miriam Malone in the 1953 hit *A Love Affair in Venice*. She starred opposite Cary Grant. They did several movies together. Their onscreen chemistry was dynamic."

"I haven't seen it. I'm not an old movie buff, but Sissy loves them. She said she'd seen all of Lorna's movies too."

The projector rolled and the film began.

"There's a part when Cary is leaving her to return to the States and the affair is over. He mentioned his wife traveled overseas and encountered a shipwreck. He traveled to Venice to mourn the loss and meets Miriam Malone, who bought a vineyard and small hotel. It was a whirlwind romance. But then he gets word that they have found his wife. She's not dead. But Miriam has captured his heart, and now he's torn."

"That's awful."

Teegan nodded. "It devastated me. But Miriam makes it easy on him and tells him to return to his first love. She sends him off with a bottle of wine they cultivated together. It was this emotional scene that won her the Oscar. I cry every time I watch it. It's heart-wrenching."

They watched in silence. Halfway through, Teegan pointed to the screen. "This is the scene in the wine cellar."

Lorna was a stunner. Her ruby-red lips and teary eyes drew Rhode in.

Cary Grant cradled her face. "I can't leave you, darling. I love you. You've healed me and brought me back to life. A life I didn't want to live. And now, I don't want to live it without you."

Lorna touched his cheek, her long lashes damp with tears. "You must go back. She needs you. And you'll find you need her."

Thunder cracked and the sound of rain erupted. She paused among the rows of wine. "I met you in the rain."

"I kissed you in the rain."

Lorna broke free and closed her eyes. "How you have brought me such joy. It's raining outside, but my heart is warm with sparkling delight. Let's drink to the occasion, love. One last drink." She opened a bottle of wine and poured two glasses. They drank it through tears and then she handed him a bottle. "Always remember me."

Cary held the wine bottle. "I could never forget you. I wouldn't want to. Oh, darling." He grabbed her with intensity and kissed her passionately, then left without looking back, the bottle of wine in hand.

Teegan wiped her eyes. "She was a fabulous actress. But I think she's giving us a clue. When she had the house built, it included a cellar. In fact, a lot of what Lorna has around her estate is from movies. She aspired to be done with that life, but the acting in itself she never stopped loving or missing."

"Will the baby monitor work in the wine cellar?"

"Yep."

Rhode motioned for her to lead the way. At the back of the house, a door opened to old wooden stairs and the temperature plummeted. Teegan switched on the light at the top and they descended slowly, Teegan leading the way.

Rows and rows of large shelves held bottles of wines. So much wine, one would never drink it in a lifetime. Rhode felt the dry ache in his throat and cleared it.

"You okay?" Teegan asked.

"Yeah." He said a silent prayer for strength. The scent of fermentation and grapes filled his senses as the memories of the dry, fruity drink hit him like a gut punch. Like Joseph, he needed to flee. "Actually, I'm not feeling well all of a sudden. I need some air. Do you mind if I wait upstairs?"

She paused and studied him.

Rhode should take the moment to confess the truth and that he was tempted to have a drink. He regretted the current situation and wished he'd have no taste for it anymore. He longed for the struggle to end. Embarrassment coupled with weakness and knowledge of Teegan's opinion on those who imbibed cemented his tongue to the roof of his mouth.

"Are you claustrophobic?" she asked with a smirk.

Right now, in this moment? "Yes," he answered honestly. The walls were closing in on him and he might have a panic attack.

"Go on. I'm pretty sure I know what I'm looking for."

He sighed. "Thank you." He rushed back up the stairs, closing the door behind him, and beelined it straight for the kitchen where he turned on the faucet and splashed his face with cold water. Would this ever go away? Would he have to run away like a coward every time he desired a taste? Frustration knotted his shoulders and neck muscles, and he squeezed his eyes closed.

Hairs on his neck prickled and he spun around just in time to see a man looming over him, a creepy white jester mask with an insidious red grin and black diamonds painted around the eyes.

Rhode reached back to waylay him, but the jester got the jump on him, clobbering him with something hard.

Those black diamonds around his eyes were the last thing Rhode saw before he drifted into his own blackness.

Chapter Six

Teegan sneezed as dust and cobwebs tickled her nose. The dim light concentrated on the stairs, shadows branching out before them onto the concrete flooring. Must and the scent of fermentation permeated the cellar.

She hoped Rhode was okay and not too overwhelmed, but she wondered if it might be more than that. Something felt off. She'd honed the knack for sensing when a person was withholding information. She'd had to since it had been just her and Misty since childhood.

Oh, Miss.

Teegan had tried dozens of times to prompt her twin to move back. She'd had it in her head that while she couldn't fix their mother, she could Misty. That wasn't true though. The reality was that a person couldn't help another person who didn't want help, or she'd have seen her mom make progress. She never had and she'd drank herself to death.

Teegan studied the dusty wine bottles, some worth thousands of dollars. Crazy how a fermented grape could go for twelve grand. In the movie, they had held a dark green bottle with a purple cork. The wines were in order of year and she was looking for 1953—the year the movie had been released.

There was 1956…54…

Boom!

Excitement built in her chest and she wished Rhode was down here to share this moment. Was that weird? She slipped the bottle from the wooden holder.

An empty bottle, but the one from the set. It had probably been filled with grape juice.

Teegan popped the cork and found a rolled-up white paper inside.

The next clue!

Heavy, slow footsteps clunked on the wooden stairs.

Rhode had overcome his fear.

"Rhode. I found it. I was right!"

Rhode didn't respond and her scalp tingled as the chilly air swirled around her. "Rhode," she whispered, her throat tight.

The footsteps silenced.

Teegan shifted but couldn't see past the looming shadows peeking out from the corners. The rows of wooden shelves blocked her vision.

She gripped the wine bottle and shoved the rolled-up clue into her waistband. She tiptoed to the end of the row with her back flush to the end cap. Her heart hammered against her ribs and she covered her mouth to keep from gasping.

Rhode wasn't down here with her.

But someone was.

If she screamed, would he hear her? Whoever was in the cellar with her definitely would and she'd give away her position. It was a matter of time before he found her anyway.

Shuffling along the concrete ignited a jolt through her system and her fight-or-flight kicked in. She bolted from the shelves just in time to bounce into a large frame dressed in black.

The terrifying jester mask with the wicked smile painted in ruby-red stared at her. In his gloved hand there was a very large butcher knife, glinting in the dim light.

He raised it and she shrieked; the wound in her flesh where he'd already torn through throbbed. She bolted the way she'd come and rounded the shelf. He raced after her. Circling it, she aimed for the staircase. As she reached the bottom stair, he gripped the back of her hair and yanked her toward him. She stumbled and fell as the knife swooped through the air, narrowly missing her stomach. She scrambled on her hands and knees for the inner cellar. Once she was on her feet, she darted down a row of wines.

Creaking and groaning gave her pause, then she pivoted as the shelves shuddered then toppled over, bottles crashing to the floor and scattering glass shards across the red-stained concrete. Like blood, the wine oozed and pooled at her feet.

She screamed again as another row crashed down, clipping her back and forcing her to drop to the floor, pinning her. Agonizing pain shot up her right leg to her head as it smacked against the bottom of a rack, the bottles falling like dominoes in front of her.

The jester loomed over her; the knife blade glittering. She raised her hands in defense and shrieked, "Please don't. I have babies. Please!"

"Teegan!" Rhode thundered.

"Rhode!"

Pain blinded her. Spots dotted her vision as the last thing she saw was the shiny, bloodstained knife raised above her head and heard the words of the jester.

"…gets…last…now…"

"You're okay. Stay still," Rhode said. He pushed the wooden wine shelf from her leg. "Can you move it?"

"Where is he? Where are my babies?" How long had she been out? She was alive!

Rhode held up the monitor. "They're fine. But if you can move, I want to check on them."

She nodded and moved her leg, wincing. "It's not broken, but it hurts. Where did he go?"

"He was gone when I got down here. Maybe three, four minutes ago. Is there a cellar door that leads outside?"

Teegan pointed to the east side of the room and Rhode raced to it. "It's locked. How did he escape then?"

"I'm not sure," she said through the pain. Every muscle in her body ached and her head pounded. "I want to stand. Want to see my babies."

Rhode helped her to her feet; her ankle smarted. Relief flooded her when she could put weight on her foot. Not broken. Bruised for sure. "What happened to you?"

"He came into the kitchen and got the jump on me. Knocked me out. I'm so sorry. I said I'd protect you and I failed, Teegan." His voice was low and full of disappointment.

"Rhode, you couldn't have known. How did he even get in the house? The doors were locked."

"I don't know. Can you make it upstairs?"

"I don't know."

"Can I have permission to carry you?" he asked.

How embarrassing. But she wanted to be close to the babies. "Okay."

He swept her up as if she weighed nothing and climbed the stairs. "You're shaking," he said. "I'm so sorry."

"You saved me. He was going to kill me, Rhode. Right before I blacked out, he said something, but I couldn't hear it all. His voice was fuzzy in my ears. I did make out three words. *Gets. Last. Now.* What does that mean?"

"I don't know." He reached the top of the stairs and eased her onto the couch in the loft then covered her with a blanket. He checked the babies' room and returned. "All is well in there. Stay here and I'll clear the house." He drew a small can from his pocket. "Pepper spray. It shoots thirty feet. You spray and move. He'll be blinded and unable to tell where you moved to."

Gripping the can, she nodded, and Rhode began clearing the second floor then went downstairs.

Which one of the family members would be this vicious? This cold-blooded? The money, the home and estate weren't worth this. Not even a little.

Finally, Rhode returned. "It's all clear, and I called Dom again. Told him the jester wore gloves, but he's sending the crime scene techs anyway. Be about thirty minutes." He slumped next to her and searched her eyes. "How are you feeling?" He lightly touched a cut on her cheek and she winced. "Let me fix you up." He stood and helped her to the bathroom.

"Sit," he ordered, and she sat on the toilet lid. He opened the medicine cabinet and retrieved hydrogen peroxide. He found a rag and ran it under warm water.

"I can do this myself, Rhode." But her hands wouldn't stop trembling.

"I know." He knelt in front of her and held her hands until the warmth of his steadied her. "It'll be boo-boo fixer practice for the kids."

She actually smiled. "My dad wasn't around to fix boo-boos."

He held her gaze and she inhaled the subtle scent of his cologne that lingered on his clothing, which evoked a sweeping memory of dancing in his arms, even though his face was fuzzy.

"I'm not going anywhere, Teegan," he whispered. "Maybe your dad told you the same thing. I don't know. But I'm here. I'm going to be the dad those babies deserve to the best of my ability, but I'll be honest, I don't have much in the way of money. I do have love and all of myself. And anything I do have is theirs."

Tears washed over her eyes and she bit her bottom lip to tamp down the sobs. Her dad had never said he'd stay. Never said much at all. "I believe you."

He applied the warm washcloth to her cheek, dabbing delicately, and brushed a stray hair stuck to her skin before slipping it behind her ear. "I don't remember that night, but I must have been knocked for a loop by you. You're...so beautiful." His finger trailed her jawline. "So sweet."

Teegan's chest fractured, the ache painful but thrilling. He poured the peroxide on the rag and pressed it to the abrasion, holding it in place while arresting her gaze and maybe...just maybe...cuffing her heart.

No. She couldn't let that happen. A few compliments didn't equal commitment. And even if it did, she'd been committed to and left before. By family. By her fiancé. She couldn't be crippled emotionally again.

"I have the clue," she said instead, snuffing out the flame that had been flickering between them. She pulled the slip of paper from her waistband.

"Where did you find it?" Rhode removed the rag and stood, rinsing it out and hanging it on the towel rack then examining his reflection—and the goose egg—in the mirror. They both needed an ice pack.

"In a stage prop wine bottle."

He frowned at his face in the mirror and she had a feeling he was beating himself up for being caught off guard. "What's it say?"

"'Oh, how I can make an entrance. I'm a showstopper, darling.'" Teegan frowned and turned the paper over. Blank. One line.

"Do you know what movie that's from?"

"Not off hand." Disappointment dropped heavy in her stomach. "Do you have your phone?"

He nodded.

"Can you Google it?"

Rhode pulled his phone from his pocket and googled the line. His lips turned downward. "Nothing."

Teegan sighed. She had hoped it would be as easy as the first clue.

Nothing was easy. Story of her life.

She wouldn't give up though. Teegan had never been a quitter. "I'll figure it out. I may have to sift through some of her movies."

"*We'll* figure it out. For now, let's wait on the forensic team and then try to sleep."

Rhode was right. There wasn't more she could do tonight. She'd fall dead asleep if she turned on a movie. Her limbs felt like lead and her brain was foggy. Teegan needed rest and pain relievers. The babies would wake and be full of energy regardless of her exhaustion and aching body.

But they'd found the clue. Lorna wanted them to find something greater.

What treasure could be as great as what Lorna had already left her?

Rhode's eyes cracked open when one of the babies cried through the monitor. Last night, after the forensic team had left, Rhode had taken the baby monitor from Teegan and persuaded her to hit the hay for uninterrupted sleep. He glanced at his cell phone. Way too early to be awake, but he rolled off the couch in the loft area and rubbed his eyes as he padded to the nursery. He hoped they'd be okay with seeing him and not their mama. They might not be timid around strangers but they were used to seeing their mama in the mornings. Not him.

He cracked open the door and Brook stood in the portable crib, her little hands wrapping over the top. River slept through her whimpers. When he was younger, Rhode could sleep through a bomb too. "Hi, baby girl," he whispered. "It's Daddy." He hoped Teegan didn't mind, but he was their father and he wanted them to know it. Brook shied away and a pang hit his gut. "It's okay, baby girl. Come on." Holding out his arms, he waited until she reached for him and allowed him to lift her from the crib. The act melted him into a puddle of slush. River slept soundly, his little chest rising and falling rhythmically.

Rhode grabbed a diaper and wipes then slipped from the room. In the loft, he laid her on the couch and changed her wet diaper then sat her on his lap. "You feel better now?"

She rubbed her sleepy eyes and grabbed at his hair.

"Yeah, we got a lot of it, kiddo." He kissed her forehead.

"Juice."

"Okay, princess, let's get you some juice." He was about to clip the monitor to his waist when he heard River.

"Ma-ma. Ma-ma!" No cries, just demands.

"Let's take bubba with us, okay?" He hurried into the room where River stood, banging a dinosaur on the crib. A fat grin filled his face when he saw Rhode and Brook.

"Hey, bud." He put Brook down and picked up River, taking him to the changing table. "I thought you were gonna sleep all day." He kissed his cheek and changed his diaper. "You want juice too?"

"Juice."

"I hear ya, bruh." He put him on his hip, snatching Brook back up, and carried them down the stairs. "Y'all are work. No wonder Mama is still asleep."

"Ma-ma," Brook said.

"I know you want Mama. She's going night-night." Once he arrived in the kitchen, he buckled them into high chairs and went to work hunting down sippy cups and pouring apple juice. "You hungry?"

"Hun-gy," Brook said as she accepted the cup.

Rhode pulled eggs and butter from the fridge and a loaf of bread off the counter for scrambled eggs and toast.

By the time River dumped his eggs and Brook had eaten most of her toast, Teegan entered the kitchen. "I can't believe I slept this late."

He held up the pan. "You hungry? I think I got a second round of eggs and toast in me."

She nodded and spoke to the babies, kissing heads that had eggs and toast smooshed in their hair. "Thank you." Her eyes pooled and Rhode laid the spatula on the counter and closed the distance between them.

"What's wrong?"

"I just... I haven't slept in for almost two years, and I'm overwhelmed at your kindness."

His heart cracked. How exhausting it must be to do this day in and out alone. Single moms deserved the world. Rhode had only managed wake-up time and breakfast, and he was whipped. He'd picked up sippy cups and baby forks ten-thousand times. "Well, I'm here now. You don't have to do this alone, and while you haven't said I can't be involved, you haven't made it clear that I can."

Teegan poured a cup of coffee and sipped. "Rhode, I want you to be in your children's lives if you want to be. And by that, I mean fully and wholeheartedly in their lives. No walking out when it's tough. No neglecting them. My dad walked out when we were little, and it was devastating. My mom was an alcoholic and I can't even begin to describe what that was like for us. They need stability and security. Can you provide that for them?"

His dry throat ached. He was a recovering alcoholic. He had no plans to return to the drink. But he imagined her mother had said the same things before falling prey to the false soothing effects liquor brought. If he admitted he had the same problem, Teegan would never allow him to be a part of the twins' lives. Yeah, he could take her to court, but she had a strong case and the funds to hire power attorneys who could tie him up in legal fees he'd never dig out from.

But she deserved to know the whole truth. And he would tell her. He would. Once she saw how great of a dad he could be.

"I won't tell you I'm some superhero, Teegan. I assure you, I have faults. I've made mistakes and I have a past I'm not proud of. But I want to be a full-time dad." He meant every single word.

"We all have a past. You know the things I'm not proud of. And if you want to be a father, I want you to be. They need one. I know what it's like to long for both parents. My dad walked out. My mom…she tried. She did. She'd get sober for a few months. Once, for a whole year, and I thought 'now things will be right.' She was present and active in our lives and then she lost her job due to budget cuts and it sent her into a tailspin. It was like she died after that, and it crushed me and Misty."

"I'm sorry," Rhode said. "Alcohol makes people act in ways they normally wouldn't."

"We both know that. I'm glad it was just a one-time mistake for us."

He swallowed hard. "But we have the babies and they're perfect."

She nodded and sipped her hot caffeine. "That, they are. Except for when they're being complete terrors." She laughed and put the coffee cup on the counter. "So what's the plan for today?"

"Well, Beau is still running down leads on Misty in California, and Dom is working the case here. I want to stay close to you—professionally, of course."

Her smile was tight. "Of course."

"But later this evening, we're putting up the tree. We used to do it on Christmas Eve, but the past two years we've done it early—the week before. And we open one gift each then watch *A Christmas Carol* and Sissy and Mama bake cookies. Us boys aren't allowed because we're terrible at it. It's pretty much a loud and obnoxious hoopla but it's our thing. I'd love for you and the twins to be there."

Teegan's eyes lit up. "I would love that, but I have no idea what to buy your family. I barely know them."

"No one will expect you to bring gifts, Teegan. But I have some shopping to do for the kiddos."

"Okay then. Later today, I need to watch some of Lorna's old movies and see if we can figure out which movie that last clue is from. I wonder how many clues there are."

"With Lorna, who knows?"

Teegan nodded. "If you're good with the babies, I'd like to walk down to the stables and talk to Harry. With last night's attack in the house, he needs to know to be careful."

"I don't know that it's a good idea."

"It's not even 8:00 a.m. I won't leave the property."

Rhode frowned. "I don't love it, but you're right. Unless... do you normally go for a walk this time of day?"

"Ha. I wish."

"Okay, then you have no routine he might know about. Take the pepper spray I gave you last night; it'll make me feel better. And maybe don't go in the labyrinth. Didn't work out well when Sissy did that." She'd been attacked by a serial killer stalking her. "How do you know Harry is down there?"

"He's like clockwork. Arrives 6:30 a.m. every single day except Sunday."

Rhode couldn't hold her hostage. "Be careful. I'm going to clean up these kiddos and get them dressed. I can't promise you they'll match, but they'll be clothed and in dry diapers."

"Fair enough."

She walked out the back door and Rhode's stomach pinched. Then he looked at the twins and groaned. Eggs, toast and sticky juice covered them from head to toe. Weren't sippy cups supposed to be spill-proof? He sighed and shook his head. "Y'all are the absolute messiest."

River clapped and Brook joined in as they giggled. No way he could be irritated at that. "It's going to take all day to clean you up, you rug rats."

His cell phone rang. Beau. He answered. "Hey, man. What's going on?"

"Have you had the news on this morning?"

"I haven't even had time to brush my teeth. I have twins. You just wait. In a few months, it'll be you."

"How did you know we were pregnant? We were waiting to tell everyone at Christmas. I mean we don't know how many babies there are." His voice carried, swelling pride and joy.

"I'm a twin. We have a sense about each other, and I *wish* two babies on you. It's awesome and scary and exhausting." He laughed and Beau chuckled. "Also, maybe don't tell Sissy you both are pregnant. She might be inclined to rip your head off."

Beau laughed. "Valid. I'm down with whatever. I'm actually pulling into the driveway. I wanted to share the news in person."

"I'm heading to let you in." Rhode hung up and unlocked the front door, welcoming Beau inside. He was dressed in his usual trendy jeans and a fitted sports coat over a white dress shirt. "Babies are in the kitchen, follow me."

When they entered the kitchen, the babies stopped banging their cups on the high chair trays long enough to see who was with Rhode.

"Dude, did you feed them or bathe them in their breakfast?"

"Both?" He shrugged and headed for the sink to wet a washcloth. "What news needs to be shared in person?"

"Where's Teegan?"

"Talking to Harry. With pepper spray and instructions not to go into the labyrinth."

"Yeah, I'd rather not go through that again." He shivered. "So… I found out a woman was murdered two days ago in Austin. Adeline James. Stabbed to death. Dom called the detective working the case. She's the same age as Teegan and they went to the same high school, but that could be coincidence. What's not a coincidence is bluebonnets left in a pool of blood, just like with Misty."

Rhode's stomach knotted. "Have you looked into the family members individually?" He scraped the food from the trays and wiped them down.

"Yeah. I found a photo of one of Lorna's great-grandchildren with our victim. It was taken about three months ago."

"Charlie?" Rhode asked.

"No. Peter."

Hmm. "Anything else?"

"Yep." Beau shot him a sheepish grin. "I sometimes have insomnia so what else am I gonna do but work?"

"I hear ya."

"Peter dated Adeline for about eight months and, according to Adeline's roommate—who happens to be a night owl—she was the one who broke things off. She said Adeline wasn't feeling it anymore. The spark was gone."

"She say how he took it?" Rhode took a fresh rag and went to work cleaning Brook.

"Not well. According to the friend, he called her repeatedly and sent a bouquet of bluebonnets to her work."

Teegan never mentioned dating Peter or being sent flowers by him. Was there a connection? "Keep digging and let me know what turns up. I want to go with you when you talk to Peter Landoon, but I also don't want to leave Teegan alone."

"Understood." Beau stared at the babies. "If the dogs were here, they'd lick them clean. Save you some time too."

"I don't see Teegan loving that idea."

"They'd be like Roombas for messy babies. Plus, I read that dogs' tongues are cleaner than humans'."

"Why are you reading about dog tongues?"

"Insomnia?"

Rhode sniffed. "Hey…do you smell that?"

Beau inhaled. "Maybe the gardener is burning leaves."

"No one is here but Harry Doyle." He frowned and walked to the kitchen door. A plume of smoke billowed. "Beau! I think the stables may be on fire."

Teegan was out there. Rhode knew it had been a bad idea and kicked himself for allowing it.

"Go! I'll call 9-1-1, and I got the babies. Go!"

Chapter Seven

Teegan rounded the second set of stables. The horses always calmed her. They were sleek and beautiful. She inhaled the scent of leather and hay, but it was mixed with smoke. She hadn't seen Harry out there yet, and he would never light something on fire with the horses nearby and dry hay that would catch quickly and spread.

As she turned, fire crackled along the roof of the stable. She opened her mouth to scream for Harry, but a gloved hand clamped her lips closed. The faint smell of cigarettes attacked her senses. Using her elbow, she rammed the man holding her hostage in the ribs and his grip released. She sprinted toward the house, refusing to look back.

Horses ran along beside her, pushing ahead as the fire had spooked them. Had Harry let them out this early? He didn't usually. Had someone else?

Where was Harry?

Footsteps pounding on hard-packed earth let her know she needed to pick up speed. She'd never been much into exercising, and running was for crazy people, but she wished she had more cardio in her life right now. Her chin wobbled as she sped up and her legs protested by burning and threatening to buckle, but she raced for the gardens, weaving through the rows of flower beds, pots of gorgeous blooms and the fountain with benches surrounding it. She shot into the labyrinth.

The one place Rhode had told her not to go.

But she knew it well and walked it often. Taking rights was the key, but since she was moving into it backward, she needed to make lefts. Without thought, she raced down one concrete-laden aisle flanked by massive, perfectly manicured box hedges that stood nearly ten feet tall.

Teegan's heart beat out of her tight chest.

"Teegan!"

Rhode. Rhode must have seen the fire from the house. She called back and hoped he'd played Marco Polo as a child. She couldn't give away her exact location, yet hollering would also give her position away to her assailant.

She turned the corner. Footsteps pounded the ground and she pushed her back flush against the hedges as a dark figure ran past her. She prayed he wouldn't backtrack and find her. After waiting a few seconds, she continued through the labyrinth. All she had to do was reach the beginning and she'd be out. If her attacker hadn't returned the way he'd come, he'd end up stuck.

Darting a glance behind her, all was clear. She pivoted and smacked into a chest, yelping.

"It's me. It's me. Are you hurt? Did you see who did it?" Rhode asked.

Siren peals echoed in the distance. Her lungs begged for breath. She nodded. "He's in here. Ran right by me."

Rhode started in the direction she pointed but she grabbed his arm. "Unless you know this puzzle, it's a death trap. You could get lost or blindsided. Or he could find his way out and you'll end up stuck."

"Not my first time in this thing, Teegan. I really wanted that treasure."

Suddenly it dawned on her. Rhode was out here with her.

"Where are the babies?" Panic pushed her words out in short pants.

"They're okay. Beau came by and is inside with them. He called the police." He took her hand. "Let's get out of here."

They returned to the kitchen where police officers—including Rhode's cousin, Dom—stood talking with Beau. Firefighters had used the side road to the stables.

"Harry." Teegan gulped in air. "I didn't see Harry. I'm worried something bad happened."

"Don't worry. We'll find him," Dom said.

Rhode led Teegan into Lorna's sitting room where the babies were being chased by Beau, his expression frazzled.

Her heartbeat slowed and peace washed over her seeing her kiddos safe and having fun amid the danger lurking outside. Danger that had almost been her ending.

"Hey," Rhode said and Beau turned.

"These kids are going to win awards in track. I'm telling you now." Beau chuckled as River and Brook ran for Teegan.

Teegan scooped them up, one in each arm. Who needed the gym and weight training when one had twins?

"Did you find him?" Beau asked.

"No." Rhode huffed. "If he's on the property, they will though. The question is why set the stables on fire?"

"I own them now," Teegan said. "Any one of the Landoons might have. They let the horses out. They didn't want them hurt. I don't know if the fire was meant to lure me out or I was in the wrong place at the wrong time."

"It's possible they were burning them down to discourage you. And then when you showed, it was convenient to take it a step further. We need to find out what happens to the estate if you die."

"She had no clause, Rhode. Nothing stating it reverts back. I need a will drawn up immediately."

Rhode agreed.

What was she supposed to do to keep her children safe?

Lorna's estate didn't feel safe at all. And the security system wasn't being installed until Monday.

"Did you know an Adeline James?" Rhode asked.

Teegan frowned. Why was he bringing up an old school friend? "Yeah, but we lost track of each other a few years ago. You know how it is when lives change and people move. Last I heard she was in Dallas. Why?"

"Because she was killed and bluebonnets were left at the scene," Rhode said.

"And she dated Peter Landoon," Beau added. "What can you tell us about him?"

Peter? Peter dated Addie? This was new information.

What did it mean?

The babies squirmed to break free and she set them down. They bolted into the living room, chasing each other and giggling before River found his little bike and climbed on. Brook got on behind him and they started scooting across the floor. She was glad to have thought to bring a few of their toys to keep them busy. The rest were back at the ranch. Lorna had always gotten such a kick out the kids. Never minding their toys and the sometimes clutter.

"I didn't know about them. I don't see Peter often, but he's always been kind. You think Peter killed Addie, Lorna and my sister?"

Rhode flushed against the wall, as the kids zoomed by nearly taking out his legs. "I don't know. But the flowers left at both crime scenes and the fact they'd both been stabbed multiple times tells me it's connected. I'm unsure of Lorna. It's possible that Misty and Addie's killer couldn't bring himself to stab Lorna. He might have been too personally connected to her, as in family."

"So there's no chance Misty walked in and saw something and was killed for simply being in the house."

"I think so," Rhode said. "I'm just not sure if the killer targeted her thinking it was you or knew it was Misty."

"Or we could be missing something," Beau added, dodging the little plastic bike. "Now we have track runners and NAS-CAR drivers. These kids!" He laughed. "I'll keep digging."

"What should I be doing?" Other than trying to stay alive.

"Maybe Lorna's treasure hunt will turn up something vital to the investigation. Work that movie line and see if you can find the next location."

"There's a legit treasure?" Beau asked, his blue eyes brightening. "I thought that was a rumor."

"It's not," Teegan said. "We have no idea what it is, but it's obvious Lorna wanted me to find it. She left the first clue in a private letter to me."

The question was what would Lorna have known long ago when she hid the treasure that would be relevant to the case now? Teegan wasn't sure they linked, but it did give her something to do to keep her mind off the fact she was being hunted down by a savage killer and that her children might be in danger.

And where was Harry Doyle?

The rest of the morning had been a whirlwind of activity. Rhode had met with Dom to get updates and he'd help him pick up Teegan's car, which had been repainted. He didn't go to the Cedar Springs PD much anymore—not so much due to being ostracized but out of shame.

Rhode had made amends to the people he loved and to colleagues, but he could never make up for the pain he'd caused, the disappointment and the money it had cost those he loved most. He would forever be in debt to Beau, who had paid for his rehab, and to his family for never giving up on him. For the intervention and the tough love.

But for the pain he'd inflicted on his mama—that was one he would never forgive himself for. She'd aged years during his spiral, worrying over him, and he imagined she had calluses and rug burn on her knees from the hours of devotions on his behalf. He'd never again take for granted a praying mama. Her persevering prayers and her stubborn head to not give up had been answered. He had no way to pay her back except to live in the way he knew a man of faith should live and to be the kind of father who brought his own children before the Lord on a daily basis. He'd be proud of rug burn and calluses formed in bowing before God and making intercession.

After lunch, the babies napped and Teegan watched several old movies—and googled a few to help speed up the time. While she did that, Rhode's brothers and Beau came by to discuss the case. Harry Doyle hadn't been at work this morning like usual. He said he'd felt ill and slept in. Rhode thought that sounded too convenient, but Harry had nothing to gain by setting fire to the stables. He had a job no matter who ran the business.

Initially, they believed one of the Landoon family members had known—or suspected—Lorna was going to amend her will and killed her. Stone said Lorna's fall appeared to be accidental, but everyone knew she never went upstairs. They were considering the possibility that someone had hit her on the head, carried her upstairs then thrown her down the stairs, staging it. Misty, who had arrived to surprise her sister, had entered the house and seen the display. She'd been collateral damage.

The other possibility was that the will had already been changed, and Misty had been killed under the assumption she'd been Teegan. The killer couldn't have thrown them both down the stairs. It would point back to the will.

But stabbings were personal.

One had to get up close, look their victim in the eye, and the number of stab wounds—over seventeen, not counting self-defense wounds on her hands and forearms—indicated rage. Very personal rage. That made sense if a family member believed Teegan was gold-digging or going to be left the estate, businesses and all the money.

Any one of the Landoons had motive and opportunity. They all had access to the house. Lorna was lax on security. But another victim who Teegan knew personally had been stabbed multiple times and Texas bluebonnets left behind at the scene.

That didn't feel like it tied to Lorna leaving the estate to Teegan.

Peter Landoon was connected to Addie and Teegan. Could Addie have known something and her death had been to shut her up? Had Peter assumed Addie and Teegan were still friends? Would he have even known they'd been friends? Rhode wanted to know more about Addie and how she tied to Teegan. For the past hour, he'd been researching everything he could on Adeline James.

She and Teegan had attended high school together. He'd found an online yearbook with several photos of them together with two other girls. They'd belonged to the Beta club and a scholastic bowl team. Only Teegan hadn't been a cheerleader. But Misty had. Misty, however, wasn't in the same photos with Teegan and her friends. In fact, he'd only found a handful of photos of Misty and two had been with Teegan. The others were of Misty with a rougher crowd of teenagers. Rhode wasn't one to stereotype, but stereotypes were stereotypes for a reason.

Addie had worked as a receptionist at a dental office near Austin after moving from Dallas recently. She had a roommate, whom Beau had talked to earlier, and he was going to talk to her coworkers as well. Teegan said that she'd lost touch with most of her friends from school. They'd gone off to college and run around, having a good time, but she'd worked two jobs and had had to grow up fast. She hadn't had time to waste and she hadn't had the money to throw away on concerts, habitual takeout and movies.

"Hey," Teegan said as she entered the upstairs sitting room. He'd been working in the loft area while the babies napped in the nursery. "I found it."

"The next clue?"

"Yep. It's from the 1957 film *Make a Splash* about a starlet whose last film tanks and she's humiliated and hides out on a small farm in Upstate New York while figuring out what to do with her life. I think the clue is hidden in the swimming pool drain."

The swimming pool drain? How would anyone put paper in a wet drain? "Are you sure?"

"I'm ninety-nine-percent certain. She says, 'Oh, how I can make an entrance. I'm a showstopper, darling.' Then she dives into the pool and, when she comes up, her manager hands her a towel and tells her that her movie didn't go over, and there won't be a sequel. It sets the course of the rest of the movie. It's really good. She entered the pool, and the word *stopper* makes me think of a bathtub stopper—or a drain plug."

Teegan's guess wasn't out of the realm of possibility. "Do you think Lorna did it herself? Back in the day?"

"I do. She was an avid swimmer, which is part of the reason they gave her the part. She could easily have put on scuba gear, waterproofed it, and then shoved it inside."

"What if the pool needed maintenance? It could be found."

"If she had issues with the drain. They don't drain a pool to put in new liners. It's worth the swim to find out. The pool is heated."

"I'll call Bridge. He's the scuba dude and he's already combed her stupid lake already. This will give him new satisfaction that his diving wasn't fully in vain." Rhode chuckled. Bridge would be all over this.

"Okay, but we should wait until evening when no one is around. Bridge scuba diving will call attention. I don't know where loyalties lie. I know I kept everyone on and they're thankful, but several employees adore Evangeline and especially Charlie—down at the stables." Teegan sighed and pointed at the nursery. "They were super tired. They'll be much easier to manage tonight at your ranch. Don't get me wrong, they'll be buck-wild but less temper tantrums."

Rhode grinned. "My mom raised a rowdy bunch of boys. We can handle feisty twins."

"You say that now."

The entire family was inside and as they entered with the babies, the Christmas "Chipmunk Song" played and he cocked his head. "Last Christmas, this song didn't pan out well with us."

His remark about their fun brotherly wrestling match last year sent laughter through the home. It was warm and cozy; the fireplace going, though it wasn't truly cold enough. Sissy caught his eye and grinned. "Bridge turned on the air-conditioning so we wouldn't burn up from the fireplace heat. He said it would balance out. Stone grumbled over electric bills."

"Sounds about right."

Teegan had Brook, and his mother and Emily were going nuts over her. Sissy snatched River from Rhode. "You going to announce your big news?" So much for letting Sissy pretend to at least surprise him.

"I should have known you knew. You havin' sympathy pains? Urinating more often? Feeling nauseous?" Sissy held River's little hand and kissed it.

"No, but I often felt that way when I was on the sauce, which…can we not bring up my issues with Teegan? I haven't told her. Hasn't been the right time." Rhode wasn't sure if it would ever be the right time. Fear had built a big, impenetrable wall between his mouth and Teegan.

"I didn't expect to be all, 'Have a holly, jolly Christmas and, oh, by the way, Rhode's a recovering alcoholic.'" She snorted then froze.

Rhode's hairs along his arm prickled and he slowly pivoted. Standing directly behind him was Teegan.

Chapter Eight

Teegan must have heard wrong. It was a joke pertaining to their one night in Dallas. "Is that true?" she whispered, her throat and chest tight.

Rhode glanced at Sissy and her eyes pulsed with apology. It must be true. Rhode returned his attention to Teegan, his neck red as a lobster. "Can we talk?"

What was there to say? He was an alcoholic. Her body shook and turned cold. She was going to have a panic attack at any moment.

"Hey," Sissy said, "you don't look well. Come outside on the back porch and sit down. I'll bring you some water." She whistled and her dogs came running, following them outside. Sissy guided Teegan by her elbow and eased her into the chair. "Lady, up."

Lady jumped into Teegan's lap.

"Just stroke her and take deep breaths. I'm going to grab that glass of water." She rushed from the deck and Teegan obeyed her instructions to breathe deeply as she petted the dog. Lady curled up in her lap and laid her head on Teegan's chest; her warmth radiated through Teegan's long-sleeved T-shirt. A smidge of tightness in her chest loosened, but this was shocking news that changed everything. He'd said he had a past and made mistakes, but this was different. This was... this was just like Mom.

Rhode stood cemented to the porch, licking his bottom lip, his fists clenched at his sides. Sissy returned with the water and knelt.

"Drink this. Little sips. Deep breaths in between."

Teegan sipped the water, the cool liquid satiating the burning fire in her throat.

"Better?"

"Some."

Sissy glanced up at her brother. "I'm going to leave you two alone." She squeezed his biceps and hurried inside.

"That's not how I wanted this to go down." Rhode tiptoed toward her.

Teegan gripped the glass tighter as memories surfaced. Mom forgetting them at school. Promising she'd stop. Getting sober and relapsing. No Christmas smells like here at the ranch: cinnamon, cloves and orange. No presents. No coming to games to see Misty cheer. All the fear, disappointment, anger and guilt resurfaced. She couldn't let her children go through those same agonies. This must be her punishment from God for her mistake. For picking up a hot guy at a bar after being drunk when she'd promised herself she never would touch a drop.

She might deserve this, but her twins did not.

"How exactly did you want it to go down? Why did you lie to me? You're a drunk *and* a liar?" The words shot out cold and sharp. Sharper than she'd intended, but fury bubbled to the surface. Not only at Rhode, but anger at herself and at her mother. The news had stoked the already simmering rage.

Rhode's lips pursed and his cheek pulsed. "I didn't lie. And I'm not a drunk. But I was. The day after our rendezvous, my brothers found me and I went straight to rehab. I haven't had a drop in over two years. Since that night. And you asked if I'd drank since then. I said no. That's not a lie."

"But you hid it from me! You know how I felt. I was up-front." She held Lady closer to her chest. "I can't let my children repeat my history. I won't."

"So now they're your children. The past couple of days, they've been ours." His own tone was sharp but not cold. It sizzled in red heat. "I wish I could go back and never have tasted a drop of liquor. But I did. I had no clue it was going to dig its claws into me and keep a hold until I lost everything. And I have. Lost everything. I regret it every single day." He pinched the bridge of his nose. "I planned to tell you, but it hasn't been the right time. I wanted you to know the real me so you could see I'm not who I once was, and I was afraid to tell you for fear you wouldn't let me see *our* babies."

"I'm not sure I'm going to." She placed the glass on the table next to the outdoor chair and stood, keeping Lady in her arms for support and warmth. Everything else about this moment was icy and empty. Could she take a chance and believe him? Her mom had held out for quite a long time, too, but in the end, she'd given in. How could she be sure Rhode wouldn't fall into the trap again? "Do you have cravings?"

He glanced away.

The cellar. The smell of the wine. "You didn't have claustrophobia, did you? You lied because the wine was enticing."

Rhode raked a hand through his hair, his longer bangs hanging in his eyes. "I didn't lie. The room was closing in on me, but, yes...it was because of the ache. The scent of the wine."

"Then you battle it still. You still want to drink."

Rhode's eyes shone. "Sometimes," he mumbled.

Teegan drew in a deep breath. Rhode was undeniably ashamed, but so had her mother been when she'd been sober. Maybe that's why she'd gone back to the bottle. Being numb was easier than carrying the pain of hurting loved ones. But that was a selfish move to play. "I think you're a decent person, Rhode. I do."

His eyes held hers, pleading. "I didn't drink any wine. I literally ran away."

"And can you honestly say you'll run every time?"

Rhode ran his tongue along his lower lip. "I hope so."

Hope wasn't enough for Teegan. "I need to be alone." She put Lady down and the dog trotted to the back door to be let inside. "I need to think."

She clambered off the back deck, putting space between them, and strode toward the barn. This was too much for her to even understand. She honestly blamed herself. If she hadn't made a terrible choice, she wouldn't be dealing with this. But then, she also wouldn't have the twins, and while the way they'd been conceived wasn't ideal, she didn't regret the babies. They were the most precious things in the world to her. A gift of God's mercy and grace, even in the jacked-up times. Teegan was thinking of the babies now.

Rhode wanted to be in their lives and might be great for a time. But what happened if he succumbed and spiraled? The babies would suffer. And they wouldn't understand why.

Teegan hadn't. When her mom was sober, she was amazing and, when she wasn't, she was neglectful and distant. Teegan always believed she hadn't met the standard of good enough for her mother. So she'd tried to be as good as she possibly could be in hopes Mom would come out of her room and love her. She'd kept the house spotless and the dishes done. Worked extra hard on her grades and joined academic clubs instead of sports. But the truth was it wouldn't matter how clean the house was or how great her grades had been.

Time passed, and she'd never measured up, which had led to crippling insecurity and the fight against becoming a people-pleaser. In college, a Christian psychology professor had spoken about insecurities and their consequences. Teegan had finally realized the problem hadn't been her, but her mother. Mom's disease had controlled her and no one but God had the power to help her fight it for good. Yet Teegan had spent all those years believing she could make her mother better. Make her love her.

But Rhode was a man of a faith—she didn't doubt that. And yet he couldn't even stay in a cellar without fearing he'd give in. He wasn't free; he was biding time. Teegan should extend him grace, but what if that grace opened the door for her children's pain? Teegan needed to shield them and protect them. What was she going to do?

She slunk onto a bale of hay outside the big red barn. Inside, horses pawed at stall doors and rustled the straw. The wind picked up and rattled the doors. How was she supposed to go back inside and pretend nothing happened? How was she going to bake cookies and watch movies and let her babies attach to this family—to their father—now knowing this enlightening information? The knowledge sent a ripple of confusion and disappointment through her. Teegan wasn't sure what she was hoping for. Nothing concerning them as a couple, but at least a committed and entirely involved dad.

She'd received a massive amount of money. An equally massive estate and a successful business in the blink of an eye and yet she felt more hollow and alone than she ever had before. No amount of money could fix this. Or the fact a killer was... She paused.

The hairs along her arms spiked as she immediately realized a presence. Teegan jumped to her feet as someone rushed her, knocking her to the cold, hard ground.

Her eyes widened under the moonlight as the jester's mask came into full view. The white mask he wore contrasted with the dark hoodie.

"I'm going to get the last laugh," he said through a raspy

voice as he brought up the large butcher knife, the blade glinting under the pale light.

She screamed and grabbed his forearm, trying to hold off the sharp blade, but he was strong. Unimaginably strong for her petite strength to match. A crack of gunfire erupted, giving the jester pause. Another shot fired and Rhode hollered her name.

The jester jumped to his feet and pointed the knife at her. "This isn't over." He hurled an insult and darted into the darkness.

Where he belonged.

Teegan sprang to her feet, her stomach in a tangle of knots and sweat slicking down her temples as she darted toward the sound of Rhode's voice. She ran straight into him and shrieked.

"It's okay. It's me. You're safe."

His brothers flew by them. "Which way?" Bridge hollered, gripping his gun in his right hand.

"Behind the barn," Teegan said.

Bridge didn't slow and, like lightning, he vanished into the night.

Stone veered left, to hedge the other side.

Rhode cupped her face. "The babies are safe. Emily and Beau are inside to make sure everyone indoors is protected. Did he hurt you again?"

Teegan rubbed her head where it had smacked the solid earth as she'd fallen. Her hip smarted but, overall, she was in working order. "No. He came out of nowhere. How did he know we were here?"

Rhode released a long, heavy breath as he led her to the house. "He's watching, Teegan. He's watching."

Leading Teegan into the house, Rhode scanned the perimeter. All was quiet. Too quiet, and he sent up a silent prayer for his brothers' safety. This killer had a particular brand of weapon—a knife. But that didn't mean he wasn't also carrying a gun.

Seeing Teegan shake, he longed to hug her and protect her, but he didn't want to upset her further. She no longer trusted him—at least concerning their children—and Rhode understood.

She wasn't being ridiculous, over-the-top or excessively cautious. Teegan had endured the destructive consequences of alcoholism. While she hadn't revealed every detail of her childhood, she'd offered enough for him to feel the full impact it had seared into her soul.

Rhode wasn't naïve. Although he was now sober and relying on God, he had seen many men in rehab who had returned to the bottle when things grew difficult. Rhode kept his guard up on the daily, reminding himself he wasn't over it. The war still raged, and every day was a battle he had to trust God for. He completely understood Teegan's fear and hesitation.

He had no way of convincing her he wasn't like her mother. Because he knew how dark a path the drink had taken him on, the changes it had made, the man he'd become and hated but couldn't shake. Could he look her in the eye with utter confidence and tell her he would never succumb to temptation? No. He hoped. He prayed. But he wasn't arrogant enough to stake their children's lives on it. She'd been right. He couldn't even handle a wine cellar and wine had never been his drink of choice.

Rhode opened the kitchen door and Teegan went straight to the table. He grabbed a glass from the cabinet and flipped the water on, filling it to the brim, then he handed it to her. "Drink this."

Her hands trembled, and the water sloshed over the top of the glass, splashing onto the old farm table. "He said, 'This isn't over' and that he was going to get the last laugh. I think that's what he said before I passed out the last time too. What does that mean? The last laugh."

Rhode shook his head. "I don't know. Maybe, in his twisted mind, he believes you think receiving all of Lorna's fortune is some kind of joke or that you're laughing at the family. Maybe he thinks you've known all along you'd be receiving the inheritance—that you convinced Lorna through a long con to give up her money to you. It happens all the time, sadly."

"But Misty died before they read the will."

"We need to contact the attorneys and find out if any of the family members had recently inquired about the will. They could have persuaded the attorney to share the information."

Teegan sipped her water. "No one is above attempting a bribe in the Landoon family. If someone from the firm—not necessarily Lorna's personal attorneys—needed some money or wanted it, they might cough it up. I don't know how many attorneys are in the firm."

"We can find out." Rhode glanced up and Emily peered around the corner, her fiery red hair hanging around her shoulders, her brown eyes meeting his. He shook his head and she nodded. He noticed the gun in her hand. She'd steered Mama, Sissy and the babies into the living room. Beau must have gone out the front door. Rhode didn't see him and he couldn't hear his voice. Only the sounds of the Whos in Whoville singing "Welcome Christmas" and Sissy and Mama's voices accompanying the animated families.

But this wasn't the Grinch attempting to steal Christmas. This was a brutal killer bent on stealing the mother of his children. Rhode had to stop him. He would stop him.

"Are the children safe anywhere, Rhode? Am I?" Teegan pushed the glass away and covered her face with her hands. Her shoulders shook as she cried. But Rhode didn't offer physical comfort. He was unsure how to approach her now. Was he a friend or foe? Would she use all that new money to make sure he had no rights to his children? His past could easily be used against him. Her accusations of his sins would be right.

She could take them to a judge and declare him guilty, stringing his past transgressions like a litany of his life.

Neglect of his family.

Neglect on the job.

Blundering a homicide investigation and allowing a killer to go free.

A one-night stand he couldn't even remember, and not just with Teegan. His past wasn't splotchy—it was stained and smeared red. Rhode didn't have a leg to stand on. He wouldn't be able to deny he'd missed the mark frequently.

He might lose his children before he ever began to truly know them.

And he could not blame Teegan for her actions. He might have done the same thing if he were in her place. For now, he had to focus on protecting her and catching this jester.

The back door opened and Stone entered first, a scowl along his brow. Bridge entered next and shook his head.

The jester had slipped them. Again.

"How you doing, Miss Albright?" Stone asked and rested his meaty palm on her shoulder.

She raised her head, tears streaking her dirty cheeks. "Not well, if I'm being honest. I'm working to be brave, but I'm not."

Rhode begged to differ. Teegan was the bravest woman he'd ever met. Resilient and determined. She had grit. She plainly didn't see it or believe it about herself.

"We'll keep working," Stone said.

Beau entered from the family room. "Nothing out front and no cars parked along the roads. He must have parked in field grass."

Mama entered the kitchen just then. Her jet-black hair—popped with a few silver strands—pulled back in a tight bun like her expression. "Teegan, sweetheart." She sat beside her, pulled her close then wrapped motherly arms around her.

Teegan crumpled against her and cried, letting it all out while Mama stroked her long blond hair.

"It's okay, baby girl. You just cry it out," Mama whispered and prayed over her. Rhode wanted to be the one to soothe her, but it was his fault she'd even been outside in the first place. And then it dawned: she'd probably never had a mother's comfort and his mama was nothing if not a nurturer.

Stone, Bridge and Beau slipped into the family room, and Sissy clapped. "Yay. Christmas was saved. Say yay!"

The children clapped and hollered, "Yay!"

Rhode was intruding. He, too, exited the kitchen and entered the family room. The twins looked up and grinned, and Brook ran right for him. "Ho me."

He scooped her up, his heart growing like the Grinch's. His love for the babies burst from his chest. "Did you watch the Grinch?" He kissed her tiny brow and held her close. She didn't flinch or pull away. Rhode had Brook's trust. He wanted Teegan's too. He had no way to know how to garner it though.

"Why don't we watch *Frosty the Snowman* while we wait for Mama and Teegan?" Sissy said. Emily agreed and pressed the remote to stream the old cartoon. River busied himself banging the coaster on the already-nicked coffee table. He and his brothers had wrecked all of Mama's furniture growing up. Banging, clanging and jumping from anything solid as they'd played superheroes or cowboys.

Rhode settled in the overstuffed chair. Brook nestled on his lap. But his thoughts weren't on the snowman come to life. They were on the woman in the kitchen who needed a superhero.

And Rhode was the furthest thing from a superhero.

Chapter Nine

"Dude, this is awesome. Also, what's my cut of the treasure for diving and retrieving it?" Bridge asked. "I feel a big Christmas gift coming on."

Rhode glanced at Teegan as they stood by the Olympic-size swimming pool outside Lorna's home. In the past few years, the pool area had undergone an upgrade that replaced concrete with stone and added bright blue lounge chairs. The space now resembled a community center rather than a family gathering spot.

For the holiday, they'd strung white twinkling lights and changed the lounge cushions and towels to red and green since a heated pool meant swimming all year round.

Bridge sat with his back to the water, scuba gear secured. He was ready to find the clue from the 1957 film *Make a Splash*. When Rhode had told him that the treasure was real, Bridge had turned back into that seventeen-year-old diving in Lorna's lake to discover riches untold. It had been almost three years since he'd seen Bridge's eyes light up like this. He'd been a shell of himself since the Christmas night Wendy, his former fiancée, had written him a note that she was leaving and not to come looking for her. He'd left the FBI around the same time and joined the family business with Stone.

None of the family had ever asked questions. If Bridge wanted them to know the details of his murky past, he would have told them. That's who Bridge was.

After last night's debacle, Teegan hadn't broken all ties. She wanted Rhode to handle the case. As far as their personal relationship, she wasn't rude, but the warmth growing between them had turned lukewarm. He hadn't brought up his role in the twins' lives. Teegan needed space and Rhode could give her that. He'd give her whatever she needed to make the right decision.

Rhode wanted to be a father.

"You get no cut of the treasure. This is something you do out the goodness of your heart," Rhode said.

Bridge adjusted his scuba mask. "That blows." He shoved the breathing apparatus into his mouth and entered the water as they watched him dive to the bottom of the ten-foot pool. The sun had set over an hour ago, and the employees had left the premises. Rhode didn't want curious eyes roaming and spilling the tea to the Landoon family that a treasure was real and they had been given clues. Teegan already had a massive target on her back. No need making it even larger.

Most of the day, he'd read files and kept in touch with Beau, who had been leading the case, and then he'd taken Teegan with him to shop for the twins. He'd purchased them a double-side car for outside and she said they'd love it—after he'd insisted he was buying them Christmas gifts no matter what. After, he'd helped her wrap presents—again at his insistence—and they'd had lunch at the ranch and he'd rocked the babies to sleep for their nap.

The water rippled and the lights of the pool cast shadows over Bridge, but he'd reached the drain. "I hope I'm right about this," Teegan said.

"I'm sure you are. It makes sense."

Awkward tension built, swirling like a winter breeze between them as they waited on Bridge.

Several minutes eked by.

"I think he has something." Teegan leaned over the pool, gawking below, and it appeared Bridge did have something. It evoked the image of the money tubes used by banks, but it was shorter, slenderer, and completely black like rubber.

Waterproof.

Bridge resurfaced and held it high, removing his breathing apparatus and grinning. "Victory!"

Rhode and Teegan laughed. Bridge swam to the side of the pool and handed Teegan the tube. "Figure you should do the honors. Can I stay and hear the next clue?"

Teegan chuckled. "Of course."

Bridge emerged from the water, took off his gear and eagerly waited next to Rhode.

Teegan opened the rubbery tube and inside a waterproof vial was a rolled-up slip of paper. She removed the clue, opened it, then read its contents. "'I can be myself when you're around. I can admit to the darkness that lurks in my mind and know you won't judge me for it. Oh, how I long to clear the cobwebs, step on the cockroaches of my stained past and tunnel my way to the light. Won't you help me find the light? I'm innocent.'"

Bridge scratched his head. "What in the world?"

Rhode stood, stumped. "Do you know what this quote is from? Which movie?"

Teegan's lips swerved to the left and she read it silently. "'I'm innocent.'" Her eyes looked out into nothing. Rhode wished Teegan would find him innocent, not judge his stained past. But that seemed impossible.

Teegan tapped her index finger against her chin. "She was in a film where she played an heiress accused of murdering her husband. I only remember that because she starred opposite Paul Newman. She has quite a lot of fond stories about him. He played a detective she fell in love with, but she murdered her husband and was manipulating the detective to believe in her innocence. I can't remember the title."

Rhode wasn't manipulating her to be in his children's lives. He swiped his phone from his back pocket and googled Lorna Landoon and Paul Newman. Several sites appeared. "*D is for Deception.*"

"Yes." Teegan snapped and pointed at him. "That's right. But where is she talking about?"

"A garage maybe?" Rhode shrugged. "Cockroaches. Cobwebs. Dark. Or a basement. Is there a basement, or could it be the wine cellar again?"

Teegan frowned. "No. Lorna would be more creative. She wouldn't even drink the same blend of tea each afternoon. It wouldn't be the wine cellar."

"Tunneling to light sounds underground," Bridge offered with a boyish grin on his stubbly face.

"It does." Rhode scratched his temple then massaged it. He had a major headache threatening to burst through and his throat began the all-too-knowing dry ache. How many times had a small drink eased the thumping behind his eye or the tight muscles in his neck causing tension headaches? How many times had one little drink turned into an entire bottle or two and hours of blackness because he'd passed out?

More than he could count. He swallowed hard and reached into his pants' pocket, retrieving a stick of gum. Something to do, something to swallow.

Teegan eyed him and he caught the slight flash of judgment in her baby blues. But maybe it was his own paranoia.

"I'll keep thinking, and I might even find blueprints to the house in Lorna's office. She designed this entire estate, including the labyrinth. She was a savvy woman." Her eyes filled with moisture, but Rhode kept his hands, which wanted to reach out for her, down at his sides, balled in fists.

Bridge checked his waterproof smartwatch and frowned. "She was definitely a cool lady. Look, I'd love to stick around, but Stone and I have to go to a recovery site. He just texted the scene is clear. Sissy's already there with the mother."

The young boy had died of suicide after being bullied online. His mother had heard the gunfire but was too late to intervene. Rhode inwardly cringed at the tragedy. He needed to stay on this case and keep the mother of his children protected.

"We'll keep you posted," Rhode said as Bridge carried his gear to his car.

"Should we search?" Rhode asked just as his phone rang. "It's Beau." He answered. "Hey, is this about Teegan's case? If so, I'm going to put us on speaker."

"Cool. It is," Beau said.

Rhode pressed the speaker button. "Okay, go."

"I told you about that boyfriend of Misty's that was trouble. Well, it's not him."

"How do you know?" Rhode asked.

"Because the Cedar Springs police found him an hour ago in the woods behind Lorna's estate. He's dead."

"Dead?" Teegan said and pressed her hand against her mouth. "Kenny Lee? Isn't that the name of the guy?"

"Yes," Beau said. "He was stabbed in the woods and left there, likely on the same day your sister was killed."

"So it wasn't a murder-suicide. Not if he has multiple stab wounds, right?"

"He didn't. It was one cut to the carotid. He followed her, killed her, and then went into the woods and slit his own throat. It's been done before in this manner. Dom said he'll know more once the autopsy is completed, but he's not ruling that out."

Teegan shuddered. "But it's not him. Someone is still coming after me and with a big fat knife."

A heavy sigh filtered through the line. "Yeah, I have a theory about that. Let's say Kenny Lee followed Misty to Texas. He killed her. Then he ran. You said you saw Charlie Landoon pass you. What if Charlie was in the house and witnessed Kenny kill her? He could have followed Kenny into the woods, stolen the knife, killed him and is using it now. For all he knows, no one will ever find Kenny's body. With Kenny's prints on the knife, it would lead to him."

But they had found the body, so the potential jig was up.

"They're keeping it out of the news, but the media will only allow it so long," Beau added. "If Charlie—or someone else in the family—is doing it, they don't know Kenny has been found. Yet."

Rhode rubbed his temples again. "Did they find bluebonnets near him? And why would Kenny or Charlie kill Addie James?"

"Maybe it wasn't Charlie. Maybe some other Landoon, like Peter, had been at the house. Charlie is the only car and person you saw, Teegan. But that doesn't mean he was the only one there."

Teegan's mind spun. There were numerous variables. The suspects endless. The motive unclear. "Have the police talked to Peter?"

Beau cleared his throat. "Apparently, Peter is out of the country on business."

"Then he can't be the person after me."

Rhode's expression seemed a cross between apology and disbelief, looking at her like Rachel looked at Joey on *Friends* when he said something stupid. Next, he'd be telling her, "You're so pretty." Rhode sighed. "Just because someone says he's out of the country and, even if we can find a plane ticket or manifest with his name on it, it doesn't mean he's actually out of the country. People lie and fake their whereabouts all the time, especially if they're using private or chartered planes."

True. And Peter absolutely had the funds to bribe private charters. A Landoon flying commercial would be like someone not covering their heart during the National Anthem or a preacher taking the Lord's name in vain. "Well then, what do we do?"

"What we always do," Rhode said. "Ferret out the truth and watch our backs."

"When I know more," Beau said, "you will too." He ended the call, and Rhode shoved his phone into the back pocket of the worn jeans he'd been wearing with a pair of old cowboy boots and a long-sleeved Henley that was as black as his hair and eyes.

Teegan couldn't let physical attraction dictate her life. Misty had done that and it ended in a Kenny Lee. Not that Rhode was a Kenny Lee. He'd never hit a woman, but then, if he wasn't sober, she didn't know what he would be capable of doing.

Teegan checked her phone. No texts from Sissy or Emily, but she didn't want the babies to be an imposition. Rhode's mother, Marisol, had been overwhelmingly and unexpectedly kind. When she'd pulled her into an embrace after Teegan's attack on the ranch, she'd felt safe and loved in a nurturing way she never had before. Mom's affection had appeared during short bursts of sobriety. Being loved by Marisol had been exactly what she'd needed.

"I should pick up the children. I don't want them to overstay their welcome and it's going to be their bedtime soon."

"Teegan, those babies have been the best thing in our family in a long time. They are not, nor will they ever be, an imposition on our big ole family. They fit right in."

A big family. A loving, supportive family. The Spencers loved each other, despite their shortcoming and failures. Could Teegan also extend that grace to Rhode as his own family had? They were adults, and if he ended up in the gutter again, they would be able to handle the disappointment. Children didn't understand. They blamed themselves.

"Let's see if we can't figure out where the next clue is. Maybe we should watch *D is for Deception*. The backdrop during this scene might give us an idea of where to look in the house or on the property. I'll call and tell them we'll pick the twins up later."

Teegan reluctantly agreed. The movie and treasure hunting might take her mind off the chaos going on in her real life. She headed for the theater room and found the film, then got it ready.

Her phone rang, and she saw it was the attorney's office. Her stomach bottomed out. "Hello?"

"Hi, Miss Albright. It's Scott Carmichael. I'm sorry to call after five. But business hours are laughable in this line of work."

"No worries. Is everything alright?"

Scott sighed. "Yes, but because we handled Lorna's estate and you haven't fired us, we're your attorneys now and you should know that the Landoon family has officially contested the will and hired big guns. Bernstein, Wilcox and Bailey."

"What does that mean exactly?" Was Teegan out of a home again? Would the money be frozen? Not that she'd used any of it yet.

"You can only contest a Last Will and Testament during the probate process if there's a valid legal question about the document or process under which it was created. They're stating she didn't have testamentary capacity."

"Mental capacity?" Teegan asked.

"Yes. It's a common legal reason to contest a will," Scott said. "But they're also stating 'Under the influence,' which means someone had unduly influenced her at the time of signing. A common example would be a full-time caregiver who has taken complete control of all an elderly parent's assets, decisions and day-to-day life, and has been fully in charge of him or her, influencing them to agree to just about anything, including signing a will that might not be what they want."

"But I didn't!" Teegan's heart slammed into overdrive. "I never discussed this with her. I assumed when she passed, I'd be looking for a new job. And she was sharp as a tack, Scott. Surely, you know this or Sylvia, who often handled Lorna's affairs at the firm."

"We know this, Miss Albright."

"Call me Teegan." They were around the same age and if things were about to get sticky—which they were—they might as well be on a first-name basis with one another.

"Teegan, then. I didn't call to upset you but to inform you. I don't see the court throwing it out. It will look at all the facts in the case and decide based on what is provable. Wills are, generally, upheld, and sibling disagreements after a parent's death usually subside with time."

"So I have nothing to worry about?"

"No. But you need to understand that the assets will be frozen until court."

"Can I live in the house still or do I need to find a new place? I have babies and no job." Panic fluttered in her chest.

"You have until December twenty-fourth by 8:00 a.m. to be out. The family thinks that's generous."

That was two days away. She had to find a new place by Christmas Eve morning? Where would her babies celebrate? Rhode would offer the ranch and she would have to accept, without a doubt, but that felt wrong since she'd all but told him his relationship with the babies was in limbo. She wasn't a user like that.

"Lorna's money is frozen, so you cannot spend it or have control over the thoroughbred business, but the good news is, neither can the Landoon family."

"I understand. Thank you."

"If you need anything, call the office."

Teegan hung up and laid her head on the counter in the projector booth. Two days.

When Rhode entered the room, she raised her head. He was grinning.

"The kids are having a ball and so is the family. They've offered to keep them overnight. And if Stone is offering, he means it. He's not what I'd call a pushover."

Teegan didn't think so either. "If they're sure, then that's alright by me. They sleep well anywhere, so I'm not worried about that, but tell them if they get fussy and ask for me, I'll come and pick them up."

Rhode ran his thumbs along his phone's keyboard then pocketed the device. "Done. What's going on?"

"One of Lorna's attorneys called." She relayed the message to Rhode. "I'm not worried about the money. But to leave on Christmas Eve? I'd had such plans for River and Brook. I over-indulged in gifts and wanted them to have a stable Christmas, and we're like a ship out at sea during a tropical storm. Tossed here and there and…it's all the things I don't want for them." She laid her head on the table again and tried not to bawl and squall. This was embarrassing and overwhelming, and she'd all but told Rhode he couldn't be a father. If he couldn't be a dad, then he couldn't be her comfort or confidante either. That wasn't fair to him or to her.

"You had no way of knowing you'd inherit this money or that there would be a freeze on the accounts."

Which meant they'd have to cancel the security company coming. She had no means to pay them.

"Sometimes things beyond our control happen and we have to make do. You know the whole lemons and lemonade spiel."

"I have all the lemons and no sugar for the drink."

"Now's probably not a good time to say, 'I'll give you some sugar.'" He softly snorted, and she actually found she could laugh.

He'd given her some sugar once before and that had led to more sugar than they should have partaken and resulted in twins. "Let's just watch this movie—I googled where the line fits. It's about three-quarters through and I've set it to start there."

Lorna was in a large dining room, her hair swept up and her lips a perfect shade of crimson.

Paul Newman rushed into the room, his chest heaving. "Darla," he whispered. "They found the gun. Your prints

are on it. Have you lied to me all this time? How can I have
fallen in love with...a murderer?"

Lorna's eyes pooled as she drank a deep finger of whiskey.
"How can you even ask me that? You know me. I can be myself
when you're around. I can admit to the darkness that lurks in
my mind and know you won't judge me for it. But you're judg-
ing me now. How can we have a future without mutual trust?"

"There is no future when they match the gun with the bul-
let that killed your husband. I know you haven't been squeaky
clean but..."

"Oh, how I long to clear the cobwebs, step on the cock-
roaches of my stained past and tunnel my way to the light. Oh,
won't you help me?" She kissed Paul Newman, leaving red
lipstick on his mouth. "I'm innocent. I know how it looks." She
gripped his suit lapels. "But you must believe me. I don't care
what anyone else thinks of me. Only you, Thomas."

Paul pushed her away and turned his back. Lorna dramati-
cally cried out and rushed from the room, tripping over the
dining room rug. Paul's character—Thomas—dropped to his
knees and held her. "I believe you. I do."

Then he showed her with a passionate kiss that had Teegan
wondering if it was acting or if there might be something behind it for real. Lorna had only been married a brief time to a
famous director, but shortly after the twins were born, he filed
for divorce. She and a nanny raised the children, but Lorna
had many suitors before and after her marriage.

That's when she noticed the rug.

"Rhode. That rug. It's in the dining room. Of this house."

Rhode followed Teegan into the room that overlooked the
front of the estate. A massive dining room table was the focal
point. The gold Christmas runner on the tabletop and pots of
real poinsettias created a festive atmosphere. The large Ori-
ental rug underneath the table was in shades of navy, blue
and burgundy.

Glancing at the large foyer, he snapped his fingers. "Let's move the table into the foyer so we can roll back the rug."

Teegan nodded and went to work moving the twenty dining chairs to the sides of the dining room and then, together, they lifted the table and pivoted toward the foyer. Once the table was removed from the rug, they worked to roll it up under the windows.

"I don't see anything." Teegan huffed and planted her hands on her hips.

"Were you expecting some kind of hatch or trap door handle?" Dropping to his knees, he used his cell phone's flashlight to study the hardwood.

"I was hoping for one. Leave it to Lorna to not be easy." She mimicked Rhode and began searching the floor with her hands.

If there was a secret passage that led to a tunnel under the house, this was where it had to be. Rhode and Teegan pressed and pulled on every piece of flooring, but nothing turned up.

"What are we missing?" Rhode sat on his heels and scoured the room, searching for any kind of clue. Had Lorna Landoon been mentally unstable? Had she started to bury a treasure and then petered out? Did they have the clue wrong?

Teegan tiptoed along the uncovered floor, slightly pressing with her feet for give, a frown lining her brow.

Rhode stood, his right knee cracking. "Maybe the rug is the clue to the right location but we have the method wrong." His hands glided along the cream-colored walls and he paid close attention to the chair railing. Moving a large hutch with china, he felt along the back of the wall and continued around the room until he reached two sconces flanked by a painting almost as tall as himself.

"Hey, weren't these in the movie too?" he asked.

Teegan glanced up, frustration still twisting her face. She eyed the sconces and tilted her head to the side. "Yeah. Good eye."

He chalked it up to his mom dragging him and Sissy along as children to estate sales. Mama loved antiques. After a moment, he pulled on the right sconce and it gave way. A creaking and groaning filled the air as the painting cracked open.

"It's like something out of that movie *Clue*. Did you see it?"

"I did. Loved that game as a kid. I beat Bridge and Stone every time, but Sissy knew my tells and she was harder to fool."

"It's a secret passage from the conservatory to the kitchen!" Teegan mimicked Miss Scarlet. Rhode wasn't sure that was the exact line, but he smiled anyway.

Rhode put some muscle into it and opened the painting—a front for a heavy wooden door. Cobwebs shivered at the draft, and he held up his cell phone light. "Stairs."

Concrete.

"Well? What are we waiting for?"

"Nothing, I guess. Let's do this." Rhode drew his weapon and glanced at Teegan. "Just in case."

"In case of critters or killers?"

"Both. I don't like either one."

"Same." Teegan inched up behind him as if he were an invincible shield and he couldn't deny he liked the way she trusted in him, confident he could and would protect her. If only she'd trust him in other areas.

Rhode started down and Teegan followed.

Her hand rested on his left shoulder, her cell flashlight shining from her other hand as they descended the cement stairs. The walls were cool and concrete, covered in cobwebs and a few spiders. Chill bumps raised on his arms. It definitely felt like winter down here.

A squeak sent Teegan's grasp tighter on Rhode's shoulder. "What was that?"

"What do you think it was?"

"A mouse or a rat."

"You'd be right."

Teegan shuddered and scooted closer to him, her sweet scent teasing his senses. "Why do you think she had this built?"

"Good question. Could be because she had the funds and simply wanted to. Could be to hide things like treasure. The question is, does the family know it's here?"

"No one has mentioned it, but surely one of them does. Why would Lorna not tell anyone, including the family? Plus, the blueprints are in the office."

"Why didn't we just look at that then? Didn't you say you planned to?"

Teegan chuckled. "I don't know. I guess the hunt feels so Indiana Jones-like. All we're missing is the hat and the whip."

"And the cool leather jacket," Rhode added.

"Well, there's that. You'd look good dressed like Indy."

Rhode's gut tightened and the air grew thick.

Teegan cleared her throat. "I just mean that you're adventurous."

Rhode was pretty sure she was covering for blurting out a compliment at best, flirtation at worst, because she'd all but told him he couldn't be in their lives personally. She was like a bad case of whiplash.

The old concrete steps spiraled then ended, leaving a long dark corridor that stretched forward. "Doesn't look like any light at the end of the tunnel," he said.

"Do we keep going or turn back?"

He shined the light along the walls and the floor. "We came for a clue—or the treasure. Let's find it."

Using their cell phone lights, Rhode felt along the wall.

A scraping along the cement caught his attention. "Did you hear that?"

They paused, listening.

"No," Teegan whispered and scooched closer to Rhode. "What was it?"

"I'm not sure." He put his index finger to his lips. "Turn off your light."

"Are you insane?" She drew out the *s*.

He held her forearm. "I won't let go of your arm. Just turn it off." He switched off his cell phone light and she finally extinguished hers.

Tangible darkness engulfed them and she shivered against him. Holding her wrist, he felt her quickening heartrate thump against his fingers. Skittering along the walls brought ice to Rhode's spine but he focused on the scraping noise—like boots scuffing cement.

Their breathing overrode the rodents and bugs, and the shuffling silenced. Rhode must be hearing things. No one knew about this tunnel. And even if they did, no one could possibly know that he and Teegan were planning to come down here.

Unless they were being watched or the killer had camped out in this place. And if that was the case, they'd willingly walked into the lion's den.

"I don't hear anything, Rhode, and I'm starting to freak out. This was a bad idea."

She might not be wrong.

"Just give it a few more seconds. Please," he murmured.

The noise had come from the way they'd entered. Their only choice was to keep moving forward and hope there was light at the end of the tunnel—literal light. Otherwise, things were going to get dicey.

Thunk. Thunk.

Teegan gripped his biceps. "I heard that. I heard it that time, Rhode. We're not alone down here."

"No. No, we're not."

Chapter Ten

"I want you to keep going forward. I'm going to stay right here and when he catches up to us, I'll be waiting," Rhode whispered.

Teegan's stomach jittered. "No. I can't leave you. What if he kills you?"

"What if you stay and he kills us both? Do we want our children to grow up without any parents?"

Rhode made a valid point. But she didn't want him to risk his life. She might be unsure of how much time he could be with the children given his past, and the fact he admitted to wanting to drink, but she definitely didn't want him dead.

"Why don't we both leave? Just hurry to the end and find a safe place? You don't have to be a hero."

"I'm not trying to be a hero, Teegan. I'm just trying to keep the mother of my children alive. Go. I don't know how much time we have. Whoever is down here clearly knows about the tunnel and that means he might have better knowledge of where it leads. He's at an advantage."

Teegan could argue, and they'd both catch their deaths, or she could trust Rhode. He'd been a detective and a good one—she knew it deep down. He was capable and trustworthy—at least when he was sober.

"Okay." Teegan turned and prayed God would keep them safe. The tunnel narrowed and something crunched under her shoes. Probably a cockroach or some other creepy-crawly she despised. Bugs gave her the heebie-jeebies. Why on earth would Lorna build a tunnel under her estate? It's not like tornadoes were prevalent in the hill country.

As she felt along the wall, she noticed a dip. It wasn't sharp or jagged, just a little uneven. She paused, listened. Nothing. No footsteps. Not a single peep. It raised the hairs on her neck and arms.

What if the jester had hurt Rhode? Killed him? Wouldn't she have heard something?

She should keep going but the dip in the wall... She ran her hands until she felt an opening. But to know for sure if a clue was inside, she'd have to go in blindly. Curling her nose and glancing behind her, she fought the anxiety rising in her belly.

She should keep going, but they might not have another chance. And what if the person down here was searching for the clue too? Teegan had to pause. Had to find it first.

She groaned, pulled her sweatshirt sleeve over her hand like a glove and then reached inside. She couldn't feel anything with the heavy material over her fingers. Just great.

Inhaling a deep breath, she released the fabric and sticky cobwebs entangled her exposed flesh.

With cobwebs came spiders and other icky creatures. Pushing past fear, she maneuvered her hand, thrusting it deep into the tight space, and her fingers brushed against something rubbery and long, like a tube.

She grasped it and yanked it out. The clue. She had another clue.

Teegan could open it later. For now, she had to do as Rhode had instructed and haul it out of this tunnel. She wasn't sure how long she'd been digging around in the wall. Couldn't have been more than seconds. Clutching the tube, she darted one last glance toward Rhode, who was engulfed in darkness with a psychotic person who got his thrills and chills wearing a jester mask and carrying a butcher knife. Did no one tell him that was Horror Movie 101, making it cliché?

Of course, she had all the bravado she needed at the moment. She wasn't the one in the tunnel confronting the killer. She was the one running away.

Darting down the corridor, she kept her hand along the wall to help guide her and hoped nothing lay in front of her to trip on. She silently prayed for Rhode as gunfire echoed in the tunnel, deafening her. She shrieked and cried out, "Rhode!"

Did she go back? Keep running ahead? Rhode would be furious if she returned for him, but she couldn't leave him alone in the tunnel with a killer. Unless…had Rhode shot him?

A scuffle sounded. Two men.

Neither dead—yet.

She switched on her cell phone flashlight and used it to search for anything that might serve as a weapon. Lying in the corner was a piece of rock that had fallen from the wall. Teegan wasted no time, retrieved it, then switched off the light and kept to the side of the tunnel wall as she headed in the direction of the fight ensuing up ahead.

Rhode's phone must have fallen in the commotion. A faint glow from the tunnel floor peeked through the darkness and illuminated a narrow path for Teegan to follow.

Rhode punched the jester in the face, and he dropped, but then he grabbed Rhode by the legs and brought him down with a hard thud.

Straddling Rhode, the jester raised his arm. And Teegan went in for the strike. She slammed the rock into the back of the jester's head and he collapsed to the floor but then regained his footing and came for Teegan.

His presence moved into her space like a whirling tornado and slammed her against the cement wall, her head banging against rock. Little white pinpricks of light dotted her eyes and she fought to keep from blacking out. Hands wrapped around her throat but then suddenly he was ripped away from her.

Rhode!

Unable to see, she could only listen to the grunts of two men battling it out to the death. She could not, would not, stand there doing nothing. She switched on the flashlight again, found the rock and looked up to see the man in the hoodie straddling Rhode. Teegan rushed him, using the rock and slamming it into the back of his head again.

He fell to his side, unmoving this time.

"Rhode. Are you okay?"

Rhode grunted and stood over the attacker, who was lying on his stomach, listless. Panic replaced relief. "Oh no. Rhode! Did I kill him?" She hadn't meant to kill him, even if she had been defending Rhode.

Rhode rolled the man over using his foot.

But he wasn't wearing a mask or wielding a knife.

Teegan used her flashlight and stared at Dexter Landoon's bloody face.

Dexter Landoon was the jester? He'd killed his own mother and Misty? Possibly Addie too? Why?

"I'm so confused right now."

Rhode released a heavy breath and checked Dexter's pulse. "Join the club." He peered up at her. "He's alive."

"Good. Now he can go to prison where he belongs."

"Speaking of being where one belongs, what happened to following directions? You should be out of the tunnel and to safety by now. *Where. You. Belong.*" His voice was raspy and clipped, and the scowl on his face revealed just how thoroughly upset he was.

"First of all, you're not the boss of me. Second, I heard a gunshot and fighting. I couldn't tuck tail and leave you here alone. And before you go all 'I'm a dude and can take care of myself,' don't. You needed help and I helped you."

Rhode gawked at her, blood trickling from his bottom lip.

He undid his belt and used it to secure Dexter Landoon's hands behind his back. "We'll discuss this more in depth after we question him and once my lip stops bleeding. Are you alright?" He finished securing the knocked-out-cold Dexter and stood, running his cell light over her face. He paused at her neck and his eyes flashed with dark fury. Running his index finger along her throat, he frowned. "He hurt you," he murmured.

He had. But right now, she was feeling far from hurt. A flurry of flutters filled her belly at his touch along her skin. Not so much his actual touch but the way his eyes went from fury to something that unsettled her and drew her. His thumb grazed her jawbone, his eyes on hers, and his Adam's apple bobbed hard when he swallowed.

"I'm fine," she squeaked through a dry mouth.

Rhode inched into her personal space. "Are you sure?" he whispered.

She couldn't deny she was woozy, but it had nothing to do with Dexter choking her or slamming her against the wall. The air thickened, sweet and warm. Rhode's minty breath with a hint of cinnamon brought back a rush of memory.

He's a coward. And a fool for walking away from you. You're smart, funny...and beautiful.

"You think I'm beautiful," she blurted breathlessly.

"I do."

"And smart."

"Absolutely—minus the stunt you just pulled."

She grinned. "And funny."

Rhode squinted and framed her face. "Yes." His dark eyes held her captive and every brain cell withered and died at his expression. Not a man eyeing a woman he wanted to hook up with. This was something deeper. Stronger. Pure. It terrified and enthralled her all at once and her heartrate spiked until it throbbed in her ears.

A long, dark lock of hair hung in his eyes and she slowly slid it behind his ear. "I had to save you."

His nose grazed hers, his lips a hairbreadth from hers. "Then I owe you a thank you," he murmured, his lips touching hers as he pronounced each word.

Teegan's eyes automatically closed as she fell headlong into the moment. "I suppose you do."

Sliding his hand from her cheek into her hair, his lips pressed against hers. Soft but urgent. Warm and full.

"Hey! Let me go!"

Dexter had woken.

Rhode broke the kiss that hadn't really gotten off the ground yet, but she was certainly floating.

And floating had never landed her anywhere solid. She'd fallen into a whirlwind romance with her former fiancé, Darryl. He'd left her before the wedding.

It was time to find sure footing.

Rhode Spencer wasn't it.

Even if she wanted to trust him. Even if he'd proven trustworthy. He had an anchor tied around his neck and it was only a matter of time before it dragged them both under.

Rhode towered over Dexter Landoon. He'd hauled the jerk up and had him sit against the tunnel wall. He had every intention of calling Dom, but he wanted to question Dexter first. A PI had a different set of rules and the word "lawyer" meant nothing to him.

He glanced back at Teegan, who stood with her arms crossed at her chest and a thumbnail in between her teeth. Had they almost kissed five minutes ago? He'd been terrified to see her still in the tunnel and then furious, but her loyalty, concern and bravery had filled his heart with admiration and mad respect. Teegan was a fighter. A survivor and an all-around awesome woman. She was also stubborn, rebellious and defiant. And he kinda admired that too.

No denying she revved his pulse like a V10 engine.

He hadn't been able to resist her. But he was impulsive and

his restraint was pretty much nil, which is why he'd ended up down the path he'd been on over two years ago. Teegan could not become his new addiction, but he'd wanted to taste her more than a drop of liquor. Wanted to find comfort in her embrace and share a tender moment to show... What? Words formed in his mind but they were words he couldn't attach to. Word that were not "thank you." One didn't thank a person with a kiss—not like that. The atmosphere had been crackling like a raging wildfire in a drought.

It had been a good thing for Dexter Landoon to wake.

"Why am I bound? I'm calling the police."

"You were trespassing, for one," Rhode said, now focused on the problem at hand. "Assets are frozen, but Miss Albright has until Christmas Eve to vacate. And lurking in a dark tunnel at night is suspicious to say the least. Why are you here? How did you know about the tunnel or that we were down here?"

Dexter leaned his head against the concrete wall. "Miss Albright assaulted me. I'll be bringing charges against you both. I have the gash on my head to prove it."

"You have no gash, I checked. And we were acting in self-defense. Why are you trying to kill Miss Albright?" Rhode shined the cell flashlight in Dexter's direction but not into his face. He'd only received a squint and Rhode wanted to see his natural facial reactions.

Dexter's eyes grew wide. "I didn't kill—or attempt to kill—anyone. Everyone in my family knows about this tunnel and the other secret passages that lead here and to the stables."

"There are multiple passages?"

"Yes. They all lead to this one connecting tunnel."

That explained how an intruder showed up in Teegan's room and how he disappeared so many times with no trace. He was using the secret passages to this tunnel.

"In my mother's earlier days, she didn't want the staff seen. You know, like at Disney World. They use underground tunnels to travel from place to place. She still had some of her snobbery in her. Staff should be working without being seen. Eventually that changed and she stopped using them. But our children would occasionally still play down here. How do you know about the tunnel?"

"Doesn't matter." And he was the one asking questions. He'd patted him down. No weapon. No butcher knife. "You're not dressed in a fancy suit. You're in the same kind of clothing the jester wore when he tried to kill Miss Albright. When he murdered her sister and your mother. Explain."

Dexter heaved a sigh. "I don't have to explain anything, but I will. I'm dressed in black because I didn't want to be seen. I am in the tunnel because I wanted something from the house before Evangeline takes the place, so I thought I'd sneak in and grab it and go. I had no idea the two of you would be down here. It scared me. Why are you here?"

"Doesn't matter. What is it you wanted?"

Dexter's face turned smug. "Doesn't matter."

Fair enough.

"If you need something you don't want your sister to know about, we might be able to help you retrieve it. If your story checks out, and right now I'm not so sure." Dexter might be the killer. Or he was here to kill Teegan to protect his grandson, Peter, who had ties to Addie and Teegan and free access to the house. He could have killed Kenny Lee, Misty's ex too.

"Evangeline is a money mosquito. She'll suck the estate dry. And while I'm not salivating like wolves over fat lambs, I do want a few things. One of which is a deed to a property my mom owned in Austin. It belonged to her daddy and is worth a fortune. Evangeline doesn't know about it."

"Why not?"

"My mother never told her, but I knew. I've seen the files. Upstairs. The maps and the deed as well as any other documents. I wanted them before Evangeline takes possession. That property is worth far more than all of Mother's assets combined. Oil property."

Dexter was going to sneak and steal it. No wonder he hadn't seemed interested over the reading of the Will and Last Testament. All he'd wanted was the old Landoon real estate.

"I thought Mother would will it to me. I was surprised that she didn't. If you give me that, I'll help you fight Evangeline and Glen. I'll back up that Mother wasn't out of her mind or under mental duress at the time."

Teegan looked at Rhode for guidance.

"That will be something Teegan needs to think about for more than two seconds, and you haven't been cleared as the jester. Just because you don't have the mask and knife doesn't mean you didn't do it."

Dexter snorted. "Fine. Do whatever tests you need. You want DNA? Swab me. Need fingerprints? Have at it. I did not kill anyone. I shouldn't have been skulking around like a two-bit criminal, I agree. But I feared if I mentioned it to Teegan, it might end up being discussed and Evangeline would get wind of it."

Rhode wasn't so sure he believed Dexter. Often, criminals who thought they couldn't be caught were willing to give DNA samples as well as take polygraphs. Cold and calculated sociopaths often passed them. And there might not be any DNA on either victim. His prints would be in the house and should be. He was Lorna's son.

"I'll consider it," Teegan said. "I never asked for or expected to receive all of Lorna's things. I was as shocked as anyone else."

Dexter shifted and readjusted his bound hands. "I believe you. My mother was mischievous and a drama queen until the end. We loved it as children. As adults, we weren't as amused by it. Evangeline believes this was Mother's last little fun with the family."

Like a last laugh. Exactly what the killer had said to Teegan.

"Cutting you out of a will? That's going beyond hidden property, tunnels and rumors of treasure," Teegan said.

"I didn't say *I* believed that. I think Mother was sick of Evangeline, Glen and Charlie's mooching and money-grubbing hands. I don't understand why she cut myself and Peter out. We've been good with our inheritance. We didn't squander it and we work. We've invested and doubled our money. But I suppose she had her reasons." He closed his eyes. "My head hurts."

He was all too calm about this. And he had been skulking around. Rhode wasn't sure he was lying, but he was certain Dexter wasn't telling the whole tale. Rhode wanted to see those property maps himself. If it was worth more than Lorna's estate and the money she'd left, including the thoroughbred business—that would be over a billion dollars easy. The Landoons could split that and still have money to last long after they passed on. Unless they squandered it, but Rhode couldn't imagine going broke in this lifetime with that amount of money. They'd have to buy yachts and trips and a slew of property to run through that kind of wealth.

They were willing to kick a single mom of twins onto the street at Christmas, so it was possible they were just fat enough at heart to glutton themselves on the finances with anything and everything they laid their eyes on.

"If you're cleared by the police, we'll discuss it. I won't say anything to Evangeline and…and I'll find the files and take them with me. For now." Teegan's shoulders had pulled back and she'd raised her chin. It was more than he'd do for a man who might have murdered his own mother and two other women. But it was Teegan's money now. If it was truly oil property, then Teegan and the babies were set for many lifetimes. Generations to come would never worry about finances again.

Rhode wasn't sure how to feel about that. He barely had two pennies to rub together. What could he possibly provide except anxiety to Teegan, who would constantly fear a relapse? It wasn't like he didn't have that same fear. Even in this moment, his nerves purred at the thought of amber liquid burning its way down his gullet to his belly, creating a heated and soothing warmth. Languid.

She'd have nine ducks and a cow if he revealed that temptation, that urge. Instead, he pushed it out with a reminder that God's grace was sufficient for him. In this moment. This lie that swirled around his mind telling him that one drink wasn't going to kill him. It would ease his anxiety and fear.

Lies. God was his peace. God was his calm in the storm. And the thirst was like a tempest he'd never experienced before. Tossing him like a rag doll. Coaxing him to jump overboard into still waters.

But Jesus led him beside real still waters. Waters of the Word that would renew his mind. Keep him focused on things above.

"Did you hear me, Rhode?" Teegan asked and cocked her head, studying him. She had his number. Recognized the signs of craving. How could she not?

Rhode hadn't heard her. He'd been in a battle.

"I said, we need to get out of the tunnel and call the police now. Let Dom figure it out."

"Right. Yes. Sorry." He shook his rattled head, hoping the thoughts would shake out and bring him back to a level head. Back to the moment. He cleared his parched throat and hauled up Dexter. They walked back the way they'd begun and returned to the dining room. He closed the painting behind him.

Rhode sat him in a chair, leaving the belt on his wrists. He called Dom and woke up him up, giving him the rundown. "He'll be here in twenty minutes, but he asked if he should just temporarily move in."

"Can I talk to you?" Teegan asked. "In private?"

Was she going to call out his earlier war with the bottle? Nerves knotted his gut, but he followed her a few feet away, out of earshot but where Rhode could keep an eye on Dexter. "What's up?"

"I found it," she whispered. "The clue. It was inside a divot in the wall. Like in the *Temple of Doom*."

"Bugs?"

She wrinkled her nose and nodded. "But I have it. I still need to read it. Thought I'll wait until he's gone."

"Good call and good work."

"Are you okay?" she asked. "You went away for a few minutes and…and I know that forlorn expression. I saw it on my mom when she was sober but wishing she wasn't."

"I'm fine."

"She said that too." Her mouth turned hard.

"Teegan, I'm not sharing that part of my life with you. You've made it clear it's keeping me from being in my kids' lives. And while I get it—I understand your thinking and fear—know I'm thinking the same thing. I'm fearing the same thing. But more than fearing I'll drink again, I fear I won't get to know my children. I won't be a good dad. I have nothing to offer them. And you threatening me with withholding them from me, it kinda makes me not want to share my struggles with you." He folded his arms over his chest, waiting on her reply.

Her cheeks tinged pink and she kicked her toe along the floor. "I'm sorry. I don't mean to be without mercy or compassion, Rhode. Truly. But…you can't begin to know what I went through my whole life until Mom died. You can't understand how much I want my children to have a normal life. A stable life. I don't want to live in fear. You think I like the burning and gnawing sensation in my stomach? I don't." She closed her eyes. "But the children come first. Always and in every way."

"But you let me kiss you. I can't be in our children's lives, but I can do that? If that's not personal, I don't know what is."

She flinched at his harsh tone, the truth in his words.

"That was a mistake. It won't happen again. There is no you and me. Not even if I allow you in the children's lives. I can at least control that narrative. But I can't trust you. Not with my heart. And I don't want our babies to lose theirs to you either. Because you'll break them. I know it. And, deep down, I think you know it too." While her tone was low and her words soft, they hit with a one-two punch. A total knock-out. Below the belt.

He'd heard the same words from his family when he'd come out of rehab. *Trust has to be earned back. One day at a time.* And he had—earned their trust. They hadn't held his past, his sins, against him. Neither had God. But, at the moment, it felt like God was punishing him in the worst way for his mess-ups. Punishing him by revealing he had children then stealing them away.

Maybe Teegan was right.

Maybe he was a grade-A loser who had no business in their lives. He had nothing to give but the possibility of screwing them up mentally and emotionally. He had no response. No argument. He was guilty. He'd been sentenced. Now all that was left was for him to do his time. At some point, the mercy train would run out of gas.

"You go see if you can find the property records and deeds. I'll keep an eye on Dexter until Dom arrives." He turned and strode back into the dining room.

His phone rang.

Stone.

He answered. "What's going on?"

"Ambulance is on the way to us. Mama's having severe stomach pain. Emily will stay with the babies. But me, Bridge, Sissy and Beau are heading to the hospital."

Rhode relayed the situation quickly. "As soon as Dom takes him, I'll be right there."

Rhode wasn't sure he could handle one more thing.

What if the cancer had spread?

What if the killer got his clutches into Teegan?

So many what-ifs.

Chapter Eleven

Teegan rifled through Lorna's office on the second floor. She had rarely used it and once the elevator had broken down, Lorna had stopped going upstairs altogether. Said no point in it. Then why had Lorna been upstairs the day she'd died and how had she climbed up there? She wasn't decrepit, but she'd have needed a cane or walker for balance.

Sifting through the filing cabinet nearest the maplewood desk, she tried to hurry and find any documents on property that Lorna's father had owned. Property that produced oil. This felt so wrong, as if she were violating Lorna's privacy, but this was all hers now. Or might be. A judge might decide to throw out the will and revert back to the original document.

Who were the beneficiaries? Who would the money have gone to? That person might be their best suspect. It couldn't be Evangeline. Teegan's attacker had clearly been a man, but that didn't mean Evangeline hadn't hired someone to do her evil bidding. For the right price.

Dexter Landoon all but promised he hadn't hurt anyone and, on some level, she believed him. He was fit and in great shape. He could be the jester. But why wear the mask? Why that mask? Why not a balaclava, which would be more difficult to track? How many jester masks could be out there? Why such a terrifying one at that? Was there meaning behind it or was it something the killer'd had on hand—although who had plastic jester masks on hand besides serial killers and psychos or just big fans of trick or treat?

Finally, in the bottom filing cabinet drawer in the back, Teegan found the folder with all the property information and a deal with an oil company to drill. How had Lorna kept that from everyone but Dexter? She hurried from the office when she heard Rhode.

"Teegan, Dom's gone with Dexter." He stood at the bottom of the staircase, his cheeks pale and his eyes pulsing with concern.

"What's wrong?"

"My mom is in the hospital. Stomach pain. I—we need to go. Is that okay?" he asked.

Marisol was in the hospital? "Of course. Yes." She rushed down the stairs and held up the file. "I have this. Dexter was telling the truth—at least about this." But right now that didn't matter. All that mattered was Rhode's mother and her health.

In the car, Rhode white-knuckled the steering wheel and raked his bottom lip between his teeth repeatedly.

"I'm sure she's going to be okay, Rhode."

Rhode kept his eyes on the road and nodded. "What if the cancer has spread to her stomach? What if...what if this is the end? I've already lost my dad and my sister Paisley. I can't lose my mama. I just can't," he whispered on a shaky breath.

She couldn't back up her claim that Marisol would be okay. The truth was she had no idea. She could pray for mercy and hope for the best, but nothing was a sure thing. No guarantees in this life. Silently, she prayed for Marisol and the family, and specifically for Rhode. This kind of stress was the same kind that had sent her mom spiraling into the drink. Seemed like Rhode had had more than his fair share of pressure squeezed on him and this was yet another massive hit.

Lights came into view from behind, blinding her. "Ugh. Don't drivers know to turn off their brights?"

"You'd think, but we are on country roads and it's hard to see deer. I'm more irritated they're on my behind. Step off already," he muttered and increased his speed.

"Should we be—" Teegan's words died on her lips as a vehicle rammed them from behind. Yeah, they should be worried.

Rhode held steady as they lurched in their seats. Teegan once again silently prayed for their safety. The vehicle rammed them again and Rhode lost all control and careened into a ditch.

The jarring reverberated through her bones and even her teeth rattled on impact. "Rhode?" she said and winced at the pain radiating through her body.

"Yep," he said through a grunt. "You okay?"

"Not really."

The lights zoomed past, an engine revved and then faded into the distance.

"He's gone." Rhode rotated his shoulders, wincing again.

"You say that like you're disappointed." Teegan's muscles spasmed and her hands trembled as the aftershock dissipated and her brain processed what had transpired. They could have been killed.

"I'm not disappointed. I'm confused. Why run us down and not finish what you start? Why not come on down here and put a few bullets in us?" Rhode pinched the bridge of his nose.

"Who cares? I'm glad he didn't. Maybe he thought our crash would kill us. I feel dead." Teegan rubbed her neck, which had bunched and tightened. She was going to be in a world of pain come morning.

Rhode backed up but he couldn't drive out of the ditch. It was too steep. He punched the wheel and the horn gave a weak beep. "I don't have time for this!" Digging out his phone, he pressed Stone's name and, on the second ring, his brother's voice came through the line. Deep and baritone. A little menacing. Like Stone.

"Where are you?" he barked. "They took Mama back. We're all here in the ER waiting."

"We got run off the road. I'm out on Highway 4 and can't make it out of the ditch. I'm going to call a tow truck. I'm sorry."

"No. Don't be. Are you two hurt? Do we need to come?" Stone asked.

"No. The driver ran us into the ditch and kept driving. Don't you find that odd?"

"I do. But let's thank the Good Lord for the grace and we can discuss ideas later. You sure you don't need me?"

Rhode sighed. "No. He's gone and, if he does come back, I have my gun. I need to call the towing company. I just wanted you to know why I'm not already there. It's out of my control." He grimaced and muttered, "Like everything else in my life right now."

Teegan inwardly flinched. The added stress was her fault.

"Well, the babies are fine," Stone said. "They were asleep when the hullabaloo went down. Don't worry about them."

"Good to know." Rhode ended the call. "Guess you heard all that. Stone's voice carries."

"I did."

Rhode called the towing company and, when he disconnected, leaned his head back against the headrest. "Be thirty minutes." His words were tight. Every minute here was a minute that slipped away at the hospital.

"I'm so sorry, Rhode. All this added pressure on you is because of me. If you want to drop the case, I can find another PI or just trust the cops to do their jobs. Maybe I could take the kids and go somewhere." Even as she said the words, she knew they meant nothing. Teegan didn't have the finances to up and run off with her babies. Lorna's assets were frozen and that meant Teegan was too. She wasn't even accruing new income. Maybe she should again consider returning the excess toys to the stores. The children didn't need them. The splurge had been more about Teegan's meager past than the babies' needs. It might give her a little extra to stretch.

Rhode rubbed his eyes with the heels of his hands. "Teegan, you can stay with us until the contesting of the will is lifted. You said so yourself that the attorney doesn't see the judge throwing it out. It's going to take time, and if the Landoons can push it faster, they will. In the meantime, one of them is threatening you."

"You mean trying to kill me." She had a shallow stab wound to prove it.

Rhode shifted in his seat, his face scrunching at the movement. She was already feeling stiff and sore in her neck.

"About that. I think one of them is threatening you to push you to give up the estate or to forfeit the will, giving it to them. But I think someone else in the family wants you dead. It's not enough to scare you. He—or she—doesn't believe you'll ever scare badly enough to give up a fortune and they aren't taking their chances on a judge."

Two family members. "That's why you're confused about the vehicle running us off the road but not shooting us or something."

"It also explains the damage and threatening notes—warnings to scare you. But then, someone else with a jester mask and a really big knife wants to end things permanently. And I don't know which family member is which or if they're all in on it together somehow. They have a unified cause—getting you gone and their greedy paws on that money and property."

Teegan quivered and ran her hands along the tops of her thighs. "I know this is going to sound shallow, but I can't let whoever is doing this ruin Christmas for me and the babies. This will be the first one where they can open gifts and actually enjoy it. Last year they were confused and ate the paper. Granted, River might eat the paper still but..." She smiled.

Her kids could bring her joy even in this nightmare. "Obviously our safety—their safety—is the utmost importance, and I know they don't have a clue when Christmas falls or the true meaning of it, but I guess…"

"You're the little girl who was disappointed each Christmas. You're giving yourself what you never had," he murmured. "You deserve a special Christmas. Every Christmas should be special, Teegan. I want you to have that. And we'll do everything we can to make it happen."

Why was Rhode showing her such compassion and grace? Maybe she should show him the same understanding and kindness. Give him the benefit of the doubt.

But the moment the thought came, a dreaded darkness flooded her mind and heart. Sad memories washed over her. Mom had been sober for a month and the house had been clean, they'd had food in the fridge and she'd even baked cookies. Misty had turned her nose up and stayed in her room.

"Don't get used to this, Teegan," she'd said. "It won't last. It never does. Stop hoping. It only ends with you locked in the bathroom sobbing and thinking it's your fault. It's not. It's never your fault or mine. So, no, I don't want a cookie. I don't want any sweet hope. Because that cookie won't last and neither will the sweetness." She'd slammed her door shut again and Teegan had eaten cookies and milk with Mom. They'd laughed and watched old movies—where her love for them and theater began. Everything had been picture-perfect.

The next morning, Mom had passed out on the couch with an empty bottle of Wild Turkey, the cookie platter as empty as Teegan's heart.

Rhode rubbed his eyes and groaned. He was still sore from the crash on Saturday. That night had been a blur. After the tow truck had arrived and given them a ride to the hospital, Mama had been taken for tests and, hours later, they'd declared she had no cancer in her stomach and the pains were likely side effects from the chemo, which was a relief and also grievous. Mama was hurting and there was nothing they could do to change that except some pain pills she hated taking due to grogginess and fuzzy brain. While she lived, she wanted every moment to be lucid. The first thing she'd asked was how the babies were doing and could they get her home to them.

River and Brook were her saving grace.

And Rhode's.

They'd all stayed home on Sunday. Sore, exhausted and frazzled, they'd watched church online and taken it pretty easy, sticking close to Mama.

Moving like Frankenstein, he padded to the kitchen. The house was extra quiet for a Monday morning, and the sky was still dark with a small hint of gray light poking through.

Tomorrow was Christmas Eve and Teegan would be homeless until the court ruled on the will. He'd asked her to stay at the ranch—welcomed it—but she was hesitant. Probably from guilt. His nose drew him to the coffee maker. No one would be up this early except Stone.

"Hey," Stone said as he walked inside from the back porch with Rhode's Labs at his side. Rhode scratched their ears. He'd been gone more than usual and these guys were all about the love, pushing on him and poking their noses under his hands for rubs and licks.

"Hey."

Stone had clearly had a cup or two already. He wore sweats and a hoodie and his stubble had turned into more of a beard. "Everyone's still sleeping. It's been a rough weekend."

As if he needed to tell Rhode. "You think Mama will be okay?"

"Praying so. But there's no guarantee. She's tough and a fighter." Stone sipped his coffee. He was the realist of the family, but they needed that level head. "How's Teegan?"

"I haven't seen her yet this morning but based on how I still feel, I'm going to go with sore and miserable."

Stone smirked. "I meant in general. With everything looming and having to be out of the house. She agree to come here? It's the safest move for her."

Rhode sighed and poured a cup of hot caffeine. He sipped and savored it. "I think she feels guilty for accepting our kindness. Now that she knows about my alcoholism."

"I'm sorry about that."

"She needed to know. Ripping off the Band-Aid was probably best. I'm not sure I'd have ever told her, for fear. She isn't sure she wants the children in my life. She's lived with an alcoholic parent and is afraid. Thing is, I don't hold her fear against her. I'm scared too. What if I do mess up? What if in four years, I don't flee temptation and fall off the sobriety wagon? I can't crush my family again and definitely not my own children. Maybe it's best if I'm at a distance—whatever that might look like. It might be the safer choice for everyone."

Stone poured another cup of coffee and then leaned on the counter, his green eyes piercing Rhode's. "You're aware of the problem. You have a support system. As always, we're going to be with you every step of the way. At some point, you have to live your life, Rhode. You can't exist in limbo. You can't base every choice on whether or not you might succumb at some time in the future. That's not healthy. And it's a sure-fire way to end up back on the drink. Because there's no hope in that."

Stone was right. It killed him that his children might not know him. And if he was being honest, it hurt knowing Teegan might not want to know him better either. Because he wanted her to. He wanted to know her even more as well. He already admired her stamina and strength. He loved the way she loved their babies, and his heart broke at her shattered childhood. A loving and attentive family that got in each other's business too often and could be annoying had raised Rhode, but they were loyal to one another and, at the end of the day, had each other's backs. Their growing-up years had been built on a solid foundation.

Teegan's had been shaky at best.

"You may be right, Stone. But Teegan will not see it that way. I have no idea how to win her trust. I mean I have her trust today. She doesn't trust me for tomorrow or the next day though. Her fears have swallowed up her future too."

"Then maybe just live each day for today. Isn't that what Jesus said? Each day has enough trouble of its own, so don't be worrying about tomorrow's trouble? In twenty-four hours, you'll be upon it. Then you can fight it when it comes. You're a fighter, Rhode. But more importantly, Jesus is a fighter and a finisher of our faith. And if He's fighting for you, you can make it. You can overcome each day and each temptation."

Rhode trusted God to help him each day and, some days, minute by minute. "I know you're right. I just don't know if Teegan will believe so."

"Well, she's a believer. So God will talk to her. Trust that He'll work things out. He's a rewarder of those who believe."

"Thanks." Stirring caught their attention and Teegan entered the kitchen, moving as stiffly as Rhode had been.

"Morning," Stone said. "You need some ibuprofen?"

"I just took some. But thanks."

Stone turned to Rhode. "Until you get your vehicle back, feel free to use the family truck. And, Teegan, the door is open for you. You're welcome to stay here with the kiddos as long as you want or need to. We love 'em. And it's been so good for Mama to have vitality running through the house again. Another generation of Spencers wreaking havoc in the ranch. Sounds about right." He grinned and patted her shoulder before leaving them alone in the kitchen.

Rhode pointed to the coffeepot. "Help yourself. Won't help the stiffness but it won't hurt either."

She nodded and poured a cup into a Christmas mug. She wore leggings and an oversize sweatshirt with reindeer and stars. Her thick wool socks were Christmas-themed as well. She wore a messy bun that worked for her but shadowy half-moons hung below her eyes. "What do you have planned today?" he asked.

"Stay alive, find the person or people who want me dead, and maybe find our next clue."

The clue. He'd forgotten she'd found it in the tunnel below the estate.

"Did you hear anything new about Dexter from Dom?" she asked, pouring a heaping amount of cream into her coffee.

"They cut him loose. He's technically not trespassing since the estate is frozen right now and, according to him, he was acting in self-defense. Since he didn't actually hurt anyone then there's no crime, but Dom's looking into his history. Seeing if he was anywhere near Addie or her place around the time of her death. And he's looking into where he was the day your sister and Lorna were killed."

Rhode wished they had more concrete news and a better lead, but for now they had nothing. Peter Landoon had dated Addie, which connected to Teegan since she and Addie had been good friends in high school. But it stopped there. He was their solid suspect and, so far, Dom hadn't found a decent alibi.

Teegan put her mug on the counter. "I guess we wait. And I also guess we stay here. I feel torn about that. I don't mean to use you—"

"You're not. But I do want to be in my children's lives. I don't plan to ever touch alcohol again and, let's say I never do… Then what? My children have been spared my presence on the chance I might fail, but if I never do, then everyone has lost. Either way, it's a no-win situation to not be able to have them in my life." He silently prayed she'd see the truth.

She nodded. "You're right. They need a father and you're clearly a good one. If you never touch it again but they don't know you, it's a fail. And if they do know you and you fall away…it's an even greater pain. I have to decide which is a lesser evil, so to speak, in their lives. I'm struggling, Rhode. To be perfectly honest."

"I know." Now was not the time to push. Only God could change her heart and mind. Pushing for what he wanted would only drive her away. "So what's the clue?"

"Let me get it from my purse." She grunted as she stood and hobbled to the counter, pulling out a tube similar to the one they'd found at the bottom of the swimming pool. She opened it and read, "'My life is a maze of mistakes, but I don't mind, honey. I found you at the end.'"

"Maze. The labyrinth?"

She nodded. "I actually know this one. It's from Lorna's 1963 film with Rock Hudson. *Once Upon a Mistake*. She said she had the maze built because of the mistakes in her life she'd made. Life was a set of paths. If you chose the right path, it would lead to the garden of life. That's why she had an English garden planted outside the labyrinth. But I wonder if this movie didn't somewhat inspire that. It was a few years after she made this film that she gave her life to the Lord and her entire world and purpose changed."

"You want to add searching the labyrinth to our checklist today while we still have the time to be on the property?" he asked. Beau was heading up the investigation and Dom was working it through the law enforcement channels. He had the time.

"Yeah. I also have a meeting at Lorna's law office. Scott returned my call and left a voice mail late last night. We have a court date for the day after New Year's."

"That's fast."

"Not like criminal law. That's what he said anyway. But, yeah, let's see what we can find."

His phone buzzed with a text from Beau and he read it. "Hey, Teeg. Do you know an Olivia Wheaton?"

Teegan paused and nodded. "Yeah. She was at the reading of the will, remember? Lorna gave her two million dollars. She's the estate manager. I helped her get the job, since we were friends in high school. Why?" Her face paled.

"Because they found her dead in her apartment an hour ago."

Chapter Twelve

Teegan's brain wouldn't process Rhode's words. Olivia was dead? "I don't understand." After the initial text, Rhode had called Beau for more information.

Rhode helped ease her into the kitchen chair. "Just breathe."

She nodded and inhaled deeply, but her chest ached. "How? When?"

Rhode pulled the other kitchen chair around and straddled it, then held her clammy hands. "Beau said her cat was wandering the hallway and a neighbor going out for a morning jog saw her. She tried to take her back. The door was cracked and she found Olivia."

Teegan's chest tightened. "Was she stabbed?"

"Multiple times, and bluebonnets were left at the scene, like Misty and Addie. The police and forensic team are there now. Stone just texted. We've been called in to clean the scene. I'll need to help my brothers, but Emily has the day off and she's going to be on protective duty. She's tough, capable, and shoots better than any of us Spencer boys."

He meant to lighten the heavy atmosphere and bring her comfort, but the fact she needed protection and that Emily might have to gun someone down on her behalf turned the coffee in her stomach.

"What can you tell me about Olivia? You'll have to tell this all to Dom. He'll want to interview you, so get ready for recounting the statement multiple times." Rhode waited while she swallowed and balled her hands at her sides.

"We went to school together. Her, Addie and me were tight. Practically inseparable. After high school graduation, Olivia went off to college at A&M. She got married after she finished school and they lived in Waco, but about six months ago, she went through a divorce and she moved back to Austin. We reconnected and since she had experience being an estate manager, I got her a job onsite. It's good money. Lorna pays—paid—well, and she and Lorna got along like a dream. She moved to Cedar Springs, so it'd be less of a commute."

"Children?" Rhode's brow furrowed.

"No. They never had children. That was part of the problem, I think. He didn't want them and she did. She thought he'd change his mind. He didn't." Teegan covered her face and the dam of tears burst. Had Teegan unknowingly put her in the crosshairs of a killer? She'd never forgive herself for that. "I don't understand. Why her? Why Addie?"

"I don't know why her. Addie had a connection to Peter Landoon. Olivia, too, just by working here, but do you know if they might have had a personal relationship?"

He rubbed her upper shoulder but nothing brought comfort at the moment.

She shook her head. "I know Charlie had taken an interest in her. He'd asked her to dinner a couple of times, but she wasn't ready to date yet. She was still grieving her marriage."

"How did Charlie take it? Did she say?" Rhode asked.

"He understood. Charlie went through a divorce two years ago. She said he was sympathetic and they were on good terms. Which is surprising because he's skeezy to me. But then, she needed a friend and sometimes our need..." She trailed off as it dawned she was no different than Olivia. Sometimes a person's need blinded them to truth, deceived them.

Was her need to protect the children from Rhode based on her own pain blinding her?

"Take your time." Rhode sipped his coffee. "We can connect the women to two Landoon men personally. And, who knows, maybe Peter can be connected to her and you didn't know. He's at least seen her on the property. They all have. But why kill her unless they're so greedy they wanted the two million too?"

Teegan wiped her tears and peered up at Rhode. Turmoil swam in his ebony eyes and she could tell he was keeping something from her. "What is it? What aren't you saying?"

"Nothing. I don't want to scare you. I'm just thinking."

Understatement of the century. "I'm already afraid, Rhode."

"You're the center. You own everything. You were friends with Addie. Addie dated Peter. You got Olivia a job and you were friends with her. Misty was your sister. They all died in the same manner. Only Lorna's death was different. Something else is going on here. I wish I knew what. It's like I can taste it but can't pinpoint the flavor."

"Tastes metallic to me." Like blood.

"We should know more later. Do you want to be alone?"

Yes. No. The sound of babies crying drew her attention.

"I'm happy to take baby duty and feed them if you want to lie down."

"Actually, the babies will soothe me. Their joy is contagious and, right now, I'm pretty low on joy. Even if it's the time of year that brings great joy." She stood and Rhode followed her to her room. The twins were already standing in the crib they'd been sharing. The room wasn't exactly spacious, but it was cozy and comfortable.

"Ma-ma. Ma-ma!" Both babies reached out with huge grins. Not any idea that evil lurked right under their noses. They had no cares and simply trusted Mama would take care of them. They were safe. Loved. Knew they'd be provided for.

Childlike faith.

Right now, Teegan's faith was a bit wobbly. She lifted Brook from the crib and Rhode reached for River. He went right to him as if deep within he knew Rhode was his father.

"Hey, little man. Did you sleep good?" Rhode asked and kissed his little cheek then frowned. "Wow that diaper is heavy." He glanced at Teegan. "When do babies potty train?"

"Depends on the baby. I think I could actually train Brook now. But, River...well you just have to change the rivers flowing in his Pampers."

Rhode chuckled and snagged a diaper then laid River on one side of the bed while Teegan took to changing Brook on the other. Once they were in fresh diapers, they all headed for the kitchen. River repeating "juice" over and over.

"We're gonna getcha some juice, bud." Rhode rubbed River's dark hair and when he wiggled for freedom, Rhode put him down and Teegan let Brook loose. They chased after Rhode's Labs and the good sports seemed to enjoy the game of tag.

"If I could bottle that baby energy, I'd be the richest man in the universe," Rhode mused.

"Right?" Teegan said with a smile.

"How about I make pancakes?" Rhode asked. "Do they like pancakes?"

Teegan laughed. "Yes, but it's going to take an army to clean the syrup out of their hair and anywhere else."

"Hey, if your food isn't sticky and messy, what's the fun in eating it?" He went to the pantry and retrieved a griddle. "I could always put maple syrup in the batter to make them sweet already."

"Will that work?"

"Will that work?" he asked as if her skepticism was ridiculous. "I don't know. I've never done it." He laughed and Teegan's knotted neck relaxed at the breath of fresh air. The joking and normalcy of making breakfast was what she needed to battle the unsurmountable fear and dread.

As Rhode worked at making pancake batter and adding a heaping amount of maple syrup to it, she kept an eye on the kids. The toys his family had purchased kept them occupied and River had a special love for Rhode's oldest Lab. He leaned against the furry friend while crashing trucks against one another.

Teegan made them juice cups and enjoyed how much the children felt at home, as if they'd always come to the ranch, had sleepovers here. Belonged. And if truth be told, Teegan felt a part of the family too. Other than Lorna's hospitality, Teegan hadn't felt so welcomed by anyone else.

Bridge entered through the back door into the kitchen. "Pancakes. Score!"

Rhode pointed a finger at him. "I didn't remember inviting you to breakfast, bro. Besides, pancakes are carbs. Don't want to ruin that nice figure," he teased.

The Spencer men were fit but Bridge had taken it to a whole new level. His guns bulged through his Henley, but he wasn't like bodybuilder big. Just seriously dedicated to weights. "Har har. Where's the kiddos?" he called loud enough for them to hear. "I have presents. Maybe toys!"

As if they understood, they came toddling into the kitchen. "How did my brother father such cute kids? I hope you have your mommy's brains or you're done for." Bridge baby-talked and laid two gift bags on the table then scooped up a twin in each very big, very strong, arm.

"You want a present?" he asked them.

Brook nodded and River pulled at his short beard.

Rhode snorted. "I'll have you know my mind is sharp and could outmatch you any day."

"You wish. Stick to pancakes." Bridge sat the kids on the table and handed them each a little red gift bag. River pulled out the white tissue paper and shoved it in his mouth. "Aw, you take after your dad after all," Bridge teased and removed the paper from his mouth and wadded it up. He was a natural with children. Teegan wondered why he wasn't settled and a father himself. He helped River look into the bag and her son removed the little Dallas Cowboys nerf football. Navy, silver and white.

Brook was already tossing the tissue paper out. She, too, had a Dallas Cowboys football. In pink.

Bridge grinned. "Equal opportunity here."

Teegan snickered. "Thank you."

The kids attempted to clamber off the table and Bridge scooped them up and set them down, and off they went throwing footballs and giggling and talking gibberish that they seemed understand. She and Misty had had a language only they could interpret too. Her heart ached for her sister, her friends. Lorna. When last she'd talked to her attorney, he'd informed her that they were holding a graveside funeral tomorrow morning. Family only.

Teegan wasn't even able to say a final goodbye to Lorna and it ripped out her heart. Her only solace was knowing that Lorna wasn't really in the cemetery but in Heaven and one day Teegan would see her again. Once the service was over, she'd go pay her respects privately and leave flowers.

Rhode plated several pancakes and handed one to Teegan. "It worked."

She bit it into it, tasting the sweet maple flavor. "No-stick pancakes. You're brilliant."

"Teegan, you're the first person on the planet to call my brother brilliant," Bridge said. "That doesn't really speak well of you." He shoved an entire pancake in his mouth and winked at her. Oh, this man was a character. The whole family was fun.

Emily padded into the kitchen. "Morning. She held up River's football. You forgot to teach him how to yell 'incoming' before he throws." She rubbed her head. "He's got good aim. I'll teach him to shoot in the spring."

Teegan laughed at her dry humor. Bridge shoved Emily playfully as she poured her cup of coffee.

"Hey, easy. You don't want me to spill a drop of this go-juice. I need it."

After she poured in a large helping of cream and sugar, Rhode snorted, "You want some coffee with that cream and sugar?"

"You want to live five more minutes? Target someone else." Emily made a dramatic display of taking that first delicious drink.

After feeding the babies—and an easy cleanup thanks to Rhode's pancake ingenuity—they dressed them for the day.

Rhode and Bridge grabbed their coats and Rhode hung back. "I'll be a phone call away if you need anything. Emily will keep you safe."

"You two seem close."

"Well, we weren't always." He glanced at Emily playing catch with the babies, smiled with fondness, then followed Bridge to the crime scene.

To Olivia's crime scene. This couldn't be real.

She plopped on the floor next to the fiery redhead and mindlessly played ball with the children. Emily tossed the pink football into Brook's lap. "Hey, Rhode will make sure to keep you and the babies safe. We all will. I know how hard it is to trust though."

"Yeah. How do you know?"

"Because I was a target of high-profile people during an investigation that included the late eldest Spencer sister, Paisley. Working for the Public Integrity Unit—well…the fact there has to be a PIU says it all. And I'd just found out my father had a whole separate family for my entire life. To say I had trust issues is an understatement. But Stone was patient with me. Like Rhode's patient with you." She leaned back and grabbed the ball River had tossed, missing.

"Rhode said y'all got off on the wrong foot."

"I cut his legs out from him, actually. I let his alcoholism shape my thoughts concerning him. He was friends with our suspects—yes, plural—and I let his past cloud my judgment. I thought he was either involved in the murders or tipping off his buddies with investigative information. We had some serious verbal blows. In the end, I was wrong. And he showed me grace. He also showed me a lot of ice. But I deserved it."

They sat quietly.

"He's a God-fearing man who stumbled in a really big way and it robbed him of everything he held dear." Emily chucked the ball again further to make River run for it.

"I'm scared he might slip again."

"No one is more afraid of that than Rhode, Teegan. And you can't measure him with the yardstick of fear. That's not fair." Emily's soft brown eyes met hers. "He loves these babies and if I had to guess…he loves you too."

"No. We're not a couple. It was just a one-night thing that humiliates me to this day."

"Because you made a grave mistake and got drunk. God forgave you. He forgave Rhode too. Maybe it's your turn."

Maybe Emily was right. But how did she overcome this fear and dread?

The scene from earlier had been as gruesome as the first site where they'd cleaned up the blood from Misty and Lorna's deaths. Olivia Wheaton had at least put up a fight. Based on the setting, Rhode surmised she'd opened the door to someone she'd known. No forced entry. She'd let her killer inside. Then it had taken a dark turn. After the few hours of cleaning, he'd been wiped out, but there was no rest for the weary.

Mama had called to tell him that the Christmas festival was happening downtown tonight and that they wanted to take the babies. That Teegan had already agreed.

Rhode had called Teegan to arrange to meet her at the Landoon estate to find the next clue and then to go with her to the meeting at Lorna's attorney's office. He'd also mentioned grabbing a bite of dinner and meeting the family at the Cedar Springs Christmas Festival.

She'd agreed to that too. Was she softening up to the idea of him as part of the twins' lives? Or...part of hers? How did he feel about that? Up to now, his heart had been set on being a father but he couldn't deny that Teegan rang all the bells in his heart. But he had nothing to contribute, especially if the court decided to keep the will as it was. Then came the biggest hurdle. Would she wholly trust him? Because if she had any inkling that the shoe would drop and he'd fall off the wagon, he could not, would not, be with her. How was he supposed to be with someone who didn't trust him?

But then, did he fully trust himself? In this moment, yes. His sobriety was such a gray area.

He pulled in behind Teegan's car, Bridge's Pilot and a sleek black SUV. Who else was at the estate? Bridge must have come to protect Teegan, but the other vehicle...

His stomach knotted and then jumped to his throat as he bounded out of the vehicle with his gun pulled. The front door opened and Beau and Bridge walked out with a hulk of man he recognized as Axel Spears. Beside him, the bodyguard who had been assigned to Beau's sister, Coco, after her attack had put her in a temporary coma. Since she'd awakened, she'd been doing great and was now heavily involved in their church. It was nice to see his childhood friends serving the Lord.

Libby Winters, the lady bodyguard, approached with bright blue eyes and a dark ponytail bobbing. "Mr. Spencer," she said and reached out her hand for a firm handshake. He reluctantly accepted it.

What was going on?

Axel Spears, former FBI, extended his massive paw. And Bridge thought *he* was buff? This guy blocked the sun. He and his silent partner, former CIA operative Archer Crow, ran Spears & Bow bodyguard and security services international. But why were they here? His confusion must have been obvious.

"We've been hired as added security. Here is a photo of Amber Rathbone, our other female team member who may assist."

Early to mid-thirties with dark eyes and hair.

"And your other male colleague?" Would Archer Crow be watching over Teegan?

Axel and Libby exchanged a knowing smirk. "He sticks to the background, but even if he was on duty—you'd never know it. He's known for being a phantom."

Rhode let it go. "I don't understand. Did Teegan hire you?" Not that he was against added protection. His ego wasn't so large that he felt intimidated. The more safeguards the better, but they weren't cheap. At all. Only someone with Beau's... "Beau hired you."

Axel nodded once. "He did." He exchanged another smirk, this time with Bridge, as if they knew each other well.

"Do y'all know each other?" Rhode asked. Bridge never mentioned it.

"From our FBI days," Bridge said.

That was it? Seemed like more to him. "I assume Teegan knows."

Axel nodded and ran his hand through coal-black hair. Darker than even Rhode's, it was almost blue it was so black, but it had a few pops of premature silver. "Libby will be on the house with the babies just for precaution. We don't feel they're in direct danger. But we don't want to underestimate this guy. We've talked with Miss Albright and she's given us all the information she can, and Beau has updated us on the case."

Bridge slapped Axel on the back in a friendly gesture. "We'll talk soon. I need to get going."

"Yeah, we will. I want a yes next time I see you."

Bridge shook his head and smirked. "I know you do. No one ever said you weren't persistent." He slid behind the wheel and Rhode frowned.

"Been trying to get your brother to come work for us. Part-time if he wants to keep working for the aftermath recovery." Axel sighed. "You have any questions?"

About a million. Bridge leaving the business? How long had Axel been asking him? A lot of what Bridge did in the FBI was classified and, from what he could tell, Axel's work might have been too.

"No. Not right now. We have phones and you'll be wherever we are. That works."

They shook hands again and the bodyguards swaggered to their trucks. He remembered that kind of confidence but his had been shattered when he'd wrecked his career. He was building it all back though. A career and the confidence.

He heard Libby Winters laugh and turned. She shoved Axel into the truck. "Shut up," she teased. She must have some serious power packed into that petite frame to budge Axel. If body-guarding didn't work out, the World Wrestling Federation would hire him.

Rhode entered the house. Teegan met him in the entry, eyes wild, and gnawing on her bottom lip. "I need expensive bodyguards!"

He had a sneaky suspicion she would be more alarmed by added protection than the comfort of security. "It's Beau's way of helping me out more than it is to scare you. He thinks I'm worried I'm not enough." He kicked at the marble floor. "Maybe I'm not." At least, not in her eyes.

Teegan licked her lips. "You remember that verse in the Bible where the man said I believe but help my unbelief? That's how I feel about you. I trust you. And I don't. I hate that. And it's about me, not you. Which sounds so cliché, but it's true. I have to work through what's springing out of me. My fear. My doubt. My projection onto you. I don't know how long that will take."

"I appreciate the honesty." He swallowed the lump in his throat and exhaled. "Okay, let's find a clue."

"Right. 'My life is a maze of mistakes, but I don't mind, honey. I found you at the end.' Let's head to the labyrinth."

He followed her outside, the wind whipped and the temperature had dramatically dropped in the past couple of days. It was in the mid-fifties, which for Texas was cold. He wore a navy sweater with a navy-and-white-checked dress shirt underneath and jeans and a brown leather coat. Teegan wore a pair of faded jeans and a cardigan over a T-shirt. She shivered.

"You want to go back inside and grab a jacket?" he asked.

"No."

He shrugged out of his coat. "Hold up."

She paused and he moved into her personal space, encircling her with his arms as he draped the jacket over her shoulders and she slipped her arms inside the sleeves. He held the collar of the coat with his hands and searched her eyes, hoping to find unadulterated trust.

"It's warm," she said.

"I generate a lot of body heat," he said.

She swallowed hard. "I think maybe I remember that."

He arched an eyebrow. He'd had some of his hazy memories surface in the past week too.

"I remember this smell. Leather and something…like…sandalwood maybe. Just you, I guess," she murmured.

He brushed a windblown strand of hair from her eye. "Maybe." He held her gaze a moment more, the air swirling with tension—the good kind. The kind that turned into kisses and, if not controlled, something far more unbridled. He dropped his hands and his gaze. "Lead the way," he said, purposefully ending the intense moment.

She nodded and turned on her heel, guiding him expertly through the maze. Wind rustled in the boxwoods and the sky was painted muddy gray.

"I hope it doesn't rain out the festival tonight. Sounds fun."

"It does. I couldn't say no. I love Christmas festivals and

parades. Your mom seemed excited. I hope her strength holds up so she can go."

"Me too." His mom's cancer always loomed like a dark shadow in his mind. No one was getting out of this world alive, but he wanted more time for her and with her. Wanted her to see his babies grow up. Wanted them to know and remember her.

But life didn't always work out perfectly. Rarely did it. He hoped anyway.

At the end of the labyrinth, Teegan paused. "I think it will be here, since she said 'at the end.' I'm just not sure if it's the very end, so let's start on each side and work our way forward to the very end of the labyrinth. And we can't forget it could be buried under concrete or something. You never knew with Lorna."

He was finding that out. Rhode dug into the thick boxwoods, pushing into the gnarled branches and feeling around. "The tops are often trimmed, so I think if she tucked a clue into the hedges, it would be the middle or the bottom to avoid being found before she wanted someone to, or being destroyed with hedge trimmers."

Teegan was already on her hands and knees working her way up in a grid. He mimicked her on the other side. They spent the next thirty minutes switching from comfortable silence to small talk. Teegan shared baby stories, including her pregnancy and the hardships of carrying twins.

"I wish I could have been there to help you through it."

"I know. I would have told you but…"

But they'd had no idea who each other was or how to find one another.

"Hey. Wait a minute! There's something… I can barely feel it. My arms aren't long enough."

Rhode crawled over and reached his arm inside, feeling her fingertips against his, and his pulse spiked. "It's like a hard case."

"Yes," Teegan said, her eyes wide and full of excitement.

Pushing further into the hedges, he clasped the small case and maneuvered it through the branches until he pulled the box free. He handed it to Teegan. "You open it. She wanted you to."

Teegan smiled and opened the tiny safe that was clearly weatherproof but not locked. She pulled out a tube like the others and unrolled the paper. How many more clues did Lorna have on the property?

"'All that I have, I give to you, darling. Two wrongs don't make a right, but you in my life is anything but wrong. You have my whole heart. You're buried deep within me and I will always love you.'" Teegan low hummed. "I think I know the movie, but the location is a blank."

"What movie?"

"*Mr. Right*. From the late fifties. She starred opposite Cary Grant again. I think this movie may have been inspiration for using mostly right turns to get through the labyrinth."

Rhode scrunched his nose. "You don't think it's somehow going to be buried with her, do you?"

"Ew. No." Teegan's face softened and a tear sprang in her eye. "Sorry, it's just I wasn't even invited to her funeral, and all I have of Misty is ashes in a small urn."

Teegan had had little time to grieve her sister or Lorna. He couldn't imagine. "I wish it wasn't that way, and I wish you had some time to process, but even now…time is short. We have to head to the attorney's office, then dinner and the festival."

"I know." She blew a heavy breath. "As far as the movie line, I'll chew on it. This one is tough. I believe she intended it that way. But she must have trusted that I could figure it out."

"You will."

Rhode only hoped they'd stay alive long enough to do exactly that. This killer wasn't going to give up.

Chapter Thirteen

Teegan fidgeted as they entered the imposing brick attorney's office in downtown Austin. Inside the lobby, an ostentatious Christmas tree at least thirty feet tall twinkled with soft white lights. Rhode pressed the elevator button and the doors opened. They rode it to the tenth floor. Leave it to Lorna to hire sharks. But then, she'd known what she was up against. Her own family had smelled the blood in the water.

The halls were abuzz with attorneys flitting around with papers and cups of coffee. Reception pointed them to Scott Carmichael's office, and he welcomed them inside. Teegan glanced around the clutter and disorder. Not exactly what she'd been expecting.

"Have a seat, Teegan." He swept his hand out. "And Mr. Spencer. Sorry about the mess. I haven't finished unpacking and making this my own. It used to belong to James DeVoe. He died in a tragic accident a couple of months ago. Did you know him?" Scott pushed a few boxes away and then took a seat.

"No. Lorna might have. Usually she saw Sylvia."

Scott smiled as he rifled through a drawer, retrieving an ink pen. "I've only been with the firm about a month, but I assure you I have read up on the case and am prepped."

"I believe you."

Scott went through the case in great detail and explained the law in the style of *Law for Dummies*. He took statements from her, and jotted everything down. He noted all the attacks and Rhode's theories about two Landoons trying to kill her: One through scare tactics and the other with a knife.

Scott's eyes widened with each new attack Rhode relayed. "I'm sorry. Do you have any evidence this has been done at the hands of the Landoon family? Anything I can concretely bring the judge?"

"All circumstantial," Rhode said.

Scott nodded and made another note. "I'll contact Detective DeMarco and have him send me police reports." He closed his notebook and smiled, a lopsided sweet smile with perfectly straight teeth. He'd had braces. No one's teeth could be that perfect, and it reminded Teegan of her imperfections and the lack of funds she'd had to right them. "Teegan, you have a strong case and I don't see the court throwing out the will. Anything else that might help me?"

"In full disclosure—if it comes up at the hearing," Rhode said. "We have reason to believe Lorna also buried a treasure of sorts on her property. Nothing was mentioned in your reading, but I wondered if she had any notes about it with instructions for you to remain silent."

Scott's eyebrows raised. "She didn't mention she had a treasure, but I've heard the rumors since I was a kid. I grew up nearby and I'm pretty sure it's been national news—well, tabloid national news."

Teegan had seen it in tabloids before too. "We've found clues. That personal letter was about treasure."

"Well, if you find it before the will's decided, you won't be able to spend it or keep it. Maybe slow your search down." He winked.

Not a terrible idea.

"Who did the estate go to prior to the changes?" Rhode asked.

Who had the most to lose was his real question.

Scott flipped through a mountain of papers in a thick file and his lips twisted to the side. "Evangeline and Dexter received the lion's share then the rest was split equally between the grandchildren and great-grandchildren. Harry Doyle was given sole ownership of the thoroughbred business, including all thoroughbreds. Nothing is in here about Teegan or the estate manager, Olivia Wheaton. But this was written before either was in her employment."

Whoa. That was a massive change. And if she wanted Harry to stay on because he was a good man, then why take him out of owning the business, and give it to Teegan? That was odd. Unless Lorna felt Charlie or another Landoon could swindle Harry out of it, but not Teegan.

But if Harry knew this, he'd never mentioned it. Could Harry have motive? He could be connected with Olivia but not Addie. He had no reason to kill either of them.

Rhode dipped his chin. "That's what we needed to know. Thank you for your time."

They shook hands and left his office, bumping into Sylvia Bondurant, who had handled most all of Lorna's private things. "Mrs. Bondurant, how are you?"

"I'm well." She glanced toward Scott's office. "How is the case going? I heard the will had been contested. I'd have been more surprised if it hadn't been. All of Lorna's family members are piranhas and always have been. Her biggest regret."

"He's doing a great job. When she rewrote her will, you were present. She wasn't under duress."

"No. She was sharp and bright, and I plan to testify to that." She nodded resolutely. "It's hard not being on the case but we thought it best since I needed to be a witness. Scott taking over made sense. He's new and unbiased. Teegan, she wanted you to have it, and she trusted you to steward it well. She thought of you as family." Her smile was tight. "I have to run. Good to see you. Kiss the babies for me." She bolted down the hall.

As they left the building, Teegan frowned. "I'm surprised Lorna didn't leave anything to Sylvia. Not that you have to leave money to your attorney, but Sylvia has worked with her for over a decade and bent over backward for her, showing up whenever Lorna called and catering to her every whim. Seems like she'd show her some appreciation monetarily. If I win the case, I'm going to see she receives a gift. She deserves it."

Rhode opened the passenger door for her and she slid inside. "You're a generous person, Teegan, and she knew you wouldn't be stingy." He jogged around the front of the vehicle then slipped behind the wheel. "We're running late. Festival is underway. You want to eat there? I'm sure they'll have vendors and all sorts of food."

"That sounds good." But she was miles away in thought.

"Hey, are you okay?"

"I don't know. I have this nagging feeling. Like I should know something that I don't." She popped her knuckles. A habit she thought she'd kicked.

"You've had a lot happen and you've had no time, like you said, to grieve or process. It's like when you're rushed to get out the door but you feel like you left something behind. Once things slow down, you won't feel that level of anxiety."

He was probably right. "I guess." But she wasn't sure.

While Rhode drove, Teegan ruminated on the meeting and who might be behind all of this.

They parked in a public lot in downtown Cedar Springs. The streets were lined with cars and people wandered in droves to all the shops, which had been festively decorated. The air was frosty and carried scents of pine, cinnamon and barbecue. Her stomach rumbled as she inhaled the tangy smell.

A food court had been set up in one section and was congested with food trucks and vendors selling cookies, hot chocolate and other baked goods.

"You see the fam?" Rhode asked.

The fam. He had made her a part without batting an eye.

Not *his* family. Just the fam. She could use family right now. She was basically orphaned. "I don't."

Rhode pulled out his phone. "I'll text Stone."

"You see the Spears & Bow peeps?" she asked, darting her gaze among the throngs of people chattering, laughing, and kids romping and shrieking with excitement.

"No, but if they don't want to be seen, they won't be. Axel all but said that." Rhode's phone beeped and he read his message. "Mama is moving slow. They're still about twenty minutes out. Let's find food and we'll meet them in line for Santa in twenty."

"Perfect. I'm starving."

After pushing their way through the crowds, they stood in line for barbecue sandwiches piled with pulled pork and topped with tangy sauce. Rhode had slaw on his but she was not a fan of slaw. She squeezed ketchup onto her hand-cut fries and dug in. "This is so good."

Rhode nodded through a full mouth and handed her a napkin. She dabbed at the sauce spilling onto her chin. No one said barbecue wasn't messy. They perched at a picnic table and ate their dinner while watching the festivities and listening to the live band sing Christmas songs. At the moment, the lead was crooning "Holly Jolly Christmas" in Michael Bublé fashion.

When they were finished eating, Rhode threw away their trash and they strode for the other side of downtown where Santa sat in a wonderland nestled into a Christmas tree lot, complete with fake snow. Teegan paused at a tent full of Christmas quilts and holiday-themed pillow covers. "These are beautiful," she commented. The price tag was too big for her—at least, with her limited funds and Lorna's assets frozen.

Rhode nodded and they strode on.

"Hey, there."

Teegan recognized the voice and turned with a grin. Harry Doyle stood with his hands in his pockets. Harry was like a beach after a storm. Completely disheveled and weathered from years outdoors. He smelled faintly of hay and leather.

"Harry. What are you doing here?"

"Needed a little breather. My son is meeting me here in a few minutes. Tradition."

Harry was always big on traditions. Teegan admired that. She wanted to start traditions with her own children. Maybe the festival would be their first.

"I'm so sorry about Olivia," he said. "She was a good person."

"She was."

"I heard about the will. Charlie came by the stables an hour or so ago. Told me what was going on. I still have my job, but I'm sorry about yours."

"Well, it's not over yet," Rhode said. "Teegan will be back in the house after Christmas."

Harry's eyebrows raised. "The Landoons have always gotten what they wanted. I wouldn't hold my breath. I hope I'm wrong, though, of course." He waved a hand as if it was nothing, but his expression was grim and he'd yet to make full eye contact with her.

Teegan clenched her teeth and forced a smile. "Of course." Harry had always been a nice man, but it seemed like he wasn't rooting for her to win. Or maybe she was simply paranoid, and with every right.

As they headed for the Santa line, Rhode glanced back. "Was his behavior odd to you?"

"Yes, actually. What is that about?"

"I don't know. Probably nothing. Stress. And he's hunting for his son, so he wasn't paying much attention. Didn't the attorney say he was on the docket to testify on Lorna's behalf?"

Teegan nodded. "Harry saw Lorna every single day without fail. They were friends."

"Did he have access to the house?"

"Of course. Lorna trusted him." She studied his wary eyes. "What are you thinking?"

"I'm not sure. But he seems to be pitting his money against you. And that raises my suspicion. I wonder if he's been bribed somehow. With the horses or money or both. We should, at the very least, tell Mr. Carmichael our suspicions. The last thing we need is him getting caught unaware if Harry plans to perjure himself."

Teegan agreed and then heard, "Ma-Ma!" She turned as the Spencer family came into view. Beau and Sissy let the twins down and they rushed to Rhode and Teegan. They each scooped up a baby and Teegan watched as Rhode's face brightened. She knew that look. The same one she had each time she saw them.

Pure joy and unconditional love.

She took in his family. Marisol with her cane for support. Stone and Emily, Beau and Sissy and Bridge. That was what family should look like. It nearly brought her to tears the way they loved the babies and her.

"I never realized how hard is to wrangle two small children who can't even outrun me." Stone grinned. "I was half tempted to rope 'em like calves."

Teegan laughed at his teasing.

"They are slippery," Bridge said. "It was like watching him try to capture greased pigs in a 4-H contest. I have video." He held out his phone.

"You do not," Stone protested. "I told you not to video me!"

"Oh, but I did." Bridge waggled his eyebrows and pressed Play. Teegan and Rhode watched as Stone tried to chase down the babies to put on their shoes. A pink football flew and pegged him in the head.

"Bridge! I have enough to deal with here," Stone griped. "I'd rather wrangle killers. It's easier. Is it wrong to cuff a kid?" he muttered.

Teegan snorted. He was going to make a great dad. The enjoyment in his eyes overrode his complaining.

"It's baby shoes, bro. You've lost your edge," Bridge said.

"You better not be videoing me, Bridge." A football pelted Bridge in the head, causing the camera to shake.

"Okay. Okay!" Then the video ended.

Stone shook his head but chuckled. Emily tucked her arm into his and beamed.

Yep, Teegan would say kids of their own were in the near future.

"I'm going to take Mama over to the benches so she can watch. No point standing in this line for eternity when you can have a front-seat view," Bridge said.

Marisol kissed Teegan's cheek. "You get used to the rowdiness and picking. Teasing is our way of lovin'."

"I see that." And she loved it. "Can I bring you a hot drink? Cider, hot chocolate, tea or coffee?"

"No, dear. I'm happy to sit and see my grandbabies squirm on Santa's lap. The boys have taken a poll on if they'll cry or not."

Teegan laughed again. "They don't meet strangers."

"Just so you know," Sissy said, "I voted they wouldn't cry, but River would pull off Santa's beard."

That was more likely than tears. "Good call." They'd know soon enough.

Well, Sissy won the poll. River had successfully ripped away Santa's beard while he'd worked to keep Brook from removing his glasses and destroying them. Rhode had wondered if it had been a planned blitz attack from his little minions. Mama had loved every second and remarked how much they reminded her of him and Sissy at that age.

After the Santa debacle, they'd all eaten cookies and listened to the live music before taking the babies to see the reindeer and to make reindeer food, which consisted of oats, edible glitter and a carrot. The extremes parents went to in order to make Christmas special was beyond him. The greatest miracle of Christmas was Jesus Himself.

But Rhode was all on board with helping the kiddos scatter the food on the ground, knowing the wind would blow it all away, and he'd probably even take a few bites from the carrot to prove Rudolph had had his snack. Like his dad used to eat one of the cookies, take a bite out of the second and drink all the milk. The first thing Rhode had always done on Christmas morning was race to see if Santa had eaten the cookies and drunk the milk. Then Dad would read them the Christmas story from the Bible before a free-for-all broke loose on the gifts.

Once they returned to the ranch, the babies were wiped out and whiny. Teegan put them down, wanting some time alone, and Rhode was now discussing the case with his brothers and Beau.

"Any news on Kenny Lee?"

"Same knife that killed Misty, Addie and Olivia was used on Kenny. So he's been ruled out as the murderer," Beau said. "If I had to guess, I'd say he stalked Misty here and got in the killer's way. He then disposed of Kenny's body. I'm not sure why though. Why not leave him dead in the house?"

"Maybe he thought he could hide him and frame him. Any blood evidence could be assumed Misty had hurt him during the attack. No body meant he could be on the loose and doing this." This made the most sense to Rhode.

Stone and Bridge agreed.

Teegan entered the living room. Rhode's old and gray dogs ambled up for petting. "Sweet ole boys." She rubbed their heads.

"I don't like to think of them as old. Just wise. Old means their time is growing short and they've been my best friends for so long—"

"Because humans don't like you," Stone teased.

Teegan chuckled.

"Anyway," he stressed, ignoring his brother's smart remark, "I can't bear to lose 'em."

"You'll have to bury 'em with our other gone-but-not-forgotten friends," Bridge said somberly.

"Death is hard no matter animal or human." Teegan sighed. "So, were y'all discussing my case?"

"We were," Rhode said. "Is there anything about Addie and Olivia you can tell us that might be important?" The two women had connections to the Landoons. Rhode could buy that Peter may have killed Addie as a jilted boyfriend. But why kill Olivia unless she'd seen or heard something she wasn't supposed to?

Charlie was still on the table too. Could he have done something that Olivia had witnessed or said something she'd overheard?

"Nothing that would cause their murders."

"Were they close with Misty?" Rhode asked.

"Misty was hard to get close to. She was guarded, and could be tough to deal with at times."

"Meaning?" Rhode leaned his elbows on his knees.

"She was the Regina George of our school." Teegan darted her glance around the room. Rhode's eyes narrowed. And, based on his brothers equally confused expressions, they were lost too.

"Know my crowd. I forget not everyone is a movie buff like me. Regina George is a character in the movie *Mean Girls*. She was *the* mean girl and her friends—loosely called friends—were loyal out of fear of consequences. They hung out with her and went along with her nastiness. Sort of like Olivia and Addie with Misty. They cheered together. Neither had a real mean streak. Misty...could be mischievous in a dark way. I hate even talking ill of her. She had way more good parts."

"I'm sure she did," Rhode said.

"Well, if that's all, I'm going to try and sleep." A divot

formed along Teegan's brow, revealing the same expression from earlier at the festival.

Rhode excused himself and followed her down the hall to the guestroom. "Hey. You still feel like you can't make a thought or memory surface?"

"Yes. How did you know?"

"I'm getting pretty good at reading you."

"Part of your job and all," she said.

"No. I mean yes, it is, but no. I just… I just like to know what you're thinking and feeling." He inched closer and inhaled her sweet scent. "If I'm being honest. But I haven't forgotten we're just friends. We are that, aren't we?"

She held his gaze. "Absolutely."

"Good. And the feeling you're having?"

She squinted and shook her head. "It's like a memory rose from the depths. It's hovering just underneath the surface. Unsettling, but important. I can't make it bob above the water and reveal itself. But, again, the past few days have been a blur. A million things going on, being said. It might be nothing."

"Try to sleep. That always helps me. You want me to bring you some spearmint tea? Mama says it always helps her rest."

She touched his arm. "No. But thank you. I appreciate your thoughtfulness." Teegan slipped into her bedroom and closed the door with a quiet click.

Why did he feel like he'd lost something he never had?

Chapter Fourteen

Teegan flew up from a fitful sleep, sweat pooling in the hollow of her throat and on the back of her neck, hair sticking to her skin. She couldn't remember her dream, but it was important. Ugh. What was it? What had she remembered subconsciously?

She couldn't bring it to the forefront, but she did know where to find the next clue. She checked the clock on her cell phone. Almost 4:00 a.m. Now was the time to do the search, before light broke through the sky and the estate became a hustle and bustle with people, which meant eyes. And where they were going would stand out to anyone. Plus, she only had four hours to be out of the house. It was Christmas Eve.

After quickly brushing her teeth and changing into sweats and a hoodie, she tiptoed to Rhode, who was sleeping on the couch with his laptop on his chest. She appreciated his commitment to find the killer. And somewhere out there one of the Spears & Bow bodyguards kept watch.

He reminded her of River, the way he snoozed. His hair fell in his eyes and stubble covered his normally baby-smooth face. One man should not be this attractive. Surely, other women must think the same thing. No matter, he was stupid good-looking to her. Not to mention, patient and kind and funny.

"Rhode," she whispered as she shook him.

His eyes quickly opened, revealing he'd only been dozing. "I know where the next clue or treasure is. I know what the attorney said, but I want to go anyway. Just to see if I'm right. We have to go now though. And...and we'll need shovels."

Rhode sat up ramrod. "Shovels? What time is it?"

"Four. It'll take a bit of time and I'd like to do it before dawn and the babies wake, but someone needs to know we're gone in case they wake early. I don't have much time before I'm thrust off the estate."

Rubbing the scruff on his chin, he nodded. "Give me five minutes, and I'm going to text Libby and let her know we're going out onto the property so she doesn't shoot if she spots us. I have a feeling she's a 'shoot first and ask questions later' kind of woman."

Teegan smirked. "Yeah, she seems tough."

Rhode padded to the bathroom with his black duffel bag. When he returned, he smelled of mint and he'd changed into jeans, a violet Henley and a flannel shirt with the same color mixed in. "Okay, Emily has the baby monitor. Let's go dig it up. Where are we going? You haven't actually said yet."

"A cemetery."

Rhode did a double-take. "A what?"

Teegan grinned, excitement building. This could be it. The treasure. "Now you know why I left you in suspense. Come on. I'll explain when we get there."

After arriving at the estate, they headed to the gardener's shed. "The clue was, 'All that I have, I give to you, darling. Two wrongs don't make a right, but you in my life is anything but wrong. You have my whole heart. You're buried deep within me and I will always love you.'"

"How does that play into a before-dawn dig in a cemetery?" Rhode asked. "Don't you already think we're living a horror movie? You now want to add a creepy cemetery? I'm already freaked out." Rhode hunched against the early morning wind, his flashlight poking out of his sleeve; he'd pulled his hands into them.

"That's fair, but last night you talked about not wanting to discuss the fact your dogs are getting old and Bridge mentioned burying them. The only thing Lorna loved more than her children were her two greyhounds, Chaplin and Claudette—after Charlie Chaplin and Claudette Colbert. They were her pride and joy and, when they passed, she buried them on the backside of the property. Headstones and all. They're buried deep within her, but also in the ground. They had her whole heart. I'm ninety-seven-percent sure it's there."

"That or we're pulling a Randy Travis for nothing."

Teegan snorted and handed him a shovel from the shed. "I'll be singing 'Diggin' up Bones' all the livelong day now. Thanks for that."

Rhode smirked.

Teegan closed the door, her own shovel in hand. "It's out past the English garden near the woods. I didn't see Libby's car. But I know she followed us here."

"It's her job to stay hidden and that includes her vehicle. She'll be doing perimeter sweeps. We should take her coffee after we're done. It's cold and who couldn't use the caffeine?"

"Good idea."

They marched toward the east side of the property and Teegan shivered and paused.

"What's wrong?" Rhode asked.

She wasn't sure but the hairs had raised on her neck. "I feel...watched."

"Might be Libby. Remember, they watch but we can't see them. You probably feel her eyes on you. Who would know we'd be out here this early? I didn't even know."

"Fair enough."

They passed the garden, scents of flowers crawling through

the air. Teegan's nose started to run from the cold. Back near the woods, she pointed to the rectangular iron gate. Inside were flowers and a big tree, a bench and two headstones. "Lorna would come out here before she grew too old and visit them. Talk to them. She said it was a peaceful time that she treasured. Another reason I think we've found the right place. She treasured her dogs."

"If I dig those dog bones up and the note says they're the treasure as some kind of Lorna joke, I'm gonna be fit to be tied FYI." Rhode opened the gate and it yawned an eerie, lingering squeak, sending a shiver through Teegan.

"I'll start with Chaplin. You dig up Claudette," she said, and drove her shovel into the hard-packed earth. Her sore muscles from the car crash and being stabbed protested, but she continued. Scoop by scoop, removing soil. "Digging holes to bury a dog—or a body—is a lot of work. There has to be a better way for serial killers to hide their victims."

Rhode paused and studied her, the flashlight beams shining up from the ground, illuminating the amused gleam in his eye. "Really? That's the topic you want to land on?"

She shrugged then kept digging.

"How far would a woman—or someone who hired the gardener—bury a dog? Surely not six feet," Rhode mused. He continued digging, his scoops bigger and faster than hers.

"I don't know. Far enough that another animal wouldn't dig them up. But how far down is that? I'd google it but I forgot my phone in the car."

"Not smart." His lips twisted to the side and he went wide-eyed.

The unsettling sensation returned with a vengeance. "Rhode? What's wrong?"

He patted his back pockets and then his coat pockets and frowned. "My phone must have fallen out." He grunted and picked up his flashlight, scanning the ground for his cell.

Teegan resumed digging and hit something hard. "Hey. I

think I found something." She dropped to her knees. "Can you hold that flashlight over me? I can't see."

Rhode stopped hunting for his phone and shined the light over Chaplin's grave. No dog bones, thank the Good Lord, but she spied a black box like the one in the hedges, only bigger. Maybe 8.5 x 11. She hefted it out of the open grave. "A clue."

"Well, don't leave me all alone and in the dark. What is it?"

His words struck her. "What did you say?"

"I was kidding."

"I know." A memory finally bobbed to the surface, clear enough for her to see. "I remember something."

"Go on."

"A dance. Like a Sadie Hawkins dance, only called the Bluebonnet Dance. I didn't want to ask a boy so I didn't go, but Misty, Olivia and Addie did."

"What happened?" Rhode asked.

"Misty did what Misty was famous for. Being a prankster at someone else's expense. I didn't know about it until it was too late. Misty wouldn't tell me who she'd asked. Said it was a surprise and if I wanted to know to come to the dance. She knew I wouldn't. I would have stopped it. She knew that too."

"Stopped what?"

Teegan leaned on her shovel with one hand and held the dirty box in the other, the memory turning her stomach. "Misty had asked a boy named Anthony—as a joke. Anthony was sweet but he was socially awkward and he had a severe underbite, so some of the bullies called him Moonface. It was horrifying."

"If you didn't go to the dance and she didn't tell you who her date was, how did you find out?" Rhode asked.

"After the dance, Misty called me and told me a bunch of kids were going treasure hunting on the Landoon estate. Mom had been asleep for a while and I wanted to go. So, I locked up any liquor I found and headed to the estate. Just like I told you."

Rhode frowned. "If Misty was a popular cheerleader and he was a kid who was bullied, why would he believe she actually wanted to attend with him?"

Teegan's stomach lurched at that cruel night. "Because, unbeknownst to me, she was pretending to be me. I was always nice to Anthony. We talked about old movies and books. He was obsessed with the *Lord of the Rings*. I ate my lunch in the library and he often did too. Different reasons, same safe space."

"That was pretty vile of her. Sorry."

"No, you're right. It was."

"What happened at the dance?"

Teegan wasn't completely sure since she hadn't attended but Addie had confided her side of the story later. "Addie gave him a note from me, aka Misty. It told him she would rather spend the night alone with him, like we'd spent time alone in the library, and to meet her at nine o'clock at the Landoon estate. They could treasure hunt together and watch the stars."

"He bought it?"

"He had no reason not to. And, Rhode, you have to understand he was socially awkward, a total introvert. Not to mention, he trusted me. This was an introvert's dream! No crowds. No forced dancing or chitchatting with other students who often made fun of you."

Rhode heaved a heavy breath. "I kinda don't want to ask what happened next."

It was tragic. "Misty had clued in some of the football players and other friends. They arrived before nine and hid around the lake, in the boat and in the boathouse. When he sneaked onto the dock where she'd instructed they meet, she'd already laid out bluebonnets and was in the water. She told him to hop in—for skinny-dipping. She'd laid her dress on the dock, too, but she had on a swimsuit."

"He didn't," Rhode said, his eyes wide.

"Why wouldn't he?"

"Go on."

"He stripped down and so many kids jumped out, laughing and heckling. Addie said it was horrific. Misty was in the water, cackling, and said they didn't need the moonlight with his chin. She actually said that. And he thought I had talked to him that way." Teegan wiped away a few tears. "It gets worse."

"How?"

"Because he started crying then jumped in the lake. Addie said they thought he was swimming out to Misty to do something bad, but he didn't surface. Finally, a football player had the sense to realize he was drowning himself! He dove in and brought him out of the water, but he wasn't breathing. He gave him CPR and he came to. No one even called an ambulance, Rhode! He could have died."

"What happened when he woke?"

"By then, most everyone had scattered. He ran off with his clothes, crying. That's when I arrived. I didn't even realize it was Anthony until Addie and Olivia found me and confessed what Misty had done pretending to be me."

Rhode low whistled. "That is seriously messed up, Teegan. Did you confront Misty?"

"That was the only time in my life I laid hands on her. We came to blows and I shoved her hard into the bedroom closet. We didn't speak for over two weeks. And when I returned home that night, Mom had found a bottle I hadn't and was drunk. I should have stayed home. Misty had wanted me to be there. Wanted me to think it was as funny as she did. Or maybe she'd wanted to be mean to me too. I don't know."

Rhode shook his head. "Did you try to make it right with him later?"

Teegan had wanted to but it had been the last week of school for seniors. "Anthony didn't return to school the following Monday, and he didn't walk with us at graduation. He disappeared."

"Why did you think of it now?"

"Because Addie told me that while he was on the dock, before he'd seen Misty in the water, he'd said not to leave him alone in the dark. He was scared of the dark. She said they'd snickered at that, but tried to keep it quiet so he wouldn't hear them out there. I guess being out here at night and those words brought it all back. Sadly, I haven't thought about it in years. And we never spoke of it again."

But she was certain Anthony had thought about it often and carried the pain and humiliation with him. She hoped he hadn't let it define him…but the bluebonnets. Misty. Addie. Olivia. She'd been so focused on the Landoon family threatening her, it hadn't crossed her mind this might not have a thing to do with the inheritance left her. But it explained why someone had threatened her to scare her, and why someone else wanted to butcher her and left behind bluebonnets.

Rhode's mind reeled a million miles a minute. The sick tragedy that had happened well over a decade ago and the fact he'd been looking at these attacks all wrong. They needed more information on this Anthony guy. Where did he live now? Work? Had he been in contact with Addie or Olivia—or even Misty? He needed Beau and Dom on it immediately.

"What's this guy's last name, Teegan? Do you remember?"

"Um…" Her eyes grew to the size of balloons and her mouth dropped open.

"What is it?"

"I can't believe it. It's Doyle. Anthony Doyle."

"Doyle as in *Harry* Doyle?" Could this Anthony have been his son or grandson? Harry was in his mid to late sixties, if Rhode had to guess. He'd been weird at the festival and that's when Teegan had had those strange vibes. It was convenient that a gunshot had sounded out at the stables but the attacker hadn't been shot. If Harry was the attacker and heard the sirens, the shot could have been a cover for him. He was helping to protect Teegan. But really, he was the one after her. He was always in the stables according to her but was conveniently missing during the attack.

Harry had been employed by Lorna for years. He would have known about the multiple passages that led to the tunnel. The attacker had disappeared from the wine cellar, but the door had been locked. There must be other ways in and out of the house.

Revenge for a loved one was a strong motivator, and Harry was in great shape.

Snapping of twigs jarred Rhode from the conversation. He placed his finger to his lips and drew his gun. They stood listening to wind rustle the leaves. The noise could be deer or other nighttime critters still creeping around before dawn.

But Rhode's gut warned him it was dangerous. Eyes were on them and they weren't Libby Winters'.

"Stay here. I'm going to check it out."

"Let's just go back to the house," she pleaded.

"If he's out here stalking you, I'm finding him. And if I have to put him in this dog cemetery to keep you safe, I will. Sit tight. I'll be right back."

"Everyone knows no one comes back in a horror movie after saying they'll be right back, Rhode!"

A flock of birds burst from the branches as if spooked.

A predator.

"Rhode," Teegan whispered with urgency. "Maybe we should just—" She screamed and pointed behind him. Rhode spun around in time to be charged by the jester, who knocked his gun from his hand.

Teegan squealed.

The blade came down quick and hard, entering Rhode's gut, but he didn't feel pain. Adrenaline had already kicked in, protecting him to fight or take flight. Then the jester ripped the blade from his flesh and he did feel that.

Searing. Throbbing pain.

Raising the knife again, the jester brought it down and struck his shoulder, shoving him to the ground.

"Run, Teegan! Go!"

When the blade raised again, Rhode grabbed the jester's arm, holding it back. He never saw the sucker punch coming. Everything faded to black.

The jester raised his face, hidden beneath a terrifying mask, the knife dripping with Rhode's blood. Teegan bolted, dropping the box. She didn't want to leave Rhode, but if she stayed, the jester would kill her too.

Rhode.

Dying in a pet cemetery if he wasn't already dead—he'd hate that. Teegan had to flee and find help. "Libby!" she screamed as fear consumed her and adrenaline boosted her speed as she ate up the ground. But Libby knew Rhode was keeping a watch over Teegan and could be in a sweep a mile away on the other side of the estate.

In the early morning haze and hustle, Teegan had rushed off without her phone and Rhode had lost his. Teegan couldn't fight a killer and try to recover Rhode's phone or gun.

The jester was hot on her heels and gaining. Teegan darted toward the lake and the boathouse, hoping to hop in the boat and get as far out on the lake as she could. He'd never make it to the other side on foot before her.

She hollered again for Libby, her voice carrying on the dark wind. Her pulse pounded in her ears, but she kept her eyes locked on the boathouse where they kept the keys.

Behind her, heavy footfalls fell faster, harder, and her blood turned cold.

Moonlight glittered on the water even as the clouds morphed from inky black to slate gray as the sun worked on its approach to dawn. Up ahead, the boathouse came into view. She could make it. But what if Rhode was dead? What if it was too late?

Images of River and Brook kept her rushing forward with

all her might. As she reached the boathouse, she glanced behind her. The man in the white mask, bathed in an eerie glow, approached, and her hands fumbled to open the door, but she managed it. On the right hung a pegboard full of keys, one set belonging to the speedboat.

Grabbing the keys, she turned to race to the boat, but the jester—Harry—now blocked her path. Could she appeal to him as a parent? She, too, had kids now. She had to try.

"Harry, please, don't do this."

He slowly cocked his head, his grip tightening on the knife. Ice raced through her veins.

"I just figured out today that it's you. I understand your fury. I do. But you need to know the truth about that night. I've always wanted to tell it to Anthony, but he vanished."

He stood eerily silent, his head still tipped to the side.

She continued. "Misty pretended to be me. I would have never done something so cruel. Please don't do this. I have children and while I know I'd want revenge for their humiliation, killing isn't the answer."

He inched toward her and she shuddered. "Take the mask off, Harry. Let's talk like adults." If she could appeal to any sliver of humanity left in him, she would, but not when he was wearing a mask of wicked confidence. "Please." No last laughs tonight. Just truth. And, hopefully, forgiveness.

Harry reached for his mask and Teegan felt a tiny sliver of relief. He knew her. Knew she wasn't capable of menacing behavior.

Slowly, he pulled the terrifying plastic face from his and Teegan stumbled backward, shock quaking in her veins.

"Not who you expected? Crazy what a jaw reconstruction, working out and a new haircut will do for the appearance."

Scott Carmichael's handsome face stared back at her.

The transformation was astonishing. But the weird nagging she'd felt in his presence now made sense. She'd known him all along but couldn't place him. It wasn't Harry jarring memories, but Scott.

"But your name?" What was happening? How could he work at a top law office in Austin with a phony name?

"Anthony Scott Doyle. After the terror you and your friends reigned, I was too embarrassed to stay the same person. I changed my last name, taking my mom's maiden name. I went to law school, searching for ways to make you pay legally, but you know what? There's nothing one can do to scum like you for bullying a person almost two decades ago."

"I didn't—"

"Stop lying!" he bellowed, raising the knife. "I'm so sick of lies and pranks. Of people like you. I got the wrong sister the first time, but I'm not sorry."

Actually, he hadn't killed the wrong sister. The irony was terrifying and tragic.

"Misty was nothing but a vicious viper with a pretty face. But you can't pretend, can't get out of this. You knew things I hadn't told anyone."

True. Misty would have had to gain his trust somehow. "She must have overheard us talking in the library. I didn't share our conversations with her." But she had shared them with Olivia and Addie. They must have confided in Misty.

"Liars never stop lying. I was humiliated. For years. And that was just the cherry on top. I couldn't even go to my own graduation for the embarrassment. That's what you and your sick friends did to me!"

Teegan remained silent.

"You ran a long con on me. Made me into the butt of all your jokes. I trusted you, Teegan. Thought you were different. But you aren't. Your kids will be better off without you." He stepped forward and she retreated. "You ran a long con. So, I did too."

"I don't understand."

"For being smart, you're pretty stupid," he said through a sneer.

Where was Libby? Where was any help? She inched her arm behind her back, feeling along the wall for anything that might be handy to use as a weapon. She was cornered like a mouse with a big cat, fangs bared, ready to pounce.

"When Dad told me you'd become the caretaker for Miss Landoon, I set it all in motion. I stopped at the stables a few times. Knew Lorna's attorney. A real shame James DeVoe died, but it made a spot available for a new attorney. Me." His wicked grin revealed that the lawyer's death had not been accidental. Scott had killed him. As far as knowing about the tunnel, he could have always known because of Harry. He'd been employed at the estate for decades. "But I had already been working that angle, schmoozing one of the named partners. So when he died... I was right there with the plans to become Lorna's main attorney, get close—to you. Maybe even get to know you. Pretend to like you. Pretend to be your friend—or more—and betray you too. I knew Sylvia would never give up those billables, so I set another plan in motion, but then Lorna went and fell down the stairs and I found a new way in."

Be unbiased and run the reading of the will. "Why didn't Harry speak to you at the reading of the will? If you're his son."

"Dad knows some of what happened that night—that I'd been embarrassed. He presumed it was because I wasn't a good dancer and awkward around people, and I let him believe it. With the changes to my name and physique, I asked him not to let anyone know we were related, including the Landoons. He always respected my wishes. I suspect because he had a hunch the night of the dance was far worse than I let on."

Teegan's mind reeled. Harry had been cordial but never overly friendly. "He fired a warning shot at you! He could have killed you. His own son. He'd have never gotten over that."

"There's always risks involved. It was worth it."

If he was willing to let his father almost kill him, then why hadn't Scott copped to killing Lorna? "You act as though you didn't murder my employer. An innocent woman!" She continued searching for a weapon, but nothing.

Scott made another move toward her. She was trapped inside the boathouse. Only one exit that he was blocking. "I didn't kill Lorna. I'd decided you weren't worth the game, the seduction. It was time for you to die. When I arrived, she was already at the bottom of the stairs and your sister was standing over her. I assumed you'd killed her for the cash. Which wasn't surprising. But I guess your sister did it or maybe the guy who'd been there with her."

No way. Misty would never! She had no reason to kill Lorna—or anyone. Teegan didn't believe him.

"Kenny Lee?"

"Don't know or care. He saw me and was running for the car. I couldn't let him get away and I knew Charlie was on the property. I used the golf cart and dumped him in the woods."

Wait. If Kenny Lee was running for Misty's vehicle, then he must have been with her. They must have gotten back together. Or there would have been two vehicles. But Teegan would never fully know. Kenny and Misty were gone.

Finally, her hand grasped something slender and wooden. An oar! She gripped it and kept to the shadows, waiting for the right moment to strike and praying Libby would come this way to do a perimeter check.

"Did Harry keep you in the know? Is that why Lorna cut him out of the second will? Had she overhead something and that's why you killed her? Because my sister would never have done that."

Scott laughed and her blood curdled. "After what you say she did to me, you don't think she'd shove an old lady down the stairs? Either you didn't know her at all or you're lying about your involvement that night of the dance. Bluebonnets were a nice clue, but you never put it together. You wrote me off. Forgot about it all. But I never forgot. I've remembered it every day of my life."

"I—" She had forgotten. Instead she said, "I'm sorry. And I'm sorry if it cost your dad the business. Your heartache and grief. I am sorry." And she was. None of that should have happened.

"Dad didn't want the stupid business. Too much headache. When Lorna told him she'd willed it all to him, he asked her to amend it to keep him with a clause he couldn't be let go, but he never wanted the headache of owning a business. He wasn't about the money—not like her family."

That actually made sense. Two feet. That's all she needed and then she could use the oar to clobber him and escape to the boat.

"You were going to actually be my lawyer in court?" Part of that long con.

"No. I never planned to go to court. You're going to be dead. It won't matter. Talk time is up." He rushed her and she thrust the oar out, knocking him off balance; the knife clattered to the dock. She raced for the boat, keys in hand, and ready to speed to safety, call the cops and ambulance, and free them from this nightmare.

Scott's hand latched onto her shoulder and she screamed.

Gunshots rang out. One. Two.

Scott's hand released and she turned as he fell to the dock in a crumpled, dead heap.

Libby!

Teegan snapped her attention toward the figure on the dock. Not Libby.

Rhode!

His body was bent forward, one hand holding his stomach. His purple Henley was darker in the middle now from the blood. In the other hand, he held his gun.

"Rhode!"

"It's over," he rasped and collapsed on the dock with a thunderous crash.

Teegan's heart stopped and she froze for a second before launching herself in his direction. She dropped to her knees in a pool of blood. "Rhode! Rhode!"

But he was unresponsive.

She could not lose him. The babies couldn't lose him. She'd been such an idiot. "Rhode, please stay with me. I... I love you. I need you. We need you." She brushed her lips to his clammy brow. "Please don't die. Please live."

"Let's just chalk this up to God's perfect timing, which pretty much seems to be later than we want," a woman's voice remarked with utter calmness and even a hint of humor. "I found blood at the pet cemetery and then heard you scream."

Libby emerged from the shadows, her light conversation as if no one had nearly died or was dying. But then she spotted Rhode and her expression sobered and she darted into action, checking Rhode's pulse. "He's alive. Apply pressure." Libby guided Teegan's hands to Rhode's abdomen then checked Scott's pulse. "He's not." Two bullet wounds side by side filled his forehead. One from Rhode. The other from Libby.

Teegan couldn't control her tears as she peered down at Rhode. Helpless. Lifeless. He'd risked it all to protect her. "I can't lose this man. I love him."

Libby's face contorted, pain unmasked. "Sometimes the people we love most...they don't always make it."

Chapter Fifteen

Teegan tiptoed into Rhode's hospital room. After the police and EMTs arrived at the Landoon estate, Rhode had been rushed into surgery. Thankfully, he would fully recover from the injuries and would be allowed home the day after Christmas. Best gift ever. Teegan had been stuck at the police department, going over her statements for what felt like hours, and all she wanted was to kiss her babies and be at the hospital for Rhode. Libby had sat with her the entire time, which was not in her job description, but it meant the world to Teegan to have her support and her help in filling in the gaps.

Libby had foregone using the golf cart because it hadn't blended into the shadows like patrolling on foot. Lorna's property was so vast, when she'd heard the faint scream, she'd come running. Libby could run a six-minute mile. Impressive.

Teegan's friend Yolanda had picked up the children so the Spencer family could all be with Rhode. She'd taken them to her parents' home for some Christmas Eve festivities. It was now nearing evening, the day had been long, exhausting, and not exactly full of the Christmas spirit.

Rhode slept peacefully. She ran her finger through his hair, so thankful he'd been spared.

"Hey," she said.

Rhode's dark lashes fluttered and then his eyes opened. He studied her face and smiled. "Hey."

"How you feel?"

"Like I was stabbed in the shoulder and the gut, but it's all good." He shifted on the bed and winced, but in true Rhode Spencer form, he had his wits about him—and his wit.

"Can I get you anything?"

He patted the bed and she eased beside him. "Stone and Bridge are in the waiting area. Sissy and Beau went to pick up food, and Emily's now at the ranch with your mom."

"Is Mama okay? I know I probably set her back."

"She's fine. A strong woman who raised a strong family. Dom was here too."

"What did he say? About the case? Is it really over?" Rhode asked.

Teegan nodded. "He questioned Charlie after I told him Scott denied killing Lorna. It fit. No knife. But Charlie lawyered up fast. They brought in Evangeline and pitted the two against each other. When Evangeline heard she'd be tried for the murder, she started talking. According to her, Charlie sneaked onto the estate because he'd overheard Harry on the phone with Scott about asking Lorna to take him out of the will as inheriting the business. That she'd done it. Charlie knew the will had been amended and wanted to see it himself."

"And Lorna?"

"That wily woman saw him, got suspicious, and had the audacity to climb those stairs and confront him. It turned into an argument and, according to Evangeline, Charlie shoved her and she fell, but it was an accident. He panicked and left, calling his mother and telling her what had happened. She instructed him to stay silent. So she's in trouble but not as much as Charlie."

"And the other threats like painting your car and running us off the road?"

"All Evangeline and Charlie to scare me, as you thought. They hoped it would cause me to give up."

"Was Harry involved?" Rhode asked and cleared his throat. "Can I have a drink?"

"Of course." She poured him a cup of water and helped him sip.

"Thanks. So, Harry?"

"Harry didn't know the real story about Anthony's past at the estate or that he was the one killing people. He said the name change was to sound more like a prominent attorney. And, to be honest, I think that's somewhat true." She relayed everything Anthony, aka Scott, had told her on the dock. "I think Scott mostly wanted to be someone else. He hated the boy who was picked on and all he represented, and Harry did know about him being bullied in general. So he agreed to all the changes and wishes of secrecy." Teegan brushed a bang behind his ear. "This was all a revenge plot."

"Not exactly," Rhode said. "Beau came by a little earlier. They found items in Scott's house. Photos and trophies."

"Like serial killer trophies?"

Rhode nodded. "During Scott's college years, two girls were stabbed and bluebonnets left near the scene. But it wasn't multiple stabs."

Teegan covered her mouth with her hands. "You're kidding."

"That's not all. While Scott clerked for a judge in Dallas, one of the paralegals also died by a stab wound and bluebonnets were left behind. So, I don't think it was just revenge. I believe Anthony Doyle, aka Scott Carmichael, was a serial killer and used revenge to kill more women, including attempting to murder you. I think the revenge was how he personally targeted you, Addie and Olivia."

A serial killer? Had that night broken him so badly he'd grown an urge to kill? No. He'd had a choice to make. He could have overcome his past. Teegan had. Instead, he'd chosen to make heinous choices. What was done to him had been vicious and wrong, but everything he'd chosen to do was on him.

"What about the VICAP? I thought it would have let you know about similar murders."

"Sometimes law enforcers get behind on paperwork and entering information into the system. If it's not entered into the database, it's not there to find. Who knows, there might even be a larger trail of murders in the places Scott lived and worked."

Teegan sat stunned, her hand still in Rhode's. She had so much she wanted to say. So much to apologize for.

"I do have some good news—other than I'll live."

She chuckled. "What's that? I could use some good news."

"Dom said in light of the circumstances, you get the estate. No court date. It's yours. No moving into the ranch, and you can do whatever you want for the babies."

Tears sprang to her eyes. Christmas in their home. The only home the babies knew. But that paled in light of what she wanted to say. "I have good news too."

"Yeah?"

She wiped her eyes and laid a hand on his cheek. "I love you."

His eyes widened and shined with moisture. "You do?"

"When you dropped on that dock, I thought you were dead. And, in that instant, I realized I wanted you in our lives. Completely. Not me as your accuser but as your support system. Our children need you. Not any dad. You. God is going to help us walk this journey out and I want it to be together. If I haven't hurt you so badly you don't want to try."

Cupping her neck, Rhode gently drew her to his mouth. When his lips met hers, he whispered, "This is the best Christmas gift ever. I love you, too, Teeg. So much." Then he kissed her with such tenderness and care, she almost cried again. This man was not perfect. He had a past. A dark past. But the enemy did enough accusing and guilt-tripping of his own. She was not going to add to it. She would be his biggest champion, right next to Jesus.

When he broke the kiss, he grinned. "Sorry I ruined Christmas. I know you had all these grand ideas. Nothing went your way."

True. "I've learned Christmas doesn't have to be perfect by what I do or buy or when I put up a tree. It's not about a day. It's about who."

Rhode's mischievous eyes sent a flutter through her. "You're not going to go all 'Jesus is the reason for the season' greeting card on me, are you?"

She laughed. "No. But it's true."

"It is." He kissed her hand. "I want you to know that I don't want your money and you can never think I would be after it because I don't have much. So I'm fully onboard with a prenup."

Teegan snorted and started to bring a witty comeback but then his words dawned and her heart galloped in her chest. "Rhode, you said prenup."

His grin turned wily. "Well, yeah. I'm going to marry you. Duh."

She couldn't contain the joy bubbling all through her. "Well, I'm gonna say yes. Duh. And I don't want a prenup. If we're together it's til death do us part, and all that I have is yours too. Lorna would want it that way."

"I guess that's settled then." He kissed her again.

Teegan broke away. "We can't spend Christmas Eve making out in a hospital bed."

"Why not?" His tone was innocent but teasing filled his dark eyes. "Then what will we do?"

Teegan removed a thick envelope from her handbag. "Open it."

Rhode did as he was told and perused the stack of papers. "It's a screenplay."

"Lorna's treasure we found in the pet cemetery. I had Libby

retrieve it after all the chaos. It's a screenplay she cowrote with one of Hollywood's most famous directors—Charles Kendrick. A Christmas screenplay!"

"Wow. This will be worth a lot of money." Rhode low whistled. "What are you going to do with it?"

"I think Lorna wanted me to find it because of my love for theater and movies. We had that in common. I can't say it would have ever seen the light of day had I not come along."

"But you did. And I have a feeling I know what you're going to say."

"What's that?"

"You're going to go back to the local theater and pitch this play and perform it. Next Christmas, if I had to guess."

Teegan's eyes pooled again. This man truly knew her. And so had Lorna. She would represent her and her hard work well. "That's exactly what I want to do. What Lorna would have wanted."

"Lorna knew you would treasure it and do the right thing, not try to sell it and make a fortune, like her kids would have. Lorna's legacy will live on, through you. Can't beat that kind of treasure." Rhode ran a hand over the old typed pages. "Can we force Bridge and Stone to be Christmas carolers?"

"I thought you wanted to help her legacy not hurt it."

Rhode chuckled. "You are amazing. I can't wait for you to be my wife."

She leaned down and kissed him again. "So you know, my calendar is wide open."

* * * * *

Romantic Suspense

Danger. Passion. Drama.

Available Next Month

Colton's Last Resort Amber Leigh Williams
Arctic Pursuit Anna J. Stewart

Mistaken Identities Tara Taylor Quinn
Kind Her Katherine Garbera

LOVE INSPIRED
Hunted On The Trail Dana Mentink
Tracking The Missing Sami A. Abrams
Larger Print

LOVE INSPIRED
Texas Kidnapping Target Laura Scott
Alaskan Wilderness Peril Beth Carpenter

LOVE INSPIRED
Ambush On The Ranch Tina Wheeler
Cold Case Disappearance Shirley Jump

Keep reading for an excerpt of a new title
from the Intrigue series,
THE MASQUERADING TWIN by Katie Mettner

Chapter One

"Getting shot sucks," Selina grumped, shifting to find a more comfortable position. "What's worse is this damn hospital bed. It's like a board with sheets."

Efren glanced up from his crossword puzzle and raised a brow. "Next time, don't walk in front of a bullet."

Her eye roll was epically dramatic. She noticed her reflection in the mirror across from her bed and gave herself a score of twelve out of ten. The airtime before those drugged-up eyes returned to center had earned her the two extra points.

"If I recall correctly, I didn't, but I'll keep that in mind. What were you and Eric whispering about while everyone else tried to save my life?"

His sigh was notably a six out of ten on the exasperation scale. "Has anyone ever told you that you're incredibly dramatic?"

"Not before today. It must be a new skill. You didn't answer my question."

"Nothing," he said pointedly. This time, he didn't even look up from the crossword puzzle.

"Seemed like a lot of nothing considering the time it took. I was surprised you parted ways without a hug or a secret handshake."

When he lifted his head, agitation was written all over his face. Good, she was getting to him. Maybe he'd finally leave her hospital room for more than ten seconds. "Is this contrary banter supposed to convince me to leave?" She raised a brow as an answer. "You'll have to try harder. I've protected kids with more game than you've got."

He was so irritating! Selina forced herself to take a deep breath, or at least as deep as she could without pain.

Don't let him see you sweat. It's bad enough he sees you in pain. He doesn't need to know all your weaknesses.

Efren Brenna had been a burr in her side since the day he started working for Secure One. He'd moved down a spot now that she had a bullet wound in her side, but at least that would heal and the pain would disappear. Not the case with Brenna, it appeared. His reputation was that of a hero, and his ego matched. Okay, that wasn't fair. He was a hero. He'd saved countless lives while bleeding out from a traumatic leg amputation. On the other hand, his ego was too big for her liking. It filled up the room and left no space for anyone else. At least that was her story, and she was sticking to it.

She studied the man who sat engrossed in the newspaper crossword puzzle. Selina knew he was also paying full attention to everything around him in the hospital room and the hallway. She could see his profile from her bed, and she had to admit that some might consider him handsome. His brown hair was cut short in the back with a swoop of hair over his forehead. His skin was the perfect shade of desert tan, and his brown eyes were giant with lashes that any woman would kill for. He was tall to her five and a half feet, but thin and wiry. Under his left pant leg, he wore a high-tech above-knee skin-fit prosthesis with a running blade attached. He always wore his blade when they went on missions, and since he hadn't returned to Secure One, he hadn't changed into his everyday leg. She suspected Eric would return with it soon but wouldn't ask. She didn't want him to think she cared one way or the other about his comfort when she was the one in the hospital bed.

"If you must know," he said, setting the paper aside and leaning forward in his chair, "we were talking about the case—"

Motion caught her eye and she peered through the narrow window in the door. What she saw had her heart rate climbing fast. She put her finger to her lips, her gaze glued to the nurses' station outside her door. Efren swung his head around slowly. Selina wondered if he saw her, too. If she was real. A woman with long blond hair that fell in waves against her back where it blended into her white fur coat stood tapping her bloodred nails on the counter. The door was open a crack so they could hear the discussion between the nurse and the woman.

"I'm looking for Eva Shannon. I was told she was brought to this hospital."

"I'm sorry," the nurse said. "I can only give out information to family. Are you a direct family member?"

"Yes, I'm her sister," the woman answered in a rather bored tone.

Efren raised a brow at Selina in question, and she swallowed hard. There was no way that woman was her sister. She'd put her sister in a body bag eight years ago.

"Let me check," the nurse said, typing into the computer. "I'm sorry, but I don't have an Eva Shannon on this floor. You could try two floors up. That's Med-Surg. She might be there since that's overflow when our floor gets full."

"I'll do that," the woman said.

Selina recognized the signature sass, and sweat broke out on her brow as the woman turned and sashayed toward the elevator. That woman was her sister. The one who was supposed to be dead.

Efren stood by the door until he heard the elevator's ding, then closed the door the rest of the way, jammed a chair under it and spun on her. "Get ready. I'm going to let Eric know we're moving."

"Get ready? Moving? I just had surgery to remove a bullet from my gut. I'm not going anywhere!"

Efren stalked to her bed in a way she'd never seen him move before. A lion patiently hunting prey came to mind. When he stood over her, his entire demeanor had changed. "Did you hear who that woman asked for?"

Selina swallowed before she answered, afraid nothing but a scream of terror would leave her lips if she didn't. "Eva Shannon. I don't know who that is, so I don't know what you're so worried about, Efren."

He braced his hands on the bed and leaned in until he was inches from her face. "You wanted to know what Eric and I were whispering about earlier?" He raised a brow, and she nodded. Having him this close to her was unnerving, and she blinked, afraid to breathe. "It was about the moment before you were shot. Randall Jr. said Ava Shannon right before he put a bullet in you. It was a question, not a statement. Vic also kept mumbling about you being dead, which tells me two things. That woman out there is Ava Shannon, and the woman I'm staring at is Eva Shannon. Cute play on the names. I give your mom props for that. I don't need to know the rest right now, but I need you to stop playing games. Let that fear you keep trying to swallow down motivate you to get up and get out of here before they finish the job!" The growl of exclamation was intense before he turned and picked up his bag, pulling out an encoded phone all Secure One operatives used.

With the phone to his ear, he stared her down, and she closed her eyes because if looks could kill, he'd do a better job than Randall's bullet had. The woman from a few moments ago filled her mind as terror shot through her soul. It was like looking in a mirror in a house of horrors. Ava was supposed to be dead. Selina had been the one to shoot her in the chest. The ME had assured her the bullet had done the trick and ended her reign of terror—all evidence to the contrary. Ava was alive and well, wearing her signature fur. That meant one thing. She was out for blood. Ava did not take well to being wronged, especially by her family.

Her mind warred with what she had just seen and what it already knew. How? Where had she been all these years? That night, the night they raided Randall Loraine's home, things hadn't gone as planned, but Selina wasn't sad to put her twin in a body bag at the end of the night, even if it put a target on her back.

"Listen, Eva, we have to talk about your sister," her *police chief said as they strapped on their vests and readied their weapons.*

"What's to talk about?" she asked, tightening the straps.

"You can't be a risk to the lives of the team. If she's going to distract you, you need to stand down."

"You should know me better than that by now," she answered, and then lined up with the rest of the team.

Eva could only hope her sister was inside those four ostentatious walls. The task force could prove she knew about the counterfeiting ring, but not that she had her hands in it. She did. They'd find that proof tonight. There was no way Ava Shannon-Loraine would let her husband run the ring alone. She was too controlling—too diabolical—to let an opportunity to manipulate and dominate Randall Sr. pass her by. They should both be behind bars, but first, they had to find the proof. Once they did, Eva had no problem being the one to put Ava in handcuffs.

The team spread out around the perimeter of the Loraine mansion. It had so many doors to cover that they'd had to pull in the SWAT teams from two separate counties. The last thing they wanted was for Randall or Ava to escape and disappear when they'd been building a case against them for over a year. If they went underground, they'd be in the wind forever.

Intel told them the couple spent their evenings in the library. Eva snickered to herself. She was the intel. She's spent enough time inside the mansion to know Ava and Randall's routine. Their sniper on the hill had confirmed they were there. That meant entering the front door, turning right down a hallway, and right into the first door. The room was small, which left them little room to hide, but Eva suspected they had a way out that even she didn't know existed.

With a nod from the chief, they rammed their way

into the house from both ends. Eva tried to tune out the shouting and shrill alarm as she swung into the room where her sister and brother-in-law sat enjoying a glass of bourbon they'd bought with blood money.

"Freeze! You're under arrest!" her chief yelled at Randall as he crawled through a hatch in the floor.

Two SWAT guys hauled him out before he could shut it and handcuffed him before he got a word out. Eva swung her gun around the room. "Where is she?" It wasn't a question as much as a rebel yell at the man who had somehow helped her twin escape.

"Tag, you're it. Run, run as fast as you can, big sister, but little sister can't be caught." Randall's words were spat at her with so much distaste it made Eva laugh.

"You don't know me very well then, Randall." She swept her gun and flashlight down the hatch, but her twin was nowhere in sight. She didn't let that stop her. Eva's feet barely touched the ladder's rungs before she jumped onto the concrete floor below. The tunnel only went one way, so on instinct, she ran, knowing it was leading her toward the property line to the south. Ava couldn't have that much of a jump on her. Maybe thirty seconds. How far could she get in that time? With her gun tight to her chest, Eva noticed movement ahead of her. The swish of long blond hair as she climbed a ladder before popping out into the night.

"Ava, stop! You're surrounded!" she yelled to her twin, but Ava didn't stop.

The adrenaline had Eva's legs and heart pumping as she ran full out toward her twin, knowing that if she escaped, Eva would never be safe. She'd always have to look over her shoulder for a bullet that one day would come. Ava believed in an eye for an eye, but if her family betrayed her, she would burn down the world.

Eva reached out, her fingers grasping Ava's long hair. She pulled her backward and to the ground, where she landed with an oof. "Stay down!" Eva yelled, pointing her gun at Ava's center mass.

"What are you going to do, sis? Shoot an unarmed woman?"

"If she doesn't stay down, I won't hesitate," Eva growled. Her body shook with anger, but her gun remained steady.

"What happened to you?" Ava asked, shaking her head in disdain.

"What happened to me? I'm not the one on the wrong side of the law, Ava."

"You think you're holier than thou because you're a cop. You have no idea what real life is like for me. You're about to find out."

Ava launched herself at her twin but didn't get far before Eva squeezed the trigger. The bullet knocked her back, and shock filled her eyes as she glanced down at her chest, where blood turned her white cashmere sweater bright red.

"You shot me," she hissed, that shock turning to fury. "I can't believe you shot me!"

"I warned you," Eva said, her gun still pointed at her twin. With one hand, she pushed the button on her walkie. "I need EMS on the south side of the property. I have Ava Loraine. She has a bullet wound to the chest."

"Selina!"

She started at the name, opening her eyes to stare right into Efren's brown ones.

"Sorry, what did you say?"

"I said it's time to get you up and dressed. We have to go."

There was a knock on the door, and Efren had his gun out and was next to the door before she saw him move. He opened the door a hair, but Selina couldn't see who it was.

"Quickly," he whispered, and opened the door wide enough for a nurse to slide through. He had the door shut and the chair under the handle before the nurse made it to the side of her bed.

"I have your discharge papers," she said cheerily, as though there wasn't a man with a gun in her room.

"Discharge papers?" Selina asked, her heart pounding in her chest as she pushed herself up in the bed.

The nurse shook the papers in her hand. "Everything you need to finish your recovery elsewhere. Eric told us to be alert for anyone asking about you who looked suspicious," she explained as she busied herself with the machines by Selina's bed. "When that woman looked exactly like my patient, I decided chances were good that was who he was referring to. I know you're an APP, so I'm confident you can take care of your wound, correct?"

Selina nodded, and the nurse smiled. "Good, let's get your IV out and find you something to put on that's a little less memorable." The nurse turned to Efren. "I have enough medication for the day, but she will need more than this."

Efren dug in his bag and pulled out a slip of paper. "Call it into that pharmacy, under that name. We'll pick it up."

The nurse stuck it in her pocket and set about removing Selina's IV and checking her wound. The drugs had made her head hazy, but she forced herself to concentrate. Her twin had returned from the dead, and now Selina and Efren were in her crosshairs. Her gaze drifted to Efren, his backpack on and ready to go while he glared at her in confusion and anger. She was going to have to trust him to keep her safe, but she suspected she was anything but when it came to Efren Brenna.